BLOOD TIES

AGENTS OF THE CROWN BOOK II

LINDSAY BUROKER

Blood Ties
Agents of the Crown, Book 2

by Lindsay Buroker

CHAPTER 1

I DON'T THINK IT'S FAIR THAT your noble righteousness ruined my life."

Zenia cocked an eyebrow at her friend as they walked around a fountain marking the entrance to the Silver Ridge shopping district. The armor-clad zyndar warrior at the center of the water feature appeared far more interested in slaying trolls and golems than highlighting discounts and bargains. Not that either was to be had in the exclusive district.

"Are you referring to me letting that elf princess have her artifact back?" Zenia asked.

"Unless you've done something else to ruin my life lately." Rhi Lin, monk of the Water Order, thumped the butt of her bo against the cobblestones for emphasis.

A bejeweled woman in furs that were far too warm for the late spring day curled a lip at the overly boisterous thumping and murmured something to the gilded ladies browsing with her. Nobody dared say anything, not when Rhi wore her blue gi and wielded that bo with authority, but Zenia had already heard a few snide comments about commoners in the wrong part of town.

"You still have your job at the temple," Zenia said. "Regular pay, a room to stay in, monkly vows of chastity to follow. I fail to see how my actions affected your life in the least."

"I don't work with *you* anymore." Rhi's tone held genuine anguish as she gave Zenia an exasperated look. "Why did you let yourself get kicked out? After ten *years* of working as an inquisitor and establishing a reputation as the best in the city? And *twenty* years in the temple. They took you in and taught you to read, didn't they? How could you just leave?"

As if she'd had a choice.

"I'm trying to decide if my personality is truly so endearing that you're having difficulty living without me there," Zenia said, "or if you got stuck working with someone unappealing."

Rhi cleared her throat so vigorously she drew another lip curl from a well-dressed passerby, a man this time, arms full of recently acquired boxes of hats. Everyone in the city seemed to see the end of the war and the crowning of a new king as an excuse to shop.

"Marlyna," Rhi confessed, naming the hard-nosed inquisitor who had interrogated Jev. The woman was known for inflicting pain and leaving mental scars when she scoured a suspect's mind for information. "I'm her new bodyguard when she goes out on assignments. I don't think Archmage Sazshen thought this through. Shouldn't your bodyguard care if you live or die? And not be rooting for the felons to horribly embarrass you?"

"Fortunately, as a consummate professional, you would never allow your feelings for someone to get in the way of doing your duty."

"After five years of working together, shouldn't you know me better than that?"

"You were always a professional with me." Zenia slowed to a stop in front of a store with a diamond shape carved into the wooden sign above the doorway. "Aside from the occasional sarcastic comments you issued while pummeling felons into submission."

"They were *frequent* sarcastic comments. But only issued before and after pummeling. Talking while fighting is a good way to get your legs swept and a dagger stuck in your throat."

"I'll keep that in mind. This is the place."

Rhi eyed the sign and the large window skeptically. A few necklaces featuring simple opals and sapphires lay on velvet cushions on the display ledge. Zenia shuddered at a phallic pendant carved from ivory. She'd had enough of ivory carvings of late.

"You sure you can afford anything here?" Rhi asked. "I almost wet myself when I saw the price for orc ears back on the corner. How can any self-respecting baker ask twenty krons for a fried pastry dusted with cinnamon and sugar?"

"Discussion of urination habits may get you some disapproving frowns in this part of town," Zenia said, choosing to respond to the second topic rather than the first. Because she feared the answer to the first would be *no*. But she had to ask. She worried she wouldn't be able to perform her new job adequately without a dragon-tear gem hanging around her throat, one that lent her the power to read minds when she questioned witnesses and interrogated suspects.

"What does it say about our city that it doesn't get you frowns everywhere?" Rhi asked.

Zenia shook her head and stepped inside, the shop cool and shady after the warm sun. To her surprise, a man and a woman in brown gis almost identical to Rhi's blue uniform were pointing at items in a display case in the back.

"I wouldn't have guessed monks could afford jewels," Zenia murmured.

"Trust me, they can't. I make less than you. Or than you did. I'm sure they're here on behalf of the Earth Order archmage or someone else with access to the donation trays at their temple."

Zenia frowned at the idea that someone might pilfer money meant to assist the Orders in providing aid for those less fortunate. She didn't think Archmage Sazshen had done that. The Water Order Temple leader certainly hadn't worn jewels. She'd been modest in dress and appearance and fair in... most matters. Zenia knew she should resent her old employer, but she couldn't help but wish things had turned out differently and that she was still at the temple, still on the path to becoming archmage herself one day.

"Are you going to make a lot more at the castle?" Rhi asked curiously. "Is that why you think you can afford this?" She pointed the tip of her bo around the shop, drawing a frown from the room's other occupant, a raven-haired woman in a richly colored silk dress and slippers. The clerk. Or perhaps the owner.

"I don't know yet what my salary will be, but I'm not expecting largess."

"You said yes without knowing what the king is going to pay you?"

"One doesn't ask impertinent questions of the king when he's offering a job perfectly suited to one's talents." Talents Zenia worried would be insufficient now that she no longer had the use of one of the temple's dragon tears. She let a hand stray to her chest, to where the oval-shaped gem had once dangled.

"Asking what your salary will be isn't impertinent."

"It is among the zyndar and even more so among royalty. When they work at all, it's supposed to be for the glory of their kingdom, not because they need money."

"Four elemental hells, are they going to pay you at all?"

"Yes." Zenia hesitated. "I think so."

By the founders, should she have asked? She had assumed…

"For someone with the intelligence to outmaneuver criminal masterminds, you can be dense at times, Zenia."

"I hope your new inquisitor enjoys your bluntness as much as I do."

Rhi opened her mouth to respond but closed it when the owner sashayed in their direction.

Zenia braced herself for a suggestion that they would find shopping in a less ritzy district more to her monetary tastes.

When she'd worn her blue inquisitor robe, nobody had questioned her right to go anywhere in the city she wished. But she not only didn't have a robe any longer, she didn't even have much of a selection of civilian attire. Her brown and beige cotton dress was almost ten years old, and the hem and collar were starting to fray. Now, she wished she'd bothered to shop and purchase clothing a little more often, but it had hardly been necessary when she dressed in the same robe every day for work.

The owner pointed toward the door, her lips parting in preparation to issue her decree.

"This is Zenia Cham," Rhi said, speaking first. "She wants to see your dragon tears."

The owner blinked and lowered her pointing finger. "*Inquisitor* Cham? I—my dragon tears? Are you here to take inventory? See my books? I assure you there's nothing nefarious going on. I only have three dragon tears in inventory. I know that's far more than most sellers, but I assure you, they were all legitimately acquired from zyndari ladies who've passed on and whose heirs had no aptitude for magic. I paid a fair price to the families—*more* than fair—and my markup is quite modest when you consider how much the rent is in this exclusive neighborhood."

"I'm not an inquisitor anymore," Zenia felt compelled to admit.

Once, she would have been proud that her reputation had reached all the way to the Silver Ridge, but it would do her little good now. Could she one day establish a new fearsome reputation as one of the king's Crown Agents? She didn't know. She feared the agents worked largely in secret and weren't supposed to be seen or heard until they pounced on some threat to the kingdom.

"I'm just a shopper," she added.

The owner's eager-to-please expression faded. "You're not here about a case?"

"No, I'm interested in seeing your dragon tears as a potential buyer."

"She'll need one for the work she's doing for her new employer," Rhi said. "King Targyon."

The owner's lips formed a round, "Oh."

Rhi smirked smugly as the woman turned, murmuring, "This way," and headed toward a door in the rear of the shop.

Zenia didn't know if she should thank her friend for name-dropping or not. She hadn't minded relying on *her* reputation, but she didn't like the idea of receiving preferential treatment because she worked for Targyon. It reminded her of the zyndar favoritism that she hated. Besides, it wasn't as if she'd even seen the king since the morning she and Jev had dined with him, and Targyon had hired them.

They followed the shopkeeper through the rear doorway, and Zenia jumped when she spotted a bodyguard—or maybe security guard?—looming just inside, his thickly muscled arms bare, a pistol and heavy cudgel belted at his waist. He narrowed his eyes at Rhi and her bo.

She winked at him. "Hello there, Muscles. What are you doing in the back instead of displaying those forearms up front?"

"Muscles are uncouth," he rumbled in a voice deep enough to belong to a dwarf. "Zyndari Grayela said."

Zenia took that to mean the Silver Ridge customers might not find it appealing to see armed beefy types roaming the shops. But if the owner truly had dragon tears, Zenia wasn't surprised she kept someone fearsome nearby.

"Over here, ladies." The shopkeeper—Grayela, presumably—waved them to a small vault built into the stone and plaster wall. "I would usually ask to see proof of finances from commoners," Grayela said, eyeing them up and down. "But if you're here on behalf of the king…"

Zenia frowned at her back as Grayela inserted the first of two keys into the vault door. Zenia hadn't said that. She didn't even think Rhi had implied it.

"Is he looking to acquire more dragon tears?" Grayela asked. "One would expect the Alderoths to have a whole stash in the castle somewhere—most of the old, wealthy zyndar families do—but maybe his father and cousins died without telling him where it is? That would be tragic, wouldn't it? Though you'd think someone with a dragon tear could use its magic to find other magic gems located in the castle. Unless they're stored elsewhere. I could see the princes having died—all at once, speaking of tragedy!—without writing down the family secrets. Or sending them off to Targyon at the front. I don't think anyone ever expected that boy to be crowned. I bet there's a lot he wasn't told."

"I'm sure," Zenia murmured, wondering if Grayela had heard any useful rumors about the three princes' mysterious deaths from a "disease of the blood" that only affected their family.

It was the very mystery King Targyon had asked her and Jev to investigate first. In less than an hour, she was to meet Jev at the office of the doctor who'd treated the princes, so they could begin asking questions. She'd wanted to go right at dawn, but he'd been pulled aside that morning for some zyndar-only meeting with the king. She, being a mature and self-assured woman of thirty-two, wasn't envious, jealous, or feeling left out. Or so she promised herself.

"Here we are." After turning a second lock, Grayela opened the vault door and drew out three boxes, each carved from ivory with gold or silver clasps and hinges. She produced a keyring and proceeded to open the boxes one by one and hand them to Zenia. "As you can see from the carvings on the fronts of the tears, that one holds a loom and was used by a master weaver. This next one has a quill and is more versatile—anything to do with books or writing and recording or even teaching should work. This last one is for more of a warrior woman—Zyndari Masarathi had quite the reputation for winning fencing competitions even against male competitors—with its sword carving. I'm told that one is quite powerful, so it is accordingly valued. Of course, if none of these work, you can see the city's master gem cutter, Akura Grindmor. For a reasonable fee, the dwarf is rumored to be able to fill in the old carvings, using magic to ensure the gems are fully whole again, and then carve new ones."

"What's a reasonable fee?" Rhi asked as Zenia considered the gems.

A sense of bleakness came over her as she realized she could no longer sense magic, not without a dragon tear of her own, and had no way to tell if these were real. Given the reputation of this shop, she was inclined to believe they were, but she would need someone else with a dragon tear—someone she trusted—to verify that before she sank her life's savings into a purchase.

"For a remake and re-carving? Around ten thousand from what I've heard. It's only five thousand if the master cutter is starting from scratch with an untouched dragon tear, but it's exceedingly rare to find one that hasn't already been carved these days."

"Ten thousand?" Rhi asked, her bo drooping. "How much for just the gem?" She eyed the sword one.

Zenia had only heard of a couple of monks receiving dragon tears from the archmage, as the temple usually sought out gems that would be useful to its mages over its fighters. Even then, few mages received them. To be offered one was a great honor. Once again, Zenia felt a twinge of distress over losing the regard of Archmage Sazshen.

"For that lovely one?" Grayela pointed at the sword-carved gem. "Seventy-five thousand krons."

Zenia planted a hand against the cool stone wall to brace herself. She'd only made five thousand a *year* as an inquisitor. Rhi's salary— her mouth was dangling open at the price too—was only half that. The temple had included room and board and their uniforms in with their compensation, but even with all that Zenia had saved over the years, she didn't have that much money, not even close.

"The quill is a mere sixty, and the loom fifty." Grayela arched her eyebrows at Zenia. "Forgive my uncouthness in discussing sums, but that must come out at some point, especially when I don't know the depth of your coffers and if I can simply bill you. How much did the king say you have to work with?"

"I..." Zenia didn't know what to say. This was *Rhi's* ruse.

But Rhi only shook her head slowly.

Zenia lowered her hand from the wall. She should have known the prices would be exorbitant. And unattainable. Coming here had been a mistake. There was no way she could ever save enough. Even if she somehow could, the quill was the only gem she could imagine meshing with her abilities and needs, and it wouldn't be as tailored to her as her last dragon tear, carved with the eyetooth of justice, had been.

"We'll have to clarify that with him and see if any of these carvings suit his needs." Rhi gripped Zenia's arm and nodded toward the door.

Zenia allowed herself to be led toward the doorway while biting her tongue to keep from protesting Rhi's continuing ruse. Zenia hadn't grown up zyndar with notions of their Code of Honor planted in her head, but she was proud that she'd achieved all she had without bending her morality. She hated to think she might start her new life with lies and misdirection.

"Thank you for showing them to us, Zyndari Grayela," Zenia said, bowing on her way out.

"...he better listen to our archmage," the male monk muttered as Zenia and Rhi returned to the main room. "He's only sitting on that padded throne by the grace of the Orders."

"If he's smart, he'll remember that. The archmage isn't asking for anything unreasonable."

Zenia paused, the reference to King Targyon piquing her interest and reminding her she had something more important to do than shopping.

But the monks turned, noticing Zenia and Rhi, and stopped their conversation.

"Rhi Lin." The woman bowed to Rhi.

Zenia wondered if they knew each other. Female monks were rare among all the Orders, the training being rigorous and the tests geared more toward men.

"Danja." Rhi bowed back, including the male monk in the gesture. "Choris. Anything interesting happening at the Earth Order Temple these days?"

"No," Danja said blandly. "Anything of interest with the Water Order?" She looked at Zenia but didn't direct any questions to her. Her expression seemed dismissive.

Zenia held back a frown, not sure if the monk recognized her or not. If so, she wondered if she was now considered an outcast among all the Orders. Could word have traveled so quickly about her parting from the Water Order?

"Nothing at all," Rhi responded with an edged smile.

They bowed to each other again before turning away.

Outside, Zenia squinted at the bright sunlight.

"I need to get to the temple so I can trail Marlyna—don't even think of calling her Marly for short—around the city," Rhi said. "I'll leave you to your new investigation." She paused, looking like she wanted to say something else.

"Will you be all right?" Zenia asked. "I know Marlyna isn't as warm and chatty as I am—"

Rhi snorted.

"—but she's good at her job and gets sent out on a lot of missions." Zenia kept herself from saying Marlyna was brusque and sometimes cruel and that she would love a chance to pummel the inquisitor on the wrestling mat after what she'd done to Jev. "At least you won't be bored."

"Boredom isn't what I was worried about. And that's the question I was thinking of asking you."

"If I'll be all right?"

"Yes. You may have noticed—" Rhi tipped her bo toward the shop door, "—that the archmage hasn't been quiet about you being kicked out of the Order. She made it clear she's irked with you and that you're not to be trusted. Also that you may be sympathetic to elves."

"Ah." Zenia knew she'd earned Sazshen's wrath, but she hadn't expected the archmage, a woman in her late sixties, to be vindictive or hold a grudge. The knowledge stung. They had worked together for so many years. But it had only been a few days since Zenia had done what she believed was the right thing. Perhaps in time, Sazshen would mellow and realize that giving that artifact back to its rightful owners would not likely result in the world ending.

"I think she wanted to make sure you wouldn't easily gain employment with any of the other Orders," Rhi said. "Probably because you know a lot of the Water Order's secrets—I assume that's the case, since lowly monks aren't *told* any secrets—and she wouldn't want that information being shared with the other Orders."

"There's something to that, I suppose, though it's not like I would have gossiped."

"Your employment in the king's service was unexpected." Rhi grinned. "People in the temple were flabbergasted. Even Sazshen."

"Are you supposed to be sharing all this gossip with me?"

"Oh, absolutely not. I've been forbidden from talking to you."

"Truly?"

"Yup. You're just lucky Marlyna is so odious and humorless and that I felt the need to seek you out."

"Don't get in trouble—or worse—because of me, please." Zenia felt bad enough about her own ruined career. She did not want Rhi to lose hers simply for associating with her.

"If I do, do you think the king has a position open for a monk?"

"Uhm, I don't know. He's got a bunch of dour-faced guards that trail him around the castle. I don't know what training they had before being added to the staff."

"I can be dour. Let me know if you hear of a position." Rhi waved her bo. "I'm off to see if I can requisition one of those orc ears for free. A donation for the temple, if you will. Maybe if I offer the vendor a fortune and the favor of the Blue Dragon founder, he'll be eager to share with me."

"Monks aren't allowed to tell fortunes."

"Yes, but those who are only vaguely religious rarely know all the rules." Rhi winked and trotted off up the street.

Zenia blew out a slow breath, worried that her friend would get in trouble, worried that she would be ineffective at her job without a dragon tear, and worried that she was now considered an outcast by every member of the four Orders in the city. Aside from the personal implications, that status might make people less likely to cooperate with her when she did work on the king's behalf.

"This day is off to a good start," she mumbled as she headed off to meet Jev.

CHAPTER 2

JEV CLIMBED UP THE FIRE-ESCAPE ladder, heading to the rooftop of a three-story building across the alley from a row of backyards belonging to elegant stone townhouses. Soft clinks sounded on the rungs below him as Cutter followed, his hook doing as well on the ladder as his right hand once would have.

"When I said I'd come with you because we were going the same way," Cutter huffed from below, "I didn't expect you to take a detour."

"It was a whim." Jev touched the folded paper in his pocket, a single address written upon it. Not that much of a whim, he admitted silently.

Cutter grunted something indecipherable even to someone who spoke numerous languages, including Preskabroton Dwarf.

"You didn't need to come up. I said you could wait down there." Jev pulled himself over the lip of the building and onto the flat roof. A fishy breeze wafted up from the Anchor Sea as he headed to the far side. The harbor and the mouth of the Jade River Delta were visible from the lofty perch. As well as those backyards....

"How would that assuage my curiosity about what you're up to?" Cutter followed him across the rooftop.

Jev knelt at the edge, looking out over the alley and into a particular yard. A mix of brick pavers and neatly trimmed grass, it was empty of life aside from a few seagulls plucking at a trashcan lid. He'd hoped to catch a glimpse of more.

It was the middle of the morning, he told himself. She might not be home. She might be caring for the children inside. Or she might be having wild passionate sex with her husband.

Jev rolled his eyes at himself, disgusted that his mind traveled down that road. He didn't care about *that*. Or he shouldn't. He just wanted to know if she was doing all right. If she was healthy and well. With *him*.

"Are we looking for someone?" Cutter crouched beside him, his long red beard brushing the textured roof at their feet.

Jev hesitated, reluctant to explain even though he'd shared his past with Cutter before. He felt a little embarrassed about this diversion and wished he didn't have a witness for it. His meeting with Targyon had ended early, and it so happened that the address he'd been carrying in his pocket for three days was near the doctor he planned to visit next.

The doctor he planned to visit next with *Zenia*. What would she think if she knew he was checking up on the woman he would have married if he hadn't been ordered off to war?

"Naysha," he finally told Cutter.

"That the woman who didn't wait for you?"

Jev grimaced. "Yes."

"Huh. A dwarf woman would have waited, but ten years isn't that long for a dwarf. I hear it's different with humans."

"It's a long time for humans," Jev agreed. "I don't blame her for not waiting. I just…" Wish she'd waited more than six months before starting to see someone else, he finished silently.

But he didn't want to go into more detail. He hadn't noticed that Cutter was a romantic in any sense. As far as Jev could tell, Cutter's quasi-crush on the bearded female Arkura Grindmor had more to do with what she could teach him in the gem-working shop than any notions of bedroom frolicking.

"She's not expecting you, eh?" Cutter waved to indicate their rooftop perch.

"No."

Jev had thought about walking up and knocking on her door, but he didn't want to intrude on her life or assume she would want to see him after all this time.

"Is this what humans call stalking, then?"

"It's not stalking if you work for the king."

"Oh? Did he ask you to peep into her backyard?"

"No."

Cutter arched his bushy red eyebrows.

"Don't you have a master gem cutter to meet up with?" Jev asked a touch grumpily.

"At noon, yes. She doesn't rise early—dwarves aren't much for abiding the workings of the sun—as I found out when I showed up at dawn and she yelled at me through a window."

"You would think if she wanted to find her special diamond tools, she'd be amenable to being up at all hours." Jev felt guilty that he had foisted the job of assisting Arkura with her search on Cutter. His friend had asked for an introduction to the master cutter, not a quest. Still, Cutter seemed pleased by the chance to prove himself to the legendary dwarf.

"She's a master and in high demand," Cutter said. "She must be used to picking whatever hours she wishes to be awake."

Before Jev could respond, the back door of the townhouse opened. He crouched lower, held his breath, and gripped the lip of the rooftop.

Naysha, the woman he hadn't seen in ten years, walked out accompanied by three children, their ages varying from four to eight. He knew that from letters his cousin Wyleria had sent over the years. She had been the one to report that Naysha had married someone else, and she'd updated him when the children had come along. She kept tabs on a lot of the zyndar families the Dharrows interacted with. He had always flinched away from the gossip on Naysha, not wanting to know about her new life, but at the same time, he hadn't been able to stop reading those letters. It had always stung that Naysha herself had never written, instead leaving his cousin to send along the news.

"She doesn't look very healthy," Cutter observed. "Too skinny. No beard."

Jev slanted an oblique look at his comrade. Naysha had always been beautiful, and she still was. Her figure was fuller, less wispy than it had been when they'd been in their early twenties, but that was to be expected. She was a mother now.

The breeze played with her long hair as she led the children to the back gate. They skipped and laughed, and she smiled gently.

Jev swallowed, remembering how much he had adored that smile once. When he had been younger, he'd thought she would be the only one he would ever love. And for a time, she'd led him to believe she felt the same.

As the family opened the gate and headed into the alley, off to the children's school perhaps, Jev leaned back so Naysha wouldn't see him if she looked up. And because he felt like a heel for spying like this.

"You going down to talk to her?" Cutter asked.

"No." He'd seen that she was healthy and well, that she lived in a nice home and that her new husband—what was his name? Zyndar Grift Myloron—was presumably taking good care of her. That was all he needed to know.

"Then this is *definitely* stalking."

"No, it's not. Because we're done." Jev backed away before rising to his full height and heading to the ladder.

He didn't know if he was glad or not that he hadn't seen the husband. He vaguely remembered Myloron as handsome and overly blessed with muscles and athleticism. If that was still true, Jev didn't want to know about it. He also wouldn't have wanted to witness them kissing before the man headed off for whatever business he attended to daily.

"Good. You don't even need to care for her anymore, right? You've got the equally un-bearded Zenia."

"Hm." Jev couldn't truly say that he *had* Zenia.

"Hm? I heard you two were lip wrestling in your castle the other night. That's how humans profess love, isn't it?"

"It's how they profess mutual interest and attraction. Love sometimes comes later."

Jev definitely wouldn't mind further exploring the possibility of mutual interest and attraction with Zenia, but he didn't know if he had it in him to experience true love again, the fiery passion bordering on obsession that had consumed him in his youth. He also didn't know how much interest Zenia truly had in *him*. That night in the castle, she had been injured and had her guard down when he kissed her. She didn't let her guard down often, so he didn't know if he could expect that event to repeat itself.

He glanced at Cutter. "How do dwarves profess love? My languages tutor failed to mention that."

"Usually by making things for each other. I made the first dwarf maiden I fell in love with a spice rack. She likes to bake, you see."

"That's sweet."

"Sweet? It was manly and virile. It weighed twenty pounds, and I carved it out of stone."

"Did she make you something in return?"

"Yes, frosted rock thumpers."

"Those are kind of like our cupcakes, right?" Jev, for all the traveling he'd done in the army and all the languages he'd learned, had never been into one of the great underground cities the dwarves had carved deep into the mountains around the world.

"Ten-pound cupcakes that fill your gut like a good borscht."

"Is weight an important element in all dwarven gifts?" Jev asked as they climbed down to the alley.

He headed in a direction that would take them to the doctor's establishment without crossing Naysha's path. The last thing Jev wanted was for her to know he'd been checking up on—but definitely not stalking—her. If she was curious about how he was doing these days, she could come out to Dharrow Castle to ask. He wouldn't inflict himself on her in her new life.

"Nothing says you care like heft," Cutter said. "You should buy something hefty for Zenia. Or even better *make* her something."

Jev looked down at his hands. His father could make something out of wood, and he had cousins that were artists, but Jev didn't have a knack for craftiness. As numerous lopsided building projects from his youth attested. He blamed his colorblindness. He felt he was doing well if he could match his clothes, something that had been easier when he'd been in the army and expected to wear the same uniform every day.

"I should probably ask her on a date first," Jev said.

"If you made her something she liked, it would be easier to ask. Making leads to acceptances."

"I don't know how to make anything."

They turned at an intersection and entered a more peopled part of town with tenement buildings on one side of the street and law, bookkeeping, and apothecary offices lining the other.

"That's moderately pathetic," Cutter said.

"When you grow up zyndar, nobody expects you to do anything except lead your people into battle and manage the estate for the family. There's the office. Dr. Bandigor."

"Looks like he does well for himself," Cutter said. "That's Kandoorish marble, imported more than two thousand miles from the mountain jungles of Izstara. And those are gold and diamond door pulls.

I think that's the work of Master Craftsman Borgis the Melder out of Frumtar, one of my people's largest cities."

"He was the king's personal doctor." It amused but did not surprise Jev that Cutter could name all the architectural elements of the building. "I imagine that pays well."

Jev climbed the steps and knocked on a door made from thick teak carved with ornate safari scenes of people riding elephants while orcs and lions peered at them from the grasses.

"We're going right in?" Cutter asked. "You don't want to stalk him before talking to him?"

"I don't think that will be necessary."

When nobody answered, Jev tried the fancy pull. The door opened easily.

A wide, shadowy hallway led inside, the marble floor swept clean, no dust dulling any of the busts resting on pedestals lining one side. And yet, the place felt abandoned. Not a sound came from any of the rooms off the hallway.

Had the doctor fled town after the princes' deaths? Or maybe he was simply taking off for the last day of the holidays following the coronation.

"Jev?" a familiar voice called from somewhere in the interior.

"Zenia?"

"Back here."

He strode down the hallway, regretting that he'd made her wait because of his unplanned stop. She had, he recalled, wanted to start their new assignment as soon as the sun came up. Or possibly much sooner.

"We have a problem," Zenia added in a quieter tone.

"Already? We just started."

"She probably knows you haven't made her anything," Cutter said.

"Ssh."

They passed a couple of waiting and examining rooms. The last door on the right stood open, and Jev peeked inside.

"Uh." He expected to see Zenia, but instead, his gaze locked on a man lying face-up on the floor. A *dead* man.

There was no mistaking the pool of blood on the marble tiles or the hole in the side of the gray-haired man's skull. An intricately inlaid gold pistol lay next to him, inches from his open hand. Glassy eyes stared up at the ceiling beams.

Zenia stood a few feet away, her chin propped on her fist as she gazed down at the corpse.

Jev hurried to her side, lifting an arm in case she needed support. He had the urge to pull her into a hug and turn her face from the grisly sight.

"I've examined the body as much as possible without disturbing it," she stated matter-of-factly. "I believe the time of death was very early this morning or possibly late last night."

She looked at his extended arm and lifted her eyebrows.

"Ah." Jev lowered his hand, feeling silly.

After ten years as an inquisitor, she must have seen a few dead bodies. He didn't think the religious Orders' law enforcers were assigned murder cases frequently, but he supposed it happened.

"It's definitely Dr. Bandigor," Zenia added. "I'm familiar with him."

"Ah," Jev said again for lack of a better response. He wouldn't have been. After ten years out of the kingdom, he wasn't familiar with many people in the capital anymore.

"He shoot himself?" Cutter asked from the doorway.

"It looks that way, but…" Zenia lifted a palm toward the ceiling.

"You don't think so?" Jev asked.

"Oh, it's possible. I imagine he's been under pressure and scrutiny since he was known to be the royal family's doctor and the princes all died in the same month. It's possible he felt intense guilt at not knowing the cause or being able to save them. Or maybe he *did* know the cause and, for some reason, he chose not to save them. Then when he heard we were starting an investigation, he worried we would find out the truth, and he would be financially ruined if not hanged." She lifted a shoulder. "That's mere fanciful speculation, mind you, and nothing to truly be considered unless we find evidence to support it. It's also possible someone else shot him and tried to make it look like he committed suicide."

Jev nodded, his brain slowly spinning into gear as he got over the surprise of finding the man dead.

"If someone did kill him, they left his dragon tear behind." Zenia waved toward a chain visible around his neck. "I checked. He's got one with a vial carving—a medical enhancement. It would be worth a lot, even sold on the black market."

"Have you checked his work space yet?" Jev waved toward a large mahogany desk and chairs near the window. Stuffed bookcases rose on one wall, and a huge hearth took up much of another. "I assume this is his office."

"Not yet. That was next on my list. The ashes are cold in the fireplace, there are no signs of a fight—no objects on the floor or anything knocked over—and there's also no sign that his assistant, who works in the front office, has come in. I did check the desk up there. There are appointments scheduled for today, so it's odd that this wasn't discovered before our arrival."

Jev smiled at her, appreciating her analytical mind, even if he would have liked an excuse to hug and comfort her. "Maybe the assistant came, found him like this, and ran away because he or she was scared."

"She. And it's possible. She could have gone to report to the watch, too, which could mean we'll have uniformed company soon."

"I believe we outrank that company now."

"Didn't you always?"

"I suppose."

Zenia gazed at him with inscrutable green eyes, and he had the sense of being studied by a scientist. She'd been much more approachable— much more kissable—when she'd been tired and wounded, with her hair fallen down around her shoulders instead of up in that no-nonsense bun. She'd once admitted that men were afraid of her reputation and didn't ask her on dates often. He could see why, though he enjoyed trying to get her to smile, trying to break her determined focus.

Or at least he had when she'd been arresting *him*. Now that they were on the same side, he would feel guilty about distracting her.

"Even if you're zyndar," Zenia said, "the watchmen might not appreciate you impeding what they'll see as *their* investigation."

"True."

Zenia pointed at the desk. "Do your snooping quickly if you plan to."

"Yes, ma'am." He smirked and gave her an army salute, open hand to the side of his temple.

She wasn't one to bow to the zyndar or hesitate to order them around.

One of her elegant eyebrows twitched, but all she said was, "I'm going to check the rest of the building for clues."

She nodded at Cutter, who stepped aside as she walked out, even though she didn't ask him to. She had a way about her that cleared obstacles, zyndar, commoner, dwarf, and otherwise. In only a few short days, he'd come to admire her determination, even if it occasionally came with haughty chin tilts. As someone who'd traveled in zyndar circles his entire life until he'd joined the army, he was accustomed to haughtiness in all its incarnations.

"You should definitely make her something," Cutter said after she left.

"Because that's the only way I'll win her heart?"

"Because that's the only way her heart will notice you. She's got a singular focus, eh?"

"True. What do you suggest? A spice rack?"

"Does she bake?"

"I don't think so."

"Probably not then." Cutter backed into the hallway. "I'm off to help Master Grindmor. I'll leave the dead bodies to you."

"Thank you."

Jev opened drawers and looked for clues, but he came across nothing more than typical office supplies and notebooks pertaining to patients. He skimmed through the recent entries on the chance some bitter man or woman the doctor hadn't been able to help had come back to take revenge, but he doubted complaints of digestive discomfort and corns lent themselves to murders.

Nonetheless, he wrote down the names of the patients from the last two weeks as well as those the doctor had planned to see that day. Dr. Bandigor had people booked out for weeks, so it was unlikely he had been planning this end for a while. Had he been planning it at all? Jev found it very suspicious that the man had killed himself the night before he and Zenia had arrived to question him.

"Why do I have a feeling our first case isn't going to be an easy one?" he murmured.

CHAPTER 3

ENIA LIFTED HER CHIN AND did her best not to feel daunted as she and Jev walked through the massive gateway into the castle, the guards watching without doing anything to stop them. Jev, gazing at the flagstones with his hands in his pockets, probably expected no less—zyndar were invited to the castle for social gatherings, after all. Zenia kept waiting for someone to question her right to be there.

This was only her third time entering the great fountain- and garden-bedecked courtyard and only her second day on the job. The first had been tediously full of meetings and introductions to all her new colleagues—her new subordinates, she reminded herself—when all she'd wanted was to get to work on the case she'd already been assigned. There were thirteen agents working in the king's information office, directing international spies and overseeing intelligence gatherers in Korvann and in greater Kor. Supposedly. She had gotten blank looks when she'd asked who had been investigating the deaths of King Abdor's three sons. Had they been an accident or had someone arranged the strange virus that had only targeted those with Alderoth blood? If the latter, was young Targyon now in danger himself?

Nobody had admitted to knowing anything, and a young woman named Lunis had implied the former Crown Agent captain, Zyndar Garlok, hadn't assigned anyone to research the incident. Zenia hadn't met the man yet. He had been out of the office, apparently spending the coronation holidays at home, so she didn't know if he was aware yet that he'd been replaced.

Lunis had shown enthusiasm when Zenia said the agents would start investigating the princes' deaths. It boggled Zenia's mind that nobody had been doing so earlier. Had somebody—this Zyndar Garlok, perhaps—deliberately kept the agents from the task? Or, with nobody on the throne following the princes' deaths and prior to Targyon's coronation, had they all failed to take the initiative? The thought galled her, and she planned to give Garlok a verbal lashing when she met him, zyndar or not.

"Lost in thought?" Jev glanced at her as they walked through the courtyard, passing vibrant birds of paradise and belladonna lilies already in bloom.

Zenia almost mentioned her suspicions about Garlok, but since Jev was also zyndar, and they all seemed to know each other, she hesitated to berate the man. Targyon hadn't seemed impressed by him, but Zenia ought to wait until she'd at least met him to form an opinion. And voice it.

"This morning, I overheard a comment from a couple of Earth Order monks," she said instead, something she'd meant to bring up to him as soon as they were away from the prying eyes in the city. "It has me itching to go talk to their archmage."

"Was it related to the princes' deaths? Or did you hear that they're hiring over there, and you're already ready to abandon me—and the king?" He grinned at her, but something akin to genuine concern lurked in his dark brown eyes. Did he truly think she would do that? Apparently, he hadn't heard about her new status as outcast among the Orders. Not that she would leave the king after two days even if she were offered her old job back.

"They implied their archmage wanted something from Targyon and expected him to deliver. Since he owes the Orders for his appointment."

"Do you think the Orders could have had something to do with the princes' deaths? That one of the archmages might have wanted Targyon on the throne for a specific reason?"

"They're the ones who collectively decided to put him there, and I imagine they *all* have their reasons, but I'm not assuming anything about the princes' deaths yet. As a former inquisitor sworn to defend the kingdom and the tenets of the founders, I'd like to say *no*, it's impossible that a representative from one of the religious Orders would think of murder. But I can't. We would be best not to rule out anything this early in the investigation."

"True."

"Do you want to come with me to question the various archmages?" Zenia asked. "Or do you think our resources would be better spent if we split up? One of us should do some research on the disease and try to figure out if it truly was a virus of some kind. Are you qualified to do that?"

"I'm not qualified for much in this new job, but I can question some experts."

"I didn't think zyndars were ever self-effacing," Zenia said, surprised by the comment. He'd worked in the army's intelligence unit—led it, from what she'd heard—so he couldn't be *that* unqualified for this kind of work.

They turned down a side aisle in the courtyard garden, toward doors that would lead to the intelligence office rather than straight into the great room.

"The Code of Honor doesn't require self-effacement. I'll see what I can find out about the illness, but it can wait a few hours if you want me to come with you to talk to the Order archmages. I'm tall enough that I can loom fairly effectively, and the scar makes me look like a brutish combat veteran." He touched the wound on his right cheek—it looked like a sword had once come close to removing his eye.

"I don't think so," Zenia said.

Jev stopped at the path that led to the side entrance. "You don't think I can loom? Or you don't think I'm brutish?"

"I don't think I need you to come."

"Ah."

Belatedly, it occurred to her that he might have *wanted* to come. She couldn't imagine why, as she knew her company wasn't witty or scintillating— unless compared to the interrogation-loving Inquisitor Marlyna. But on the chance she'd made him feel rejected, she explained further.

"I just don't want to waste your time dragging you around the city. I'm used to having Rhi. She used to go everywhere with me for looming purposes."

"Was it hard for her to loom when she's three inches shorter than you?"

"No, she's stouter. And has that big stick." Zenia smiled briefly. "But now, she puts herself in danger even talking to me."

"In danger? How?" Jev leaned forward, and she imagined she could see hackles bristling protectively.

"Not physically. But of losing her job. My choice has marked me... Well, I guess Archmage Sazshen has been vocal about how disappointed she is with me, and she's made it clear that people working for the Orders, including my old friends, should avoid me."

"I'm sorry. That must be hard."

Zenia shrugged, for some reason uncomfortable with the sympathy in his eyes. "I just have to make sure Rhi doesn't have a reason to seek me out. She's known to flout the rules."

"I gathered that when she stalked down those bare-chested men playing ball on the beach. Monks are supposed to be celibate, aren't they?"

"She interprets that word loosely."

"Well, if she can't go with you, then you'll definitely want my company." They reached the side door, a single guard posted next to it, and Jev held it open while smiling at her.

Despite her focus on the case, Zenia found herself pausing to admire the gesture. Scar or no scar, he definitely wasn't brutish. His neatly trimmed beard highlighted his strong jaw, his straight white teeth gleamed during his frequent smiles, and his dark eyes were always eager to give off an alluring twinkle. Few men had ever twinkled at her.

"I'll accept your company, thank you. Will tomorrow morning work? I want to go over whatever reports on the archmages I can find in the office before going to speak with them." Zenia wondered what the Crown Agents' report on Archmage Sazshen might look like. Would they have it all wrong? Or would she be amazed by how much the agents knew about all the religious leaders in the capital?

"Tomorrow is fine. In the meantime, I'll see if anyone took any samples of the princes' blood before they were interred. It's a long shot, I'm sure, and even if they did, I don't know how helpful it would be to study under a microscope weeks later, but you never know. A medical expert might find it useful."

"That's a good idea." Zenia had occasionally talked to experts in medicine and science when she'd been on cases, and she'd often found it illuminating.

"Thank you." Jev beamed another smile at her as they walked down a windowless hallway, a few guttering lanterns slightly brightening the way, and she resolved to compliment his ideas more often. He smiled often, surprising given how soul-stealing the last ten years must have been for him, but these private just-for-her smiles were a new thing. And she couldn't deny their appeal.

"I've been meaning to ask you something for a while," Jev said, slowing before they reached the closed door that marked their new office.

"A while? It's only been a week since we met."

"True, but it was an eventful week. I barely slept at all while we got to know each other intimately. And nakedly. For some people, those would be the same thing."

Zenia remembered being stripped in front of the Fifth Dragon crime lady, Iridium. There had, indeed, been nothing intimate about that, except that she could say she'd seen Jev naked and that he had an attractive body to match the smile.

"Go ahead," Zenia said, realizing he was waiting. For her permission to ask his question? It seemed strange to think someone from the zyndar class would bother.

"Would you like to get dinner one night after work?"

Her first thought was to respond that she got dinner every night after work, but awareness trickled into her. "On a date?"

"Yes. I—"

The door opened, and one of the older and more portly agents ambled out, already reaching for his buckle as he headed for the closest latrine. He saw them and lowered his hand from his belt.

"Zyndar Dharrow," he greeted respectfully as Jev and Zenia stepped apart so he could pass. He looked at Zenia. "And Zenia." He smiled, his gaze dipping toward her chest briefly. Not briefly enough.

"Miss Cham, if you please, Mr. Brokko." She didn't bother to disguise her irritation at the casual address. As newly appointed leaders of the intelligence office, she expected to struggle to get the two zyndar men working there to address her with any respect, but the others were commoners, the same as she, and as their boss, she deserved a respectful address. Granted, she hadn't had a chance to prove herself yet, but she would. They could show some politeness until she did.

The man snorted and looked at Jev. "Uppity, isn't she?"

Jev's eyes widened in indignation, and she once again imagined him like a guard dog with hackles rising. "Miss Cham is your boss, Brokko. I've seen her punch people for irritating her."

"I'm not worried about a girl's punch."

"*I've* punched people for irritating her," Jev said, his voice low, his eyes hard.

Even though Zenia preferred to take care of herself and didn't like relying on anyone else, she couldn't help but feel warmth at having Jev come to her defense. He was always so quick to smile and joke, but she'd seen his serious side a few times before and found it intriguing.

"Huh," Brokko said, stepping back and glancing at her. "Must be nice to have a zyndar leashed up and ready to fling into battle." His second nod toward Jev wasn't as respectful, but he hurried past without delivering further insults.

Jev watched him leave, his eyes slitted. He had once suggested that he could be *her* zyndar if she wished it, but she was fairly certain he had been joking, trying to make her feel better after she'd been caught in that rockfall.

"Is it too soon to start formulating lists of suspects from within the office?" Zenia asked when the man had disappeared into the latrine.

The thirteen agents that worked inside were all people they had inherited from King Abdor and that they didn't know well. That *Zenia* didn't know well. Any one of them could be an informant for the underworld crime guilds or someone else.

Jev arched his eyebrows. "Is that a joke or do you have a reason to suspect our colleagues?" he asked, keeping his voice low. "A reason such as someone might have warned Dr. Bandigor that we were coming? Which might have prompted him to take his life before being blamed for something? Or did someone want to keep him from revealing what he knew?"

She nodded, glad he'd also found the man's death—and its timing—suspicious, even if they hadn't been able to determine if it had been suicide or murder. "Not many people outside of the office know we're on this assignment."

"True." He gestured to the office door. "But we may want to spend more than a day on the job before accusing our colleagues of crimes."

"How political."

"You've discovered my true worth. As a diplomat." Jev smirked, but it was perhaps not as much of a joke as he thought.

She'd seen him trade a few words with Master Grindmor and win the dwarf to their side, and dwarves were not known for being easily winnable. She suspected the army had chosen him for linguistics training only partially due to an aptitude for words. They'd likely thought he would do a good job speaking—and swaying people—on their behalf.

Maybe taking him along to interview the archmages *would* be a good idea. Less for looming and more for smiling and charming people.

"An odd claim given that you just threatened to punch someone," was all she said aloud.

"I merely informed him that I *had* punched people, though now that I think about it, I don't know if I've brutalized anyone on your behalf. I remember trying to step in with those Fifth Dragon thugs that kidnapped us, but you punched them first."

"Do you want me to hold back next time?"

"Would you? So I'm not proven to be a liar?"

"I'll do my best."

He bumped his shoulder against hers, smiling again, and they strode into their new office.

CHAPTER 4

I'M NOT GOING BACK DOWN to see her." Jev sipped calmly from his wineglass, though he was ready to get steely if Cutter pushed it.

"But you said she liked you. She flirted with you and wanted to have sex with you."

"She wanted to add another zyndar notch to her bedpost." Jev looked out the double doors of the tasting room, open to the setting sun, warm rays bathing the lush rows of green vines outside. From their vantage point at a booth in the back, they couldn't see the city, though the winery wasn't far outside of it. Jev had agreed to the meeting place because it was easier for Lornysh not to have to travel through the city.

He hadn't arrived yet, but they expected him soon. Cutter had been the one to request the meeting, but Jev didn't mind. He didn't want to ignore his comrades because he was busy with his new job, especially since they were still relative strangers to Korvann. And since Korvann didn't have any love for strangers right now.

"Isn't it desirable for humans to have sex with many women? I've observed your kind aren't as monogamous as dwarves."

"I prefer monogamy myself. Leads to fewer hard feelings. Weren't you just this morning arguing for me to make something for Zenia?"

"Yes."

"She might not like my spice rack as much if she learns I've been having sex with many women." Jev shuddered at the idea of going back into the warren of tunnels underneath the city to seek out Iridium for sex or anything else.

"Have you started constructing it?"

"No, it was a busy day."

"Don't forget a slot for tarragon. Some people leave that one out. Here's what I wanted you to look at." Cutter pulled a folded paper from his pack. He'd been carrying all his belongings around since arriving in the kingdom despite having the use of a room in Dharrow Castle.

Maybe he didn't trust Jev's father not to throw him out. Or burn all his belongings. The old man's venom was directed more at elves than dwarves, but he had taken on a xenophobic streak in his old age. Or since his wife had left him for an elf. Only to be killed by her own mother who had wanted to stop it...

Jev rubbed his temple. His head still throbbed whenever he thought of the insanity he'd unearthed in his own household. He wished his brother Vastiun had never gotten caught up with that elf princess and her quest. If he hadn't, he never would have sailed off and joined the army only to die in the war. Of course, Mother would still be dead, by Grandmother's hand.

"This map," Cutter said. "It's of the sewers and aqueducts for your city. I paid some kid who said he'd worked for the Fifth Dragon to fill in some of the *extra* tunnels that none of the maps in the library mention." He scowled at Jev as if this was his fault. "But I know it's far from complete. A dozen dwarves mining a lifetime couldn't have made all the tunnels under your city."

Glad for the excuse not to think of his family—and that he'd agreed to go to dinner at the castle later that night—he leaned forward to examine the paper. "You hope mapping the underworld lairs will help you find Master Grindmor's missing tools?"

"I do. If they're underground in that guild's lair somewhere, and I've got a map, I could tunnel in from the side, avoid dealing with criminals. Not that I'm afraid of them, mind you."

"Has anyone delivered any threats to Arkura? Or suggested she trade her services for information again?" Even though Jev's mind was on his case, he would do his best to offer helpful comments on Cutter's problem.

"Not since Iridium tricked Master *Grindmor*—" Cutter frowned at Jev's audacity at calling her by her first name, "—into carving a dragon tear for her. And raising golems. And lots of other things."

Jev nodded. "I was there for their meeting."

"The master is positive now that Iridium had the tools all along and has hidden them someplace new. I wouldn't have a chance at convincing a human to tell me anything." He tapped his hook on his chest. "But maybe you could convince her. You're good at talking people into things."

"Thanks, I think."

"Remember when you convinced that elf warden to surrender?"

"He had eight rifles pointed at him from all sides. I didn't have to do much convincing."

"Yes, you did. He was going to cut his own throat so he couldn't be interrogated by us."

"True." Jev sipped his wine.

"And then instead of interrogating him, you played chips with him while chatting with him in Elvish and getting him drunk. I seem to remember he told us quite a bit." Cutter grinned as if he missed those good old days.

Jev couldn't claim to miss the war, a war he'd never believed in, but he had felt... competent there. He'd known his job and how to do it. Here, in this new position for the king, he worried he wouldn't be sufficient for the task. He wished he had some of Zenia's confidence.

"Will one of you move over, or do I have to stand here all day?"

Jev turned to find Lornysh waiting by the head of the table. How long had he been there? In his green woodland clothing, he blended in with the fake vines twining all over the walls and ceiling of the tasting room.

"If you stood more loudly, people would notice you," Cutter grumbled, sliding over while keeping a hand on the open map.

"That wouldn't be good for my health." Lornysh took the seat beside him.

He wore a cloak, the hood pulled up, but even so, Jev worried someone in the busy tasting room would glimpse the pointed ears thrusting out of his silver hair. Fortunately, most of the people here had been tasting all afternoon on this last official day of the coronation celebration before the city returned to normalcy. Some of them had likely been drinking all three days of the affair.

"I'm seeking to fill in this map," Cutter informed Lornysh, "but Jev won't go sleep with a criminal for me."

"That's selfish of him."

"*Exactly*. Jev, what if I help you make a gift for Zenia? Something good that she'd like. Then will you sleep with this Iridium?"

Jev leaned back, draping his arm over the back of his booth, and noticed Lornysh's eyebrows arching.

"Is that logic strange to elves too?" Jev asked.

"Most of what comes out of Cutter's mouth is strange to elves."

Cutter scowled at him. "I'm regretting sharing my bench with you."

A waitress wandered past, and Jev held up a finger to preemptively order a drink for Lornysh, more because he didn't want the woman coming over to engage him and his ears in conversation than because he thought Lornysh would enjoy it. His friend had snooty tastes when it came to alcohol. And food. And art. And everything else.

"Do you have a pencil or charcoal?" Lornysh asked.

"Yes…" Cutter squinted at him but dug into his pack again and pulled out a charcoal stick.

Lornysh wordlessly took it and bent over the map.

"What're you doing?" Cutter gripped his forearm. "I had to pay a grubby overcharging human for that map."

Lornysh looked coolly at the hand on his arm before shifting his icy blue gaze to Cutter. "Filling in the missing tunnels for you."

"How would you know where they are?" Cutter asked, but he released his grip. "You haven't been here any longer than I have."

"I have been using the underground passages to get into interesting places around the city since my hood is not typical of spring fashion here, it seems, and has made many people suspicious."

"Imagine," Jev murmured, leaning out to take a glass from the waitress before she came close enough to look at Lornysh. He laid a dragon-headed kron coin on her platter.

She smiled shyly. "Thank you, Zyndar."

"What counts as an interesting place in a human city?" Jev set the glass in front of Lornysh, though he'd already bent his head to sketch tunnels on the map.

Lornysh glanced at the glass, sniffed without reaching for it, then wrinkled his nose and returned to the map. "The Museum of Exotic Creatures, the orchestra hall, the Fourth Garden Amphitheater, and a business with a ceramics tour."

"We've been here less than a week." Cutter leaned his elbows on the table, watching the drawing intently. "How have you had time to see all that?"

"I don't think Lornysh sleeps much," Jev said, voicing a suspicion he'd long had.

"I meditate."

"I don't think Lornysh meditates much," Jev amended.

"It is sufficient for my needs."

"If I went to a theater of human plays, I'd certainly fall asleep," Cutter said.

"But not if you went on a ceramics tour?" Jev asked.

"Ceramics can be interesting. It's working with materials from the earth."

"Do you know anything about medicine, Lornysh?" Jev asked. He didn't expect the answer to be yes, but he'd found in the past that Lornysh had an ecumenical education. It would be convenient if he could offer some insight into his case.

"Human medicine? Little."

"Medicine in general. I imagine that what applies to elves applies to humans for the most part. We can't be that dissimilar since we can have offspring together."

"We?" Lornysh lifted his eyes from the map.

"Well, not *we* specifically. You and I would have trouble in that department. But our races. There are all manner of mixed human-elves wandering the world."

"Yes," Lornysh said, his tone cooling.

Did he not approve of such mixed bloods? Likely not. He did seem to be a purist. Jev had always been surprised he'd managed to talk Lornysh into joining Gryphon Company during the war—especially since his introduction to the army had been when soldiers captured and brutally interrogated him. And now, with the war over, Jev kept expecting him to offer a parting and return to his elven homeland. Or, if he wasn't welcome there, head off on travels to parts of the world he hadn't yet seen. Lornysh couldn't find the ceramics museums of Korvann *that* exciting.

"What do you want to know?" he asked.

"Targyon has asked me to investigate how his cousins all came to die last month and to figure out if he could be in danger for the same 'disease of the blood' as it's been called."

"As your kingdom's new monarch, he'll likely be in constant danger from many sides. I assume bodyguards and food testers flank him most of the day."

"From what I've seen, yes. But the princes must have had those things too. Dazron, the eldest, at least. He was all but running the castle and the kingdom while Abdor led us around Taziira."

Lornysh set down the charcoal and steepled his fingers. "I have only passing familiarity with the medical sciences, but I suppose even that's more than what most humans have. I can offer a few thoughts, but I anticipate you'll want to find a human expert."

"I do plan to visit an expert, but go ahead." Jev had long since stopped being offended by Lornysh's arrogance and belief in his own superiority.

"As I'm sure you know, there are afflictions that affect some races and not others. Only dwarves, for instance, can contract *mynoresta* and get serious infections from it. It's not that the fungus doesn't get into all of our bodies when we inhale spores, but humans and elves aren't bothered by it. It's believed that dwarves, because they left the surface long ago and spent so much of their evolutionary history underground, didn't need to develop an immunity to many of our above-ground microscopic nemeses. That can make dwarves more susceptible to illness when they travel among us. Meanwhile, they are unaffected by the methane that one often encounters underground, a gas that is deadly when elves and humans are exposed to too much of it. Presumably, it was so advantageous for dwarves to be immune to underground gases that those with a tolerance were more likely to live into adulthood and reproduce. Those without a tolerance may have died before having children. Thus, immunity became more prevalent than not in the species as a whole."

Jev nodded, though he was getting far more of a lesson on spores and gas than he had wanted. "That explains why one race might be more susceptible than another, but what about specific bloodlines within a race?"

Cutter snapped his fingers to get Lornysh's attention while frowning at Jev. "You're distracting my elf from what's important here."

"*Your* elf?" Lornysh asked. "Did you not once say you wanted nothing to do with me until I learned to grow a decent beard?"

"That was before you started drawing tunnels on a map for me." Cutter picked up the charcoal stick and thrust it between Lornysh's fingers.

Lornysh sighed and accepted it, pulling the map closer so he could continue drawing. "Your people, Jev, spread out long ago from the jungles of Izstara where we all originally evolved from Grellan apes. Humans, elves, dwarves, and orcs all did, of course, but we grew into very different species hundreds of thousands of years ago."

Jev set his wineglass down with a clunk. Evolved from *apes*? What did that mean? That he shared ancestors with some furry primate? And was cousin to some tusk-mouthed *orc*?

Was there any human science out there to back up what sounded like ridiculous claims to him? Jev would ask Targyon what his books said about this the next time he saw him. He knew not everyone believed the Order origin story that the dragon founders had hatched in the cosmos and been instructed by the universe to create this world and all its species, but he hadn't heard any of this before. Zenia and all her Order friends would stomp up and down on Lornysh's ears if he shared the ideas in public.

"Your human ancestors traveled from their jungle origins in search of food and because of competition with the other species. They soon settled on other continents, even the already populated, and claimed Taziira." Lornysh's lips thinned, and he glanced up from his tunnel drawing, as if Jev was to blame.

Cutter snapped his fingers again at the pause and pointed to the map.

"Over countless generations," Lornysh continued, "your people continued to evolve, adapting in small ways to better fit into their new environments. This didn't occur uniformly to the whole species. Different clans and tribes changed depending on where they settled. Some of those changes were in the blood and were passed on to children and grandchildren and so on. Today, with the advent of steam power, it's easier for humans to travel around the world and create vast kingdoms and empires, so many of the old clans have dissolved. But the quirks of their blood still exist, manifesting in their descendants."

"By the founders, I'm going to need a lot more alcohol if he's going to keep talking." Cutter groaned and eyed Lornysh's untouched wineglass.

"He's drawing your map while he does it," Jev said. "What's the problem?"

"When he lectures, it's like having nails pounded into my skull."

"To sum up," Lornysh said, "your king's ancestors may have come from another continent or an area where they developed a mutation that allowed them to thrive there. Maybe it's useful here, or maybe it isn't, but it continues to exist, passed on from father to son through the generations. It's possible that an intelligent doctor or scientist may have found a blood-borne pathogen that is deadly to humans with that specific mutation. I don't believe anyone—human, elf, or otherwise—has the scientific understanding and tools to *create* such a thing, but to exploit something that exists in nature would be a possibility. Perhaps, if you were to pore over genealogy reports, you would find that this happened to your royal family in the past."

"So, it's possible that what they say is true, that there's a disease that only affected the Alderoth family?"

"Possible, though for it to be completely family-specific would be unlikely. It probably affects a small subset of the human population, and the Alderoths happen to belong to that subset."

"Could it have been an accident?" Jev asked. "Or do you think someone would have had to deliberately introduce the princes to this... pathogen?"

"Unless there are others dying in the city after displaying the same symptoms, the latter seems likely."

Jev's head was starting to hurt. This was a lot to take in. "Here's the problem with your hypothesis. The Alderoths are a very old family, as old as my own, and they've been here on this land since before Kor was a kingdom."

"That doesn't negate my hypothesis. It's possible your Alderoth family has carried this mutation for millennia. Since your royal families are known for inbreeding—marrying cousins and such—it makes sense that such a mutation would have stuck around and remained dominant among them."

"So, I should be digging into their genealogical history, you say?" As if Jev didn't have enough to do. At least what he'd expected to be a simple meeting for drinks had turned informative.

"To see if this has happened to the family before and if premature deaths were the result. Perhaps someone even found a cure centuries ago."

Jev nodded. "If we had a cure, Targyon wouldn't have to worry so much. Not about this specifically."

"Indeed. Though you might warn him not to marry any distant relatives, so he's less likely to pass the trait along to his children. Inbreeding, as it's taken humans a long time to realize, tends to cause a lot of trouble and mutations, not always advantageous ones. A greater diversity in the blood is ideal for health."

More science Jev had not heard about. As far as he knew, the royals and the zyndar had always believed their blood was superior and it was ideal to marry others from royal or zyndar families. Jev wondered what Zenia would think of all this. Perhaps that inbreeding was the reason for zyndar arrogance, a malfunction in the blood, no doubt.

He started to smile, but Lornysh was gazing gravely at him, and his lips froze.

"What?" Jev asked.

"If I were you, I would be very careful with my investigation."

"Why?"

"You know more about your own genealogy than I do," Lornysh said, "but given your family's standing in Kor and your estate's proximity to the capital and Alderoth Castle, I wouldn't be surprised if some of your ancestors had married Alderoths at some point in history. Or multiple points."

"They have." A tendril of worry wormed its way into Jev's stomach as he realized what his friend was implying.

"Then it's possible *you* may share this mutation that makes you susceptible to whatever this affliction is. And if whoever brought it into the castle is still there…"

"I see your point." Jev thought of the dead doctor, the man somehow having been warned of the investigation before it arrived on his doorstep. Yes, someone was still around who'd been involved. Or who had been responsible. "I see your point," Jev repeated softly.

"Lower your hood," a man growled, walking up to the table behind Lornysh. It was unoccupied, but other tables beyond it held crowds of people, and several were looking their way.

Jev should have known someone would find Lornysh suspicious sooner or later. He stood up and gave the man a steely gaze while noting the dagger and a one-handed hatchet belted at his waist. Clad in coarse, dirt-spattered clothing, he looked like he'd come in from someone's field. Or perhaps the winery's field.

"Is there a problem?" Jev asked.

"You've got suspicious companions, Zyndar," the man growled.

Jev flicked his fingers toward the door, the gesture only for Lornysh and Cutter. He didn't want a fight to break out. There was nothing to be gained from it except a bill from the owner and the need to carry people to a hospital.

"How boring would it be if my companions were mundane?" Jev smiled and stepped forward, effectively blocking the newcomer from Lornysh. He hadn't yet tried to touch Lornysh, but he was glowering hard enough to wilt flowers.

Lornysh hadn't turned around or acknowledged the man, but he appeared tense, his head up and alert. He slowly set down the charcoal stick.

Cutter sighed, though his expansive map appeared nearly finished.

The hatchet man glanced over his shoulder to comrades at a nearby table, and they all nodded encouragingly.

"If you're loving elves," the man told Jev, "your father's name won't help you."

"If I were loving elves, my father would beat me black and blue."

If he still could. Jev liked to think he could handle himself against the old man these days.

"As he should."

More head nods.

"We insist that your suspicious companion leave." The man slurred the word suspicious. Neither he nor his buddies appeared sober.

"We'll all leave if that'll make your evening more comfortable." Jev pulled out his purse and dropped a few coins on the table.

His self-appointed harasser seemed surprised, as if he'd been readying himself to spout more threats.

"Why don't you sit down, friend?" Jev offered as Cutter folded his map and returned it to his pack.

"You think I'm afraid of you because you're zyndar?" the man snarled. "World's changing. People got used to not bowing so much during the war, when there weren't so many zyndar in the streets. Zyndaring."

"I imagine." Jev continued to block the man as Cutter and Lornysh slid out of their seats and headed for the door.

Lornysh kept his hood up. Jev didn't see how the hatchet man could have seen his ears and known for certain he was an elf. Unless it had become common knowledge that Jev was roaming the city with an elf and a dwarf. If so, as much as he hated to contemplate it, it might be better for his friends if he parted ways with them. At least for a time.

The man's fingers twitched toward his hatchet as Lornysh walked out the door, his cloaked back to them. Maybe he wouldn't have attacked, and maybe Lornysh would have sensed an attack coming even if he did, but Jev didn't take the chance.

He stepped forward, his hand darting for the man's forearm. His foe tried to jerk it back, but Jev was faster. He clamped down, keeping the man's fingers from touching the hatchet.

"Don't do anything foolish," Jev murmured, glaring into his eyes for a second before sharing the glare with the man's companions.

"We're not the foolish ones here. We're not drinking with an elf."

"He didn't drink," Jev said, then promptly gave himself a mental kick for admitting what they could have only suspected.

The man growled and tried to pull his arm away. Since Cutter and Lornysh had left, shutting the double doors behind them, Jev let go. He issued another baleful glare to the table, for all the good it did with drunk men, and strode toward the exit.

A thud came from beyond the doors, followed by a crash.

Cursing, Jev sprinted outside, worried that lout had set his friends up for a trap.

He almost tripped over a man writhing on the path and grabbing his crotch. A second man lay crumpled against the wood wall of the tasting room. Lornysh stood over him, his expression impassive. Cutter had his fists balled as he crouched, facing the one protecting his nether regions from further abuse.

"Problem?" Jev kept his tone calm, but he looked around, worried more threats would materialize.

These men wore farmers' clothing, similar to that of the hatchet thug inside. At least his friends hadn't knocked out watchmen.

What would happen if the law came after Lornysh? Would Jev's status as zyndar and now agent of the Crown keep them from attempting to arrest him? Or worse?

"Only that Cutter chooses unsporting targets when he brawls," Lornysh said.

"I can't help it that humans are so tall. That's the level my noggin's at when I bend over to head butt someone."

Since the two men didn't look like they wanted anything more to do with them, Jev waved for his comrades to head down the path. The sooner they got out of the area, the better.

He paused when he spotted a pistol in the grass next to the man Lornysh had knocked unconscious. Jev grimaced and kicked it farther from the path.

"Just a typical evening out with Lornysh," he said, forcing a smile as they walked away. He couldn't bring himself to suggest that they should part ways and avoid each other for a while. Especially when Lornysh had given him information relevant to his research.

"That's the truth," Cutter said. "There was always someone trying to kill him in the army too. Not always the other side."

"Perhaps," Lornysh said, as they headed into the sunset, "I will accept Shoyalusa's offer."

"Who's that?" Jev asked, eyeing people riding up and dismounting by the hitching post. Fortunately, nobody did more than glance at his hooded comrade.

"The current elven ambassador in Korvann. He sought me out and suggested I stay in the embassy tower."

"A tower?" Cutter asked. "Seems like a life of paucity after living in a castle."

"I haven't been living *in* the castle," Lornysh pointed out.

Even though he sounded matter-of-fact rather than resentful, Jev winced. His father had made it clear that neither Lornysh nor any other elves were welcome inside his walls or anywhere on his land. Jev had told Lornysh that nobody would know if he was camping out in the woods, but it galled him that he couldn't truly offer his friend a hospitable place. It galled him further that at thirty-three, he still felt dependent on his father.

Jev wasn't without funds, and he'd almost run into town in a snit to rent a townhouse where he could invite Cutter and Lornysh to stay as long as they liked, but he'd known Lornysh wouldn't be interested in sleeping in a stone-walled box, as he referred to human homes. If this ambassador's tower was in the city, it likely had some lush gardens and vines crawling up the sides of it to make it more palatable to an elf.

"Do you think he knows anything about the unorthodox succession?" Jev asked.

"We did not discuss it when I met him."

"How about discussing it when you move in? I doubt you think your people had anything to do with the princes' deaths, and I'm inclined to agree, but an ambassador has spies, I assume, and might know something."

"I believe they're called diplomats," Lornysh said. "If I hear anything relevant, I will tell you."

"Good. Thank you." Jev felt guilty asking his friend to spy on his own embassy, but he owed it to Targyon to use every resource at his disposal.

"Where's the tower located in the city?" Cutter asked.

"Why do you ask?" Lornysh asked.

"I need to know where to find you in case I need your wisdom as I go seek out Master Grindmor's tools. Your wisdom or even your company. You know a quest undertaken by oneself is a lonely affair."

"You want me to finish your map, don't you?"

Cutter grinned.

CHAPTER 5

ENIA GLANCED AT JEV AS they walked together through the city, heading for the Air Order Temple. He hadn't made any jokes yet this morning, which she found she missed, and she kept catching distracted expressions on his face. A couple of delivery boys on bicycles piled high with crates almost mowed him over, and he barely noticed.

"Are you all right?" Zenia finally asked.

His eyes focused, and he nodded quickly. "Yes, of course."

"Because you seem distracted. I'm not sure you could loom effectively right now."

"I disagree, but do you think looming will be required at our first stop? The Earth Order people are the ones you suspect of plans to strong-arm the king, right?"

"Yes."

Zenia had been tempted to head straight to their temple this morning, but she wanted to check with Air first for a couple of reasons. First off, she thought the Earth archmage would be less suspicious and on-guard if he learned she was simply questioning all the archmages. Second, the Earth and Air temples rarely worked together and more often worked in opposition to each other. Supposedly, it had to do with the alignment of the stars and grudges the original dragon founders had carried toward each other. But Zenia had heard that when the city had been founded, both Orders had coveted the valley the Air Order managed to snag first, a beautiful area with a stream cutting through on its way to the sea. Ancient oaks and cottonwoods lined the banks, creating natural shade over the street and walkways.

"Given what Archmage Sazshen has said about me, according to Rhi, I may have difficulty getting any of the Orders to work with me. I may need you to be more charming than looming."

"I can certainly attempt to charm these people with my infectious good humor. I'm glad you noticed I have such an ability. I've wondered at times, since you don't usually laugh at my wit. They say a good laugh can cure many ailments." Jev offered his first smile of the morning.

"I've heard that."

"*You* should try laughing more often."

"At your jokes or just in general?"

"Both, but my jokes are a particularly fine medicine."

"It's possible I'm in the placebo group."

He snorted. "Is that why you avoided answering me yesterday when I asked you on a date?"

"No, that was because one of our colleagues came out and leered at my chest."

"I remember. I look forward to punching him the next time he does it. Don't forget that you're going to stand back and let me."

"I won't."

"Good." Jev's smile faded as they turned at an intersection to head up the road into the valley, the stream trickling alongside their route. "I admit I have ailments on my mind for a reason."

"Besides infecting people with your humor?"

"Yes."

As Jev and Zenia walked beneath the shady trees, he summarized the chat he'd had with Lornysh the day before.

"So, if you were exposed to the disease, it might be deadly to you?" she asked, focusing on that for now, rather than some of the more contentious things the elf had told him.

"Possibly. And to Targyon, of course. And any of his brothers and sisters who visit the castle."

Zenia eyed him, not surprised he would make light of the threat to himself and focus on someone else. "And possibly deadly to your family too?"

His expression grew bleak.

"I merely bring this up because extortion could be a possibility, something you should prepare yourself to deal with," Zenia said.

The Air Order Temple with its white salt-encrusted dome and travertine columns came into view farther up the valley.

"I understand. I'm going to hope that nobody else makes the leap that Lornysh did, thinking that because the Alderoths and Dharrows share some distant ancestors, my family and I might be susceptible to the disease. For all I know, we're not. My ancestors married lots of different zyndars. Dharrows are a randy bunch." He smiled again, though it didn't reach his eyes and make them twinkle the way it usually did.

"Nonetheless, you should avoid putting yourself into situations where you might be exposed."

"The easy way to do that is to solve this case as quickly as possible and make sure the person responsible gets locked up or shot."

"I'm happy to work toward that end," Zenia said.

She wondered if having a zyndar father meant she might possibly share blood with the royal family. Was it worth investigating the Morningfar genealogy? Would that information even be available in the library? To commoners?

"After we're done with the interviews, I'll poke around the castle and talk to the staff," Jev said. "See if I can get a solid description of what the princes' symptoms were before they died so I can look for a match in the history books. I suppose I could get one of our agents to help."

"Hm." Zenia hadn't asked any of them for anything yet. In theory, they had all these people at their disposal, but she had no idea what kind of vetting King Abdor had done. For all she knew, one of them was responsible for the deaths. Was it possible they had double agents in their midst? Could some other country have been responsible for this? Wanting to throw Kor into chaos over the succession?

"It will be good to have that information when I go to interview medical specialists," Jev added.

Zenia opened her mouth to reply, but a white-eyed old woman sitting cross-legged next to the stone steps leading up to the dome lifted a hand to get their attention. A cane rested next to one of her knees, and a ceramic soup tureen with a few coins in it sat beside the other.

"May I tell your fortune, friends?" she asked. "I'll charge half what the temple mages demand, and my fortunes are twice as accurate. They come to me in visions that the sighted would never see." She pointed at her milky white eyes.

Zenia kept walking for the steps, planning to ignore the entreaty, but Jev paused, then veered toward the woman. He placed a kron coin in her tureen.

"Give me your hand, love." She raised hers toward him.

"How did you know which one of us came over?" Jev asked dryly as he lowered a hand into hers. "Or do you call everyone *love*?"

"Only those who tuck money into my bowl." She lowered her head and sandwiched his hand between hers.

Given what he'd just been worried about, Zenia was surprised he wanted his fortune. She never put much stock in such things, despite having lived and worked in a temple for twenty years, but even if someone could share an accurate one with her, she would prefer not to know.

"Hm, you were born under the stars of the air sign," she said.

"Yes," Jev said.

"I see potential happiness in your stars, but the road to that place is fraught with numerous dead ends and winding mazes that lead nowhere. You must choose wisely in the days ahead and expect a storm to test your mind and body."

She lowered her hands and lifted her head.

"Thank you," Jev said.

Zenia couldn't tell what he thought of the fortune. She thought about asking him, but the temple doors opened, and a white-robed inquisitor walked out.

Zenia recognized the woman. Ji Loo. They'd worked together on a case once, one that had involved both of their Orders. Zenia had been the one to stay up late every night and rise early, dedicated to the duty until she solved it on her own. Ji Loo had been far less dedicated, wandering off for long lunch hours and shopping. Ji Loo hadn't been pleased when Zenia had told their archmages as much rather than implying they had both worked equally hard and both deserved credit.

She wasn't surprised when Ji Loo sneered and stepped in front of her on the steps, blocking her way. "Zenia Cham, dear. I heard the news, that you betrayed the Water Order and Archmage Sazshen. For your own gain, no doubt. I understand you work for the king now."

"I understand gossip spreads faster than news in the Korvann Chronicle." Zenia shifted to walk around her, wagering the true story hadn't gotten out, that Sazshen wouldn't have spoken widely about the Eye of Truth, not when she'd tried so hard to keep it a secret.

"The young king risks much in hiring you. The wrath of the Water Order. Of *all* the Orders. He would be unwise to make enemies of the archmages."

"You should have gotten your fortune told," Jev said, climbing up to stand next to Zenia, his shoulder to hers.

"So I would have foreseen an inquisitor coming out of the temple to harass me?"

Ji Loo squinted at Jev. He wasn't wearing his wolf-head brooch today, a sizable piece of jewelry that identified him as zyndar from an important family, but ever since he'd cleaned up and trimmed his beard, he looked far more the noble than he had when he first got off that ship. Would Ji Loo recognize him as such? Or care?

"So you would have gotten your hand caressed by that lady. She has some lovely lotion on her palms. It smells like lemons, don't you think?" Jev raised his hand toward Zenia's nose.

"Uh, yes."

"I think my palm is soft and moisturized now too." He shifted his hand toward Ji Loo's nose.

Her eyes widened and she stepped back, but she forgot she was on the stairs and clunked her heel against the riser. She almost pitched backward onto her butt. Jev, Zenia was certain, could have grabbed her in time to steady her, but he merely lowered his hand, watching blandly. Alas, Ji Loo recovered before polishing the steps with her white-robed butt.

Without another word, she rushed around Jev and hurried onto a path leading to a stable.

"It's possible my charisma isn't working as promised," Jev said. "She must also be a member of this placebo group you mentioned."

"It's possible all inquisitors are."

"I *am* finding it difficult to infect them with my laughter."

If the blind old woman, close enough to hear this strange conversation, thought anything odd of it, she didn't say. She merely smiled and gazed sightlessly at the stream.

Zenia took Jev's arm and led him toward the open door, wondering if she should send him in first to speak with the archmage. Or let him do the speaking while she stood back and analyzed the man. That might work well. In addition to having that charisma, he had a knack for startling emotions out of people with his irreverent comments.

They walked into the deep shade of the spacious temple, the cavernous great room with its candles and dragon statues taking up the front half of the dome. Zenia had visited before and headed across the polished travertine floor toward hallways on the other side, intending to walk straight to the archmage's office.

But another white-robed figure rose from among several people in civilian clothing, all kneeling before the candles with their heads bowed. The figure, another inquisitor, this time a strong-jawed man with shoulder-length salt-and-pepper hair and gentle gray eyes, strode to intercept them.

"Another inquisitor for me to flirt with?" Jev murmured.

"Is that what you were doing with Ji Loo?"

"You couldn't tell?"

"She hustled away at top speed. Is that the typical result when you flirt with a woman?"

"It's not my fault she didn't want to sniff my palm. It smells quite lovely right now."

"I had no idea working with you was going to be such a unique experience," Zenia said, lowering her voice since the other inquisitor was nearing them. What was his name? She'd seen him about before but didn't think he'd had this job for long. Uragran?

She stopped, forcing a smile, though inwardly, she braced herself for more insults. Inquisitors in other temples often considered each other rivals of a sort, but they also treated each other with politeness and respect. Maybe that rule no longer applied to Zenia.

"Zenia Cham?" The man offered his hand. "Uragran Uthors. You're not looking for our archmage, are you?"

"Yes, is he in?"

"He's not. He's gone to a meeting in Drovann to speak with several Air Order archmages from other cities. May I assist you? Ji Loo is the senior-ranking mage in the temple when the archmage is out, but she just left."

"So unfortunate to have missed her," Jev murmured.

"I'm next in command, I believe, though I'm told I'm not nearly ferocious enough to lead a temple." He smiled at Zenia.

It was so different from the reception she'd expected from anyone here that she stared at him with a slack mouth. She glimpsed Jev looking at her, and she snapped her jaw shut.

"Would you be able to answer a few questions?" Zenia asked, though she was disappointed the archmage wasn't there.

If the Air Order ran its temple the way the Water Order did, its inquisitors wouldn't be privy to all the secrets the archmage was. A fact that Zenia still resented. If only Sazshen had told her all she knew about that artifact from the beginning, her introduction to Jev could have been far less fraught.

"Yes, certainly," Uragran said. "I understand you work for the king now?"

"As one of his intelligence-gathering agents, yes."

"And is this—" Uragran spread a hand toward Jev, who stood a couple of inches taller than he, "—your bodyguard?"

Jev drew back his shoulders, appearing pleased by this unbiased assessment. Any second now, he would start looming.

"I'm her zyndar," Jev said before Zenia could introduce him as a colleague. "Jev Dharrow."

"Oh?" Uragran seemed taken aback, but he recovered and bowed. "It's an honor to receive you in our temple, Zyndar Dharrow. Do you wish to light a candle?"

"No, thanks. And I've already received my fortune." Jev pointed a thumb toward the entrance.

Uragran frowned in disapproval. "I'm certain we could get you a more divinely approved fortune. No charge for a zyndar, of course."

Zenia decided it wouldn't be seemly to roll her eyes at the display of preferential treatment. She ought to be happy someone here was amenable to answering questions. Unless he was *overly* amenable? Was it possible Uragran had been sent to lead Zenia astray? Maybe the archmage was even here in the temple and simply didn't wish to speak with her. Because he had a truth to hide?

"Not necessary," Jev said. "We came to see how the Air Order feels about King Targyon. We heard the Earth Order was paramount in selecting him over older and wiser relatives who might have been suited to the position."

"The Earth Order? I fear you're mistaken, zyndar. They objected to Targyon as king. It was Water, Fire, and Air that banded together and cast their votes for him."

"Ah, I must have heard incorrectly. Why did you support such a youthful king?"

"*I* had no say, you understand." Uragran touched his chest. "I'm told the archmage received a vision from the White Dragon, and there was no doubt as to the content. Young King Targyon sat upon the throne, ushering in a peaceful and economically thriving era for Kor."

"A vision?" Zenia couldn't keep the skepticism out of her voice.

Sazshen had never claimed to receive visions. The dragon founders had left the world millennia ago. Why would they be sending visions to people?

Uragran spread his arms. "I only know what I was told, though my dragon tear did not inform me of any dishonesty from the archmage. Have you not experienced visions, former inquisitor Cham?"

"No."

"No?" He truly seemed taken aback. "Not in all your years serving the Blue Dragon?"

"You probably didn't inhale enough of the blessed incense," Jev muttered to her.

She might have snorted, but it was true that the incense burned in the prayer rooms tended to prompt hallucinations. Or visions, if one wanted to interpret them that way. Many of the mages and disciples did.

"I would be happy to take you to our prayer room and guide you through a cleansing if you wish to experience a vision," Uragran told her. "And, ah, you too, Zyndar Dharrow."

"I prefer to get cleansed with beer and wine."

Uragran's forehead creased.

"Old King Abdor was the same way," Jev offered. "I'm not sure about the princes. I didn't know them as well. Did you? Prince Dazron was born under the air sign, I understand. He must have come to the temple for guidance from time to time."

Zenia hadn't known that, and it occurred to her that she should have. In the past, she had never bothered reading news or gossip about the royal family, caring little for the intrigues that the royals and the zyndars always seemed to be a part of, intrigues that her fellow commoners found so fascinating. But now that she worked for the crown and her case revolved around the royal family, she should spend all her free time learning as much as possible about them. She vowed to do so.

"He was a busy man, but he came occasionally," Uragran said.

"Did you have any trouble with him?" Zenia asked. "Did he ever butt heads with the archmage?"

"Not that I'm aware of. He was properly respectful of the archmage, despite his modest origins and Dazron's princely status."

Uragran spoke earnestly and didn't ooze guile, but Zenia once again felt disadvantaged without her old dragon tear. She had no way to verify if he was telling the truth. He could have been sent out here to deal with her not because he was in charge but because he was a good liar.

"We were devastated by Prince Dazron's abrupt passing," Uragran added. "And that of his younger brothers. They were not of the air sign, but they were, nonetheless, good people. Any one of them would have been a good leader, I believe. Certainly less stress-inspiring than… my pardon." He bowed his head. "It's not appropriate to speak ill of the dead."

"Abdor was a handful," Jev said.

Uragran shook his head, not willing to speak further on the subject, but he didn't deny that the old king was who he'd had in mind.

"Forgive me, but I have duties to attend," Uragran said, lifting his head. "I must go. Do you require anything else?"

"Just to use your latrine before I leave," Zenia said.

Uragran blinked, and his dragon tear, which lay visible over his robe, seemed to glow faintly. Zenia tried to summon a genuine need to use the facilities—maybe she should have slurped some water from the stream on the way to the temple—so Uragran wouldn't, with his gem's magical assistance, sense that she was lying.

"It's back there." He pointed to the hallway that happened to lead to the archmage's office. "May I escort you?"

"To the latrine?" Jev raised his eyebrows. "To hold the washout paper for her? I had no idea Air inquisitors provided such an opulent experience to their guests."

While Uragran blurted a flustered response, Zenia strode quickly away. She trusted Jev understood that she wanted to snoop, for he patted

Uragran on the shoulder and asked some question meant to keep him from following her.

Zenia didn't pretend to open the latrine door and step in. She hustled straight for the archmage's office at the end of the corridor. She didn't knock but tried the knob, expecting it to be locked. It wasn't. She poked her head inside.

The archmage wasn't there. She hadn't truly expected him to be, but she wouldn't have been surprised if he had been. She had a feeling Uragran was lying or perhaps giving her half-truths. Even if she didn't have a dragon tear and couldn't be positive, she believed his attempt to distract her by talk of visions had been an intentional diversion.

A half-full glass of peach juice rested on a corner of the desk next to a partially eaten plate of scrambled eggs and gort leaves. The eggs did not appear to be congealed, so if the archmage had truly left town, he'd gone abruptly and less than an hour ago.

Zenia backed out, closing the door. She wished she had a half hour to snoop through the contents of the desk, but she could hear Uragran and Jev speaking in the great hall. The inquisitor would grow suspicious—*more* suspicious—if she was gone long.

She walked out of the hallway, collected Jev, who was discussing lemon hand lotion with Uragran, and pulled him to the door.

"Did you learn anything useful?" he murmured as they stepped outside. "In the latrine?"

"Just that the Air archmage is likely in town and maybe even in the temple. I wish I had my dragon tear. I could have used it to guide me to other magical sources in the temple, such as the dragon tear *he* wears."

"So, you think someone saw us coming and the archmage has a guilty enough conscience that he didn't want to talk to us?"

"To me, at least." Zenia couldn't know if that had to do with guilt or with the fact that she was ostracized. "They thought you were just my bodyguard."

"Did I loom effectively?"

"I'm not sure. The inquisitor didn't whiz down his leg in unadulterated terror."

"True. Maybe I shouldn't have brought up the lotion. What now?"

They stopped outside once they were out of the blind woman's earshot, stepping off the road and into grass growing alongside the stream. A breeze whispered up the valley, stirring the oak and cottonwood branches. A lone olive tree rose up on the opposite side, the stout tree appearing older than the city itself.

"Let's see if any other archmages are available for a chat," Zenia said. "After that, back to the castle, I guess."

Jev nodded. "After I get a list of symptoms and make an appointment with a medical expert, I also want to hunt in the castle library for lineage books."

"Yes. It would be nice to catch someone in a lie, but maybe finding out more about the disease itself will lead us to the person who created it. Or found it and knew how to put it to use."

"Either way, I suspect it's a small group of individuals with the knowledge to do so."

"If we find that person or persons, they could lead us to whoever hired them," Zenia said.

"Let's hope so. For Targyon's sake."

Zenia knew it was selfish, but she wanted to solve this case as much for her own sake as for the king's. She felt she had to prove herself all over again in this new job, and if she didn't... if Targyon believed he'd made a mistake in hiring her, what then? It was clear none of the other Orders wanted her. Would the watch hire her? She had briefly thought of applying to be a detective there, but the Orders worked closely with and had sway over the watch. What if Sazshen had also forbidden *them* from speaking with Zenia?

If this didn't work out, she might not be able to find a job anywhere in the city.

Zenia firmed her chin as she and Jev headed to the next temple. She *would* solve this crime. And, dragon tear or not, Targyon would see how valuable she was to his team.

CHAPTER 6

JEV YAWNED AS HE ENTERED the castle's huge library, its book-stuffed shelves reaching from floor to high ceiling. Two stories of the north wing were devoted to the depository of knowledge. Fortunately, he was too tired to feel daunted by the size of the place and the size of his task. He'd trailed Zenia all over the city, questioning people in each of the four Orders' temples. Not archmages since they had all been mysteriously absent when he and Zenia had arrived.

Zenia had almost seemed relieved when that happened at the Water Order Temple. Jev couldn't imagine she wanted to come face to face with her old employer, the woman who believed she'd betrayed the temple. And her.

On the way back to the castle, Zenia had decided they should also check in with the captain of the watch. At least he'd been at his desk and hadn't hidden himself away before they came in. Not that it had mattered. The captain had claimed he didn't know anything about the deaths, agreeing only that they had been odd. Terrible bad luck or perhaps something more.

Jev hadn't found any of their talks that day enlightening. He hoped Zenia had gotten more out of them, perhaps learning something from the lies that had danced with truths. Whether she had or not, she'd skipped dinner when they'd returned and gone straight down to their new office. To see what Abdor's original agents had managed to gather since she set them on the case.

He couldn't fault her dedication to duty, but he wondered if she was sleeping. And *where* she was sleeping if she was. He knew she'd been ordered out of the temple, and she'd refused his offer of a room in his father's castle. He couldn't blame her for not wanting to go back there, but he hoped she had found a suitable place to relax.

"Lineage records, where are you?" Jev murmured, eyeing the nearby stacks and hoping a page would wander out to assist him.

He'd been in the castle library before when he'd attended balls—in the last couple of decades, it had grown trendy to host social gatherings among one's book collection, no doubt to show off one's supposed intelligence—but he'd never tried to do research here.

"Are you speaking to the books?" came a voice from the shadows.

The sun had set an hour earlier, leaving the library largely in the dark save for a few lit wall lanterns near the entry. Jev spotted a figure sitting cross-legged on a piano bench, ignoring the piano and looking in his direction.

"Tar—Sire? Should you be in here alone? Sitting in the dark?"

There hadn't been guards at the door, nor did Jev see any bodyguards lurking. He grabbed one of the wall lanterns and carried it toward Targyon.

"I'll answer your question if you answer mine," Targyon said.

"I was hoping a page would hear my mumbling and come help me. I didn't expect the books to respond. Though a talking directory would be handy."

"There is a non-talking directory if you want to try it." Targyon pointed toward a massive card catalog. "The pages only work until dusk."

A closed book rested next to Targyon on the piano bench along with a glass of a dark liquid. "I snuck out of my suite. Mostly to see if I could, to see how long it would take my suffocating protectors to find me."

"A flattering term for those who have agreed to step in front of an arrow and trade their lives for yours."

Targyon winced.

Jev lifted an apologetic hand. It wasn't his place to lecture or act the senior officer to his junior. Not anymore. "Unless the guards sleep in the suite with you, I imagine you won't be missed until dawn."

The wince turned into a grimace.

"They don't, do they? Sleep with you?"

"No. They're not allowed to sleep on shift. And they stay outside the door. There's a manservant who wanders in every couple of hours to see if I need help bathing. Or wiping my ass."

"You didn't tell him you mastered that in the field?"

"I'd like to think I mastered that by age two."

"A precocious child, were you?"

"My mother said so." Targyon smiled faintly and took a large swig of his drink.

Jev would have assumed it to be alcohol—even though he hadn't known Targyon to consume the stuff often, he could see where his new duties would drive him to drink—but he caught a whiff of pomegranate and realized it was juice. Maybe it *should* have been alcohol.

"She's not coming." Targyon set his glass down. "Nor is Father."

"To visit?" Jev thought he'd seen Targyon's parents at the coronation.

"To live here. You remember I told you they work as professors in Rokvann?"

"I seem to recall a tale of them falling madly in love and your mother neglecting to mention she was the king's sister until they were engaged."

"Yes, unlike her other siblings, she always thought our government system and the notion that some people were born the superiors of others complete ludicrousness. She didn't want to support it. Her first suggestion to me was to dissolve the monarchy and establish something democratic."

"That would go over well with zyndar families." Jev didn't mind chatting with Targyon, but he did want to find those lineage books before he fell asleep. And he still needed to locate people who'd cared for the princes when they had been sick and could describe their symptoms.

"Naturally. I'd be assassinated before I could more than make a suggestion to the court." He took another drink, a bracing one. Maybe he had dumped some alcohol into the beverage. "I'm already being pressured to sign a bunch of documents that more or less affirm that I'll maintain the status quo. I know it would be safest for me to do so, as has been hinted at not obliquely. But... even though I wouldn't attempt to push my mother's suggested reforms through, I would like to make *some* changes. To make a difference."

"Might I suggest that it would be best not to rock the boat in the first year of your reign? Let the Orders and your court relax a bit. Your advisors must be as edgy as you as they wonder what they're getting.

Later, you can gradually institute some changes, maybe once you've put more people that are going to support you into positions of power. It's favoritism, granted, but it's something that's expected. You would be foolish not to make sure you have supporters around."

"That's why you're here."

"Oh? You think I'm going to support you? As your former commanding officer, it's my job to ensure that you do your morning exercise routine and clean your boots and rifle every night before you go to bed. That's it."

Targyon's second smile seemed more heartfelt.

"I was hoping my parents coming to stay here would be support too," he said softly. "They would give me advice I could trust, no ulterior motivations. And I'd have normal people to talk to at meals. I understand why they want to stay in Rokvann, as they're both still working and have no interest in retirement. My mother's barely turned fifty-five, and Father's not much older. But a selfish part of me hoped they would come here for me." Targyon ran a hand along the closed lid over the piano keys. "I thought I might find it comforting down here."

"Among the books?" Jev knew Targyon would prefer his science texts to whatever paperwork he'd been referring to.

"Yes. And the piano. We had one in the house when I was growing up. I enjoyed playing. And..."

"And?"

"This is silly, but as a boy, I'd drape blankets over the piano and hide underneath whenever there was a thunderstorm. Or I was afraid of anything."

"So, I'm lucky I didn't find you sprawled down there among the dust balls?"

"It crossed my mind." Targyon looked wistfully between the piano legs, but he stood up instead. "I'm sorry, Captain. I whine to you every time you show up."

"You can whine to me." Jev opened his palm. "Though I hope you're less open with people you don't know as well."

"I clam up around most of them. Growing up in Rokvann was a blessing, but a curse, too, because I know so little about the castle and this life. The staff. I don't know who to trust, and I'm still concerned about the possibility of..." Targyon met Jev's gaze. "Is your case progressing at all?"

"Not as quickly as Zenia would like." Jev smiled. "I think she expected to figure everything out the same day and have a report on your desk by dusk."

"I would have been amenable to that."

"We're working hard." Jev hoped he hadn't implied he expected this to drag on for months. "In fact, I came down here to do some research related to you and your blood. I don't suppose you know where books are that detail your lineage?"

"I could find them easily enough." Targyon's ears perked as he turned toward the card catalog.

"Er." Jev hadn't meant to put him to work, but he had to admit Targyon would be a better researcher than he unless they found pages that need translation. "Good. We can look together."

"What are we looking for specifically?"

"If any of your ancestors died the same way as the princes did."

"Oh." Targyon paused with his hand on the cabinet of drawers and grimaced over his shoulder. "Do you think that's likely?"

"I don't know, but I talked to Lornysh—did you know his people have some interesting ideas about where humans, orcs, dwarves, and elves originally came from?—and he suggested we figure out if this disease had ever struck before and if there was a mention of it anywhere. It's possible someone researching your bloodlines chanced across the information and saw an opportunity."

"The elves have an evolution hypothesis. I'm aware of it." Targyon turned back to the cabinet, pulled out a drawer, flipped a few cards, then grabbed a lantern and headed for a corner of the library. "I'm not aware of any diseases that struck my family in the past, but I'm ashamed to admit I haven't studied my own lineage that much. The future has always drawn my interest more so than the past. To my father's consternation. He teaches global history at the university in Rokvann."

Jev followed his king, having a notion that he shouldn't let Targyon out of his sight as long as the bodyguards weren't around.

"Ah, here we go. Everything you wanted to know about the Alderoth family line, plus fifty or sixty tons of paper more." Targyon spread his arms, shining the lantern on a bookcase stuffed with scrolls, boxes of letters, and old books with yellowed pages trying to fall out. "I wonder if anyone has mapped it out in a nice chart? Fifteen-hundred-odd years might defy the constraints of a scroll though. That's a lot of parchment. A whole flock of sheep would have been sacrificed."

"I was going to feel guilty about foisting my work onto you," Jev said, accepting the lantern Targyon handed him, "but this is the most excited I've seen you since we spent that night decrypting that dwarven courier's message."

"You know research and solving puzzles get me excited. I'd happily work on this with you in the Crown Agents' office, but I fear people would be reluctant to speak openly with me around."

As Targyon removed books and scrolls, handing some to Jev and piling more into his own arms, Jev thought about mentioning Zenia having a similar problem when it came to Order representatives, but he doubted she would want him sharing her difficulties with the king.

"I also fear I might get myself in trouble if I were seen openly poking into the mystery of my own coronation. Like I might seem ungrateful and intractable and—" Targyon grunted as he pulled out a final thick book and headed to the nearest table. "I don't know, Captain. Am I being paranoid? They chose me, so someone must want me here. I just don't know if I'm what they expected."

"Were you what your parents expected? You're not very zyndar-ish."

"Neither are my parents. My mother didn't think my father was from a zyndar family at all when they first started seeing each other. I think she *wanted* to marry a commoner. Maybe to ensure her children would never be considered for the throne." Targyon carefully set down his collection. "Alas for her, Father is from the Mayjarin family, the seventh son of a minor zyndar prime. No chance of him inheriting. Or so you'd think." Targyon spread a few scrolls, then made a delighted noise, almost like a cat's purr. "There *are* genealogical charts. But look at that tiny writing. This is going to take a while, especially in this light."

Jev brought over more lanterns while Targyon used books to pin down the corners of four scrolls' worth of charts. They had to drag over a second table to fit everything.

"I assume we're looking for Alderoths who had oddly short lives?" Targyon glanced at Jev.

"I think that's all we can hope to deduce from those charts." Jev waved at the trees of who married who over the centuries, where they had come from, and the children they had spawned. Dates indicated how long each person had lived, but there was no other information there. "It's certainly possible that older people could have died from the disease, too, but cause of death won't be listed on there, I assume."

Targyon bent low over one of the charts. "No. And I can tell already that a *lot* of my ancestors died young. It seems that being royal wasn't an antidote to the short life expectancy that plagued the kingdom until rather recently. Nothing here about pustules on the bodies of the dead." He grabbed a pencil and a stack of papers from a box on a nearby table.

"Pustules?" Jev asked. "Is that one of the symptoms?"

"All three of my cousins had them near the end."

"Do you know the rest of the symptoms?" Jev didn't see how he could, since Targyon had been with him sailing back from Taziira when the princes had been afflicted and died.

Targyon straightened, drew a folded sheet of paper from an inside pocket, and handed it to Jev before returning to his bent stance. While Targyon started writing down names, dates, and ages of death for notable people, Jev unfolded the paper. The symptoms were listed in a neat column. Jev recognized Targyon's tidy handwriting.

"I did a little research of my own," Targyon said, anticipating Jev's next question.

"To find out if you recognized the disease?"

"To find out if… to know what to expect if some of the symptoms start appearing. In me."

"Ah."

Jev imagined how he would feel in Targyon's place, returning to his homeland only to learn that he had to go be king and live in a castle and a city that had belonged to his ancestors and relatives but never to him. Knowing his cousins had all died recently in this very castle. Lying awake at night, wondering if what had killed them was gone or if virulent bacteria still lurked in the halls, waiting to jump into his skin…

Jev didn't know if it was allowed, but he patted Targyon on the back.

Targyon looked at him curiously.

"Just checking for pustules," Jev said.

Targyon grunted. "Those come *last*. The fever is first. And fatigue."

"If it helps, you look perky for this hour."

"Because you gave me research to do."

"Have you taken the symptom list to a doctor to see what one thinks? If you didn't hear already, Dr. Bandigor was dead when we went to question him."

"I heard. I took the list to Dr. Astnar." Targyon scribbled two more names on his paper.

"The *army's* Dr. Astnar? The man who said amputation never slows a good man down for long?"

"I was fairly certain I could trust him."

"But he's a field surgeon, not a… researcher of rare diseases." Jev didn't even know what such a doctor would be called. Nor did he know for certain this disease was rare.

"Which possibly explains why he didn't have any ideas."

"Can I take this list?" Jev held up the page. "I'm planning to speak with a medical expert at one of the universities. Or maybe that unicorn doctor at the Second Korvann Hospital. Their kind are reputed to be indifferent to politics, economics, and humans in general, except as specimens to study."

"Take it. I've got it memorized. I did consider visiting Dr. Oligonite, the unicorn, but there's someone else I came up with who may even be a suspect."

Jev slipped the paper into one of his pockets. "Oh?"

"Zyndari Dr. Ghara Nhole. She's a scientist, a *mad* scientist if the tales are to be believed. She appeared in the newspapers a few years ago in relation to the wheat and barley crops that were annihilated by locusts. You were gone but may remember news of famine back here in Kor."

Jev nodded.

"She predicted that it would be a horrible year for locusts months before they showed up. Based on some climate and weather analysis, I gathered, but the common and uneducated, being what they are, came up with notions that she'd caused the locusts because she predicted them. There were riots outside her university office. Since then, she's stayed in her family's castle and avoided going to the city."

"I can imagine."

"I looked her up back then. She studied medical science as well as environmental science at Trakmeer University and was at the top of her classes. She published a research paper on ingested anti-fungal and antimicrobial substances being useful for fighting infections. She may know something about diseases that strike down certain families."

"I can take Zenia and go out and see her."

"Don't tell her I sent you. In fact, don't tell anyone I'm doing research on this at all, please."

"If anyone asks if I saw you tonight, I'll say you were merely snoozing under the piano," Jev said.

"That could still happen."

While Targyon wrote down more names, Jev sat at the table and opened one of several books that had been written over the years on the Alderoth family. If their ancestors had been known to suffer from some blood disease, maybe a scribe of the time would have mentioned it. Tomorrow, he would head out to Nhole Castle.

The sooner he and Zenia got to the bottom of this apple barrel, the sooner Targyon could rest a little easier. Not, ideally, under a piano.

CHAPTER 7

ENIA SPOONED SMALL BITES FROM a bowl of cinnamon-dusted porridge while agents ambled into the kitchen to join her. She had selected a table at the rear, so they wouldn't be interrupted often, though the banging of pots and scrapes of spoons in the main part of the kitchen did mean there would be noise. This, however, was where the staff ate, and the Crown Agents, if they chose to eat in the castle, were included in that category.

She hadn't expected to dine at the royal table every day, but she couldn't help but feel this was a demotion, at least in social standing, from being a temple inquisitor. She had been near the top of the food chain there, dining with the other senior mages at the same table as Archmage Sazshen.

Not that such things mattered, Zenia told herself firmly. Jev would likely plop down next to her with his own porridge and not think it insulting for a zyndar to eat in the kitchen with the staff. He truly was the least egotistical zyndar she'd met, though, as he'd once implied, ten years in the field had helped cultivate that. Sleeping on the ground in the elements and eating from a common cookpot must have rubbed away some of his delusions about the superiority of the nobility.

Every time the door opened, Zenia looked up, expecting Jev. She'd mentioned when they parted the night before that she wanted to have a staff meeting this morning to hear if the rest of the agents had found anything useful. She also wanted to get to know them better, to start to get a feel for who she could trust.

"What's going on, ma'am?" Lunis Drem, one of the younger Crown Agents, asked. A woman in her late twenties who wore her thick brown hair up in a strict bun, she had been promoted out of the city watch's investigative division.

She was, aside from the secretary, the only other woman in the office.

"I want to hear what you all think," Zenia said, deciding that most of the staff had arrived and that she could start without Jev, "about who wanted King Targyon on the throne and why he might have been chosen."

"The archmages of the Orders chose him, as they always do." Brokko frowned at her, managing to avoid eyeing her chest this morning.

Zenia wondered if Jev had punched him yet. Not without her there to watch, she hoped.

"But did they decide of their own accord or were there outside pressures?" Zenia asked, thinking of how seldom Sazshen had mentioned the king or her thoughts on the succession.

"I think one of the underworld criminal organizations may have played a role." Lunis leaned forward, clasping her hands. "May I share my hypothesis with you?"

Two men groaned. Zenia, believing she may have found an eager-to-prove-herself colleague she could understand completely, nodded.

"With King Abdor gone for so many of these last ten years," Lunis said, "the underworld guilds have taken advantage, many of them growing bolder and more powerful. Tiger Hunters, Future Order, and the Fifth Dragon have all increased the sizes of their territories and extended their reach outside the capital. *Far* outside. We've inspected shipments and found they have trade relations with other nations."

A door opened, and a yawning Jev walked in, his hair mussed.

Zenia waved for Lunis to continue with her report but scrutinized Jev as he approached, surprised he had been late. And also surprised he was wearing the same clothing from the day before.

As if he'd spent the night here. Or… with some woman?

Zenia frowned at herself and stomped out the jealous thought before it could take root. Besides, if he did sleep with a woman, could she blame him? She never had accepted his offer of a date.

And why hadn't she?

She would enjoy spending time with him in a non-official capacity—once they solved their current case. That wasn't the problem. The problem was that she might enjoy it too much, as she had that kiss they had shared in his castle—when she should have been going after that artifact. What if they dated and she ended up succumbing to temptation and having sex with him? She didn't want to put herself in a situation where she ended up with child, not when she had a new career to establish and certainly not when she wasn't married. And she couldn't imagine Jev proposing to her. Even if he was less zyndar-ish than most zyndar, he was still the oldest son and heir to his father's estate. His family would have expectations, expectations she did not have the blood to meet.

Even if her zyndar father had acknowledged her, Morningfar came from such a minor family that she doubted it would suffice. And she'd eat her own sandal before asking the odious turd to acknowledge her. She didn't *want* to be zyndar. To become someone without that status meant so much more.

"What are you mulling over this morning?" Jev whispered, sliding into the empty chair beside Zenia and nodding to Lunis, who was listing everything the criminal guilds stood to gain if they had a king on the throne who was friendly, or at least indifferent, to them.

He'd grabbed a bowl of porridge on the way over and dug in with a spoon.

"Underworld guilds." Zenia felt her cheeks warm. She hated lying, but she also had no intention of confessing the path her mind had wandered down when he'd walked in.

"Have they done anything inimical this week?"

"Besides stripping us naked?"

"That was last week."

"Are you sure? I think it was only five or six days ago."

He considered that. "It's been a long and eventful week."

"Yes." Zenia turned back to Lunis, not wanting to miss the report she'd asked for. The young woman barely seemed aware that she'd been whispering to Jev.

As Lunis was wrapping up, explaining some of the recent activities of the organizations, the door opened again. A castle page of twelve or thirteen burst in. He looked around the table, then raced to Jev.

"Zyndar Dharrow?"

"Tamordon?" Jev asked.

He knew the names of the pages? Zenia abruptly felt like a heel because she did not.

"I wasn't sure who to tell. Steward Merkish said for me to mind my business." The page wrinkled his nose distastefully. "But I'm zyndar. I have to watch out for my king!"

"Indeed you do. Tell me."

By now, Lunis had stopped speaking, and the rest of the agents at the table were watching the exchange. The boy noticed them and hesitated.

Jev patted him on the shoulder encouragingly.

"There's a woman seeing the king. A dangerous woman. His secretary tried to refuse her, said she wasn't on the appointment book, but then he got confused because when he checked, the woman *was* on the book. He said he was positive she hadn't been penciled in the day before. The woman patted him on the cheek and strode into the king's office. The bodyguards didn't stop her." The page lowered his voice. "I recognized her. On account of—you heard about what happened with my uncle? How he was, uhm, acquitted? Is that the word? Even though he was, uhm, doing things?"

Zenia gripped her chin, struggling for patience as the boy babbled on.

"I hadn't heard that," Jev said, "but go ahead."

Zenia suspected Jev knew the boy's name but not much else about him or his family, at least not much that had happened in the years he'd been away. The page had likely latched onto him because he was zyndar and a soldier who'd seen action during the war. A hero, Zenia decided. That was how young people would see someone like Jev. She wished someone would see her that way. Or at least that the city would decide she wasn't to be an outcast.

"It's Iridium," the page said. "The Fifth Dragon leader."

"I *knew* it," Lunis whispered, clenching her fist. "The criminal guilds are already trying to assert themselves on the king."

"Audacious that she would show up at the castle," another agent said. "That didn't happen when Abdor was king."

"Because he or Prince Dazron would have had such a person arrested," someone else said. "Can we arrest her now? The watch detectives must have enough on her to have her shot."

"Multiple times, I should think."

Zenia pushed her chair back to stand.

"We'll look into it," she told the agents and the page, then extended a hand toward the door and nodded to Jev.

"We will?" Jev gave his porridge a mournful look. He'd only taken a bite. "What if Targyon invited her to come up to the castle and doesn't want us looking into it?"

"Do you think he would have?"

"I don't know, but he's been doing some investigations on his own." Jev touched a breast pocket, but he did not unbutton the flap. "He could consider her a resource and be asking her questions."

"And did he also sneak in and alter his secretary's appointment book?"

"I don't think it's considered sneaking if you're the king, but you're right. He could have ordered the secretary to change it himself."

Zenia, aware of several sets of eyes watching them, pushed through the swinging door and stepped into the nook where she'd dined with Jev and Targyon a couple of mornings earlier.

"Is it within our right as agents to barge into the king's office and make sure the woman isn't physically or emotionally manipulating him?" Zenia asked, concerned about Iridium's appearance. She highly doubted Targyon had invited her up of his own accord, and the others were right. This was highly audacious of her. Zenia could hardly believe the castle guards hadn't arrested her instead of showing her in.

Had the woman come in through some secret tunnel into the castle? Like the ones she lived in under the city? Zenia grimaced, imagining the guild's tunnels extending all the way up to the top of the ridge to Alderoth Castle.

"I don't think so," Jev said after a contemplative moment looking out the tall window to the gardens. "We'll have to find that handbook to read up on what exactly our powers entail. Normally, one would expect one's supervisor—or in our case, predecessor—to offer a briefing to help us get our wagons onto the highway, but since Garlok decided to take off for the full coronation holiday, I haven't even seen him yet."

"Nor have I." From what she'd heard about the man, Zenia wasn't eager *to* see him.

"I suppose I can make an excuse to go into Targyon's office and check something. He and I were up late talking last night, so he shouldn't be surprised if I ask for clarification on the discussion."

"You were with Targyon? When you came in wearing yesterday's clothing…" Zenia waved up and down his form. "I thought you might have had some tryst with a woman and not gone home for the night."

"Would that have bothered you?"

"No."

His eyebrows rose, and her cheeks threatened to heat again. Why did she feel compelled to lie to him in this matter?

"Possibly slightly," she amended, certain he *knew* she was lying. "This case is so important that we shouldn't allow ourselves to be distracted by personal passions until it's resolved."

"Me having passions is what would have bothered you? Not me sleeping with some random woman?"

"Of course." Zenia smiled weakly, wanting to change the subject. Maybe she should simply tell him that she had some feelings for him, but to what end? She shouldn't act on them. Besides, in making the admission, it seemed like she would be giving him power over her. As a zyndar, didn't he already have enough power over everything?

"My days and nights have been full since I set foot on the continent again. No time to arrange trysts." He smiled at her. "I'm still trying to get one particular woman to say yes to a date."

Which she definitely should not do. But she heard herself saying, "Perhaps after this case is solved and the king is safe, at least for the time being, that would be the appropriate time for the recreational pursuit of personal passions."

"Was that a yes?"

She hesitated. A date didn't necessarily have to lead to sex, did it? They could simply hold hands or do more of that lovely kissing they'd engaged in the other night.

But what happened when he wanted to do more? She would have to tell him her stance on that matter. But, she decided as a butler walked past with a tray, this was not the place for it.

"I never know what to think when you spend a long time contemplating these requests," Jev said.

"One shouldn't rush into such decisions."

"Decisions such as whether or not you want to go to dinner with someone?"

"That's not so simple as you seem to think."

"Sure, it is. I'm a simple man."

She didn't know if that was true or not. Was *she* the complicated one? Surely, his zyndar status added layers of complication, even if he had trouble seeing them himself.

"I accept your offer of a date," she said formally.

"Excellent. As soon as I recover from my shock and delight, I'll check on Targyon. Maybe I'll ask him for clarification on some of the research from last night."

"Research?" Zenia asked.

"Yes, we ended up in the castle library together for hours, looking up his ancestors to see which ones of them died young. There were quite a few. Unfortunately, we didn't find any mentions of diseases of the blood or any other kind that were known to afflict Alderoths in the past."

"You were in the library doing research without me?" Zenia propped her fists on her hips.

Jev lifted his eyebrows. "Is it odd that you're more distressed about that than when you thought I was having a tryst with a woman?"

"No, it's not. Why didn't you come get me to help? I would have *loved* to do research in the great library here."

"My apologies." He bowed. "It was late, and I don't even know where you're living now."

Zenia lowered her hands. It was true that she couldn't be irked with him if he didn't know how to find her. "In a room I rented behind an old farmhouse near the city gate." She decided not to mention that the room was above the stable. She had chosen it over ones available in the house because she liked privacy, but she realized admitting to living in a converted hayloft might make her sound impoverished. "I don't have access to a horse or wagon right now, so I didn't want anything far from the castle."

"I think as one of the king's Crown Agents, you can use the horses in the castle stable."

Zenia was less certain about that. Riding them during the workday seemed reasonable, but taking one home each night?

"I'll give you my new address today," she said, skirting the issue.

"So I know where to pick you up for our date?"

"So you know where to find me if you're doing intriguing research in libraries."

"Should our date *involve* research in libraries? That sounds more like work than pursuing passions to me, but perhaps if we took a picnic basket and ate amid the scrolls…"

"That does sound more appealing than other dates I've been on." Not that there had been many. At least not in recent years. She'd been a normal teenager, experimenting with the boys her age around the temple, but those relationships had never advanced as far as she feared Jev, long out of his teenage years, would expect things to go.

But not, she assured herself, on a first date.

"I aim to please you." Jev bowed again and turned toward the exit, but he paused and turned back. "I told Targyon I'd visit a zyndar mad scientist—his description—whose land is about thirty miles outside of the city. He suggested her as a resource for information on the disease. I have a list of symptoms here." He patted his breast pocket again. "Targyon even suggested she might have been the one to *design* the disease, if such was done, because of her background. Do you want to come?"

"Yes," Zenia said promptly.

"I'm noticing that it's much easier to get you to agree to visit suspects with me than it is to agree to dates."

"What kind of inquisitor—agent of the Crown—would I be if I didn't jump at the chance to visit suspects?"

"Oh, I agree that such is expected. I just need to figure out how to get you to jump at the chance to date me."

"Keep talking about picnics in libraries, and that could happen." Zenia smiled at him.

"I'll remember that. I'll arrange for a steam carriage. We better head out in the next hour or so, so we don't arrive too late in the day for polite interrogation."

"I can arrange it," Zenia said, though she didn't yet have an idea how that was done or if the king's agents had free access to his vehicle house. "You go spy on that meeting."

"Spy? I said I'd *check* on it."

"What's the difference?"

"I won't be crawling on my belly and peeking under the door."

"Is that unseemly for a zyndar?"

"I should think so." Jev held her gaze and brushed her cheek with his finger.

Her skin came alive at the brief touch and the way his eyes promised more. She shouldn't *want* more, she reminded herself, but when he turned and strode for the exit, she couldn't help but gaze after him and wish he'd done more than touch her cheek. Perhaps a kiss like the one they'd shared in his castle…

A servant passing through lifted his eyebrows, catching her looking fondly at Jev's back side—and his *backside*. Zenia jerked her chin up in her most professional manner and stalked off to figure out how to arrange the use of a steam carriage.

CHAPTER 8

JEV DIDN'T TRULY WANT TO barge in on Targyon's meeting,
but a part of him believed the worries of the other agents were justified.
He'd seen through Iridium's attempts at manipulation easily enough,
but if he had been twenty-two like Targyon, he might have been so delighted
by the attention of a beautiful woman that he wouldn't have. Or he might
have been aware of her desire to manipulate but believed himself too clever
to be entrapped. Targyon could, as Jev had told Zenia, have almost any
woman he wished now, but he probably hadn't realized that yet.

When Jev walked into Targyon's outer office, a secretary sitting at
the desk lifted his head from a notebook. Two stolid bodyguards stood on
either side of the closed door behind him. Jev had a feeling they wouldn't
let him walk in unopposed. He hoped a knock at the door, if the guards
even allowed that, would disrupt any web Iridium might be weaving.

"Zyndar Jevlain Dharrow, Captain of His Majesty's Crown Agents,"
he announced to the secretary, though he believed the man had seen
him before and knew everyone in the castle. "I need to see His Majesty
briefly. I'm leaving the city shortly, and it can't wait."

"Yes, Zyndar." The secretary jumped to his feet. "I'll see if he's
available."

Jev blinked as the man strode toward the door. Almost *rushed* to the
door. The bodyguards frowned at each other, but they didn't stop the
secretary when he knocked.

Jev realized the man was concerned about what was going on inside
the office. Maybe he'd even hinted to the page that he needed Jev or
someone up here who knew the king and might help.

"Yes?" came a muffled call from inside.

"We're busy," came a second and distinctively feminine call.

"Zyndar?" The secretary stepped aside, gesturing for Jev to open the door.

He wasn't going to open it himself and announce Jev? What was this? The secretary wanted someone else to take the brunt of Targyon's ire if their young king didn't wish to be interrupted?

Jev couldn't imagine Targyon yelling at anyone, including his secretary, even if he was interrupted in the throes of passion. By the founders, Jev hoped no throes of any kind were going on.

Wordlessly, he stepped past the secretary, who regarded him with a mix of relief and hope, and opened the door. Maybe it was a good thing the man was worried about his new king.

Jev poked his head in before entering all the way. He looked past the two empty chairs facing the great olive wood desk and to the one behind it, one occupied by two people.

Iridium sat in Targyon's lap, her arms hooked around his shoulders. She looked at Jev, her expression not unlike that of a fox that had just stolen eggs from the henhouse. Targyon, who also looked at Jev, wore an expression more like that of a rabbit about to be eaten by a fox.

"I just wanted to double-check before I leave, Sire," Jev said, not commenting on their position. "Is the zyndari doctor likely to be found at her family's castle? Or does she have a townhouse in the city or other residence?"

"I..." Targyon tried to shift Iridium off his lap, but she had an iron grip on his shoulders.

Fortunately, she slipped off his lap of her own accord, folding her arms over her chest and glaring at Jev. "Zyndar Jevlain Dharrow, I don't know what made you think you could interrupt this meeting, but I'm already displeased with you. *Extremely* displeased."

"I don't know why." Jev looked at Targyon again, trying to tell if he was all right. Targyon hurried to stand on the other side of the chair, perhaps worried she would lock him down again if he remained seated. "I wasn't the one to drill holes into your lair or cause rockfalls. I simply walked out when the door conveniently opened for me. You'll recall I did not give you my word that I wouldn't try to escape."

"*Lair?*"

That was the word she objected to most from his account?

"Subterranean domicile?" he suggested.

"Palace, I should think. Do you know that in addition to reinforcing and cleaning all the old tunnels, my people have built miles of new passages. Why, I can travel all over the city if I wish. Even to remote hilltop locations." Iridium smiled at Targyon.

He shifted to the end of his desk, putting a couple more feet between them.

"Are you sure you should detail your hideout so thoroughly in front of the king? And one of his law enforcement agents? We might believe it prudent to capture you and your people for a long stay in a short cell."

Iridium's smile only widened, no hint of concern in her eyes. "The king and I were just discussing how invaluable an ally I could be to him and that it would be terribly foolish to interfere with my various interests in the city and the kingdom. But should he or his agents not realize that..." The smiled turned into something feral as her eyes narrowed to slits, and Jev thought of foxes again. "You'll find that we have taken measures to protect our borders. Without the help of a master dwarf craftsman, you would find it difficult to reach us before we could escape. And we would be *most* put out if we had to relocate." Her dangerous eyes shifted toward Targyon.

He'd recovered his equanimity and merely leaned a hip against the desk and regarded her blandly.

"I'd try the castle first, Jev," Targyon said. "Her mother lives there and can tell you where she's gone if she's not there, but I believe her lab is in the basement. Since she was exiled from the university, it seems likely she is living and working out there."

Iridium listened intently as they spoke. Jev had deliberately not used Nhole's name, and he noticed Targyon also left it out. However, if the person responsible for killing the princes had used a zyndari doctor, even their vagueness would be enough to light signal fires. Jev watched Iridium's face closely.

"Thank you for that information, Sire," Jev said. "That's all I needed to know. We'll head up there soon."

Iridium's expression grew more guarded. Jev couldn't tell if she had an idea what they were talking about or not. Too bad. It would have been nice to know if the Fifth Dragon had anything to do with the deaths or if they knew who had.

Jev wished Zenia still had a dragon tear. He would like to interrogate Iridium, if only casually. He would have to find out if others in the agents' office had dragon tears they could use for reading minds and detecting truths.

"I have another appointment soon, Javala," Targyon told Iridium.

She flinched at the name. Her real one? Judging by her reaction, she hadn't been the one to give it to Targyon.

"I'll keep your words in mind," Targyon added as he gestured toward the door.

"And my offer, I'm certain." Iridium glanced at his belt—no, his crotch.

Jev didn't roll his eyes since his father had long ago informed him that such immaturity was unbefitting a zyndar. But he couldn't resist commenting. "An offer to make him number twenty-eight?"

Targyon lifted his eyebrows.

"She has notches on her bedpost," Jev explained.

"Were you twenty-seven?" Targyon asked.

"I was not, due to the interruption I mentioned."

Iridium, perhaps irritated by them chatting about her while she stood in the room, strode toward the door. But she skewered Jev with her gaze on the way out and said, "It's twenty-nine now, Dharrow. Don't think you're the only sexy zyndar I can lure to my—"

"Lair?" he interrupted.

She smiled again, but her eyes closed to those dangerous slits. He couldn't bring himself to feel daunted by her, no matter how powerful and well-connected she was in the underworld. Maybe that made him a fool, but after dealing with the very magical and very deadly Taziir, she seemed a mundane threat in comparison.

"I advise you to watch your back," she murmured, pausing at his shoulder. "Nobody cared about you when you were some rural zyndar plumping your grapes and swilling wine, but my element doesn't care much for agents of the Crown. If we must endure them at all, we prefer they be old, fat, and easily bribed."

The glare she shot over her shoulder to Targyon seemed triumphant.

Without another word, she walked out, offering a sexy, "Hello, boys," to the bodyguards as she passed. Someone shut the door.

Targyon sighed. "I guess that was a confirmation that Zyndar Garlok isn't to be trusted. He's not exactly fat, but at sixty, Iridium might consider him old."

Old, fat, and easily bribed reminded Jev more of Brokko, the double-jowled agent who had leered at Zenia. He made a note to look into his past and his associations.

"I'll inform him of his retirement as soon as he returns from his holiday," Targyon added.

"I wouldn't take anything Iridium says as confirmation of anything, Sire. I'm sure she lies more naturally than fish swim."

"Yes," Targyon murmured and glanced at his chair.

Had Iridium been lying to him about something while she'd been in the process of… How had he let himself end up with her in his lap? Jev was tempted to ask, but he reminded himself that Targyon was his king now, not his junior officer. He shouldn't pass judgment or question him. And definitely not lecture him. He ought to go now and do his duty, nothing more.

"Did you invite her here or did she invite herself?" Jev asked.

So much for going.

"I didn't invite her, but I could have chosen not to let her in. I thought it might be educational to hear what she had to say." Targyon rubbed a red spot on the side of his neck.

Iridium hadn't *bitten* him, had she? Or sucked overly enthusiastically…

"I'll bet," Jev said.

"It's occurred to me that she or one of the guild leaders might have been behind my cousins' deaths—I understand Prince Dazron was attempting to stamp them out this past year, since their influence had grown in the city, as had the murder rate."

"Huh." Jev wished he had something more articulate to say. He shouldn't need to get his intelligence from Targyon. Wasn't it *his* job to dig everything up? "Some agents in the office do believe the criminal organizations may have played a role—or dictated a role. Zenia suspects the Orders since they specifically chose you. Also, we found all the archmages suspiciously out of town when we went by to interview them yesterday. They seem to have something to hide."

"Very possibly. Any other suspects?"

"Other than the research doctor you're sending me off to question?"

"Mm, she's not a suspect, I don't think, so much as a means to the end for a suspect." Targyon lifted his shoulders. "Iridium didn't react when we brought her up."

"No, but I think she could hide a reaction easily enough."

"Yes."

A knock sounded at the door, and the secretary opened it a crack. "Your next meeting is here, Sire."

"Thank you, Nutch."

"Nobody else who's going to try to seduce you, I hope." Jev headed for the door.

"If Zyndar Gaminrokdor does, it'll prove far less effective."

Jev paused with his hand on the knob. "Would Iridium's attempts have been effective if I hadn't butted in?"

"No. I was about to dump her on the floor. It did occur to me that maybe I could try to seduce *her*..." Targyon's gaze dipped to the sheepskin rug at his feet, his cheeks turning faintly pink. "You know, to get information. But I knew she was a master, and my attempts would be bumbling and laughable."

Jev didn't want to insult his monarch by agreeing, so he simply offered a sympathetic wave of his hand. "We can find you someone less masterful to practice on if you wish."

"No, no. I am a believer in the zyndar code and chivalrous love. It was just nice to imagine for a moment that she—a pretty woman— found me desirable as a person. I suppose I'll never know that now. It'll always be political. Maybe I should just ask my mother to arrange me a marriage before the advisors I inherited suggest it."

"Would she?" Jev thought of Targyon's description of his mother as particularly un-zyndarly.

"Maybe not. She's said that only dogs should be penned together for breeding purposes and only if they're from a particularly fine hunting line. She might set me up on dates. That would probably be worse."

Jev thought of his own upcoming date, glad it had been secured but sad a night had not been set. Alas, it sounded like Zenia wouldn't be game until they finished the case. What were the odds that all their answers would be at Nhole Castle and they could resolve everything by nightfall?

He smiled wistfully at the thought.

The door opened, and Jev stepped aside. A stocky, bald zyndar prime wearing fur-trimmed silk robes walked into the office.

"Zyndar Dharrow," he rumbled, nodding to Jev, though he appeared surprised to see him.

Jev nodded back. "Zyndar Gaminrokdor. I'm on my way out."

"Excellent."

Jev tried to decide if there was anything suspicious about the way the man said that but decided not. Gaminrokdor strode to Targyon and bowed low.

"I'd definitely get him his own chair," Jev whispered, drawing a snort from Targyon and a confused frown from Gaminrokdor.

Jev bowed himself out, thinking again of how lovely it would be to get to the bottom of everything by the end of the day.

The steam carriage came with a driver and also a fireman, someone who shoveled coal into the firebox as needed to keep the water in the boiler hot enough to power the engine. The Water Order kept horses and horse-drawn carriages and did not have any steam-powered vehicles, perhaps because monks and mages who walked around the city in garments that had changed little in a thousand years would look odd in such modern contraptions. Or maybe Archmage Sazshen simply hadn't wanted to pay for drivers and engineers capable of operating the vehicles.

Jev didn't seem to think anything of riding inside the velvet-lined carriage while others sat on a bench up front and did the work of driving it, but Zenia wondered if they should have borrowed a couple of the king's horses instead. Thirty miles was a long ride on horseback, however, and they wouldn't have arrived until well after dark. The steam carriage, she was told, could travel up to twenty miles an hour on level roads.

"Did you see Iridium?" Zenia hadn't wanted to ask at the vehicle house, since it and the nearby stable had been filled with workers. "Anything to worry about?"

"Yes, and probably yes," Jev said, "but Targyon is smart enough to avoid any entanglements."

"Are you sure? She's sexy and knows how to use her body."

"I noticed that when she was sitting on the edge of her bed and stroking her nearly bare breasts. It was a very revealing blouse."

Since Jev had already admitted he hadn't had sex with Iridium, Zenia kept herself from imagining them in bed together with their limbs entwined. Mostly.

"Is that what she was wearing for Targyon?"

"No, but today's attire was also sexy and slinky. Zyndari women would call it scandalous to dress so revealingly in the king's court. Or at all. And Targyon... I'm sure it didn't escape his notice that she's pretty, but he has nearly limitless options now that he's king. He could take six pretty courtesans to bed at once, if he wished, none of whom lead criminal organizations that want to use him as a figurehead."

The idea of bookish Targyon in bed with six women was almost as alarming as that of Jev entwined with Iridium.

"Something all young kings should aspire to do, I'm sure," Zenia murmured.

Jev flashed her a grin. "Do you know anything of Zyndari Dr. Ghara Nhole?"

"I hadn't heard of her until you gave me her name this morning."

"I only know what Targyon told me, but I'll share it with you. Or do I need to?" Jev tilted his head curiously. "I heard from Lunis Drem in the office that you went up to the library while I was seeing Targyon. Was it to pick out our future picnic spot, or were you researching the doctor?"

"I did look her up." Zenia was surprised that Jev already knew her well enough to guess, though she supposed it hadn't been a stretch. Still, it pleased her that he paid attention. "It was hard to find much since she's a contemporary of ours rather than a historical figure who's been written up in books, but I did find a textbook for Trakmeer University that she co-authored and also a dozen papers she's published."

"In other words, you know more about her than I do."

"Maybe not. I don't know anything about *her*, just about the work she's done. Her interests do seem to be widespread, and three of her papers were on diseases in humans. The only one that was in the castle library discussed a disease that is rampant in pigs and can be transferred to humans and infect them. Apparently, it's rare for the same viruses to affect multiple species."

"Was it scintillating reading?" Jev asked.

"It wasn't uninteresting, even if it's not my field. I do feel I've gotten to know the woman a little through her work. She taught at the university for a few years before leaving her job and the city."

"Because she wanted to jump into a career of creating custom diseases to infect the royal family?" Jev asked, though Targyon had already told him about the riots and Nhole being asked to leave.

Zenia wrinkled her nose skeptically. "Do you really think she has anything to do with it?"

Jev shrugged. It seemed unlikely that the first person they went to talk to—the first living person—would be the culprit behind everything.

"Targyon suggested it as a possibility, but not, I don't think, because he suspected her of having a motive. It was more that she might be capable of finding or altering a pathogen that could selectively kill. I gather from talking to Targyon—and he's far more aware of science research and those doing it than we are—and also Lornysh that there aren't many people who could do what we think happened." Jev waved a finger and said something in Elvish. It had the cadence of some oft quoted maxim.

"What was that?"

"A fenced garden does nothing but reveal the cleverest animals in the forest."

"Hm." Zenia leaned back in her padded seat, the ride thus far surprisingly smooth as they wound into the foothills outside the city. A wide glass window that could be cranked open allowed her to see the distant green mountains ahead of them. "How did you learn to speak Elvish? And a number of human languages? I don't think you've told me."

"You never asked."

"I know. That was an oversight on my part, to be honest. I should have tried to learn as much about you as possible when I was sent to arrest you. Had you been some odious mastermind villain, I would have researched you heavily on the way to the docks, but I wasn't given much time. Also, I assumed you'd be..." She eyed him as she considered her words.

"An idiot?"

"Fluffy."

Jev lifted his tunic and looked at his flat stomach.

"I said fluffy, not flabby or fat. Decorative. Like most other zyndar I've met."

The carriage wobbled, and Zenia gripped her seat and glanced out the window. Had they hit a pothole? So far, the road—one of the king's highways that eventually crossed the mountains and stretched to the towns on the desert border—had been without bumps.

The wobble came again as tall grasses alongside the road whipped in the wind. It had to be gusting impressively to affect the large steam carriage.

"I'll have to introduce you to some of the other zyndar who went to war and led companies. If we were fluffy or flabby before, the years in those elven jungles honed us." Jev lowered his shirt—too bad since it had been a nice view. "I can't say we always acted honorably though. In the beginning, we did. We had these noble ideals about striding out onto battlefields and facing the enemy in combat with arranged rules. The Taziir didn't show up at the battlefields. They shot at us from the trees, then raced off. Sneaked into our camps at night and lit tents on fire. They destroyed our food rations, slit a few throats, and disappeared into the night." He looked out the window on his side of the carriage, his eyes taking on a distant aspect.

He hadn't answered her question, but she wouldn't push him. Maybe it was too hard for him to talk about any part of the war without growing mired helplessly in a painful past. Sometimes, she was surprised he was so affable after all the time spent over there, living on the edge.

"It was frustrating after a while, and it turned some of us into monsters," Jev said. "I found myself yelling curses and firing into the forest one evening, hoping I'd randomly hit one of them and do some good. I heard words coming out of my mouth that—well, I sounded like my father. That was sobering. I decided that I wasn't doing any good just lining up and shooting into the woods. There had to be a better way. Maybe if we understood our enemy a little more, it would be easier to defeat them."

Jev smiled slightly, though his gaze remained locked on the window, on the increasingly rural landscape outside.

"I didn't realize knowing them better would result in understanding them better and seeing the world, at least a little bit, through their eyes. At the time, we had captured a young elf woman. Nobody wanted to shoot a woman, even if she'd proven she would shoot *us* with that bow of hers, so she was just tied up. Now and then, someone tried to get her to answer questions. I'd been keeping an eye on her, so none of my men—this was when I still led Dharrow Company and they truly were *my* men from my land—would harass her.

"I started bringing her food and lured her into speaking with me. I'd like to say I charmed her into teaching me her language, but I think she was smarter than that and decided it might be good for her people to have someone fluent in Elvish on the other side, so they could negotiate more easily with us. It was more difficult to learn than the human languages I'd picked up in school and when we had foreign guests one summer. Much more so. No common roots like with so many of our languages. But we had her as a guest in camp for a while since a huge snow came, and not freezing became more of a priority than battling the enemy. Eventually, she escaped—I almost had the feeling she could have all along and she'd simply been waiting to teach me her language first. Later, I got better at it when I had Lornysh to practice on, and I picked up dwarven from Cutter. He's tried to teach me to cut gems, too, but my natural aptitudes end at languages and lawn darts."

"Lawn darts?"

"Yes, you'll have to come out to the castle this summer. I can impress you with my uncanny skill." Jev smiled at her, but his gaze was drawn back to the window. "Those are some dark clouds out there. It looks like we're heading toward a storm."

"I guess it's a good thing I didn't grab horses instead of the carriage."

"Were you contemplating that? For a thirty-mile ride?"

"I felt guilty making those two men out there toil so we could ride in comfort in this gilded box."

"They do get paid," Jev said dryly.

"Spoken like a zyndar."

"I'm guessing they get paid *well* to work for the king. There's nothing demeaning about the work. Didn't you have people at the temple who did the necessary physical labor while you inquisitors basked in the life of luxury?"

"You never saw my room, did you?"

"You neglected to invite me to visit it. I'm positive I would have preferred it over the dungeon."

"Your cell wasn't so bad. It had a window."

"The company was loathsome." He grimaced, and she knew he didn't refer to her.

The genuine pain that flashed in his eyes took the fun out of bantering with him, and she lowered her gaze to the metal floor of the carriage.

"I'm sorry," she said quietly.

She regretted that she hadn't been able to stop what she knew had been a painful questioning session. *Interrogation* session. She'd been drugged at the time, so hadn't been awake or aware of it, but that didn't alleviate her guilt, and fresh irritation welled in her, irritation toward Archmage Sazshen. For years, she had considered the woman her mentor and even a friend, but Sazshen had been so quick to turn on her. Zenia realized she must never have meant that much to the archmage. It stung to know that.

It also stung to know that Rhi was the only one of her former colleagues who had left the temple and sought her out to offer condolences to her over the loss of the job. The *career*. But she supposed she was as much to blame for that as anyone else. While she'd had acquaintances in the temple, she'd let her work make her distant. Or maybe she simply *was* distant, and the work was an excuse. How often had she gone to her room at the end of the day, preferring the company of a book to the boisterous shouts and laughs of monks and mages in the dining hall? It surprised her that Jev had made so many attempts at getting through her standoffishness.

"Not your fault." Jev must have noticed her glum expression because he scooted closer and wrapped an arm around her shoulders. For a second, she thought he'd read her mind somehow and was responding to her thoughts of standoffishness, but then he added, "I'm sure if *you* had interrogated me, it would have been much more pleasurable."

She appreciated the warmth of his arm around her shoulders. "It wouldn't have been painful. I'm not sure anyone I questioned ever mentioned finding the experience *pleasurable*."

"No? That's a shame. I'll have to readjust my fantasies."

"Your what?"

"Lurid dreams about how our interrogation session might have turned into something wild and passionate."

"I…" She almost gaped up at him. She wasn't used to men speaking with her so bluntly about sex. Technically, it hadn't been *that* blunt—she'd heard worse, though usually in a deliberately vulgar and violent context—but it surprised her that he would admit to fantasies. Revolving around her.

Should she be flattered? By the founders, she didn't know how to react. He probably assumed she had more experience in such matters than she did. Given her age, maybe that was a reasonable assumption. But then, celibacy was considered a virtue for those who worked in the temples, serving the founders. Monks weren't supposed to let themselves be distracted from their training by carnal activities, and mages, especially the women, often dedicated themselves to their careers instead of pursuing marriage and having children.

But she hadn't told him that yet.

"Sorry." Jev withdrew his arm and placed his hands in his lap. "I didn't mean to make you uncomfortable. I thought—I mean, you're fairly straightforward about most things. I didn't think straightforward talk about lurid fantasies would faze you, but I should have waited until we'd kissed more than once to hint of such things."

"It's all right."

Zenia hadn't meant to stare stupidly at him and make him think... Well, she didn't know *what* he thought now. She did know that she missed his arm around her shoulders and had the urge to squirm close to him, grab it, and put it back where it had been.

"Uhm, what *is* the appropriate number of times to kiss before bringing up fantasies?" She smiled, hoping to let him know she hadn't minded or been offended by his interest.

"More than once." He smiled quickly in return, but it wasn't as heartfelt as his earlier ones had been. Did he now feel uncomfortable because he thought he'd made *her* uncomfortable?

She stared bleakly at the side of his face, wondering how to fix that.

Water spattered the window, making her jump before she realized it was just rain. Hard rain. The wind blew it sideways against the carriage.

"I see Nhole Castle." Jev pointed out his window. "Already lit up for the night. Guess they saw the storm coming. I hope this won't take long and that we can return to the city tonight."

Dark clouds filled the entire sky now, and rain pounded down on the roof of the carriage. Zenia wondered if water running into the smokestack or dampening the coal would affect the vehicle's ability to carry them back to the city.

"I hadn't meant for this to be an overnight trip," Jev added, sounding apologetic.

"Do you think they'll let us stay if we need to?"

"I'm sure there's plenty of room in their castle, and it's in the Zyndar Code of Honor that you're supposed to host fellow zyndar travelers. Whether they honor the code might depend on whether we accuse Dr. Nhole of conspiring to kill the princes or not."

Zenia didn't point out that she was not zyndari, so those rules would not apply to her. Presumably, she could stay as Jev's guest. She didn't mind the idea of spending the night, since it would afford her the opportunity to snoop if this zyndari doctor wasn't forthcoming. But then, the last time she'd roamed around a castle with snooping in mind, she'd ended up with the ceiling collapsing and almost killing her.

As the carriage rolled to a stop in a great circular driveway outside Nhole Castle, nervous queasiness crept into her stomach.

CHAPTER 9

J EV STEPPED INSIDE THE FOYER ahead of Zenia, glancing
around for possible traps. The water dribbling into his eyes made it
difficult. He hadn't dressed for the rain, and he regretted it.

Fortunately, he didn't see anything threatening in the spacious room,
just wood paneling, flagstone floors covered with rugs and furs, and
doorways and a staircase leading into other parts of the small castle.

A *keep*, some snobbier zyndar with larger structures would have called
it. Jev resolved not to wrinkle his nose and be snobby. Though he couldn't
help but twitch a nostril at a sulphuric odor lurking in the air. What *was* that?

Lightning flashed in the dark sky outside as the butler closed the
door behind them. A long rumble of thunder emanated through the stone
walls, and Jev hoped the carriage attendants found a dry vehicle house
or stable to hunker down in.

A boy of ten or eleven ran into the foyer with a stack of towels.

"Dry yourself, Zyndar Dharrow?" The butler waved the boy toward
him. "And your lady friend…?"

"Captain Zenia Cham," she said, her chin lifting in that familiar gesture.

Jev hid a smile, amused that she'd taken to her new title so quickly.
But it wasn't as if she could introduce herself as an inquisitor anymore.

"Captain?" the butler asked, his tone carefully modulated so it came
out neither curious or skeptical.

"Of His Majesty's Crown Agents," Zenia said.

"Ah, welcome." The butler hesitated, then bowed, clearly not
knowing the proper protocol for addressing a Crown Agent. He had
bowed automatically to Jev, of course.

Zenia's chin seemed to twitch an iota higher.

"We're here to see Zyndari Dr. Ghara Nhole," Jev said. "Is she here?"

"The acrid scent arising from the basement should attest to that." The butler used the same deadpan tone, but this time, it conveyed a hint of emotion. Disapproval.

"Will you take us to her?" Jev didn't know which of the several doors led to the basement. The only visible staircase headed upward.

The butler visibly braced himself. "Yes."

He extended a hand toward one of the doors to the rear of the foyer, but before he could lead them in that direction, a woman in flowing, exotically patterned garments strode into the room. Jev had seen her before back when he'd been a teenage boy attending social functions for his father, his father detesting such things even more than Jev. He couldn't remember the woman's first name but was certain she was Zyndari Nhole and married to Zyndar Prime Tigoroth Nhole.

"Dubb, we have guests? And you didn't tell me?" She glanced at Zenia, but her gaze soon locked onto Jev. She smiled, something predatory in the gesture. It reminded him of Iridium.

The butler bowed apologetically. "They just arrived, Zyndari. They came to see your daughter."

The woman flicked her fingers in acknowledgment without looking at the man. No, she was busy looking Jev up and down, as if she were considering purchasing him for some function requiring an escort. Had Tigoroth passed on since Jev was home last?

"Zyndar Dharrow, isn't it?" She came forward and extended her hand for him to clasp to his chest. "Jevlain? You've grown up so much since I saw you last. And you're *so* handsome."

"Uhm, thank you. Zyndari Nhole." Jev glanced at Zenia. He wouldn't mind it if it bothered her when another woman showed him affection, but he supposed a graying matron wearing stripes mixed with leopard spots wouldn't drive her into a fit of jealousy.

Indeed, she appeared more bewildered than bothered. Jev didn't know if that was because she found the woman's interest puzzling or if she was recovering from his fumbled attempt at flirting in the carriage. By the founders' scaled backsides, why had he told her he fantasized about her? Had he expected her to find it flattering? He should have known she would consider it uncouth. It *was* uncouth. Could he blame his ineptness on how long it had been since he'd had anyone to flirt with?

He could certainly blame his horniness on that. He hadn't been joking about having fantasies lately and was pleased and relieved they focused on her instead of Naysha. He'd dreamt of Naysha often during the years he'd been gone, even after he'd learned she had married another, and it always disturbed him when he woke up, realizing he'd been coveting someone else's wife. Even if she had once almost been *his* wife.

"Levandra, please. And oh dear, you're terribly wet." Zyndari Nhole—Levandra—frowned as she withdrew her hand from his.

"Yes, sorry. A storm opened up on top of us."

Thunder rumbled again.

"I saw. I saw. It came in quickly. Let's hope it's natural for the season and not the work of some elf mage making trouble for the kingdom."

Jev squinted at her, trying to decide if she truly believed that a possibility. She wore a troubled expression as she glanced toward a shuttered window.

"Dubb?" Zenia asked and tilted her head toward the door the butler had indicated before. She would, no doubt, prefer to get right to work questioning the doctor.

"Yes, Captain." The butler took a step in that direction.

Levandra's gray brows lifted. "*Captain?* What are you a captain of? The watch? Surely, no women were permitted in the king's army." She frowned at Zenia, now examining her with a similar scrutiny to what Jev had received, but a faint lip curl accompanied it. "You're not zyndari, are you? I don't recognize you."

"No, Zyndari Nhole. I'm one of the king's Crown Agents. I lead the organization, along with Jev."

"Jev?" Levandra mouthed and looked at him. "You let a commoner call you Jev?"

"I'd be happy to have her call me anything she likes." Jev smiled and looked fondly at Zenia, even if she was focused on that door and didn't seem to notice.

"Does your father know about this?" Levandra demanded.

Jev realized he'd made a mistake. Oh, he wasn't worried about the old man learning he'd developed feelings for Zenia, but he didn't want a lecture from a zyndari he barely knew on women suitable for a zyndar.

"He's met Zenia," Jev said and took a step toward that rear door. The butler had already opened it.

"Has he? Then he might be especially appreciative if I visited him." Levandra gripped her chin thoughtfully and looked Jev up and down again.

"Er, in what context?" Jev could guess—he'd had zyndari matrons speak of setting him up with their daughters before—but he hoped he was wrong.

"Marriage, of course. I understand you've been away at war—a very noble pursuit for one so young as you to dedicate so much of your life to. If you'd been at home all this time, your father would have arranged your marriage by now, I have no doubt. And what of you? You must be pining for the embrace of a loving zyndari woman." Levandra sent a pointed look toward the door.

Jev expected Zenia to be halfway to the basement with the butler, but she had paused to wait for him. He almost wished she hadn't.

"My work for the king leaves me with little time for pining, Zyndari. Now, if you'll pardon me, I need to see your daughter."

"Excellent, though I do wish you'd sent word ahead that you were coming. That would have been the polite thing to do, you know. I believe she's…" Levandra frowned toward the door. "She's not likely dressed for entertaining, but she rivals elven princesses for beauty when she wishes to. And she's so smart. Do spend some time with her." The woman waved as Jev hustled for the door, trying not to feel like he'd dropped his sword and shield and was fleeing the battlefield. "I'll talk to your father as soon as I can."

Jev waved—or maybe shooed—the butler who, like Zenia, had been waiting for him. The man's eyes crinkled at the corners, but he did not say anything as he led the way down the hallway. Jev wondered if he'd witnessed other zyndar guests being waylaid in the foyer.

"You seem to be quite the eligible bachelor," Zenia murmured, sounding more amused than jealous. "Impressive, considering the water dripping from your beard."

Jev frowned and scraped his fingers through his beard. He'd trimmed it short enough that he didn't think it could hold too much water, but they had been drenched during their short run from the carriage to the castle.

"The glisten of water only adds to the allure of my facial hair," he announced.

"Haven't seen a mirror recently, have you?"

Jev shot her a dirty look, but he was pleased to have her joking with him again so he didn't offer further rebuttal.

The butler stopped in front of a set of gray stone stairs curving downward from the hall.

"If you're ready?" Once again, the man visibly braced himself.

"Do you want me to go first?" Jev couldn't imagine what the butler found so distasteful—though that sulphuric odor had grown stronger—but maybe this boded well for the daughter as a suspect or accomplice in the case. If she was proven to be a criminal, would her mother forgo the visit to Dharrow Castle?

"No, Zyndar." The butler sighed and descended the stairs.

Jev would have gone second, to protect Zenia from whatever evil sights and smells might wait below, but she hurried after the butler.

"Zyndari Ghara?" the butler called ahead before stepping off the stairs and into a windowless room lit only by lamps burning some dubious oil that might have contributed to the strong odor of the place.

All manner of laboratory equipment lined shelves and tables, and the room claimed an interesting collection of less scientifically useful decor, such as a shrunken troll head, a metal golem statue, and several animal heads mounted on the walls, some furred, some feathered, and some scaled. They looked like the manifestations of a taxidermist's imagination rather than real creatures, but Jev hadn't traveled the whole world and couldn't say with certainty that the animals didn't exist somewhere.

Shelves over the tables held jars of organs from various animals—or humans. A curtain hung to one side of the basement laboratory, obscuring whatever lay behind it. Jev didn't want to know, but Zenia already eyed it with speculation.

One corner of the laboratory was brighter than the rest with a chandelier hanging over a workstation in addition to numerous lamps on the flat surface. A woman in a simple red dress sat before it, reading from a thick book while something bubbled in a beaker over a flame. She turned toward them and pulled spectacles she'd been wearing above her forehead down onto her nose.

"You have guests." The butler bowed, glancing uneasily at one of the scaled and snouted heads mounted near the door. The thing was half as large as he was. "Zyndar Dharrow and Captain Zenia Cham of His Majesty's Crown Agents."

"His what?" Ghara's brow furrowed, and her nose wrinkled up.

It was a cute expression, despite soot smudged on her cheek, and though Jev wouldn't go so far as to agree with the mother's assessment of great beauty, he wagered Ghara could find a husband on her own if she truly wanted one. She looked to be in her late thirties but more in love with her laboratory than human beings. Much to her mother's consternation, Jev suspected.

Zenia sighed. "Just call me Zenia."

She glanced at Jev, wistfulness in her eyes, and he guessed she missed being the fearsome and fearless Inquisitor Cham. Everybody had heard of the Orders' inquisitors, and nobody wanted to cross them, not even the zyndar. Based on how nobody they talked to seemed aware of the king's special agents, Jev wondered if they should be announcing who they were to everyone they met. Had Abdor preferred nobody knew about his network of agents, their office hidden away in the back of the castle much like this quirky lab? Jev hadn't heard of the office or the agents before Targyon mentioned them, though he'd been vaguely aware that his army intelligence reports went back to analysts in the capital.

"The new king sent you?" Ghara asked.

"We're performing an investigation into the princes' deaths," Zenia said.

"Huh, I'm surprised it took that long for you to find your way here. They've been dead for weeks."

"We were just hired," Zenia said, her voice chilling.

"Since Abdor died on the front and the princes all passed away so quickly," Jev said, "the Crown Agents' office has lacked a strong leader and been in some disarray." He thought of Zyndar Garlok, wondering if the man would be back tomorrow. Jev didn't think Targyon had told Garlok about his incipient retirement yet, but might the zyndar already have guessed? Maybe he was in no hurry to return to receive the news firsthand.

"Still, it isn't as if there are many people who are experts in this area." Ghara's eyelids drooped. "Have you already visited the university?

Spoken to my ex-colleagues? Professor Radnar? Erinkon? That arrogant gasbag Pulinosk?"

"No," Jev answered since Zenia had eased a couple of steps closer to a workstation full of test tubes, with open textbooks and journals scattered about. Was he supposed to take over the talking so she could snoop without being noticed? "I spoke with someone outside of the university." *Far* outside, Jev amended silently, thinking of Lornysh. "But King Targyon knows of your work and suggested I see if you have any ideas, such as whether this was a man-made virus or if such a thing is even possible." Jev shifted subtly to block Ghara's view of Zenia. "My other source thought this unlikely."

"No human can tailor-make viruses," Ghara said. "If someone was able to do that, I would have heard of it."

"What about an elf or a dwarf?"

Zenia flipped a couple of pages in one of the journals. The butler, Jev noticed, had retreated back up the stairs.

"Dwarves aren't known for their science acumen, unless it has to do with engineering. Elves." Ghara shrugged. "Who knows what they know? They don't share their publications with us. The general consensus is that they live in trees and aren't very advanced."

Lornysh would happily shoot a few dozen arrows through that consensus. Or maybe not. The elves probably liked humans underestimating them.

"I brought a list of symptoms," Jev said, deliberately not looking at Zenia as she drifted away from the table and toward the curtain, her hands clasped casually behind her back. "I was hoping you would know if they match up with some existing disease. Or a historically significant disease that's faded away and not been seen for a while but that could have somehow been rekindled."

Jev had no idea how that would work, but this wasn't his field, so he wouldn't assume it couldn't be done.

"Symptoms? What is this, the bronze age? You couldn't bring me a sample of blood from one of the deceased?"

"Er, I think the deceased have been interred for weeks," Jev said.

"You *think*?"

Jev was beginning to see why the relatively attractive Dr. Ghara Nhole wasn't yet married. And why her mother seemed a touch desperate.

"As we said," Jev said calmly, "we were only recently assigned to this case. And only recently hired and brought up to the castle. I was in Taziira until last week. The princes, I understand, all died several weeks ago."

"So, get me a sample from one of their livers. Something I can look at under my microscope." Ghara waved to one of several contraptions on her desk.

"Zyndari, I can ask, but the bodies are entombed in the royal cemetery, and I suspect that neither the king's family nor the castle representatives from the Orders will approve of someone cutting into the remains of the princes."

Dear founders, why did she want pieces of their *livers*?

"This is why scientific progress grinds along so slowly." Ghara snapped her fingers at him. "Give me the list."

Jev was glad he'd made a copy before coming out, because he was disinclined to trust her. Not that she'd said anything suspicious. She was just... grating. Zenia would snort at someone being added to the list of suspects based on that.

"Fever and fatigue, wonderful. Those are symptoms for all the viruses in existence." Ghara grumbled under her breath as she read the rest of the symptoms. "The pustules are less common at least. Hm, give me some time to do some research. I have books that list diseases with indices of symptoms."

Zenia had reached the curtain, drawing it open just far enough that she could gaze inside. Which she did with a neutral expression on her face. From his position, Jev couldn't see what she was looking at.

Ghara walked toward one of the bookcases, scowling at Zenia as she went.

Zenia let the curtain fall shut and faced her. "Zyndari Nhole, did anyone approach you and ask if you would assist in creating a virus that could be used to attack the princes? Or simply a deadly virus in general?"

"No," Ghara said promptly, not avoiding Zenia's gaze. "I told you, humans can't create viruses. You find the guest on my autopsy table interesting?" She waved toward the curtain.

"Interesting? Not particularly. But I'm going to assume he's the reason the butler doesn't like coming down here."

Ghara gave her an edged smile. "He's the *last* nosy agent who came out here to bug me with questions."

"The corpse appears rather elderly and overweight to have recently occupied such a position in life."

"His kidneys are a mess too. You should see them up close."

Zenia's gaze drifted to the shelves with jars full of organs, but she appeared unfazed. Almost disinterested. Jev wasn't disturbed by the paraphernalia, but he also didn't have an urge to go look at what sounded like a cadaver missing some organs.

"It'll take me a couple of hours to check my references." Ghara pointed toward the stairs. "Why don't you come back tomorrow? I don't need anyone distracting me." She squinted specifically at Zenia.

Zenia hesitated, then strolled toward the stairs. On the way, she looked around wistfully. Wishing she'd gotten more of an opportunity to snoop?

Jev didn't have snooping in mind, but he didn't want to have to come all the way back out here tomorrow.

"You may not have noticed down here," Jev told Ghara, "but there's a big storm going on out there. It may not be safe to ride back right now. Would you mind if we spent the night? I'll be pleased to return the favor if you're ever out near Dharrow Castle and need a place to stay."

He offered his best charming smile, though he didn't think it would do anything to soften the woman's demeanor. Maybe nothing would.

"What time is it?" Ghara moved a stack of books to reveal a wall clock. "Oh, that late? Why didn't you come out earlier?"

Jev wondered if he would have to point out that zyndar social etiquette demanded hospitality when other zyndar came to visit, regardless of the hour. And it wasn't *that* late.

"I was prying a woman out of the king's lap earlier today," he said. "It was hard work."

Zenia twitched her eyebrows. Ghara stared humorlessly at him, then pulled on a bell.

Several long moments passed before the butler's footsteps sounded on the stairwell.

"Our visitors need a place to stay," Ghara told him.

"Yes, Zyndari. I'll prepare—"

"The cottage," Ghara said firmly.

The butler hesitated. "The cottage? Your mother has already agreed to house the king's servants in the castle, in the bunkhouse wing."

"The cottage for these two." Ghara waved for them all to leave.

"Yes, Zyndari."

"I don't think she liked us," Jev murmured as he and Zenia trailed the butler up the stairs.

"She didn't like me snooping. I saw her shooting me glares. I think that's why we're being shooed to some exterior dwelling. Maybe I shouldn't have let my eyes roam in front of her."

"Did you find anything interesting?"

"No."

The butler led them through the foyer, rain audible once again, pounding on the roof and the wind blowing sheets of it against the shuttered windows. Jev didn't look forward to walking outside to get to wherever this cottage was. Not a mile up a hillside path, he hoped.

"Do you think she was lying about whether anyone had approached her?" Jev murmured as the butler led them into another hallway.

"No." Zenia didn't hesitate before answering.

Jev looked at her in surprise. "Really?"

"Really."

"Hm." He reminded himself that Zenia didn't have a dragon tear anymore, so she could be fooled by someone who was a good liar. But would a woman who'd dedicated herself to the sciences, and who clearly excelled in her field and had a touch of arrogance, bother acquiring expertise in the art of mendacity? "You don't think she's hiding anything?"

"She could be hiding all manner of things, but I don't think she was the one responsible for making the virus. She answered that question promptly and a little angrily. I got the sense she was irked she *hadn't* been consulted."

"She was irked a criminal didn't ask her to help with a crime?"

"It may have been my imagination, but I could envision her being eager for the chance to work on a challenging scientific problem, which this might have presented."

The butler passed a kitchen and dining hall before stopping at a back door. He opened it, revealing a puddle-filled yard and water spewing from gutter spouts as well as dripping from the eaves. A stable and vehicle house stood on opposite sides of a path that meandered toward a back gate and also a small, dark cottage. Twilight had come and no lamps appeared to burn behind the cottage windows. The sloping roof slumped over a narrow porch, both in need of repair.

"I wonder if our host would be offended if we slept in our steam carriage instead," Jev said.

"I'm sure it'll be fine," Zenia said.

"I'll try to envision it as a private and cozy place—and hope there are minimal leaks inside."

"I'll send someone out shortly to lay a fire and bring food and linens. Towels." The butler shrugged apologetically. "We weren't anticipating guests."

"Thank you." Zenia jogged out onto the pathway, hurrying toward the covered porch.

"She's eager to spend a romantic night with me," Jev explained to the butler.

"Yes, Zyndar. I have no doubt."

Jev couldn't tell if that was sarcastic or not. He braced himself, then ran out into the rain as more lightning flashed in the sky.

CHAPTER 10

RAINDROPS PLUNKED INTO A BEDPAN Zenia had placed under a persistent leak. A bucket in the back corner caught water from another. She had done her best to sweep the water on the floor out the door while Jev, not waiting for the staff, found dry wood and started a fire in the hearth.

The storm had brought cold air in addition to rain, making the day considerably chillier than it had been when Zenia dressed that morning. Had she known about this, she would have brought a cloak.

"Well." Jev sat back from the hearth, a fire now crackling before him. "A leaky cottage is better than a leaky tent in enemy territory. Though back in the army, I could have ordered a private to find some pitch to smear over the leak and fix my tent." He lifted his gaze toward the water-stained ceiling. "Considering how many of the shingles were lying on the ground around the structure, pitch might not be sufficient for the job here."

"We'll survive one night." Zenia decided not to mention that the cottage was larger and had nicer furniture—however aged it was— than the room she rented. "Though one does wonder if we irritated that woman more than I thought."

"I could have tried harder to be charming, but sometimes, it takes multiple exposures to my charms before a person is infected."

"I thought it was your humor that was infectious, not your charms."

"Either way, she's definitely in the same group you're in. Or *were* in. What did you call it?"

"The placebo group," Zenia said dryly.

"It's larger than I remembered from the last time I was around women regularly. Is it possible I've lost some of my good looks and allure?" He smirked, but he also touched the scar on his cheek, his eyes growing thoughtful. Or maybe concerned.

"It's hard getting older." Zenia leaned the broom against the wall and shut the door. The wind had been blowing in as much rain as she swept out. "If it helps, the mother seemed interested in your charms."

"Not really. But in case she was serious, I better send a note to my father and let him know I'm not interested in an arranged marriage with Dr. Nhole."

"Will he listen to you?" Zenia asked, morbidly curious.

"I hope so. I'd like to think he would ask my opinion before setting something up, but it's been a long time since we discussed the matter." Jev added a couple more logs to the fire. "Do you think it would be within my purview as a Crown Agent to arrest Dr. Nhole? That should make her ineligible for marriage."

"Should?"

"Technically, there are precedents of arranged marriages going forward, even though they involved zyndar detained for misdemeanors. I seem to remember a story about a couple who were both detained and got married from adjoining cells."

"And here I thought the law couldn't touch the zyndar."

"Occasionally, something particularly scandalous justifies touching."

Zenia came to stand by the fire so her clothes would dry. Just running out to the cottage had been enough to dampen her all the way through.

Lightning continued to flash outside. If she had brought an overnight bag, she would have changed clothing. There were two separate bedrooms, if small ones. She and Jev wouldn't have to share a bed, or debate which one would take the damp couch that had been positioned under one of the leaks before they moved it. That made the situation less complicated, even if a part of her wouldn't mind sharing human warmth tonight. The flames, which could only warm one side of her at a time, felt inadequate.

Jev sat on the raised hearth next to her.

"Would you go through with an arranged marriage?" The words came out before Zenia could ponder if she wanted to ask the question. She didn't want to pry or make him grow concerned that she had marriage in mind, because she didn't, but she might have been the tiniest bit alarmed when Zyndari Nhole broached the subject. Even if Jev would fight his father about the idea of Dr. Nhole as a suitable wife, there might be zyndari out there that he *would* find acceptable. More appealing to his tastes. His fiancée from ten years earlier, whom he'd mentioned briefly when he and Zenia had been in that cell together, had presumably been zyndari and acceptable to his family. If someone appealing was presented as an option, what then? Would Jev go along with it?

"It would be ideal," Jev said, clasping his hands between his knees and gazing toward the wood floorboards, "if it didn't get to that stage. Maybe I need to do more than send a note." He grimaced. "I should talk to my father in person when I get a chance, to make sure he doesn't plan something behind my back. Or, more likely, let one of my aunts plan something and then sign off on it without paying much attention."

Zenia considered that answer. "Does that mean you would go through with it? If you didn't talk to your family soon enough and they arranged something while you were busy working?"

He slanted her a bleak look. "You're making me want to run out there right now." He snorted. "But I don't think I'm in danger of anything being planned this week. The entire family is appalled and distressed in the aftermath of the confession from Grandmother Visha. Even though my mother had been out of our lives for a long time, I think it disturbed my father a great deal to learn she truly was dead—and how it happened."

Zenia noticed he wasn't answering her question. She couldn't tell if he was deliberately redirecting the conversation because he thought the answer might distress her or if he was redirecting it because the answer distressed *him.*

She vowed not to pry further. It wasn't as if he had professed his love for her and she had the right to grill him on his marriage plans. They hadn't even had their first date yet.

Wind battered at the back of the cottage, and something snapped above them. Another rotten shingle flying free?

"It would be a hard choice to be honest," Jev said, perhaps bestirred by the noise. "It would depend on if I was involved with someone else." He didn't glance at her, but she felt him observing her out of the corner of his eye. "And how involved."

"If you were in love?" she suggested, despite her vow not to pry.

"Yeah. I guess if I wasn't… involved… Well, I've always known it's my duty as the old man's firstborn to take his place one day, to manage the estate and the tenants, to see over the family's business interests, and to marry and have children who will then carry on in my place one day. It's an obligation, my duty as zyndar. To reject it would be to reject everything. If I didn't marry eventually and produce offspring, my father might choose another to be his heir. He might not, as it wouldn't be an easy choice with my brother now dead, but it would be within his rights to do so."

"Do you want children?" She noticed he was being careful not to imply that he wanted to marry her—maybe if he did that, it still wouldn't satisfy his duty, since she didn't have the right blood—and he also hadn't implied feeling love for her. Which was fine. She hadn't expected it. They hadn't known each other long, and it wasn't as if she loved *him*. Yes, she'd admitted she was attracted to him, but that wasn't the same thing as love. Though he did seem like a man one could grow to love if the circumstances allowed it.

"I would like them," Jev said. "Both to satisfy all my zyndarly duties and because I found I missed having kids around when I was in Taziira. The young, dumb soldiers who worked under me weren't quite the same." He smiled at her, then lifted his brows in curiosity. "Do *you* want children?"

"I'm not sure. When I was younger, I always assumed I would have them one day, but now that I'm older… uhm, I guess it would have to be soon. In the next few years, anyway. I've always been so focused on my career, and opportunities to meet and marry someone haven't come my way often, that I started to think it wouldn't happen. And now…"

"Now?"

"Well, I have this new career where I have to start all over. I'm willing to do so and determined to make a name for myself all over again, but I guess I can't see that happening if I'm nursing babies and wrangling toddlers."

"Ah." Jev looked away.

Was that disappointment in his eyes?

He probably hadn't meant her to see it, but it stung. She didn't want to be anything but honest, and it wasn't that she loathed the idea of children. She just wasn't sure there was a way to dedicate herself to this new career and also make children *work*. Her gort leaves would all wither and die if she had to stay home to raise babies and give up her job. She also hated the idea of being dependent on someone else, which she would be in that situation. She loved that she'd made her way in the world from nothing to something. Even if that something wasn't now what she'd always expected it to be.

A crack sounded, and a shutter across the room flew open. Zenia jumped before her mind caught up to her reflexes. Just the wind.

Jev frowned as the shutter banged in the gale—wasn't there glass over the window?—and walked over to fix it. He stuck his head out and looked down, then grunted.

"The panes rotted and the glass fell out at some point. It's shattered in a dozen pieces down there." Jev tugged the shutter closed again.

"The stable looked to be in good repair. Maybe we should sleep there."

"I'd laugh, but you sound serious."

No need to mention that she was currently sleeping in a stable...

"I'd gladly take horses for roommates if it meant the ceiling wouldn't collapse." She shuddered at the memory of the last time that had happened, the very recent last time. Her gaze drifted upward. The cottage ceiling was made from wood, not stone, but those large beams would crush a man—or a woman—if they fell.

Jev followed her gaze. "I can see where you'd worry about such things. I promise to fling myself protectively atop you if one of those beams comes down."

"What if it lands on you?"

"I will have nobly sacrificed my life to save yours. This is what zyndar are supposed to do for women."

"So I'd be pinned under a beam *and* your dead body? That sounds like the reality might be less noble than inconvenient."

"You're a hard woman to please, Zenia." Jev smiled. "Would you truly sleep with a horse?"

"Not *with*. In the stall adjacent to, as long as it's clean."

A faint moan came from the ceiling, and Zenia eyed the beams again, wondering if her concerns were more founded than she'd realized.

The fire snapped, and a spark burned her back. She yelped and jumped away, swatting at her clothing. The flames twirled and writhed in the hearth, almost appearing like hobgoblins performing a sacrificial dance around a fire pit.

She shook her head at her imagination and shifted a mesh screen in front of the firebox.

"Are you all right?" Jev stepped up beside her, resting his hand on her lower back. "I can see the singe mark."

"I'll be fine as long as you don't see flames leaping toward my hair." She could feel the warmth of his hand through her clothing.

"No, your hair is safe." He lifted a hand to stroke it. "And almost dry."

"That's good," she murmured, distracted by his touch.

He let it linger, running his hand down her dark locks again.

She shouldn't stand there and allow it. Just as she shouldn't have agreed to go on a picnic with him. There were too many reasons why the two of them as a couple made no sense.

But her body betrayed her and she leaned closer, her shoulder brushing against his chest. She didn't look up because she worried that would lead to a kiss, and she wasn't ready for that again, not when kisses could lead to other things. Like finding out if a bed in either of the bedrooms was dry.

"My parents worked when I was a kid," Jev murmured, surprising her.

She forgot her decision not to look up and found herself gazing into his dark eyes. "What?"

"My father is incapable of not working, and my mother had a business. She wasn't one to sit idly around the castle and let people attend her needs. She went out and sold my grandmother's tapestries and other textiles, and she handled the books along with our accountant. My parents were around, of course, but my brother and I spent a lot of our time with tutors and nannies. When you've got a castle full of reliable people, it's not that imperative that a mother spend her entire day with her children."

"Oh," she whispered, realizing now why he was telling her this. Or *did* she realize? He wasn't suggesting that could be a solution for *her*, was he? "That's not reality for most mothers. Most people don't have castles full of people happy to work for them."

"I do." He'd stopped stroking her locks, his hand coming to rest on the back of her neck, and his fingers massaged her as his eyelids drooped and he gazed at her through his lashes.

"Isn't it..." By the founders, that felt good. "Your father's castle?"

"He shares."

"Even with commoners?" She lifted her eyebrows.

His forehead furrowed slightly, making her suspect he wasn't thinking that clearly. Maybe he was simply saying what he thought she would want to hear. If he were truly to suggest marriage one day, would she consider it?

"There are stories of commoners marrying zyndar," he finally said. Vaguely. He didn't intimate that his crusty father would be amenable to the idea.

"Stories," she murmured, telling herself she should step away instead of gazing at his eyes. His lips. The way they'd parted slightly, as if to invite a kiss. Or in preparation to give a kiss. "It hasn't happened to anyone I know."

She couldn't even remember any newspaper articles about it happening in her lifetime. The stories were all old, almost legend. Who knew if there was any truth to them? The classism in Kor ran deep, and the majority of zyndar truly seemed to believe they were too far superior to commoners to ever consider taking them as anything other than mistresses. She was far more familiar with *that* scenario. And it wasn't a role she had any interest in filling.

"How many people do you know?" His smile returned, and he wriggled his eyebrows.

He was handsome when he did that. Appealing. Kissable.

"Not that many," she replied, banter easier to handle than dealing with truths and reality. "There aren't many who want to befriend inquisitors."

"Sounds lonely," he murmured.

The simple words resonated almost painfully with her, and she suddenly felt he understood far more than he let on. That he understood *her*.

"Yeah," she whispered.

Jev shifted closer, lowering his mouth. Her last chance to step away, to return to a semblance of professional distance. But her body didn't want that. *She* didn't want that. She lifted her lips and pressed them to his.

Memories of sitting on the couch in Dharrow Castle came to mind, of his gentle touch as she tugged her robe down to her waist so he could smooth that salve over her bruised skin. She'd been in pain, too injured to find anything romantic in the gesture, or so she'd thought, but her body had responded to his touch, tingling with awareness and pleasure everywhere his warm fingers brushed.

And it tingled again now as he eased closer, one hand continuing to massage the back of her neck, the other coming around her waist, pulling her against him. For the first time, she felt the length of his body pressed to hers, how lean and hard he was underneath his clothing. Her cheeks flushed with heat as she remembered him standing naked next to her in Iridium's lair, naked and... beautiful. She wriggled closer as she returned his kiss, opening her mouth, wanting more of him to touch her. *All* of him.

A thunderous knock hammered at the door. They sprang apart, as if they both knew they'd been doing something wrong. Maybe they had been. But for a moment, Zenia stared at Jev, her eyes locked to his, and he stared back.

The knock came again, and they broke eye contact. Jev strode to the door, looking like he would clobber whoever had interrupted them.

Zenia silently admitted the interruption might be a good thing. When she stood close to Jev, her body seemed to forget what her mind wanted. She wouldn't forgive herself if she let her passion sweep her off her feet and she ended up sleeping with him. She hadn't even thought she *was* someone who could be swept up by passions. Maybe, after their visitor left, she would reconsider her thought to sleep in the stable. Or the carriage. Being in here with Jev and a bed seemed to be tempting fate.

"Yes?" Jev asked.

Zenia turned her attention to the door and stepped closer, trying to see past his broad shoulders. She expected Dr. Nhole or perhaps a servant bringing food, but a cloaked man stood there, water dripping from his hood. Or *her* hood? The shadows hid the face.

"I have a message for you," came a man's deep voice from inside the hood.

Unease sank into Zenia's stomach like a rock. This didn't sound like anyone from the Nhole residence.

Jev looked down at a sealed envelope and accepted it. "From whom?"

"I don't know. The person paid the fee. That's all that matters."

"What fee? For delivery? How did you know I was here?"

The man was already backing off the porch. Jev frowned and lunged after him, reaching for his arm. He was fast, but the cloaked man was equally fast. He sprang backward off the porch and landed with a dagger drawn.

Jev stopped. "Who are you?"

"A messenger, nothing more. If you attempt to touch me again, you'll feel the cold kiss of my blade."

"Uh huh." Jev folded his arms over his chest. "Your blade won't kiss very well if you let it rust in the rain."

The downpour had dwindled, but a heavy mist still fell. A horse farther back on the path shook its flanks, flinging away moisture.

"It's been wet numerous times, and it's known zyndar blood." The man backed toward the horse, keeping his eyes on Jev until he reached it. He sprang onto the animal's back without using saddle or stirrups, and his agility reminded Zenia of an elf, or at least someone with elven blood. But he parted with, "Watch the night, and the night will watch you."

She recognized the phrase, but it wasn't until the man rode through the back gate, a gate that hadn't been open earlier, that she remembered who used it.

"That's the parting for the Night Travelers," Zenia told Jev. He didn't turn and come back inside until the man disappeared from sight.

"That's another criminal guild in town, isn't it?"

"Yes. Long ago, they were the dominant one, but that was a century or more in the past. They're more niche now, not trying to control the entire underworld of Korvann, but they're known for having excellent assassins available for hire. No questions asked. They'll also do other tasks. Including message delivery, I suppose. I never tried to hire them."

Jev eyed the soggy yard and dark outbuildings before closing the door. "Would another guild use them? Or are they more often used by normal tax-paying subjects that have grievances they want settled? No questions asked."

"Some of both, from what I've heard."

Jev broke the seal and drew out a letter. There weren't many lines on it, and it didn't take him long to read. He held it wordlessly out to her.

"Stop your search or Targyon is next," she murmured.

Not surprisingly, it wasn't signed.

CHAPTER 11

AT THE FIRST HINT OF daylight, another knock came at the door, this one lighter than the guild messenger's booming pounds from the night before. Jev hurried from the bedroom he'd taken so he could answer it before Zenia stirred. The storm had abated during the night, and the cloaked man hadn't returned, but Jev hadn't relaxed or slept much. Partially because he'd been wondering who had known to send a message to them out here and partially because he'd been thinking about Zenia.

After the threatening message had been delivered, she'd hurried to claim a bedroom and said she was tired and would go to bed early. Jev wondered if he had offended her or assumed too much, even though she'd seemed happy enough to kiss him. She was more complicated than women he'd known in the past—he always sensed that she was conflicted about whether she wanted anything to do with him or not— but he thought, if he could figure her out and win her affection, she would be worth it. He believed she was someone honorable, someone who wouldn't break promises, even if he had to sail off to fight in another war.

And she was a beauty, haughty chin tilt and all. He had trouble believing she hadn't had dozens of men willing to risk the ire of an inquisitor to court her.

The knock sounded again, and Jev opened the door.

The rain had stopped, and birds chirped from the branches of trees in the soggy yard. Dr. Ghara Nhole stood on the damp porch, a wrap pulled tightly around her shoulders.

"I think I found your disease." She held up a thick, leather-bound tome that looked to be a hundred years old. At least.

"Come in." Jev stepped back and gestured her toward a wobbly table near one of the windows.

There wasn't yet enough daylight to read by, so he lit a lantern. A soft thump came from behind Zenia's closed door, so he assumed she had heard the knock and would be out soon.

Ghara glanced through the open doorway that led to the rumpled bed he had used. "My mother will be pleased you two didn't sleep together," she said dryly.

Jev didn't know what to say to that—certainly nothing encouraging—so he merely lit a second lantern and brought it over to the table to add light.

"She was put out with me for sticking you two out here." Ghara brought the book over and opened it to a bookmarked page.

"Why did you?"

"I didn't want your captain snooping around my laboratory in the middle of the night. I could tell she was someone who would do that."

Jev couldn't argue with the statement. "Do you have something in there to hide?"

"No, but I don't like people touching my things."

Jev debated if he believed that. Ghara's demeanor was less icy this morning, but he didn't know if he should read anything into that. Except that her chill seemed more toward Zenia than toward him. He did not know why, not when he had been the one asking most of the intrusive questions.

"Here it is." As Ghara touched a picture on a page, Zenia walked out.

She nodded to him as she came over. Like him, she wore her clothes from yesterday, and she looked to have combed her hair with her fingers, but she was still beautiful. And determined. As soon as she spotted the open book, her gaze sharpened, focusing on it like a hawk swooping down on a field mouse.

Ghara glanced at Zenia but didn't acknowledge her.

"What is it?" Jev bent over the picture, a blob-shaped drawing with tiny dots in it.

"The cause of what is called, in the local vernacular, Mountain Illness.

The diagram is impressively detailed considering the microscopes of the time were little more than magnifying glasses. I suspect it was further magnified with the help of a dragon tear. It is a spirochaete bacterium found in lakes and ponds in our Erlek Mountains and possibly in mountain ranges on other continents too. This sample came from a lake about two hundred miles from Korvann. It's a common bacterium that, when ingested, can quickly multiply and spread beyond the digestive tract to cause multiple organ failures. It's seen often in wolves and wild cats that frequent the mountains. Some recover, their immune systems effectively destroying the bacterial intruders, and some don't. Humans who ingest these bacteria are also susceptible. There's less data on them since humans are less likely to suck down stagnant algae-infested water, the typical breeding ground for bacteria. There's a note here that says it's very rare for it to develop in fresh, running water."

Jev gripped his chin and continued to stare down at the page. The text under the diagram said what Ghara was summarizing in stuffier and more academic verbiage.

"Ingest?" Zenia asked.

"Ingest. I haven't studied the organism myself, but according to this, it's not passed by skin to skin contact or by breathing it in the air." Ghara turned to the next page. "It says here that some animals tolerate it and feel little more than mild digestive distress. Others die swiftly and develop the pustules under their fur, as the princes apparently displayed." She pointed farther down the page to another drawing, an illustration of the skin markings on an animal with a patch of fur removed.

"So some people, some bloodlines, might be more susceptible than others?" Jev asked.

"It is possible. The Alderoths may have a particularly low ability to fight off the bacterium. But it's also possible other people would have died if they had been infected. Since it had to be ingested, someone has to have put colonies of the bacteria in food or water intended for the princes."

"The castle has royal food tasters, doesn't it?" Zenia asked.

"Yes, but unless the princes were diligent in using them, someone might have slipped something in. Especially if someone was close to them, a regular presence in the castle. Someone trusted." Jev tugged at his beard. This new information changed much. If it wasn't a virus, then they were looking for someone with a motive and access to the princes rather than a mad scientist. They had to treat this more like a poisoning than the spreading of a disease.

"How could someone have known the princes would be susceptible?" Zenia asked.

"A good question," Jev said. "I looked through some books about the royal family the other night, but I barely made a dent in the pile. I'd thought—or a source of mine thought—there might have been a precedent, other Alderoths that died from the disease—"

"Bacteria," Ghara corrected.

"—bacteria. If it was recorded somewhere, and someone chanced across the information, it could have presented an opportunity. Less damning than poison, if someone were to be caught with a vial of lake water, and, perhaps more importantly, slower acting. I assume?" Jev looked at Ghara.

She nodded. "Far more like a virus than a poison. It would have taken a couple of days for the bacteria to colonize the body in numbers great enough to make the host ill. I wasn't there for the princes' deaths, and I can only guess how long the castle staff kept their illnesses quiet before journalists found out, but I'd guess another three to seven days for the initial symptoms to turn deadly."

"Leaving plenty of time for whoever infected them to get away," Zenia said grimly.

Jev winced. What if the criminal had fled the kingdom right afterward? He would have to check to see if anyone had gone missing in the castle right before the princes got sick. Of course, their culprit could still be *in* the castle, not believing this would ever be linked to him or her.

"Is there a cure?" Jev asked. If the person was still there and had more of this substance...

His gut twisted as he remembered the note. The culprit might even now be close enough to Targyon to strike.

Ghara lifted a shoulder. "Magic is currently the most effective way of destroying bacterial infections. I've done some work with fungal extracts—fungi and bacteria are natural enemies, you know—but it could take months, if not years, to run experiments and find something guaranteed to work."

"They would have tried magic on the princes," Zenia said. "Dr. Bandigor had a dragon tear."

"It's possible the bacteria resisted the magic or that the doctor assumed he was dealing with a virus instead of this. It's not like mountain pond water is a frequent drink in Alderoth Castle. I assume." Ghara clasped her hands behind her back. "It's also possible the doctor chose *not* to figure out what he was dealing with. Was he questioned?"

"He would have been, but he was dead."

"You'd think multiple doctors would have been brought in to try to save the crown princes," Zenia said. "This isn't adding up for me."

"It's also possible the bacteria were armored with magic," Ghara said, "thus to increase their resistance to doctors with dragon tears."

"Who would have the power to do that?" Jev asked. "Any doctor with a dragon tear?"

"Not *any*, but I could do it if I was wearing one of my dragon tears."

"*One* of?" Zenia blinked.

Ghara nodded. "I had one carved to assist with scholarly work and one to assist with medicine."

Zenia clenched her jaw but didn't say more. Jev reached out and touched her sleeve, knowing she still smarted over losing access to the dragon tear the Order had given her. *Lent* her.

"The average healer in the capital isn't well studied on bacteria," Ghara said, "so there are few in Korvann that I believe could be responsible, but I can make a list for you."

"I would appreciate that."

"Could an elf do it?" Zenia met Jev's eyes. "Their magic is innate and comes easily for them, right? So they wouldn't even need a dragon tear?"

Ghara sniffed. "I suppose a properly trained elf would have the ability to manipulate bacteria with magic. A dwarf, too, but as I mentioned last night, they're not known for their advanced understanding of the scientific world. I'm also skeptical an elf ever grew bacteria and fungi in a lab dish and could tell you which was which under a microscope."

Jev, thinking of Lornysh's advanced, or at least different, understanding of the races and the world, was far less skeptical.

A knock sounded at the door. Their leaky cottage was popular.

Zenia was closer, so she walked toward the door first, but Jev watched, ready to spring to her defense if any trouble presented itself.

"Captain," a familiar voice said. It was the steam-carriage driver. "We've got the vehicle fired up, and we're ready to take you back whenever you're ready."

"Thank you. That will be soon." Zenia looked at Jev.

He nodded at her. They needed to get back to the castle with this new information as soon as possible.

"Yes, ma'am. We'll bring it around."

"Here." Ghara handed Jev a list with only four names on it. "I know all these men, and it's hard for me to imagine any of them helping to commit murder, but…" She shrugged. "I suppose anyone can be extorted by an underworld guild."

"Yes. Thank you for your assistance." Jev accepted the list.

He would visit the four doctors, but he also wanted to speak with Lornysh again. He had no proof that an elf had been involved—and as he'd considered before, he couldn't guess why one would have targeted the princes instead of the king making war on their people—but a means of attacking that originated in nature was exactly the kind of thing elves liked. His instincts, honed by all those years surviving on their continent, itched like mad.

"You're welcome." Ghara smiled at him and held his gaze for a moment before waving and heading out.

Zenia frowned.

Jev hoped that smile didn't mean he needed to worry about Ghara's mother visiting his father soon. He didn't have time to deal with people proposing marriages right now.

"You ready to go?" Jev asked Zenia when they were alone.

"Yes. One of us should talk to those people, but one of us needs to start interviewing the castle staff too. To see if we can chance upon the person who delivered the bacteria. We also need to warn Targyon not to eat or drink anything that doesn't come out of a common pot."

"And to beef up his security." Jev touched the letter that had been delivered the night before. "If we don't stop our investigation, he's going to be in more danger than ever."

"We can't stop. You can't give in to criminals."

"In theory, I agree, but it's not entirely our decision. It's Targyon's life at stake." Jev imagined their monarch hunkered under a piano draped with a blanket. "I need to talk to him before we do anything else."

Disappointment flashed in Zenia's eyes, and Jev wagered she had never in her life stopped an investigation because of a threat.

If the threat had been made on Jev's life, he wouldn't have, either, but he had more than himself to think about here. A lot more.

CHAPTER 12

ZENIA SHIFTED ON THE HARD chair, her butt half numb after three hours of reading. Why, when almost everything in the castle was padded, did the tables in the library have such hard chairs? Did royalty not spend much time in here researching?

She shook her head and turned the page in the scintillating tome she was reading, *Lives and Deaths of the Royal Family During the Twenty-fourth Century After Founders*. She'd already skimmed through a list of lives and deaths from the previous century, and she had books that went back further sitting in a stack on the table.

She would check those later, if need be, but she remembered Ghara's comment on how the illustrator of that bacterium cell must have had a dragon tear since magnifying devices had been in their infancy at the time, about a hundred years ago. Thus, the cause of Mountain Illness wouldn't have been known much before then. It was still possible some ancestor of Targyon's had been afflicted and died centuries back, but what were the odds that someone seeking a slow-acting way to kill the princes would have gone back that far in the history books? It was possible nobody had used the history books at all, but Ghara had said the bacterial infection was only fatal to some animals and people. That made it an iffy way to deliver death unless one knew for certain it would work on a person.

"Hm, what's this?" Zenia paused her finger near the end of the chapter on Dorsezrath the Destroyer, a king who'd reigned a hundred and fifty years ago. "Dorsezrath, known to enjoy hunting as a hobby, was on one of his frequent trips to the Izstara jungles for a safari when he contracted what was believed to be Mountain Illness. He died unexpectedly on the journey back to Kor, which led to his son Tiumen being crowned."

Zenia turned the page. The next chapter started off with Tiumen.

"Well," she murmured, turning back and sliding a piece of paper in to bookmark the spot. "There you are. The possible link."

She looked at the front of the book. The cover and spine had been hand-embossed, but the letters inside had been inked with a printing press. She suspected numerous copies of the book were in libraries around the country. And if one were to search through the entire series—she eyed the book stack—would one find that more Alderoths had succumbed to the bacteria?

As a city-dweller, her lip curled at the idea of sucking up water from an algae-covered pond, but it was only relatively recently that humans had collectively decided hygiene and clean water were important for health. Probably with the invention of those old microscopes and the realization that all manner of tiny life forms lived in droplets of water.

"Captain Cham?" a woman asked in a tentative voice.

Lunis Drem stood several paces away, a thick folder clutched to her chest.

"Yes? You have something to report?" Zenia had tasked two agents to do preliminary research on the staff and visitors of the last couple of months, and also to find out if anyone had left the castle right before the princes' deaths. Lunis hadn't been in the office at the time, so she shouldn't be on the assignment, but maybe the others had sent her up with their report?

"Yes, ma'am."

Zenia waved to one of the chairs at the table. She made sure her bookmark was in place and closed her book.

"Zyndar Dharrow said to add the Night Travelers to our list of criminal guilds that we're tracking, so I went and visited all of our spies in the city to get the latest on them and also on Future Order and Fifth Dragon."

The Crown Agents also had spies in the city? Zenia needed to find that handbook—and a roster, it sounded like—and learn more about her duties and how everything was done. As soon as they got to the bottom of this case...

"There are so many reasons they might have wanted a younger, more naive king on the throne. Do you want to see my findings? How's your investigation going? Do you think we're getting close?" Lunis slid into the chair beside her and laid her folder on the table. She looked curiously at the stack of history books but didn't ask about them.

"Yes, please tell me what you've found." Zenia smiled encouragingly.

Lunis reminded Zenia of herself, and she looked forward to getting to know the woman better.

"I *knew* you'd be interested." Lunis smiled with relief and opened her folder. "Zyndar Garlok told me not to waste his time with the guilds. He hasn't even been in the office for days, but he's certain one of the Orders is behind the deaths. Or that the founders themselves wished it or that the princes simply died of natural causes. How ridiculous is that?" Lunis glanced at the door, then lowered her voice and her head. "Sorry, ma'am. I shouldn't say that about a zyndar or one of our colleagues. I've just been so frustrated."

"I understand what it's like to be frustrated. Zyndar can be difficult."

"I *know*. But Garlok isn't as bad as that odious Brokko. He always…" Lunis glanced at her chest.

"Yes, I understand that too," Zenia said dryly. "Jev has offered to punch him if he ogles my breasts again. I can bring you in to watch, if you like."

"I'd rather punch him myself."

"Is that allowed among agents? I haven't seen the handbook yet."

Lunis snorted. "I don't think so, ma'am."

Zenia pointed at Lunis's folder. "Tell me what you've found, please."

Zenia wanted to find Jev and tell him what *she'd* found—he'd planned to talk to Targyon before heading off to question the doctors Ghara had listed—but she would be foolish not to listen to the other agents in the office.

"It's clear Fifth Dragon is particularly active right now, though it's actually Future Order that's perpetrated more crimes. And you may find this interesting. Archmage Sazshen of the Water Order has put out a bounty and ordered the watch to issue a warrant for the arrests of Iridium and Brick, the Future Order leader. She's saying they've grown too powerful and become a threat to the king and kingdom."

"Huh. That's the equivalent of declaring war." Zenia, remembering how Sazshen had once told her to choose her battles carefully, was surprised she would pick a fight with the guilds. She promptly worried about Rhi and the other monks and mages she knew in the temple. They could be targets for assassins making preemptive strikes for their guilds. "You mentioned the Night Travelers. How do they tie in?"

A throat cleared behind them before Lunis could answer.

"Captain Zenia?" a page asked. It was the same boy who'd warned them about Iridium the day before.

"Yes?"

"Zyndar Dharrow is in a meeting with the king, and they wish you to attend."

"Thank you."

"Oh, drat," Lunis said as Zenia stood up, grabbing the book so she could show them both the link to the past. "I'd hoped to share everything with you and get your opinion."

"Can you sum it all up in a report?" Zenia smiled, pleased someone in the office wanted her opinion. So far, the men had been... if not dismissive then far more likely to curry favor with Jev.

"Yes, of course, ma'am. I won't go home until I have it on your desk."

"Good." Zenia patted Lunis on the back. "Thank you."

She left Lunis pulling out a pencil and writing furiously on a blank sheet of paper.

The page led her through the halls of the castle and to the king's office where the secretary outside knocked on the inner door for her.

"Come in," came Targyon's young voice.

The bodyguards standing to either side of the door looked at the thick book in her hands but must not have deemed it a dangerous weapon they had to take from her. Surprising, given its heft. She wagered she could knock someone unconscious with it, if not with the weight then with the boring content.

Inside, Jev leaned against the king's desk with his arms folded. Targyon had his back to the door as he poked at a bookcase along the far wall. Zenia was prepared to curtsy and greet him appropriately, but he didn't look in her direction. He crouched and pulled on a yellow-spined tome.

A click sounded, and a small portion of the bookcase swung outward.

"There we are," Targyon said, sticking his hand into the hole. He unclipped a keyring from his belt and inserted a key in a lock to open a vault door.

"Is it a sign of your trust in us that you're doing that while we're in the room?" Jev asked. "Or do the cook, butler, and cleaning staff all know that's there?"

"I wouldn't want the inside of my vault to get dusty."

Zenia watched curiously as Targyon drew out a black, velvet-covered box. Jev didn't appear surprised by either the existence of the vault or by their king pulling something out of it. But he was much closer to Targyon. He likely expected to be included in secrets and intrigues.

Targyon grabbed a kerchief and dusted off the box.

"Did you find something interesting?" Jev pointed at the book in Zenia's hands.

"Not exactly interesting, but pertinent to our investigation. Are we still, ah, investigating?"

If Targyon had decided he didn't want to risk continuing while there were death threats aimed at him, Zenia didn't want to admit that she'd been investigating in the library all afternoon.

"Oh yes. His Royal Highness assured me he wouldn't hide under the piano and that he wants us to find the guilty parties. Promptly."

"The piano?" Zenia asked.

Targyon smiled lopsidedly at Jev. "Is it necessary for you to share *all* my confidences with her?"

"You just opened your secret vault in front of her. I assumed she'd been welcomed into the fold."

Zenia wanted the piano story, but Jev didn't explain further.

Targyon opened a drawer and pulled out another key, which he inserted into the lock on the box.

Jev caught Zenia's gaze and pointed to the book, raising his brows. "Want to share what you found while we're waiting for the unveiling?"

Targyon snorted. "I'm not *that* slow. It's just triple protected. I'm fortunate Dazron made a will and thought to explain the various vaults around the castle in it."

"I found an Alderoth that died of the Mountain Illness." Zenia glanced at Targyon, assuming Jev had briefed him already. "Dorsezrath the Destroyer about a hundred and fifty years ago. It happened while he was on safari on another continent and sounds like he was infected naturally rather than as the result of someone's assassination attempt, but it does suggest an Alderoth would be susceptible to the bacteria."

"Dorsezrath was my uncle's great grandfather. Uncle Abdor and his sons are—were—direct descendants." Targyon grimaced as he fitted a third key into a lock inside the box. "I guess I am too."

"So, if someone was doing their research," Jev said, "they would know the family is susceptible."

Zenia nodded, staying silent as she noticed a soft silver glow now emanating from the box. Dragon tears? When she'd had one of her own, she would have been able to recognize the magic of others nearby, but now, she could only guess.

"I have decided," Targyon said as he laid out dragon tears on his desk, "that I'm done being afraid and worrying day and night that someone is out to get me. I'm here now, and I'm going to do my best to remain here. Even if I believe I was chosen for the wrong reasons—the right reasons for some but the wrong reasons for the kingdom—I'm going to do my best. And I'm prepared to confront people and try to get the truth straight from their mouths." After Targyon had laid out eight dragon tears, he lifted his gaze and looked at both of them. "I'm going to host a reception tomorrow night, and I shall require attendance from invited guests. From all the leaders in the city and also from everyone on our suspect lists." He smiled at them.

"That's... bold, Sire," Zenia said.

"Targyon the Bold. I like the sound of that even if it lacks alliterative flair." Targyon picked up one of the dragon tears. "I've never tried to use one, and even if I have the aptitude, I doubt I could master it in two days. Zenia Cham, you have experience using a dragon tear, and I would be honored if you carried one as captain of the Crown Agents and used it to help protect my interests." His lips twisted. "And *me*. I want you at my side at this gathering, using your instincts and an appropriate dragon tear to tell me who's lying when I bluntly ask if they had anything to do with my cousins' deaths."

Zenia forgot to breathe as she stared at the dragon tears so casually laid out on the desk. Hundreds of thousands of krons in value, and he cared nothing if she knew where they were located. More than that, he would give her one to use. For as long as, it sounded like, she worked for him as a Crown Agent.

"I would be pleased to take on the role of inquisitor again for you, Sire." Zenia approached the desk, hoping one of the carvings in the gems would be identical or similar to her old one. The eyetooth of justice was a common carving for law enforcers, and she already knew it would amplify her words and allow her to read the minds of those she questioned.

"Is there one that will work for you?" Targyon asked. "If not, we can get Master Grindmor to re-carve one. I understand that takes a week or two though."

There weren't any eyetooths of justice. Damn. She needed something for tomorrow night.

Zenia lifted a hand and passed over several that were for warriors, one with a coin for a business owner, and reached for one with a book on it, thinking that would help her with research. But Targyon specifically wanted her to question people and read minds. Perhaps that one with a crown would work, granting her access to magic that would assist her in numerous ways related to serving the king.

As she reached for it, her gaze snagged on the last one in the row, a beautiful blue-green oval with tiny red veins. She'd never seen a gem like it, nor had she seen a carving as... arrogant—that was the word that sprang to mind—as this one held. It featured a dragon, its wings spread and its tail curling around to the back of the gem. Was it meant to portray one of the founder dragons? Or simply one of the wild lesser ones remaining in the world today? Who would have believed themselves worthy of wearing such a gem? What master would have carved it? And what would it *do*?

"That one's intriguing, isn't it?" Targyon must have noticed her gaze. "There were a few notes in the box. Apparently, that one is more than a thousand years old and was worn by several kings over the centuries. It grants mind powers such as dragons have, so you'd likely be able to do all the mental magic you had in your repertoire as an inquisitor. Along with some additional things, I imagine. There's a mention of a king using it to hurl his enemies about on the battlefield. With his mind."

Zenia blinked. She'd never wanted that kind of power, and the idea of having it scared her. No, she admitted. She'd wanted it once. When she'd gone to her zyndar father, begging for enough money to pay for her mother's treatment, and the man had ordered her carried off his property like a sack of potatoes. If she'd had such power then...

She shook her head. "I couldn't take a family heirloom, Sire. I think the crown would do what you need me to do."

"You wouldn't be taking it far. I know where your office is. And I was thinking that you should have a room at the castle so you don't have to travel so far every day to get here. You, too, Jev." Targyon waved to include him.

"I accept," Jev said. "Sleeping on the floor in your library wasn't that comfortable."

"You could have stayed awake all night like I did."

"Yes, that would have been much more comfortable."

Targyon smiled faintly. He did look tired. Was he sleeping at all, or was he too worried about potential assassins lurking?

Zenia reached for the crown. "Let me see if it accepts me and does what you need, Sire. Then—"

Targyon lifted his hand to block her, then pointed at the dragon. "Try this one first, will you? I'm quite curious myself, I must admit. And I feel like…" He looked toward an empty corner of his desk. "I know you sacrificed much for the kingdom, to do what was right. I appreciate that. As I said before, I don't yet have many people I know I can trust. I'd like those that I *can* to be powerful, so they can protect themselves as well as me and the interests of the kingdom."

Powerful? A little chill went down Zenia's spine. Did he know more about the dragon tear than he was saying?

"I can try it," she said, eyeing the gem with wariness. "A mage newly linked to a dragon tear usually partakes in a ceremony where she spends three days fasting and acquainting herself with its unique magical signature."

"You have until tomorrow night." Targyon's tone was dry, but he did spread his hand in apology. "The invitations were already sent out. I didn't want to give myself time to chicken out."

"We have a lot of people to talk to before then," Jev said. "Zenia, can you do your ceremony in a steam carriage in between meetings?"

"Uh." She didn't know how to explain the attuning process to them, but she remembered it well and didn't think it should be dismissed. Her druthers would be to wait until after things settled down and she could take three days off, but if Targyon wanted her to be able to use the dragon tear at his reception, what choice did she have? "I'll do my best."

"Excellent. Thank you." Targyon picked up the dragon tear—it was truly magnificent—and laid it in Zenia's palm.

A warm zing of energy emanated from it, seeming to shoot all the way through her body, and she gasped, almost dropping it. The gem flared with blue light.

"Zenia?" Jev stepped forward, touching her arm. "Are you all right?"

Zenia didn't know. She stared down at the gem, wondering if this signaled acceptance or rejection. With her first dragon tear, it had been cool and unresponsive when she first touched it. She'd had to, under the guidance of an experienced mage, learn to coax power out of it.

It didn't look like coaxing would be required here.

"I think so," she whispered as the energy slowly abated. It did not disappear all the way. A slight feeling of warmth lingered, along with something less describable. Vitality? She suddenly seemed to have more energy, and the desire to go run a few laps around the castle filled her.

"Will it work?" Targyon was watching her face.

Gingerly, Zenia closed her fingers around the dragon tear. It did not object. If anything, she felt a sense of contentment from it. But that was silly. Rocks didn't have feelings. Her old dragon tear hadn't emanated anything like that.

"I think so." Realizing she was repeating herself, Zenia nodded firmly. "Yes. Thank you, Sire. I'll do my best to use it to keep the kingdom safe."

"I know you will." Targyon returned her nod and placed the other dragon tears back in the box. He paused, holding the last one as he turned toward Jev, raising his eyebrows.

"My mother tested Vastiun and me when we were boys to see if either of us had an affinity for magic. We didn't. I'm honored, though, that you picked a dagger. You must think I'm a better fighter than I think I am. Or maybe you think I could *become* a better fighter with magic?"

"It's just what I have. Most of them are for warriors. I don't think any of these would lend themselves to linguists."

"What kind of carving *would* lend itself to a linguist?" Jev asked.

"I saw a dragon tear with lips cut into it once," Zenia said. "Technically, I believe the owner was a professional singer, but lips should work for someone learning or using languages too."

"I'm not wearing lips around my neck," Jev said. "I don't care if it *would* allow me to finally pronounce all those elven wines and names for species of trees."

"A moot point since I have no lips." Targyon closed the lid of the box. "Though we *could* get you one with a more applicable carving if you were interested. From what I've read, almost anyone can develop the ability to use dragon tears if they're willing to work at it. Some are naturals, yes, but…"

"*You* don't have one, Sire," Jev pointed out.

"No, I never wanted one. It always seemed a bit like cheating, or it would have if I'd used it for my professional goals." His tone turned dry again. "Of finishing the advanced science courses and becoming a professor." He sighed. "Do you think I could still pursue that?"

"The classes? Yes. Giving up kinging to become a lowly university professor? I doubt that's allowed."

"Damn." Shaking his head, Targyon returned the box to the vault and locked the door again. "I had hopes of being a *highly* professor, by the way. Not a lowly one."

"That doesn't make sense, Sire."

"I told you I was studying science, not language."

Zenia was only vaguely aware of their banter as she attempted to examine her new dragon tear with her thoughts, establishing a mental connection with it the way she had with her old one. It continued to glow softly, the blue light leaking out of her fist. She hoped it would grow quiescent eventually. She'd slept with her old one on its chain around her neck, but she imagined the glow being obnoxious if she was trying to doze off.

Something akin to a haughty sniff entered her mind. Once again, she almost dropped the dragon tear. That hadn't come from the *gem*… had it? No, her imagination had to be playing tricks on her.

"I'll let you two go back to your work," Targyon said. "I have another meeting. I must inform Zyndar Garlok that he's being replaced as head of the Crown Agents."

"He finally came back to work, eh?" Jev asked.

"Apparently, there was a death in the family, so he's been out of town."

"Was he here when the princes died?"

"Yes."

"Maybe *we'll* chat with him too," Jev said.

"You're welcome to."

Jev headed for the door. Zenia withdrew her attention from her fist and curtsied to Targyon. This time, he was facing her and nodded gravely in return.

Jev waited for her at the door, and they walked out of the office together.

"I guess all this means we can't have our date during the next three days," Jev murmured as they passed through the secretary's office.

"Why is that?" Zenia asked, though dating was the last thing on her mind.

"It wouldn't be much of a picnic if you were fasting and mumbling to your new rock the whole time."

"Mumbling isn't required."

Judging by the way Jev quirked an eyebrow toward her, he may have already heard a few unusual noises come from her lips. Gasps, surely. Not mumbles.

"But fasting is required?" he asked.

"Yes, but water is allowed."

"Won't it be romantic when I pour water into our wineglasses?"

"Are you suggesting I wouldn't enjoy a date with you if I weren't drunk?"

"You don't need to be *drunk*. A slight inebriation should sufficiently bend you toward appreciating my charms."

He held open the outer door so she could enter the hallway first.

Zenia stepped out, turned, and almost crashed into a scowling man in the green and silver uniform of one of the zyndar houses. Zyndar Garlok, she realized, guessing the former captain of the Crown Agents had arrived on time for his meeting.

"*You,*" he snarled at her, lifting a hand.

To strike?

A surge of alarm rushed through Zenia, and without thinking, she drew upon the dragon tear's magic, intending to throw its power into a command of stop. Instead, energy crackled in the air around her, and she sensed it completely encompassing her body. Like a shield?

"And *you,*" Garlok growled, his gaze shifting to Jev as he stepped out beside Zenia.

Jev's shoulder must have bumped the invisible shield of energy, because he wobbled and stepped away from her. A flash of surprise crossed his face, but he quickly focused on Garlok.

"Us," he said agreeably toward the scowling zyndar, issuing one of his affable smiles that tended to make him look less intelligent than he was.

The stout zyndar glared at him, at both of them. "I leave for a few days and return to hear you two lickspittles have usurped my position? Don't think I'll stand for this. I'm going to see the king right now."

"You do that," Jev said. "I understand he's waiting for you."

Zenia stepped aside, willing whatever shield she'd created around herself to disappear. Even though Garlok's fist was still clenched, he hadn't drawn it back for a punch, and now that she'd had a moment to consider it, she doubted he would right outside the king's office.

"I will." Garlok shoved past them, making a point of knocking his shoulder against Jev.

It was a hard bump, but Jev saw him coming and braced himself. The older zyndar was taller and stouter, but Jev didn't budge, and Garlok was the one to stumble slightly and adjust his gait. He launched a scowl over his shoulder and slammed the door after he strode inside.

"He's as cordial as I remembered," Jev said.

"Do you think we should add him to our list of inside suspects?" Zenia wished she had thought to ask him a few questions right there in the hallway, but she had better spend some quality time with the new dragon tear before trying to read anyone's mind. She needed to figure out what it could and couldn't do.

Jev slowly poked a finger toward her. It reached her shoulder, and he withdrew it. "Huh. I could have sworn I bumped against... something."

"You did. An energy shield. I was thinking of protecting myself, and I felt magical energy wrap around me."

"Huh," he repeated. "Did you expect it to do that?"

"No. I don't know what to expect yet. But I did think it would take a few days before I grew attuned enough to the gem to draw on its power."

"Three days, to be precise?"

"Yes. From what I've heard, you can make a connection more quickly than that, after a few hours of meditation, but that's rare." Zenia opened her hand. The dragon tear glowed contentedly on her palm.

"I guess the king gives good gifts." Jev smiled. "I'm a little jealous. I should have thought to give you a dragon tear."

"It's not a gift. It's a tool to be used in his service."

"Which is probably why you accepted it from him and wouldn't have from me." His smile grew lopsided.

She opened her mouth to object but remembered how firmly she'd rejected the idea of accepting his hospitality when he'd offered her a room at Dharrow Castle.

"Shall we go visit the doctors on Zyndari Ghara's list?" she asked, deciding to change the topic back to work.

"Eventually, yes, but I want to make a stop along the way. I want to visit the elven embassy in the city."

"Any particular reason?"

Jev nodded slowly and thoughtfully. "Call it a hunch."

CHAPTER 13

JEV ALLOWED ZENIA TO TALK him into riding horses into the city instead of taking a steam carriage. Zenia, more intimately familiar with Korvann since she'd spent her whole life within its walls, said the elven embassy was in a very old part of town, one full of narrow, winding roads that were smaller than the alleys in the more modern areas. An un-carriage-friendly area.

As they rode out the gates of the castle, they spotted a figure in blue jogging up the road, a six-foot-long bo in hand. The stocky woman had a graceful, easy gait even though she had shoulders fit for logging.

"Isn't that your friend?" Jev asked.

"Rhi." Zenia frowned and nudged her horse into a trot. "I hope she's not in trouble."

Jev didn't see anyone else on the road behind her, but that didn't negate trouble.

Rhi slowed down as they approached and wiped sweat from her forehead. The late spring air had turned warm again in the aftermath of the previous day's storm, humid with clouds playing chase with the sun in the late afternoon sky.

"What's wrong, Rhi?" Zenia slid down from her saddle to face her friend.

"What makes you think anything is wrong? I enjoy a good jog in the afternoon heat."

"If you'd jogged another hundred yards, the guards would have stopped you with pistols."

"Dodging bullets puts pep in one's step."

"Or lead in one's step," Jev said, waiting in his saddle, not sure if the women would want privacy to talk.

Rhi grinned up at him, her cheeks flushed from her run. "Zyndar Dharrow. It's good to see you. Have you and Zenia mated and made babies yet?"

Zenia made a choking noise.

Jev merely arched his eyebrows. "Were we supposed to?"

"I just assumed it was forthcoming from the way Zenia ogled your bare chest at the beach the other day."

Zenia dropped her face into her hand.

"I don't remember that," Jev said. "I remember you beating me with your large stick."

"Don't be dramatic, Zyndar. It was a slight tap on the bottom of your foot." Rhi dropped her smile and gripped Zenia's arm. "I'm glad I ran into you here because I doubt the guards would have let me in. I need to tell you something." She looked up and down the road. A carriage was making its way up from the city farther down the slope, but it wasn't yet close enough to worry about eavesdroppers.

"Yes?" Zenia asked.

"I heard someone's been saying that Archmage Sazshen put bounties out on the leaders of several criminal organizations. But she didn't. I just heard her talking to Marlyna. Vehemently. She's concerned the rumors will be enough to bring down the wrath of the guilds, and she's sending Marlyna—and me—out tomorrow at dawn to the temple in Sun Falls. She wants them to send a few monks and inquisitors, as many as they can spare, to protect the temple in Korvann and help Sazshen figure out who started the rumors."

"That's interesting," Zenia said. "One of my staff just reported those rumors to me. She didn't mention who started them. Apparently, we have several spies in the city who share information with our agents."

"Who reported it?" Jev asked.

"Lunis."

Jev nodded, remembering how enthusiastically the young agent had reported on the criminal guilds the morning before. Her certainty that they were involved with the princes' deaths made him doubt his hunch, but he'd learned over the years to trust his hunches. Besides, it wouldn't take long to check on the elven embassy.

"I'll let our agents know the rumor may be false." Zenia sounded like she was being careful not to promise too much. "Thank you for letting us know. I don't know if this ties into our case, but it could."

"It could be something new too," Rhi said. "Someone trying to get the Orders and the criminal guilds into a war with each other."

"To detract attention from something else?" Zenia asked.

Rhi shrugged. "You'll have to figure it out. You're the brains. I just whack stuff with my bo."

"Such as innocent zyndar feet?" Jev asked.

"I doubt your feet are that innocent." Rhi considered their horses. "Where are you going now? Are you allowed to tell random passersby?"

Zenia looked up at Jev. Letting him decide?

Jev didn't think it mattered if Rhi knew where they were going. By the time she could report the news to anyone, if she was so inclined, they would be done with the errand.

"The elven embassy," he said, then on a whim added, "Want to come along?"

That would ensure she wouldn't report back to the Water Order Temple until after they were done.

"With Zenia?" Rhi asked. "I've been forbidden to interact with her."

Zenia didn't point out the interaction they were currently engaged in.

"Come with me, then," Jev said. "If you feel compelled, you can tell your superiors that *we* were the only ones interacting. No need for them to know Zenia was riding beside me."

"Will this be lurid interacting? My superiors wouldn't approve of that."

"Because I was involved in the artifact incident or because you're a celibate monk?" Jev kept his eyebrows from twitching. Barely.

"Both of those things, yes."

Zenia swung back into her saddle. "It'll be dark in a couple of hours. We better get going."

Jev nudged his horse forward, setting a slow pace in case Rhi wanted to come with them.

She hesitated, then jogged to keep up. "I guess if you're heading the same way I am, back into the city, then nobody can be irked if they see me with you."

"Naturally not," Jev said, then offered a hand in case she wanted to ride behind him.

She waved the offer away. "The city has eyes. We'd better not be too obvious about our interacting."

Zenia's lips pursed in concern, but she didn't object to the company. By the time they reached the city gate, she and Rhi were trading their typical banter, making Jev glad he'd asked. He didn't want to get Rhi kicked out of the temple, but he knew Zenia missed her friend.

Jev had never been to the part of the city that housed the elven embassy, but he spotted the tower from several blocks away. The ancient stones smothered in some broad-leafed vining plant appeared to have been there as long as the city, maybe longer. It had been constructed during a time when Korvann had been less insular, and elves and dwarves had frequently passed through for trade or simply come to live and work.

He wondered how many elves lived within the stone walls now. Perhaps only those sent on diplomatic assignments. The tower rose about eight stories tall, but it was not wide, and he couldn't imagine more than a room or two on each floor.

As he and Zenia turned onto a narrow road that circled the tower, Jev realized walls surrounded the structure, sectioning off a full city block. The place had definitely been built in a time when land hadn't been so coveted. More vining plants covered almost every inch of the courtyard walls, several varieties with leaves that ranged from green to crimson red and purple.

Jev guided his horse toward a hitching post in front of a brick tavern that faced the tower. Dishes clinked inside, and people laughed over meals, not overly concerned about their elven neighbors.

"No guards at the gate?" Zenia asked, tying her horse next to Jev's.

She waved toward an open wrought-iron gate, the bars having a fluid, natural design reminiscent of branches with leaves on them. It appeared to be the only entrance to the courtyard.

"I'm sure they're there," Jev said.

Rhi came out of the long, late-afternoon shadows to join them. The sweat that had gleamed on her forehead earlier had evaporated. The pace must have been less taxing than the one she'd set up to the castle.

"Will they let us in?" Zenia asked.

"Let's find out."

Jev led the way with Zenia and Rhi walking behind him. A plaque mounted on the wall next to the gate, the vines trimmed free of it, said something in Elvish. At first, Jev thought it might be an invitation to visitors or a warning to enemies, but it turned out to be the street address.

When Jev stepped through the open gate into what he decided to call a park instead of a courtyard, the hair on his arms rose.

"There's magic here," Zenia murmured.

Jev nodded. "Could be defenses activating. Or alarms to let someone know visitors have arrived."

The ground was covered with ferns, grass, and moss instead of the cobblestone of the street and walkways outside. Trees grew twenty or thirty feet high, and all manner of shrubbery filled in the ground between them. A few winding paths disappeared into the foliage, the branches trimmed back—or perhaps magically coerced not to grow over them.

Jev wasn't surprised there wasn't a direct route to the front door. He just hoped it wasn't a maze requiring magic or a guide to reach the tower.

He, Zenia, and Rhi walked along what appeared to be the main path with fragrant flowers blooming alongside it.

"It's beautiful in here," Zenia said as they passed a bench made from thick vining plants that had been convinced to grow into the appropriate shape.

Rhi sneezed. "Damn pollen."

Jev sensed someone watching them so he didn't comment. The wooden door of the tower came into sight, but someone spoke from the foliage before they reached it.

"Human zyndar," a feminine voice said. "What brings you into this respite?"

I was wondering if any of your people hired the two-faced troll who slipped infected water into the princes' drinks, Jev thought.

Out loud, he said, "I'm seeking my friend Lornysh. He said he might be staying here now. Is he?"

He opted to speak in the king's tongue. If the elves didn't know he spoke their language, he might pick up some useful information, assuming more than one was about and they spoke to each other.

"I have seen Lornysh, but he is not here now."

"Do you know when he'll be back?"

"When he wishes."

Jev thought about backtracking to sit on that bench and wait, but they didn't have unlimited time. Even though he was proud of Targyon for arranging a reception so he could perhaps confront his cousins' murderer, Jev felt he should know, or at least have a solid list of suspects, before the event. Ideally, he would find the person responsible without the need for a shindig, but so far, he and Zenia hadn't made much progress.

"Is the elven ambassador here?" Jev asked.

"He is."

The female didn't volunteer anything extra, did she? He couldn't even see her and didn't know if there was an arrow pointed at his chest or not.

"We'd like to see him," Jev said.

"You came seeking one elf but now seek another?"

"Actually, *I* wanted to see the ambassador all along," Zenia spoke up. "Jev wanted to chat with his buddy while I did so."

"I say we just walk up and knock on the door and stop talking to the trees," Rhi muttered.

The speaker fell silent, and Jev sensed more than heard her move to another spot in the garden. The better to take aim at them? No, the guards shouldn't have orders to start a diplomatic incident by shooting a zyndar. Or anyone else.

Deciding the direct approach had merit, Jev walked to the door. As he lifted his hand to knock, a silver-haired elven woman stepped out from behind the adjacent trees. She barred the way with a strung bow. Arrows in a quiver poked over her shoulder, and she held one in her hand, ready to nock. She appeared no older than twenty, but Jev knew better.

Rhi stirred at the sight of the weapon, her fingers tightening around her bo. In the first shadows of twilight, Jev thought he glimpsed a faint glow escaping from between the buttons of Zenia's blouse. She'd found a thong to temporarily use with the dragon tear and now wore it around her neck. Would it make the magical shield again if they got into a fight?

"Greetings." Jev offered the elf woman his best charming smile in the hope of avoiding such trouble. "Are you going to keep us from going in?"

"The ambassador does not take meetings this late or without advance notice." She did not appear charmed.

"But I—" Jev glimpsed a shadow moving—no, that was someone running through the brush behind her. "Who's that?" he called.

Rhi burst into motion before Jev decided if they should interfere with someone leaving. Rapidly.

She sprinted back down the path and leaped into the undergrowth, trying to cut off the shadowy figure. Zenia ran after her.

Jev turned to follow, but the elf grabbed his arm.

"You will not harass those staying at the embassy," she said loudly enough for the others to hear.

The rattling of foliage and snapping of branches answered her.

Jev twisted his arm free. She had speed and agility, but he had strength. He blocked her when she grabbed for him again and pushed her back toward the door. As she thudded against it, he sprang back down the path after the others.

He didn't want to fight with the elves and worried there would be repercussions for this, but he also found it suspicious that someone felt compelled to sprint off when he and Zenia arrived.

More bushes rattled several meters from the path, and Rhi hollered.

Jev ran back toward the gate, thinking he would head off the fleeing person if he or she evaded the women. A flare of blue light came from the trees, and someone with a male voice yelped in surprise. Maybe pain.

The elven female raced after Jev. He reached the open gate leading to the street and whirled to face her and whoever else ran out of the trees.

The female sprinted toward him, now carrying a truncheon in addition to her bow. Without preamble, she sprang for Jev.

Not wanting to draw a weapon, he stepped forward to meet her, throwing his arm up to block. He targeted her wrist instead of the hard wood truncheon. He succeeded in knocking her arm aside but almost missed the punch she launched at his face with her other arm. She'd dropped her bow to make a fist.

He ducked, her knuckles brushing his hair, then turned his move into a head butt. When his skull struck padded flesh, he immediately felt like an ass for striking a woman in the boobs. But that didn't keep him from following up. Before she could recover, he stepped in and launched a punch into her stomach. She twisted but didn't fully evade him. His fist struck her side, and she stumbled away.

"Over the wall," she yelled in elven. "We'll keep them distracted."

The gate clanged shut behind Jev, and she sprang for him again. He blocked her next attack but glanced left and right, afraid he would miss the running man—elf?—if he gave her his full attention.

More leaves rustled, and a cloaked and hooded figure rushed out of the trees, avoiding the paths. Jev would have thought it was Lornysh, but his friend had no reason to hide from him.

Once again, he blocked the truncheon as it whooshed toward his skull. This time, he turned his block into a grab. He caught his foe by the wrist and twisted. She yelped and dropped the truncheon.

He spun her and pulled her into his grip, wrapping an arm around her waist as he yanked his pistol from its holster with his free hand.

The hooded figure glanced his way but did not slow down. Jev glimpsed the angular features of a male elf. The elf sprang for the fifteen-foot wall, a height nobody should have been able to reach. But he caught the lip and pulled himself to the top.

Jev pointed his pistol and yelled, "Stop!"

His target did not.

Jev almost fired, but could he truly shoot an elf when he had no idea what crime he had committed? If any?

The cloaked elf flung himself over the wall and out of sight on the other side. Jev released the female elf and whirled to race into the street, but he found the gate locked.

He turned back to her, worried she would take advantage of his turned back and attack again. But she stood facing him, her hands open and down at her sides. Right, she didn't have a reason to attack him now, did she? Not when she'd successfully provided a diversion so the other elf could escape.

Twigs snapped, and Rhi and Zenia appeared with another elven man between them. Dirt smeared their clothing, and leaves stuck out of their hair. Their prisoner's shirt, one almost identical to the brown tunic the female wore, had been ripped, and an abrasion darkened his cheek. He glared surlily at Jev. As if *Jev* had been the one to attack him.

"Anyone want to tell me who that was?" Jev waved his pistol at the spot where the hooded elf had gone over the wall, then holstered it. The guards both looked like they were done fighting.

"Only saw him for a couple of seconds," Rhi said. "Before I got close, Pretty Boy here leaped out and tackled me. Then Zenia tackled *him*. The other one got away." She looked in the direction Jev had pointed and grimaced.

"Pretty Boy?" Jev eyed the elf's scraped cheek and his ripped, dirt-covered clothing.

"He was prettier before we roughed him up," Rhi said.

"I'm surprise you found time to notice." Zenia also seemed to realize the fighting was over, for she released the elf and stepped away from him.

"I *always* notice the important things." Rhi wasn't so quick to release their prisoner. Her squint was more suspicious than lascivious.

"You will leave the land of the embassy," the female said. "You are not welcome here."

"I'll leave after we see the ambassador," Jev said. "We're representatives for the king, his personally appointed Crown Agents. I'm positive the ambassador will want to see us."

"He will not." The female pointed her finger at the exit. The lock clicked, and the gate swung open. "Leave, *now*."

Jev looked at Zenia and Rhi, half-tempted to force the issue. He thought they could best the two elves and tie them up somewhere in the garden, but would the ambassador deign to see them after they did that? Perhaps not. Jev feared there would already be a complaint filed with the king about this. Besides, he had a hunch the person he truly wished to speak with had just left.

"Who fled the tower just now?" Zenia walked slowly toward the elf female, commanding her attention. "And why did he run?"

Jev didn't expect her to get any further with the elves than he had, but then he remembered her dragon tear. With the shadows deepening, he once again noticed its glow seeping through her blouse.

"Did he have something to hide?" Zenia stopped two paces from the elf female. "Was there a reason he didn't want to talk to us?"

Jev did not think an inquisitor's mind manipulation magic would work on an elf—he was fairly certain Lornysh had been immune when she'd been trying to manipulate Jev on the docks—but maybe he was wrong. The female didn't answer promptly, but she did stare at Zenia with her mouth slack, her eyes glazed.

Zenia repeated her questions, finishing with a firm, "Tell me."

"Yilnesh," the woman whispered. "He didn't give his last name. He simply said he needed refuge here, and the ambassador granted it."

"How long ago was that?" Zenia asked, her eyes remaining locked to those of the elf.

"He came a month ago, then disappeared for a while, then returned. He's staying in a room on the seventh floor."

"Why would an elf need refuge here?" Jev asked. "Couldn't he return to his homeland?"

The elf female frowned over at him, and some of the spell seemed to fade. Jev lifted an apologetic hand toward Zenia. He shouldn't have interrupted her magic.

Zenia repeated the question, her dragon tear flaring a stronger blue, and the female focused on her again.

"The ambassador said he was cast out," she whispered.

"Shylena," the male elf said, stirring from what appeared to be a trance of his own. "You should not answer their questions. They are outsiders. Intruders. The ambassador will not appreciate—"

A clank-thunk came from somewhere in the garden, and both elves' eyes widened.

"The *zarl*," the male whispered. "We've displeased the ambassador."

The female shook her head, throwing off the effects of Zenia's magic. She threw a confused look at Zenia, but then a deep, ominous growl came from the trees, and she jumped. She and the male fled off the path in the opposite direction of the noise and disappeared, leaving only a few trembling leaves behind.

Another growl came from the trees, even deeper than the first. Deep and hungry.

"Can we go now?" Jev eyed the shadowy foliage.

"I'm done with my questioning," Zenia said.

"You sure you don't want to talk to that thing?" Rhi jerked her thumb in the direction of the growls. They were getting closer.

"Absolutely not."

Jev waved them toward the gate, letting them exit first so he could guard their backs. The leaves stirred among the trees at the edge of the path, and he glimpsed something blacker than the twilight shadows. After Zenia and Rhi reached the street, Jev backed through the gate, pointing his pistol at the inky form.

It growled again, low and dangerous. A pair of yellow eyes appeared, staring straight at Jev.

"I'm hoping you have orders to stay in your yard," Jev muttered, closing one side of the gate while he kept the pistol trained on whatever strange watchdog this was.

As Zenia reached for the other side of the gate to help close it, the creature sprang from the trees. It moved so quickly, it was nothing but a blur of black with those yellow eyes burning in its head.

Jev fired as he slammed the gate shut. His bullet struck the creature with a thud. It didn't slow down. As Zenia slammed the other half of the gate shut, it sprang straight for them.

"Lock," Jev blurted. "How do we lock it?"

Zenia jerked up her arm, and a glowing blue swirl of light surrounded the center of the gate. The creature slammed into the wrought iron. Jev skittered back, expecting the gate to fly back open. It shuddered, hinges creaking, but it held. Zenia had locked it or barred it somehow. The blue magic continued to glow around the gate.

The creature landed, not apparently hurt by slamming into the obstacle. For the first time, Jev had a good look at it. Because of the growls and indistinct shadows, he'd been envisioning some four-legged panther-like creature, and it *was* as black as a mountain panther, but it landed in a crouch on two legs. The arms that stretched toward the bars were more ape- or ogre-like than feline.

It rose fully on its legs, towering ten feet tall. Hairy, clawed hands gripped the wrought iron and shoved at the gate.

"Let's get out of here," Jev said.

Rhi had already sprinted ten paces down the road toward the tavern and their horses, but she paused to make sure he and Zenia followed.

Zenia's face was set with concentration, and a tendril of blue energy snaked from the dragon tear under her blouse to the gate. Jev had no doubt she was the only reason the creature couldn't get out.

He reached for her, torn between wanting to drag her to safety and not wanting to distract her from her magic. That thing, if it got out, might very well outrun their horses. Or *eat* their horses.

"I'm coming," Zenia whispered, not taking her gaze from the gate.

She backed away slowly. Jev walked at her side, keeping his pistol pointed at the creature for all the good it could do. He knew he'd struck their black-furred foe in the center of its chest.

The creature growled, shaking the iron with frustrated paws. Or hands? Jev had no idea what they were dealing with, whether it was natural and from some distant continent or if a mad elven mage had created it in a laboratory in the tower basement.

It continued to growl and snarl, but Jev and Zenia backed farther down the street until they could see nothing but its hairy fingers wrapped around the bars. Those fingers finally released and disappeared back inside the yard. The growls faded.

Laughter rang out from the tavern. It seemed nobody had noticed the creature or the skirmish going on inside the garden. Even their two horses, which had been joined by several others, were indifferent to the nearby predator. That seemed odder than the rest.

The blue energy around the gate faded, along with the tendril that had attached it to Zenia's dragon tear.

"We better get out of here," she whispered, turning to unhitch her horse from the post.

Jev already had his horse free. He thought a brisk evening trot sounded like a delightful idea.

"Rhi?" he asked. "Have you changed your mind about riding with me?"

"Yes, it sounds lovely now."

"Good."

Jev mounted, offered her a hand up, and as soon as Rhi settled behind him, he and Zenia took off.

He let Zenia pull into the lead so he could watch their backs more easily. A few times, he thought he heard some noise and a faint growl from the shadows behind them, just audible over the clip-clop of their horses' hooves, but maybe it was his imagination. Or maybe they were the noises of some stray dog or cat.

He and Zenia didn't slow their horses until they reached the city gate.

A couple of bored-looking watchmen regarded them with indifference as they trotted out.

"I'm going to spend the night at Dharrow Castle," Jev said. "Does either of you want to join me?"

"Was that an invitation for something exotic and outré," Rhi asked, "or do you think we all need to spend the night twenty miles away from that thing to be safe?"

"Ah, it was neither." Jev wouldn't mind having twenty miles between him and the elven guard dog, but he suspected it had orders to stay in its garden, and he didn't truly believe they needed to worry. Of course, that hadn't kept him from setting a very brisk pace out of the city.

"That's disappointing," Rhi said. "I've never done anything outré with a zyndar."

"You're a celibate monk, aren't you?"

"Exactly right. Which is why I've never done anything outré with a zyndar." Rhi grinned at him.

"My reason for going to the castle," Jev said, eager to change the subject, "is that I'm hoping Lornysh is there, since he wasn't, if we were told the truth, at the embassy."

"You think he might have crossed paths with the cloaked elf?" Zenia asked. "Yilnesh, was it?"

"Yes, that was the name. And yes, I'm hoping Lornysh has run into him and can illuminate him for us. If nothing else, he ought to be able to walk into the embassy without being attacked. Maybe he can ask a few questions."

"What about the doctors on Zyndari Ghara's list?" Zenia asked.

Jev hesitated. They *should* still interview those people. Even though his hunch about the elves had led him to someone suspicious, it didn't mean that elf had anything to do with their case. There were plenty of reasons a visiting elf might not want to talk to the king's agents.

"Why don't you give the list to me?" Zenia looked toward the sky, which had grown almost fully dark. "My room is nearby. It'll be easy for me to get an early start in the morning and interview them."

"You won't be busy fasting and getting to know your new rock?" Jev nudged his horse closer to hers so he could hand her the list. If he did find Lornysh, he could envision their chat leading to them spending the next day hunting down the cloaked elf. If that happened, he would have to make sure to be back in time for Targyon's reception.

"I will," she said, "but I'll work in a few interviews. Besides—" her tone took on an odd note, "—the *rock* and I are already getting to know each other."

Rhi hopped off the back of Jev's horse as he debated whether to find the note in Zenia's voice distressing.

"I'll stay in the city, too, thanks," Rhi said. "The last time I visited your castle, your father tried to beat me up."

"Didn't you knock him on his ass in a fountain?"

"I said he *tried* to beat me up, not that he was successful."

"Ah." Jev touched Zenia's arm.

She wore a distant expression, as if she were *getting to know* the dragon tear at that very moment. It couldn't communicate with her, could it? Jev had never heard of dragon tears being sentient or having the power to deliver visions the way that ivory artifact had.

"Will you be all right?" he asked quietly.

"Yes." She nodded, her eyes focusing again, and she smiled at him. "Of course. Be careful out there. The Kor highways aren't as safe as they used to be."

"I'll definitely stay away from the mangrove swamps." Jev thought about kissing her on the cheek, but with Rhi looking on, he did not. He didn't want to inspire more comments about babies or suggestions for threesomes.

He waved and headed off into the night, pondering why an elf might run from him.

CHAPTER 14

ENIA TOOK HER BORROWED HORSE into the stable to remove its gear, feed it, and give the animal a good rubdown. Previously, she hadn't thought much of her rented room above a stable, but now it was convenient since she hadn't wanted to ride all the way to the castle in the dark and then walk back down the hill to the room.

"This is where you live now?" Rhi nudged a haystack with her toe and grinned. "Which stall is yours?"

"I live up there." Zenia pointed to narrow stairs and a trapdoor leading to the converted hayloft. Aside from the lack of indoor plumbing and somewhat fragrant neighbors, it wasn't a bad place to stay. The privacy suited her, and she'd chosen it over the rooms the landlady rented inside the main house. There wasn't any indoor plumbing in there either. It had been a farmhouse until the city expanded out to usurp it into its territory, and the owners hadn't updated it much over the years.

"Do I get the tour? And is there someplace to eat?" Rhi waved a grease-spotted brown paper sack. She'd picked up dinner from a vendor on one of the main boulevards on the way over here.

Zenia was surprised Rhi hadn't headed back to the temple yet. She ought to shoo her friend away, lest Rhi get in trouble for spending time with her, but Zenia couldn't bring herself to do it. Facing that strange creature—guard monster?—in the elven yard had rattled her, but even more, her new dragon tear had her a little uneasy.

Oh, it hadn't done anything disturbing—indeed, in the short time she'd carried it, it had proven itself useful and surprisingly intuitive. It was more the hint of the great power it possessed that alarmed her. All she'd had to do so far was think that she wanted to know the thoughts of another or to protect herself from a foe, and the dragon tear had swiftly done what she wished and more. How much could it do? If it turned out to be truly powerful, was she capable of responsibly wielding that power?

"Zenia." Rhi snapped her fingers and waved her bag. "There's water in your trough but no horses drinking."

Zenia blinked and looked at the troughs before realizing it was a metaphor. "I'm fine. Sorry. Yes, come upstairs. There's a table and chairs as well as a bed."

"The luxury lifestyle, eh? Your last room didn't have a table. Come to think of it, neither does mine. But monks are supposed to lead simple lives. We're also not encouraged to write memoirs."

Zenia tried to decide if Rhi sounded disgruntled. She couldn't remember her friend ever complaining about her chosen career.

Zenia grabbed one of the lit lanterns and led the way up the narrow stairs. Rhi's bo clunked the railing a few times as she followed. Zenia pushed open the trapdoor and used the lantern to light lamps around her rented space. Stacks of hay occupied one end behind a partial partition, but the other was homey enough with, as Rhi had pointed out, more furnishings than Zenia's small room in the temple had claimed.

Rhi sat at the table and delved into her bag while Zenia jogged down to the yard to fill her pitcher from the well between the stable and farmhouse. She returned to find Rhi chomping on lamb and rice wrapped in grape leaves, doing her best to keep the loose pieces from spilling out onto the table.

"You were the one responsible for keeping the elven gate shut, huh?" Rhi pointed to Zenia's chest. "Can I see your new gem?"

Zenia poured cups of water for both of them, then pulled the thong over her head as she sat down. She was relieved when the dragon tear didn't share a sensation of distaste or disapproval when she removed it. She half-expected some kind of reaction. After the elf had gotten away, she'd received a distinct feeling of disappointment from it. Whether it had been directed toward her or toward itself, she did not know.

The sensations—*feelings*—that emanated from the gem might be more the reason for her unease than the power itself. She had the niggling suspicion the dragon tear was somehow sentient, and since she had never encountered that before or even heard of it, she worried she'd gotten a rare and special gem.

The dragon tear pulsed twice on the table, as if responding to her thought. To her thought that it was special?

Zenia touched her chin, more concerned than ever.

"It's beautiful." Rhi bent down to peer at the carving. "A dragon? I've never heard of a dragon being carved on a dragon tear, though that does seem like a natural choice. What kinds of skills does it augment?"

"So far, it's allowed me to shield myself, convince an elf to answer my questions, and keep a gate locked against a brute of a monster."

Rhi's forehead crinkled. She didn't voice her thoughts about the randomness of that list, but she didn't have to. Zenia had a feeling this dragon tear broke the mold in more ways than one. She didn't get a sense that it allowed any particular profession or hobby to be enhanced but that it might be able to enhance anything one chose to do. Was that possible? It was contrary to everything she'd learned about dragon tears.

Zenia would show it to Master Grindmor the next time she crossed paths with the dwarf. A master gem carver ought to know all about every possible dragon tear in the world.

"Can I touch it?" Rhi lifted a finger toward the gem but paused.

"It's all right with *me*," Zenia said.

"Uh, is it all right with *it*?"

Zenia hesitated. She'd never heard of a dragon tear rejecting anyone's touch, and Targyon had handled this one before giving it to her. She didn't think it would react negatively, but could she be sure? So far, it had proven itself... different.

The tear pulsed one more time, its soft blue glow outlining the dragon carving. Neither of them was touching it, and Zenia found it disconcerting that it seemed to be reading her thoughts.

"I'm not sure if that was a yes or not," Rhi said.

"Nor am I. I'd make sure you don't have any of that green sauce on your fingers before touching it. It may not want to be smudged with food."

Rhi frowned, licked her finger, then experimentally tapped the dragon tear.

"Not sure saliva is an improvement," Zenia murmured.

"My saliva is lovely." When the gem didn't react, Rhi let her finger come to rest on it.

Nothing noticeable happened, and Zenia let out a breath she hadn't realized she'd been holding.

"It's a little warm, isn't it?" Rhi rubbed the gem between her thumb and finger before laying it back down. "Like it's full of energy."

"I believe it is."

"Huh." Rhi picked up her food and returned to eating. "You sure you don't want some?"

"No, I might as well begin my fast now. Needing to solve this case is going to make a bit of a farce of the ceremony, but I'll meditate tonight and do my best to obey the tradition in spirit."

The last time she'd bonded with a dragon tear, she'd had other mages to guide her through it. This time, she had nobody. She hoped it wasn't possible to mess up. Most of what she remembered from the last time was lying on a mat and trying to empty her mind of thoughts until she could sense the faint vibrations of the dragon tear on her chest.

"I hate fasts," Rhi said. "Senior Monk Garseth is always wanting to lead us on them to spiritually cleanse ourselves. I can be spiritually clean while I'm enjoying three meals plus desserts a day."

"You monks fast often. You should be well-practiced."

"I'm well-practiced at many things. But thunking villains over the head is the only thing I truly enjoy." Rhi grimaced around her full mouth. "Maybe thunking the occasional snotty colleague."

"I hope you're not referring to me."

"You have your snotty moments but not usually with me. You *know* who I'm referring to." Rhi pulled the wrapper back up over her roll and set the remains on the table.

"If it's not working out with Marlyna, maybe you could request being transferred to someone else."

"I already did. Garseth said to at least work with her for a year since there aren't any other monks available to go out with her now. Which was a lie, or at least a partial truth. There are a couple of instructors who aren't assigned to an inquisitor and could be. Probably *should* be. Teaching doesn't take *that* much time, and it's not like inquisitors go out on assignments every day."

"A year isn't so long."

"It's forever with bad company. I'm thinking of quitting."

Zenia gaped. "Quitting being a monk? Working for the temple? You've been there for, what, fifteen years?"

"Almost, yes."

"You'd just give that up? Your entire career? Over one sour-faced colleague?"

"More than her face is sour, and she's more of an employer than a colleague. At least *she* thinks so with the way she completely zyndars over me."

Zenia rubbed the back of her neck, having no idea what to say.

"You changed *your* career after twenty years." Rhi gazed at her, her usual sarcasm turning into something akin to reverence.

The unfamiliar expression startled Zenia. "Not by choice. You know that. Sazshen kicked me out."

"Yes, but you've got an even better job now."

Zenia leaned back in her chair, the hard wood pressing against her spine. "You think so? It's an honor to work for the king, of course, but I'm not—it doesn't come with..." She groped for a way to say she missed her fame and the fact that everyone had known at a glance what and who she was, thanks to the telltale blue robe. Now... Few people were aware that the king *had* special agents. But to complain about losing her notoriety seemed petty. "I haven't even solved a case yet," she said instead. "I don't know if the job will be permanent. If the king was expecting Jev and me to find his cousins' killer or killers swiftly, I'm afraid we're disappointing him." No, she was afraid *she* was disappointing him. Jev and Targyon were old army buddies. As the junior officer, Targyon must have respected him and depended on him out there. She suspected it would take a lot for Jev to disappoint him.

"I highly doubt that's true. You don't give a dragon tear to someone who's disappointing you."

"He *lent* it to me. To use in his service. Just as the archmage once lent me the dragon tear I used in the temple's service. If I screw up enough, he'll take it back."

"Screw up? Zenia, this doesn't sound like you. You've always been so confident and even cocky for as long as I worked with you. You always believed in yourself."

Zenia spread a hand toward the dragon tear, not knowing how to express or justify the doubts she'd experienced since starting this job.

First, it had been because she hadn't had a dragon tear. Now, she had one, but it was a strange one, and she wasn't confident in her ability as a mage to use it. She also felt daunted working in the castle, in an unfamiliar office among agents whose names she barely knew. She didn't know the full requirements of her job since she'd never been briefed by her predecessor, a man who'd wanted to hit her the only time they had met. To add insult, she couldn't find the blasted handbook that might have enlightened her.

"It's just different," she said. "I was confident as an inquisitor because I'd been doing the same thing for ten years on my own and five years before that as an apprentice."

"You'll get used to everything. It's not like it's a whole new trade, really. You're just working for a different boss and operating out of a different location."

A neigh came from one of the horses below.

Rhi smirked. "And living in a different place."

"True."

Rhi's smirk faded, and she looked earnestly at Zenia, making Zenia take a moment to consider the words. It truly was a similar job, wasn't it? She'd hunted down criminals before, using clues to find them, and then sought out evidence or a confession to condemn them. Why was she finding this new mission so different? Because Targyon's life might be at stake? Because she had to prove herself to someone new?

"You may be right," Zenia allowed.

"Of course I am. Monks are wise."

"Would a wise monk consider a career change over one snotty colleague?"

Rhi sighed deeply. "I could survive her, I think, if nothing else was different, but when Sazshen kicked you out and railed over losing something that never belonged to the temple in the first place, it got me thinking. About leaving. It's not the first time. I've occasionally thought that I'd like to marry and have children one day before my mostly celibate ovaries wither up and die from boredom."

"I don't think that can happen." Zenia, certain Rhi wasn't all that celibate now, wondered just how much sex she wanted to have.

"Who can know? But seriously, especially now that I'm teamed up with Marlyna, I can't help but sometimes feel... that we're not the heroes. The valiant storybook orphans following the Zyndar Code of Honor and saving people's lives until they're noticed by the king and made zyndar—or zyndari—themselves."

"You aspire to be made zyndari?" Zenia hadn't heard of that happening to anyone in her lifetime. Most of, if not all of, the land out there was carved up between the king and the existing zyndar families. She didn't know if there was room for more zyndar even if someone did noble enough deeds to come to the king's attention and earn his good favor.

"No. I don't know—I wouldn't reject it, I suppose—but I do aspire to be a hero, damn it. Not some bitchy inquisitor's henchman."

Another neigh came from below, followed by a whinny. Maybe the horses were listening to the conversation and adding their agreement.

"What would you do if you quit?" Zenia asked.

"Work for the watch, I guess. They're always happy to hire someone with a monk's training. Oddo joined up with them last year, remember? They promoted him straight to sergeant."

"I remember." A hint of smoke reached Zenia's nose and she glanced around, making sure none of the lamps were sending black clouds into the air.

"I know the watch has its politics, too, and there are probably some people being paid off by the criminal guilds, but at least their goal is first and foremost to defend the people of the city from danger. They're not defending a religion or some vague ideal that the Blue Dragon founder may or may not have espoused when he lived tens of millennia ago."

"You certainly have my support if you want to join the watch—maybe they wouldn't throw a fit if you were friends with me."

"Don't be too sure." Rhi smirked. "I know plenty of detectives who always hated how you showed them up."

Unfortunately, Zenia had shown up a lot of people in her life. If she was to have a chance at making a few more friends—*true* friends—going forward, she might have to work on being humbler. She thought of the earnest young Lunis Drem and decided to invite the woman out to lunch once the case had been solved.

"I'm glad I have your support though," Rhi said more soberly. "I don't think it was until you left that I realized... your opinion means something to me."

"Until I left or until you got stuck working for someone odious?"

Rhi laughed shortly. "Yes, both."

She wrinkled her nose and glanced toward the closest lamp.

Zenia decided to check downstairs and make sure a lantern hadn't tipped over. It was probably just that the wind was blowing the hearth smoke from the house toward the loft, but it would only take a moment to make sure.

She patted Rhi's arm before standing. "Think about it for a while before you do anything you might regret later. There's nothing wrong with the watch, but you may find that you miss—" she waved at Rhi's blue gi, "—being a monk working for one of the temples—and the degree of prestige that comes with that. The average subject knows how much training monks get, and they're quick to step out of the way and respect the uniform."

Rhi's eyes closed to slits. Did she suspect Zenia was speaking as much about herself as about her?

"I've also heard the watch uniforms bind and chafe when they get wet," Zenia said. "They're not nearly as comfortable as your oversized pajamas."

"Ha ha." Rhi sniffed and frowned. "I definitely smell smoke."

"Me too. I'm going to check on it." Zenia draped the dragon tear necklace over her head again.

Rhi grabbed her bo, and they jogged to the trapdoor. When Zenia opened it and peered into the stable below, she saw the one lantern burning in its spot by the door. Nothing appeared amiss, but the horses were agitated, whinnying and neighing and bumping against the walls of their stalls. The smell of smoke was stronger in here.

Zenia hadn't closed the front door to the stable, since it had been open when she arrived, and the air near it was hazy. Orange light shifted and flickered somewhere outside.

Zenia skimmed down the stairs and ran up the aisle to the door. Then gasped at what she saw.

Flames licked at the walls of the old farmhouse, burning wood that had stood for countless generations. Fire lit up several rooms on the bottom floor, burning bright behind the windows.

"Help!" someone cried from the second story.

Founders, that sounded like the daughter of one of the other boarders.

Rhi cursed and rushed past Zenia and toward the back door of the house.

"Wait," Zenia barked. She knew her friend would never stand by while people were in trouble, so all she did was wave toward the well. "Wet yourself down first!"

Rhi hesitated, then sprinted to the side. She dumped the full bucket Zenia had left there earlier over her head and sprinted into the burning house without a backward glance.

Zenia, having few delusions of carrying people out over her shoulder, ran to the well to pull up another bucket. The water inside seemed woefully inadequate given how much of the house was on fire, but what more could she do?

A vibration came from her chest, the dragon tear almost humming to her. Zenia paused, her hand on the crank. What could it do in this situation?

She imagined water flowing out of the well to douse the house but didn't know if even that would be enough against the raging fire. Nor did she know if the dragon tear had that kind of power. She—

A thrum of energy emanated from the stone, radiating through her entire body. Then a great whooshing sound came from the well.

Zenia sprang back as water spewed out of it, arched over the yard and spread into a fan as it hit the house. She gaped as an entire river seemed to spatter the exterior of the structure.

Flames went out, but inside, the fire burned heartily. She imagined the windows flying open so the water could enter the building.

With another thrum of energy and a burst of blue light, the dragon tear caused it to happen. Shutters flew open, and windows not designed to open fell out, panes full of glass dropping softly onto the grass below.

Rhi ran out the back door, her blue gi covered in soot and smoke wafting behind her. She carried a girl in her arms, and a man and woman staggered out after her, the man almost on his knees.

Rhi gaped at the water streaming over the path as she set the girl down, and her mouth dropped even lower when she looked at Zenia. She shook her head and ran back inside.

Were there more people trapped? Zenia peered through the windows, but the water striking the fire created great plumes of smoke throughout the house, and she couldn't see anything. Maybe the dragon tear could shield her with magical energy and she could run inside to search with Rhi?

But before she took a step toward the building, a strange awareness filled her. Just as she'd been able to sense magic when she'd carried her last dragon tear, she was now able to sense the life in and around the farmhouse.

The landlady and three other tenants had made it out the front and were yelling to neighbors, trying to elicit help. Zenia sensed Rhi running toward an upstairs bedroom where the last person inside was trapped, the landlady's elderly father. A beam had fallen and blocked his door. He was trying to crawl under it and to shove it away so he could open the door, but it was too heavy. He yelled out for help.

Rhi reached his door and rammed her shoulder against it, trying to force it open. It only opened an inch before the beam blocked it. She snarled and shoved with her shoulder.

Zenia wrapped her fingers around the dragon tear and willed it to move that beam. Could it lift something so heavy? So wedged into that spot?

The water streaming from the well stopped. Because it had run dry? Or because the dragon tear was focusing on the beam?

A thunderous snap came from inside the house. Through her gem, Zenia sensed the beam breaking in half and both pieces flying across the room. The door opened for Rhi so abruptly she fell inside, almost landing on the man. He cried out in relief, and she dragged him to his feet. They staggered down the charred stairs and out the back door.

Zenia slumped against the well, exhausted even though the dragon tear had done all the work. She'd merely had a few thoughts to guide it in what to do. Founders, she was still floored by what all it could do. Floored and thankful. Everyone had made it out of the fire.

The house still burned in places, but the well water had doused most of the structure. Zenia had no idea if it would be livable after this.

"She's a mage," the girl blurted, pointing at Zenia.

Everyone in the backyard turned to stare at her.

Zenia lifted a hand, hoping that had been a thankful proclamation rather than a condemnation. Magic as a whole wasn't trusted in the kingdom, but dragon tears had always been an exception. They were rare but still commonplace enough that most people had met someone with one and seen them at work. Granted, few of them worked quite so dramatically as *this* one.

A soft vibration emanated from the dragon tear. It reminded Zenia of the contentment of a purring cat.

"Maybe you'll get reduced rent after this," Rhi said, limping over to the well, not quite hiding a grimace of pain.

"I bet *you* would," Zenia said. "If you decide you need a room. Watchmen and women aren't provided room and board."

"It's a bit charred and soggy for my tastes now." Rhi waved to the house. "Unless you're inviting me to share the hayloft."

Zenia opened her mouth to offer the couch, but a thought occurred to her, and the words didn't come out. She looked over the fence to the houses on either side of this one. They hadn't been touched by the fire, and she doubted the ones across the street had been either. So, the fire had originated here. It could have been caused by a lamp tipping over or a spark escaping a hearth, but a boulder settled in her stomach as she doubted anything so innocent had happened.

What if this had been for her? Meant to scare her off the case or even to kill her? If she hadn't been in the stable, she might have died in the house fire just as the rest of these people almost had.

If a spy had been observing her from the street each night, watching her walk through the front gate and toward the house, he might not have realized Zenia ultimately walked *around* the house and back to the stable. To an observer out there, she might appear to be one of the tenants with a room inside.

She swallowed at the notion of being spied upon. Was it likely, or was she being paranoid?

Being spied upon seemed more likely. Too many people had disappeared from their offices right before she and Jev had arrived to talk to them. Someone might have been watching them, either physically or through the use of a dragon tear and magic, since they first started on this case. Someone who wanted to make sure the truth wasn't discovered?

"Actually," Zenia said slowly, "I might accept the king's offer to let me stay in a room at the castle."

Rhi looked sharply at her. "Castles aren't overly flammable, I understand."

"I hope that's true."

CHAPTER 15

T HE FAMILY HAD ALREADY DINED when Jev arrived. As a dutiful and loyal heir, he shouldn't be glad to have missed the event, but he'd heard from his cousin Wyleria that meals had been strained lately.

Father had exiled Grandmother Visha to a distant hut on the back half of the property with livestock, provisions, and a garden sufficient for her to sustain herself, and he'd ordered nobody but her doctor to visit her ever again. He'd also ordered the textiles she'd woven and hung around Dharrow Castle over the years folded up and locked away in a chest never to be touched again. Even though nobody condoned what Visha had done, many of their kin thought the punishments too harsh for such an old woman. Jev didn't know how he felt, and his emotions were a tangle on the matter. He never would have wanted his grandmother harmed, physically or emotionally, but she'd shot his mother, her own daughter. It still shocked him like a bullet to the heart.

"Good evening, Jev," Wyleria said from the doorway as he dismounted and handed the reins to the stableboy.

"How are you doing, Wy?" He stepped up to the door and gave her a hug.

"It's a difficult time. To make my days more fraught, Mother has started trying to arrange a marriage for me. She's been muttering about how Dharrow Castle is cursed now that she knows exactly what happened to her sister. I think she wants me married to some zyndar far across the land so she can follow me away from this place." Wyleria's mouth twisted with distaste, either at the idea of an arranged marriage or because of her mother's superstition. Maybe both.

"Maybe you can find a willing man and arrange a marriage for yourself first." The topic reminded Jev that he needed to talk to his father to make sure he didn't accept any offers that drifted over from Nhole Castle or anywhere else.

"That's not traditionally been where my tastes lie."

"In willing men? You prefer unwilling ones?"

"I prefer... Well, it's not important. Even though I'm not the heir to the Prime, there are expectations." Wyleria smiled, but her eyes were sad.

He thought about prying, but if she hadn't shared her love interests with him before, then it meant she didn't want to. She certainly shared everyone else's interests with him. She'd been one of his few family members to write him more than once a year when he'd been away.

"What brings you in so late?" she asked. "We've been speculating that the king will give you a room at the castle since you work there now. This is a long ride to make every morning and night. Jhiroth is crestfallen though. He was looking forward to hearing stories of your tales at war, and he keeps asking if you need a squire."

"To help me and my horse into suits of armor before we ride out onto the battlefield?"

Jev might have smiled at the antiquated idea, but he felt more wistful than dismissive of it, wishing they'd faced their enemies on battlefields at agreed upon times, the way war had been conducted in past centuries. There hadn't been any suits of armor in Jev's war. Anything thick enough to stop a magical elven arrow—or a human bullet or cannonball—would have been too heavy to traipse through forests in. Even their chainmail vests had been cumbersome and noisy when they had been racing through the woods and crawling through undergrowth to find—or evade—their elven enemies.

"At seven, he probably couldn't lift a helmet, but I'm sure he would help in whatever manner possible," Wyleria said. "He's decided that working around the castle is dreadfully boring and that your life must be fascinating in comparison."

"It's had its moments lately." Jev thought of the elven guard creature. "I can ask Targyon if the castle needs any more pages, but I don't know if Jhiroth is old enough or would find that work any more appealing in the end." He patted her on the shoulder, then lowered his voice so the stableboy wouldn't hear the rest. "Have you seen Lornysh around?"

Since Wyleria had supplied Lornysh with a cloak and camping gear, she was the most likely to have glimpsed him lately. Lornysh had no need to hide from her.

"Not for a couple of days. I got the impression he was moving somewhere else. He thanked me for my hospitality." She grimaced. "All I did was give him some supplies for living in the woods. Your father's head would have turned purple and popped off if I even suggested an elf be allowed inside the walls again. Most people wouldn't consider that hospitality."

"Elves aren't most people. What about Cutter?" Jev wouldn't mind an update on Cutter's tool-finding quest, and he was also the most likely person around to know where Lornysh had gone.

"Oh, he's here. He wouldn't come to the dinner table—your father eyes him with a lot of suspicion even though he hasn't forbidden him to stay—but he's taken to helping Mildrey while she works. Well, talking to her and drinking ale while she works. It may or may not be helpful."

"It's possible Mildrey likes the company."

"Or a chance to have fresh gossip delivered to her."

"What kind of gossip would Cutter have that would be interesting to a cook?" Jev imagined Mildrey being confused as Cutter shared news of dwarves from his city back home.

Wyleria snorted and poked him in the ribs. "About you, of course."

"Me?"

"Nobody knows what you were up to while you were away. And Cutter, we've learned, worked with you in your company—Gryphon, it was called?—these last years."

"I had no idea I was interesting enough to warrant gossip."

"You *are* the future Zyndar Prime of Dharrow Castle and the surrounding estate."

"And that makes me interesting?"

She snorted. "That makes you everyone's future employer. They want to know what to expect. Not that your father seems like he'll die any time this century."

"Thank the founders for that." Jev decided not to explain how his desire for his father to live to an old age had more to do with not wanting to take over the estate than any deep feelings for the old man. That wasn't something he should admit. At the least, he wished it was something that wasn't true. But it was hard to love someone who had never loved him.

Wyleria gestured toward the rear castle door. "I think Cutter may still be in the kitchen."

They headed inside together, with the staff they passed giving Jev friendly greetings. He returned them, trying not to imagine them all trading gossip about him and speculating on his worth as a liege lord.

They passed another of his cousins, and she called Wyleria away, so Jev headed into the kitchen alone. The smells of baked bread and roasted pork lingered, but it looked like the cooking and cleaning had been done for the night. He didn't hear anyone gossiping about him, and he didn't spot Mildrey at all. He did find Cutter sitting by himself at the servants' table, a mug of ale between his hands as he stared glumly into the foamy head.

"You look depressed." Jev slid onto the bench opposite him. "Are you not finding the hospitality up to your standards?"

"Hospitality's fine. The drink's even decent, a good dwarven stout. I'm just vexed because I've been ramming my head against a wall."

"I didn't think you minded doing that."

"Not as long as the wall falls down eventually. This one is thicker and stronger than it first appeared."

"Are we talking about Master Grindmor's missing tools?" Jev assumed so, but it was possible Cutter had found another irritating wall. Maybe he'd fallen in love and couldn't get the bearded lady to send a flirtatious smile his way—whatever that would look like on a dwarf.

"Yes. We've hunted all over the city for a trace of their magic. Lorn's been helping, but neither his senses for magic nor mine have located them. And Master Grindmor's been looking, too, and it's clear she's getting frustrated. And I think she's disappointed in me." Cutter's shoulders slumped low. "She's been insulting my beard."

"I'm sorry, Cutter." And Jev was. He'd arranged for Cutter to assist the master in this matter. "As soon as Zenia and I finish with this case, I'll put some of the Crown Agents' resources into helping you. We'll capture Iridium and question her over a rack if we have to." He snapped his fingers. "No, a rack wouldn't be required. Zenia has a new dragon tear. It seems to be strong too. She questioned an elf with it and got what appeared to be truthful answers."

"Oh? Elves are mostly immune to dragon tears. At least attempts at mental manipulation. If a dragon tear is magically assisting you with your sword skills, and you skewer an elf with a blade, well, they're not immune to that."

"Most people aren't."

"What's represented on the dragon tear? I miss cutting those beauties." Cutter tapped the jewelry kit he kept in a pouch on his belt. "Nobody's brought me one to work on in a while, and I doubt they will in the city here, not with Master Grindmor's services available."

"A dragon."

Cutter blinked a few times. "A dragon? Uhm."

"Is that bad?" Jev was positive Targyon wouldn't have given Zenia anything dangerous, at least not on purpose, but maybe he hadn't known much about the dragon tear.

"It's... rare. And it might be dangerous, depending on the soul."

"The soul?"

"Have you ever noticed that animals don't get carved onto dragon tears?"

"I suppose so. It's usually a sword or book or inkwell or paint brush or something related to the wielder's profession or passion."

"Right, but even if the person getting the carving done was an animal trainer, you wouldn't put a ferret on it. I'd advise against it, anyway."

"Why?" Jev shifted uneasily on the bench, worried he would need to ride back into town that night to warn Zenia to toss her gift into the ocean.

"The magic captures the essence of the object—or animal— embodied in the carving. We make them that way on purpose to give them authentic power. If I put a ferret in a carving, I'd need to bring one in from the forest to make sure to get it right. Or—and I don't claim to know how this works—the essence of the nearest ferret around would automatically go into it."

"Essence?"

"Yes, personality if you will. It doesn't harm the animal or affect it in any way, as far as I know, but all of that particular creature's quirks and eccentricities go into the gem."

"Are you saying Zenia's new dragon tear has the personality of a *dragon*?"

"In theory. I'd have to examine it to know. If it's very old, it's possible the magic has faded and the personality has gone dormant."

Jev couldn't quite wrap his head around the idea of a dragon tear with a personality in it, but he thought of Zenia's gem glowing blue, of its magic barricading that gate. Of the zap of energy he'd felt when he brushed up against the shield it had made around her in the castle.

"I don't think anything has faded on it," Jev said.

"Ah. Keep an eye on her then. If she suddenly got the urge to burn down the castle and munch on its inhabitants, she might now have the power to do so."

"*Munch* on?" Jev gripped the edges of the table. "Is that *likely*?"

"I understand something like that happened in Drovak once to someone who thought it would be a good idea to have her cat's likeness carved into her dragon tear. She committed several cannibalistic murders before being caught and hanged. A master carver was brought in to sand off the gem and re-carve it with something inanimate."

"Shit, Cutter. You're scaring me."

"Sorry. Where'd Zenia get it?"

"Targyon gave it to her."

"Hm, maybe she can give it back. Want me to come into town with you to look at it?"

"Founders, yes." Jev stood up, almost knocking over the bench. He started toward the stable but remembered his original mission. "Do you know where Lornysh is?"

"Staying at the elven embassy, he said."

"I was just there. They said he wasn't there."

"Ever? Or just at the moment? Because he said he got a room on the fourth floor. He also said it might be a challenge to get past embassy security—"

"No kidding."

"—and that I should throw pebbles at his window when I needed his help."

"At his fourth-floor window? Are you able to see it over that tall wall around the garden?" Jev considered Cutter's four and a half feet in height dubiously.

"I can if I go up onto the roof of the tavern across the way." Cutter winked. "Sometimes, it takes him a while to come out, so I have a drink while I'm waiting."

"I wish I'd known that tip a few hours ago." Jev wondered if the elf woman had lied—maybe Lornysh had been inside the tower the whole time they'd been dealing with "security." He should have had Zenia ask that question with her gem.

Her gem. Horror rose in his throat like acid as he worried anew about Cutter's warning.

"Let's go find him. *And* Zenia."

Jev dismounted in the street in front of a smoldering farmhouse just inside the city wall, the scent of smoke strong in the air. Cutter sat astride one of Dharrow Castle's stout ponies, gripping his chin as he considered the dwelling in front of them. What remained of it. It hadn't burned to the ground, but a fire had ravaged it. Recently.

"You sure this is the address she gave you?" Cutter asked.

"Yes."

Feeling numb, Jev dropped the reins instead of worrying about tying up the horse. He walked through the open gate leading into the house and yard, dread walking with him. What if Zenia had been caught in this? Had this been some accident? Or deliberate arson? Maybe someone had *meant* for Zenia to be caught in it. Or...

Cutter's warning stampeded around in Jev's head. By the founders' scaled hides, the dragon tear couldn't have *caused* this, could it?

As disturbing as it was, he preferred the thought that someone else had been trying to get her and had done this. Or even better if it had been an accident.

Jev circled the house, then walked through it. Water dripped from holes in ceilings, and charred rugs squished under his feet. He couldn't imagine how the house had grown so saturated.

"No bodies," he whispered, checking all the rooms. "Hope that means everyone got out."

He peered into the stable in the back, and a couple of horses neighed at him. Their structure hadn't been burned, so the tenants must have decided to leave them there for the night. And then gone off to stay with family and friends? What family and friends did Zenia have that she would have stayed with? He didn't think she would be allowed to return to the Water Order Temple.

Jev tried not to feel defeated as he returned to the street where Cutter waited.

"She's not there, and I don't know where she would have gone. I'll see her at work in the morning and get the story." Jev said the words with confidence, hoping they were true and praying to the founders that she wasn't hurt and in a hospital somewhere. "Let's find—"

"There you are." A cloaked and hooded figure stepped out of the shadows of a nearby alley.

Jev reached for his pistol before he recognized the voice. "Lornysh?"

"Yes."

"I've been looking for you all day."

Lornysh looked at the burned farmhouse. "You thought I would be here?"

"No, I thought Zenia would be here. How'd you find us?"

"I have my ways. Though I didn't sense you until recently. Did you just arrive in the city? I know you were at the embassy earlier."

Jev couldn't tell from his tone if there was condemnation in the statement. As an elf himself, Lornysh might not appreciate that Jev had grappled with one of the guards and fired at the ambassador's pet creature.

"Yes, I was trying to get in to see you. The guards said you weren't there."

"I left for a few hours to attend a museum opening."

"*That* he has time for," Cutter said, "but when he's traipsing in sewers with me, he makes any excuse he can to leave."

"Sewers?" Jev asked. "I'd make excuses to leave too."

"I did help you all morning and all afternoon," Lornysh told Cutter.

"I know, I know. I'm just grumpy."

"Rare."

"Don't make me hop off my pony and club you."

"Lornysh." Jev held up a hand toward Cutter, hoping to forestall more threats. Or banter. Whatever those two considered that. "While we were there looking for you—and the ambassador—someone sprinted away. Very suspiciously. We tried to stop him, but the guards deliberately interfered. I heard one yell at him to get away while they kept us busy."

"Oh?" Lornysh must have decided the odds of someone spotting him in the middle of the night on the empty street were slim because he pulled back his hood. "It's odd that someone would have fled the tower. The embassy is considered a safe place where elves are permitted sanctuary in the city. The ambassador himself told me that when he invited me to stay."

"Do you know who it might have been?"

"I do not. I believe there are seven or eight elves in temporary residence in addition to the ambassador and his small staff. I've passed a few elves on the stairs, but I haven't been there long, and only one introduced herself."

Another time, Jev might have asked if the *herself* had been interested in Lornysh, but all he said was, "We're looking for a *himself*."

Lornysh spread a hand. "For the most part, everyone except the ambassador has been ignoring me, as I'm... persona non grata is the term humans use, I believe."

"Yes, perhaps one day, you'll explain that to us." Jev glanced to the side, but he didn't think Cutter knew the story, either.

Cutter shook his head and shrugged.

"I hunted my own kind in your war," Lornysh said. "The elves do not appreciate turncoats." He lowered his voice, almost to a mumble. "Though I don't know if that term technically applies."

Jev leaned forward, hoping to hear more. As far as he'd discerned over the years, Lornysh had been an outcast before he started working with the kingdom army. He never would have betrayed his own people if there hadn't been a reason. Jev was certain of that. If not for some precipitating event, he and Lornysh never would have met. Or they would have met as enemies in the bloody forests of Taziira. Jev shuddered at the idea of having to fight his friend.

"You say you wanted to see the ambassador?" Lornysh asked, speaking no more on the subject of his past. "And that it wasn't permitted?"

"I tried to knock on the door, but the female guard wouldn't let me pass. I told her I was there on the king's behalf. Which is true."

"It's possible the ambassador wasn't in."

"Was he enjoying the museum opening too?"

"I didn't see him there, but he has admitted he enjoys studying the culture and arts of the people where he's stationed. This is his fourth posting in a human city."

"Great to know." Jev huffed out an exasperated breath. It was late, he was tired, and he was worried. "I'm going to head to the castle to see if Zenia went there after—" He waved at the smoking farmhouse. "Lornysh, can you try to find that elf for me? Yilnesh was his name. Ask him why he ran? I doubt it has to do with our case, but I can't help but wonder why he found my appearance so alarming."

"It is somewhat frightful since you scythed off your beard like a farmer hacking at weeds," Cutter said.

Jev touched his neatly trimmed beard and only spared Cutter a brief frown before focusing on Lornysh again.

"Can you describe him?" Lornysh asked.

"He wore a cloak and had a hood pulled up," Jev said. "A look that's trendy for elves in Korvann these days."

"I can't imagine why," Lornysh murmured. "You're sure it was a male elf?"

"Not one hundred percent, but the features I briefly saw appeared male. Why, did the female who spoke to you seem suspicious?"

"Different, at least. She introduced herself to me. Nobody else did."

"Maybe she thinks you're cute."

Cutter made a noise akin to a cat hacking up a hairball.

"Cutter agrees that you're cute," Jev said.

"Someone's going to get clubbed yet," Cutter grumbled.

"Just let me know if you can figure out who fled from us, please," Jev told Lornysh. "I'll reward you with a bottle of fine elven wine from our cellar."

"You don't need to bribe me to get me to help. I've been helping Cutter, and he drags me around sewers without giving me anything at all."

"I offered you half a sandwich," Cutter said.

"After you dropped it in the sewer stream."

"Not *in* the stream. It landed *next* to it, on the perfectly harmless cement."

"Perfectly harmless cement covered with green algae and an odious-smelling fungal growth."

"Natural things," Cutter said. "I thought elves liked nature."

Lornysh shook his head. "I'll make some discreet inquiries and see if I can locate this person, Jev."

Jev almost pointed out that the inquiries didn't need to be discreet and that choking, punching, and threats would be acceptable. But he didn't want to get Lornysh kicked out of the one place that had welcomed him. Sort of. He might not know his friend's story, but that didn't keep him from feeling it was sad that he'd been cast out of his homeland.

"Thank you. I'll be at Alderoth Castle if you find out anything. Or I'll be looking for Zenia if *she* doesn't show up at the castle in the morning." Jev reached for his horse but paused. "Cutter, do you want to come up there with me? I can get a couple of agents in the office to help Master Grindmor."

"*I* want to help her."

"Fine, they'll help you help her." Jev imagined consternation among his agents as he assigned them to take orders from a dwarf traveler. Maybe Cutter could earn their favor with sandwiches, preferably ones not dropped in algae.

Cutter's unintelligible grumble might have been assent.

Jev mounted his horse to head off but paused again. "Lornysh, can you sense a powerful dragon tear nearby? Zenia has one now."

Lornysh closed his eyes and tilted his head.

After a few long seconds, he said, "There are a handful of dragon tears within my range, but I have no way to know if one belongs to her since I'm not familiar with her new one. There aren't any that *I* would consider powerful." Lornysh looked toward Cutter.

"Got a feeling you'd know this one right away if you felt it," Cutter said.

Lornysh appeared curious, but Jev didn't want to go over it all again, not until he had Zenia in front of him and could warn her.

"None of the nearby ones are remarkable," Lornysh said. "My range is only about a mile."

"Thanks for looking." Jev couldn't help but feel disappointed, but Alderoth Castle was more than a mile away, so he held out hope that Zenia had gone up there. And that nothing had happened to her in the fire or along the way.

CHAPTER 16

A MONTH AGO, IF SOMEONE HAD told Zenia she would end up sleeping under a desk in an office, she would have laughed at the notion. She, the famous Water Order inquisitor, had climbed far too high in her career to ever suffer anything less than a comfortable bed and a private room.

At least it was a desk in the king's castle. And she supposed she was *behind* it rather than under it. Also, she was only napping there, not sleeping. A mere resting of her eyelids. She would return to work soon. Or get ready to go interview those doctors.

After leaving the farmhouse, she'd come up here, planning to work, since she'd doubted she would sleep after the fire, and she had scribbled notes well into the night, but she had finally succumbed to weariness. It had occurred to her to wander off and find a staff person still awake, but at that late hour, she'd feared she would only find a few security guards wandering the halls. She couldn't imagine them knowing where sleepover guests should be placed. So, she'd grabbed a couple of cloaks off the coatrack near the office door and spread them out to sleep on. One, she was fairly certain, was Jev's, so it didn't seem too presumptuous to borrow it.

A clunk sounded, and the door to the office opened.

Zenia almost lurched upright so she could scramble to her feet, but her cheeks heated with shame at the idea of being caught sleeping on the floor like a toddler. Or a homeless person. She stayed where she was, hoping it was just a roving security guard peeking in to make sure all was well. She'd checked a clock recently and knew it was still the hour before dawn. There wasn't usually anyone in the office until after breakfast.

"You're here earlier than I am, you old coot," a man said. It sounded like Brokko, the old agent that liked to ogle Zenia's chest. "What's the occasion?"

"Just getting to work early," another man replied, "to prove to that young pup up there that I'm still capable of leading this office." That had to be Zyndar Garlok.

Zenia grimaced, hoping this didn't mean the men planned to sit at their desks for the next three hours. The more time that passed before she announced herself, the harder it would be to explain her presence on the floor behind the desk she and Jev shared. It would *already* be hard to explain. Unfortunately, judging by the sound of their footsteps, the two men continued into the office.

"Young pup?" Brokko asked. "You mean our new king?"

"Our new king, yes."

Zenia couldn't tell if Garlok sounded found the choice of Targyon unacceptable. His tone had grown guarded.

"Have you met with him? Did he tell you, uh, some new people are leading the office now? Complete strangers. Nobody's happy that Targyon didn't promote from within."

"There shouldn't have been a reason to promote at *all*. If I hadn't... Damn it, I know I failed with the princes, but who could have foreseen whatever that disease was?"

Zenia wrapped her fingers around her dragon tear, tempted to poke into Garlok's thoughts to see if he was feigning distress. Did he truly know nothing about the disease? Zenia hadn't spoken to him enough to decide if he should be a suspect, but if anyone were to have the ability to slip in close to the princes and infect them, the captain of the Crown Agents would be that person. Garlok had probably reported to Prince Dazron every morning and seen the other princes often.

"The new captains think... Actually, I'm not sure what they think," Brokko said. "Lunis and half the office believe one or more of the criminal guilds were responsible. I'm inclined to think Dazron and his brothers irked the Orders somehow and that *they* were responsible— they're the ones who handpicked Targyon, after all. Always possible the elves could have had something to do with it, too, but you'd think they would have assassinated King Abdor if they were going to assassinate anyone."

Zenia lowered her fingers from her dragon tear without attempting to read Garlok's mind. She sensed right away something she had missed the day before. He wore a dragon tear of his own on a chain with his pocket watch. She didn't know what talents it enhanced for him, but he might sense it if someone poked into his mind.

"The new captains." Garlok issued a juicy growl—Zenia hoped he wasn't planning to spit on the floor of their office. "Targyon's lickspittles. I'm sure he put them in here because he trusts them, nothing more. Though why he'd trust some former inquisitor from the Water Order, I can't guess. I bet Archmage Sazshen twisted the boy's arm and forced him to take her. So she can spy on him and everything going on up here for the Order."

Zenia stifled a snort. Garlok must not have heard any of the news coming out of the Water Order Temple lately. Unless he thought Zenia's disgrace was all part of a ruse, meant to endear her to Targyon. As if Zenia would be so dishonest.

"I suppose that's possible," Brokko said. "Either that, or he wants some pretty ass to look at when he comes down to visit us. Dazron always spent a few extra minutes leaning against Lunis's desk. Always surprised me she never took him up on his offers to follow him upstairs. Scruffy street urchin that she was as a kid, you'd think she would have been delighted to screw a prince. You think the new girl will screw Targyon? Or one of us? I hope she dresses in less clothing once summer is in full swing. She's got great tits in there and an ass that any king would want to squeeze."

Zenia closed her eyes, cheeks flaming with indignation. And embarrassment. She tried to focus on the vaguely relevant information about Lunis and found it heartening that she hadn't been anyone's mistress.

"If Targyon wants ass, fine, give her a desk here, but don't make her the captain. That's *my* job. Yes, I made a mistake, but damn it, give me a chance to prove myself."

"Is he giving you that chance?" Brokko asked. "I'd heard—uh, rumors of your retirement abound."

"Targyon asked me to retire. I told him I wasn't ready to sit at my brother's castle and play chips and drink all day while his brats run around, reminding me they're the heirs and not me."

"So, you're staying?"

"I'm staying. He said I have to be willing to work under Dharrow and the inquisitor."

Zenia curled a lip. Why couldn't these people call her by name?

"Which I will," Garlok said. "For now. But I predict those two are gone before the year is out."

"Gone? You think they'll quit? Both of them?"

"Quit. Disappear. Whatever. It can be a dangerous job."

A chill ran up Zenia's spine, and it had nothing to do with the cold floor underneath her. Was the man just throwing out words, voicing his wishes, or did he have something in mind already? Might he have been behind the fire?

Zenia wrapped her fingers around the dragon tear again, reconsidering her decision not to pry. With the powerful gem's help, she had convinced that elf woman to answer her questions, and she'd been able to see that she spoke the truth. Usually, her magic wouldn't have worked on an elf or a dwarf. With such a powerful gem, maybe she *could* slip into Garlok's thoughts without alerting him.

A chair scraped. Someone preparing to sit down?

Founders, how would she get out of here if they camped out until other people came in? Eventually, she would have to stand up and admit to eavesdropping. Or pretend she had been sleeping the whole time and come across as an imbecile. She wished they would go get coffee and oatmeal before starting work.

"You want some coffee, Zyndar?" Brokko asked.

"Yeah, I guess. Something to eat too."

The chair scraped again, and the men left the office.

Zenia crooked her head to look down at her chest, at the faint blue glow coming from the dragon tear. She was positive *it* had prompted them to leave. Once again, a thought had been all it took to evoke its magic. This was nothing like with her previous gem. Before, she'd had to truly focus to channel its power.

She let go and stared up at the ceiling. She had a long day ahead, so she had better get to work, not lie on the floor and dwell on whether Garlok had odious plans for her.

More footsteps sounded in the hallway, and she groaned to herself. They couldn't have gone for coffee and returned already. Had one forgotten something?

She lay still behind her desk, vowing to spring to her feet as soon as they left again. But the footsteps continued up the wide aisle between the agent desks and toward her position in the back of the office.

When she realized whoever was coming would soon see her boots sticking out, she debated feigning sleep or simply smiling and waving and pretending she wasn't doing something odd.

A red-bearded face came into view, leaning over one end of the desk. Cutter. Jev leaned over the other end of the desk.

"I told you I sensed her new dragon tear back here," Cutter observed.

"So you did."

"You didn't believe me."

"I was merely skeptical as it seemed an early hour for work, especially for someone who was caught in a fire last night." Jev smiled, but concern burned in his eyes as he looked her up and down, his gaze lingering on the soot spots on her blouse. "Zenia?"

"Yes, hello." She sat up and pushed herself to her feet. "How did you know about the fire?"

"I came looking for you last night." Jev stepped around the desk, bumping his hip on the corner, and enveloped her in a hug. "I'm so glad you're all right," he whispered, kissing the side of her neck and holding her tight.

The embrace and his obvious feelings surprised her since she hadn't ever been in any true danger. But if he'd seen the burned farmhouse and hadn't known she had been staying in the hayloft, she could understand why he had worried. And it touched her.

She slipped her arms around him to return the hug. "I'm fine. I wasn't hurt. Rhi was the one who insisted on running in and out of the burning building."

"Did someone tell her that pretty, shirtless men were playing ball in there?"

Zenia snorted, remembering Rhi's supervision of a group of such men on the beach. "No, but she has visions of heroically carrying people out of danger, and she got her chance."

Jev did not make any move to release her, so Zenia let herself notice the muscles of his back through his clothing. And the warm trickle of his breath against the side of her neck. The way his hand came up to the back of her head, fingers slipping through her hair as he held her gently.

Cutter cleared his throat. "We going to have our chat about the gem, or are you two both going to lie down behind the desk?"

Jev kissed her neck again, then pulled away, though he clasped her hands and didn't release them. "I wanted to find you last night but didn't know where you'd gone. Cutter and I came up here and got rooms. I had no idea until he woke me a few minutes ago, mentioning he sensed a powerful dragon tear, that you were here in the castle."

"Got rooms? I didn't realize it was like a hostel and you could simply tell the staff you wanted a room." Zenia hadn't even seen anyone awake when she'd come in, aside from the guards at the gate and the exterior doors, all of whom had recognized her and hadn't seemed to think it odd that she'd come in to work in the middle of the night.

"I rousted one of the stewards from bed," Jev said. "You know we arrogant zyndar are used to imposing on people."

"You do impose, though not as arrogantly as I expected when I first met you."

Cutter huffed and folded his arms over his chest.

Zenia realized she was gazing into Jev's eyes, and she looked down. They had work to do and…

She turned curiously toward Cutter. "What chat?"

"I know a thing or two about critter carvings in dragon tears," Cutter said. "Figured I should warn you."

Jev nodded.

"Critter?" Zenia lifted her gem, the elegantly carved dragon prominent on the flat front.

"That's a critter," Cutter said. "A big, scaled critter."

"Give her the short version for now, please," Jev said. "It's getting light out. We need to visit Nhole's list of doctors and also get ready for Targyon's shindig. Unless you're planning to wear that." He extended a hand toward Zenia's rumpled, soot-stained dress.

"No." She gaped down at herself in dawning horror. It hadn't occurred to her to think of attire for the event. She was used to her inquisitor robe counting as formal wear and being acceptable for all events, public and private. All she had were shabby dresses from many seasons past. She opened her mouth to complain that she had nothing to wear, then snapped it shut, annoyed by how the words would sound. As if she were a teenage girl going to a ball at some zyndar castle and worrying obsessively about clothing possibilities.

"Do you have a dress for such an occasion?" Jev asked, as if he could read the emotions passing across her face. Maybe they were obvious and he could.

"No. Why don't we have uniforms, Jev?" Every agent in the office dressed in whatever they wished, with clothing ranging from elegant and expensive suits hand-tailored for rich zyndar to extremely forgettable attire likely plucked out of bargain bins. "Like the watch. They have an everyday uniform, and then a formal one for when they go to see the king or some important person in the city."

Zenia tugged at her hair—it was in need of a brush—and looked bleakly at him. *He*, no doubt, had fancy zyndar clothes he could wear.

"I'm sure we can find someone in the castle with a dress you can borrow." Jev patted her shoulder. "Though I'm positive you would be perfectly effective at questioning people if you were completely naked."

"Is nudity allowed at royal parties?"

"I haven't seen it before, but considering how stuffy these gatherings tend to be, it could only improve the event."

"Somehow, I'm skeptical that King Targyon would share your opinion."

"He's twenty-two and male. I promise you he wouldn't object to female nudity."

"Nonetheless, I shall see if there's someone here who can lend me a dress."

"Wise," Cutter murmured.

Zenia faced him. "You have something you want to tell me about?"

"To *warn* you about."

Zenia's feeling of bleakness returned. "Go ahead."

As Jev and Zenia rode through the city, heading back to the castle after questioning the doctors capable of, according to Zyndari Ghara Nhole, creating a protective magical casing around bacteria, he tried not to feel like they had wasted most of the day. None of the men and women had known anything about the princes' deaths, as Zenia had confirmed with the help of her dragon tear, but three out of the four had eagerly filled their ears with far more information than they ever wanted to know about bacteria, Mountain Illness, and manipulating microscopic lifeforms with magic. The fourth man, a busy professor, had shooed them out after ten minutes, saying they could attend his lecture if they yearned for more of his wisdom.

Jev did not yearn.

"Why are we taking the long route back?" Zenia asked when Jev turned his horse at an intersection where going straight would have made more sense.

"I want to go past the elven embassy."

"Not so you can thrust a stick through the gate and rattle the bars to irk the guard creature, I hope."

"I would never do something that immature. Besides, a sword would rattle far more effectively than a stick." Jev tapped the short sword sheathed opposite his pistol.

"What, then? It's clear we weren't welcome." Zenia gazed at him with her green eyes, and Jev was reminded of the way she'd questioned people today. She'd asked the same types of questions as she might have before, but everyone, save the distracted professor who'd been looking at test tubes instead of them, had grown mesmerized, enthralled as the power of her dragon tear seeped into them.

It had been advantageous, but Jev found it disconcerting too. He had seen dragon tears used countless times in his life, but not by someone he hoped to entice to become more than a friend. It occurred to him that she could use that power on him if she wanted. Not that Jev thought Zenia would do that—he didn't question her morality in the least—but he'd now listened to Cutter explain the "critter-carved" dragon tears twice, and the second time hadn't made it seem any less dangerous. The thought that Zenia wore something around her throat that was somehow inspired by or even linked to a *real* dragon... He found it alarming.

Her eyes had widened, too, as Cutter had explained, but she'd assured them she hadn't had the urge to light anything on fire. Apparently, she— and the dragon tear—had been responsible for putting *out* the fire in the farmhouse the night before.

"Jev?" Zenia prompted.

"Sorry, I was contemplating your jewelry."

She grimaced, probably not wanting to discuss it again. "I'll tell you if it compels me to do something odd, like flicking coins off the top of a treasure mound with my tail."

"If you grew a tail, I'd like to think I would notice the oddness without you telling me."

"A tail might be worth it if it came with a treasure mound."

"Are you... uhm, I don't think we've been paid yet, have we?" Jev groped for a delicate way to ask after her financial situation. "Are you doing well? Need anything?"

"My funds are sufficient for the summer," she said, her back stiffening slightly.

He lifted an apologetic hand. He'd already figured out she didn't like to ask for anything or be perceived as needing anything. Especially not by him. He had a feeling she might share such problems with Rhi, but Rhi wasn't a zyndari who'd never known what it was to be short on funds.

"Good."

Her shoulders relaxed. "Sorry for snapping. I was mostly thinking that with a treasure mound, I could buy fancy clothes suitable for royal parties. I hate to waste my money on frivolous things. I'm positive that clothing appropriate for a royal reception is expensive."

"Before we left, I asked one of the castle stewards to find you a dress. No need to purchase one." Jev hoped she wouldn't find borrowing distasteful. He knew his cousins would have. Wyleria was reasonably practical, but some of the others had numerous outfits they had only worn once.

Zenia's mouth twisted. "The steward is a man. He might find something... impractical."

"I don't think clothing worn to royal shindigs is supposed to be practical."

"What if there's not a place for my pistol?"

"Pistols may not be permitted." Jev choked at the picture of her accessorizing a fancy dress with a gun belt.

"Not even for agents?"

"Uhm, we can ask, but likely not. As for why I want to stop by the embassy, I'm hoping Lornysh will notice we're around and come out to see us. I asked him to figure out who that Yilnesh was and why he ran."

"Ah."

"I'm hoping he'll come out without us having to knock on the door or deal with elven security again."

"How will he know we're outside?" Zenia touched the bump on her blouse from her dragon tear.

Cutter had sensed it from afar. Maybe she thought Lornysh would too. Jev thought Lornysh had to be actively searching to sense magical items, but he didn't know. If needed, he would try Cutter's method of gaining his attention.

"You'll see." Jev winked and turned them into an alley.

They came out near the tavern that shared a street with the tower's front gate. He tied his horse in the same spot as the day before but ambled into the tavern instead of toward the walled elven garden. Zenia followed him, her expression skeptical.

It was mid-afternoon, and only a handful of patrons drank in the dim interior. The boisterous laughs and shouts they'd heard the night before hadn't started up yet. Jev, aware of the bartender eyeing him, went to order two beers. He doubted they would be allowed to amble up to the rooftop without making a purchase.

Zenia's expression grew more skeptical.

"You think he'll hear the sounds of our joyous drinking and rush over to join us?" she asked.

"Probably not. I'm not that loud when I drink, joyously or otherwise."

"That's true. The one time I saw you drinking, you were passed out on the beach with the girls at the next towel over ogling your chest."

The bartender pouring beer into ceramic steins lifted his eyebrows and looked toward Jev's chest.

"It's more impressive when I'm not wearing clothing," Jev explained, though he promptly decided an explanation hadn't been necessary.

"Feel free to demonstrate." The man plunked the beers down on the bar.

"Uh." Jev looked at the clientele in the tavern, all of them male, nursing their drinks.

"I don't know if anyone here wants to see that."

"Don't be too sure." The bartender smirked at him. "Free drinks for a show."

"I, er." Jev shouldn't have been rattled, but he was, especially with Zenia standing a couple of feet away and watching, her expression shifting to one of amusement. "I'll pay."

He fumbled in his purse and laid coins on the bar without looking at them. He grabbed the drinks and hustled toward the winding stairs in the back.

"You paid too much," Zenia said, following him.

"To escape without any more comments about my chest? I don't think so."

"I think you could have gotten a free meal as well as beverages if you flirted with him."

"I'd much rather flirt with you."

"Even though I don't own a tavern and can't offer beer in exchange?"

"I can overlook such minor shortcomings."

Jev led her up the stairs to a rooftop patio with a few wobbly tables and chairs spread around. A broken umbrella leaned against the wall next to the door, failing to offer any shade.

Jev set the drinks down and headed to the lip of the roof overlooking the street. And the elven compound. Trees blocked the view of the windows on the first few levels of the tower, but he could see two windows on the fourth floor. He hunted around for the pebbles Cutter had mentioned and found a few broken pieces of mortar.

The two windows were identical, so he didn't know which one connected to Lornysh's room. Maybe he would get lucky. If he could throw far enough and accurately enough. He'd hate to admit that his dwarven friend had a better arm than he did.

As he prepared to throw, Zenia cleared her throat behind him.

"I don't think that's going to be necessary," she said.

He turned and spotted someone standing next to her, the dark hood and cloak appearing odd in the bright sunlight. Lornysh pushed his hood back.

"He says he also came in the hope of glimpsing your chest," Zenia said.

Lornysh gazed flatly at her, glanced at the bulge of the dragon tear under her blouse, then nodded a greeting to Jev.

"I think he's more interested in your chest." Jev dropped the pieces of mortar and joined them.

"What?" Zenia stepped back, flinging a hand to her chest before she seemed to realize what he meant.

"I did sense it when you were several blocks away," Lornysh said.

"Her chest? That's impressive." Jev grinned at Zenia. "Clearly, yours is more remarkable than mine."

She recovered her equanimity and lowered her hand. "The bartender didn't think so."

"He is a man of questionable tastes. Lornysh, do you have good news for me?"

"I have a report for you."

"A good one?"

Lornysh turned a palm toward the sky. "This morning after breakfast, I knocked on the doors of the guests staying at the tower, ostensibly to introduce myself. I assumed you would prefer subtleness and for me not to allude to the fact that we know each other."

After having been chased out of that garden by that creature, Jev wouldn't have minded if he'd greeted his elven neighbors with fists to the nose, but he nodded and waved for Lornysh to continue.

"Most of them were terse with me, though that likely has more to do with me than your case. One did not answer the door, though I sensed he was inside. There are two others I didn't get to introduce myself to because the ambassador came out and suggested that his guests prefer not to be disturbed, as it was already grueling for them to feel comfortable in a human city."

"More likely, it's grueling to get past that guard creature every time they go in and out," Jev muttered.

"It does not attack guests," Lornysh said mildly.

"The person who didn't answer the door sounds suspicious," Zenia said.

"Yes," Lornysh said, "and perhaps the ambassador is too. He was courteous enough to me until I started asking questions about his guests. This afternoon, he was noticeably cooler and more reserved when we passed on the stairs."

"A cool and reserved elf," Jev said. "Imagine that."

Lornysh arched a single eyebrow.

"Is there any way you can get us in to speak to him?" Zenia touched her chest. "If I could question him, we could learn a lot. He must know at least something about all of his guests."

Lornysh hesitated. "I'm certain he does, but he also has a powerful dragon tear. I do not know if you would find it as easy to extract answers from him as from the female guard. Further, he's three hundred years old and wise in the ways of humans. He would be difficult to tease secrets from even if he didn't have a dragon tear."

"Do elves need dragon tears?" Zenia asked. "I thought you all had inherent magic."

"We do, to some extent. Some never learn to use it. Others obsessively study to the detriment of all other skills they might learn. The dragon tears can amplify the magic we are born with so they are useful tools. There are other tools, but as a people, we started using the dragon tears more often after humans started sneaking into our homes to steal them. We reasoned it would be easier to safeguard them if they were around our necks instead of in safe boxes under the hammock."

Zenia shifted her weight and looked away. Was she wondering if one of Targyon's ancestors had once stolen the dragon tear she now wore? More likely, some adventurer seeking royal favor had done it, then given it to an old king as a gift.

She recovered and looked back to Lornysh, lifting her chin. "I'm willing to risk dealing with this wily and powerful ambassador of yours. If he has answers that could solve our case..."

Lornysh looked at Jev.

Jev scratched his jaw, not liking the idea of thrusting Zenia in to question someone with inherent magic *and* a dragon tear.

"I believe the *zarl* might appear if I attempt to bring you two into the tower," Lornysh said. "It remembers those who've proven themselves unwelcome intruders before."

"All I did was try to knock on the door," Jev grumbled.

Lornysh spread his hands. "Before the ambassador grew frosty with me, I learned that your king invited the ambassador to his reception tonight."

"Oh? Is he coming?"

"He is. He hasn't yet met Targyon, he said, so it would be a dereliction of his diplomatic duty not to go and make his acquaintance. Further, it's a foregone conclusion the Taziir king and queen will expect a full report on him."

"So, if we're there," Zenia said, meeting Jev's eyes, "we'll get a chance to talk to him."

Jev held back a grimace as he again imagined her facing off against a powerful, old elf. "Yes."

She would be standing at Targyon's side when she did her questioning, Jev reminded himself. The ambassador wouldn't want to start an international incident by attacking her with Kor's king watching. The Taziir had to be relieved the humans had finally withdrawn from their lands. Surely, they wouldn't want to stir up more trouble.

"Any chance he's taking any guests?" Zenia asked.

"I doubt our wall climber is anyone the ambassador wants to introduce to the king," Jev said, imagining that the ambassador was stuck with some criminal he couldn't turn away because he was one of his people. But maybe not. The guards had gone out of their way to protect the elf. Was it possible he was someone important? Someone visiting from the elven royal family? But if so, why would the person have felt the need to flee when Jev and Zenia arrived?

"The ambassador did not inform me if he intends to take guests," Lornysh said.

Jev nodded. "All right. Thank you for risking his ire on my behalf."

Lornysh bowed.

"I wish I could invite *you* to the reception at the castle," Jev said. "I wouldn't mind having you there as backup in case there's trouble, but I wasn't in charge of invitations. Any chance the ambassador will take you?"

"I think not."

"Oh well. Stay safe, eh?"

As Jev and Zenia left the tavern and reclaimed their horses, Zenia set a fast pace out of the city. He hoped she wasn't worried about finding a dress for the party—or how to accessorize it with a pistol. He doubted she cared about fashion in the way some women did, but he believed she wanted to appear professional and not look out of place standing at Targyon's shoulder as he spoke to people.

He smiled sadly over at her as they rode, wishing she would let him buy her a dress. Or anything she wished.

Would that ever change?

CHAPTER 17

A KNOCK SOUNDED AS JEV WAS dressing in the Dharrow family uniform he'd barely had the presence of mind to bring back with him from Dharrow Castle the night before. He crossed the small guestroom he'd been given and opened the door.

"His Majesty wishes to see you as soon as you're able, Zyndar Dharrow," a page said.

Jev glanced at a clock on the mantle. Less than an hour until the reception. He hoped this didn't signify some fresh trouble.

"I'll be there soon," he told the page.

He quickly finished dressing, glad he'd already had the castle barber trim his beard and hair. Even though his father hated the pomp and pretense around zyndar social gatherings, he'd always insisted Jev look the part of their old and distinguished family when he attended them. He was going as an employee today rather than as a guest, but he couldn't imagine looking anything but his best.

Targyon wasn't in his office but in his private suite, and again, Jev hoped nothing was amiss. One of the two bodyguards at the exterior door waved him in without a word.

"Sire?" Jev found Targyon in a sitting room, standing at a window and looking out toward one of the gardens as the sky darkened. Targyon was already draped in royal blue, purple, and gold and appeared ready to walk out among his guests. "Everything all right?"

Targyon turned to face him. He looked tired rather than energized for the evening. Had he been up nights, worrying about the case Jev hadn't yet solved?

I'm sorry, Sire, he thought. *I'm doing my best.*

"Fine," Targyon said. "I want your opinion on something. One of your agents came up to see me, to make sure my guards knew to watch for strangers that weren't invited yet somehow ended up with their names on the list, as they might be aligned with criminal guilds. Do you think it's likely Iridium will show up again? And if so, should I question her—or have Zenia question her—or should I have her turned away at the door? The latter is my inclination, but if it's possible information could be gleaned…"

"Zenia's having good luck talking to people now, whether they want to talk to her or not, so that might be a good idea. But…" Jev rubbed his chin. "Which agent came to you?"

He hadn't been in the office since returning from the interviews, but hadn't Zenia mentioned spending the rest of the afternoon in there, reading reports? If she'd been there, any agent with a concern should have gone to her, and then *she* could have decided if it was worth bothering Targyon.

"The woman. Lunis Drem is her name, I believe. She was very earnest and seemed concerned for my safety."

"Ah, she's been pressing the hypothesis that the criminal guilds are behind your cousins' deaths. I heard part of her report the other morning, but I didn't hear much in the way of concrete evidence."

"Do *you* have any concrete evidence?"

Targyon's tone was curious, not condemning, but Jev winced anyway.

"I wish I did. I've encountered some oddness in dealing with the elven embassy, but we haven't been able to pull anyone aside for questioning yet. I'm hoping the ambassador will be here tonight and that he won't run off if I try to corner him."

"Please don't corner anyone violently. Unless you're certain they're a criminal. Even then, if it's an ambassador…"

"I don't plan to use violence. I want to plant Zenia and her new rock in front of him."

Targyon smiled faintly.

Jev opened his mouth to ask how much Targyon knew about the dragon tear, aside from what he'd told them, but he noticed a gleam of sweat on Targyon's forehead. Uneasiness squirmed its way into Jev's belly.

"Are you feeling well, Sire?"

Targyon hesitated. Damn it, why did he hesitate?

"I'm fine. Just tired. It's been a stressful couple of weeks. And I'm nervous about tonight. I know I arranged this, so I have nobody to blame but myself, but my guts are tying my stomach in knots over the idea of confronting people, of bothering everyone and casting blame and then not finding a culprit. Or of finding a culprit and not wanting to. Whoever did this, when we find them... I'll have to order them executed. I—" Targyon swallowed. "I never wanted that responsibility."

"You'll do fine, Sire. And just worry about the reception for now, eh? You can be charming and personable and let us—let Zenia—do the questioning." Jev felt bad suggesting that Zenia should be the one out there making enemies, but that was the new job they had both signed up for. He would stand at her side if she found any trouble. Or even if she didn't.

"Charming and personable? Me?"

"You weren't bad with your coronation speech," Jev offered.

Even if Targyon had been reading prompts someone had written for him, he'd smiled and seemed genuine and warm and approachable. A monarch who cared.

"I wasn't talking to people then. Not people who would talk back. I was looking at the heads of a crowd in an unfocused manner." Targyon took a few steps to a chair, gripping the armrest for support before sitting down.

"Are you sure you're all right?" Jev eyed his forehead again.

Targyon must have noticed the look, for he wiped his brow. "Fine. I'll be fine. I'm just hot from all these layers of royal formality." He waved at his attire. "Thank you for coming up, Jev. If I see Iridium, I'll have the guards let her in, but send her straight to you and Zenia before she can cause trouble."

"Or get in your lap and kiss your neck?"

Targyon blushed. "I definitely won't allow that to happen."

Jev wanted to linger and make sure Targyon truly felt well, but Targyon shooed him toward the door. Reluctantly, Jev left, but he vowed to stay close to him tonight.

Zenia tugged at the tight collar of the dress she'd been stuffed into like sausage going into a particularly vicious and vengeful casing. She wondered if the uptight maid attempting to wrangle her hair into something in line with current fashions would protest if Zenia added a belt and pistol to the ensemble. Maybe a pistol was redundant when she had a dragon tear that could protect her, but she was accustomed to wearing one inside her robe when she worked.

She supposed, if Jev was right and there was a rule against agents being armed in the king's presence, she shouldn't tempt castle law. She wished she knew the law for certain. She should. She needed to find that Crown Agents handbook. One of the agents in the office had promised there was such a thing but hadn't known where it had gone.

That afternoon, while a steward had been hunting around for a dress that would fit her, Zenia had spent a few minutes searching for the handbook, but she'd also been busy going over the files of her fellow agents, something she'd been meaning to do for days. She didn't trust Garlok or Brokko, but she hadn't found anything condemning in their files. She almost wished she had. It might have led her to suspecting—suspecting and *proving*—that one of them had been the insider.

A pinch at Zenia's back made her curse. "Does it have to be so tight?"

The maid cinched the straps tighter. "Yes, ma'am. It'll show off the curve of your bosom, making the men see what an appealing lady you are."

"I don't want to be appealing. I want to blend in. I'll be there to spy, not get my chest gawked at."

"A spy with a good chest gets plenty of information, ma'am. Just ask those guests a few questions while they're half drunk and admiring your assets. They'll be too distracted to do anything but answer truthfully. Or at least, they'll let their guard down. There. Done with your dress and your hair. We'll do makeup next, but go look at yourself in the mirror there. What do you think? You're a fine catch, ma'am. How come you're not married?"

"I've been busy with my career." Zenia lifted her chin.

As if *marriage* was important to contemplate right now.

"Are you at least seeing a handsome man? You can't be nothing but your work. Where's the fun in that? Life's to be lived wild and hard, so you've no regrets." The maid winked and pushed Zenia toward the mirror, then veered toward a vanity full of makeup tins and brushes.

Zenia doubted she could do anything wild or hard in the sausage dress. If she had to run or fight tonight, she would be in serious trouble.

She stepped in front of the mirror and grimaced. The dress did not display much skin, but it definitely showed off her figure, there was no doubt about that. Unfortunately, she looked more like a high-profile prostitute than one of the king's secret agents. Her boobs, thrust north all the way to the Anchor Sea, had never appeared so large and prominent. She hoped the maid was right, that men would be distracted by them, and she could more easily pluck thoughts from their minds.

A contented vibration of energy came from the dragon tear.

She thought of Cutter's warning, about it possibly having the personality of a real dragon, but he had to be mistaken. It *did* have a personality, maybe even a degree of intelligence, but it reminded her more of a faithful dog than a savage predator.

"Here we go, ma'am." The maid approached with a huge tin containing enough rouge to paint a house.

Zenia, realizing she'd been a grump—somewhat justifiable, given that she couldn't take deep breaths right now—forced herself to say, "Thank you for your assistance this evening." What was her name? She'd introduced herself. "Hava."

The maid smiled. Zenia must have gotten the name right.

"You're welcome, ma'am."

Zenia endured a few more minutes of primping before being let free into the wilds of the third floor of the castle. She passed guards, butlers, stewards, and other people whose jobs she did not yet know on her way down to the first floor. The reception was being held in one of three ballrooms, so she assumed people would dance after they stuffed themselves with food and wine. She hoped the dancing wouldn't get in the way of the questioning. Not only would Jev's elven ambassador be here, but the archmages of the four Orders would be here. Zenia would finally have her chance to speak with them. They wouldn't be able to evade her easily here.

Several of the guards checked her out as she passed, though they were quick and subtle with their interest, since they were professionals on duty. As much as she would have preferred her form-hiding, faithful blue robe, she admitted it was a little flattering to have so many gazes following her. That robe had done more than hide her form, and after having men avoid her—*inquisitor* her—on a regular basis, she had let herself believe she had grown too old to attract a man.

What would Jev think of her in this dress? Her body warmed a few degrees as she imagined *his* gaze following her.

He hadn't spoken of their date since coming back from the Nhole estate, since their kiss in front of that crackling hearth. Since he'd hinted that the woman he married would have plenty of help with childrearing and could continue to work at her career. That was something Zenia had never considered, since it certainly did not apply to commoners, but she'd found herself wondering if it might be a possibility. If she and Jev were to marry…

But she didn't truly think he had been implying that *they* might marry one day. Even though he hadn't bluntly said it, she'd gotten the impression that to marry some commoner, he would have to give up his position as his father's heir. He might even be ostracized from his family. Even if he was crazy enough to be willing, she could never ask him.

As she descended the wide stairs to the first floor of the castle, and the murmurs of dozens of conversations from the nearby ballroom came to her ears, a dashing figure stepped away from the wall and bowed to her. Jev. She'd been so distracted by thinking about him that she hadn't *noticed* him waiting there.

He wore his green-and-silver Dharrow house uniform, which had a quasi-military aspect to it, but he looked nothing like the scruffy soldier she'd tried to arrest when they met. His hair and beard were trimmed, he was impeccably pressed and tidy, and his boots gleamed under the light of dozens of candelabras and wall sconces brightening the hall.

Dashing was the word that came to her mind for him. And… *sexy*.

"Good evening, Captain Cham." Jev straightened and offered her his arm.

Zenia smiled. "Good evening, Zyndar Captain Dharrow."

"That's a mouthful, isn't it?" He let his gaze drop, drinking her in from head to toe, though he was careful to keep his expression polite and amiable, rather than letting it turn into a leer. Still, warmth rushed through her body again, and she wished they were somewhere else, somewhere private.

"Is it terribly selfish of me to wish we were attending this reception together for recreational purposes rather than because we're on duty?" Jev asked.

"Probably. And unrealistic as I would never be invited to a party like this if I weren't on the king's payroll."

"I don't know about that. You look stunning in that dress. I'm sure you look stunning out of it, too, but I'm afraid to bring up nudity these days, as you never know the comments you'll receive from random eavesdroppers." He looked down the wide hall toward a couple of stony-faced guards watching them without appearing to watch them.

"Are you afraid another man might ask to see your chest?"

"Terrified."

Zenia rested her hand on his arm, happy to let him guide her into the ballroom, though she would spend most of the night at Targyon's side, listening to all the conversations he started. Or, knowing her, butting into them. She was more than ready to question the archmages and might not wait for Targyon to get started. The one exception was Archmage Sazshen, whom Zenia would prefer never to speak with again. But she would be here. And she was as much a suspect as the rest of them were. Zenia would have to talk with her.

Jev nodded toward the open doors of the ballroom, and she walked side by side with him.

"Keep an eye on Targyon tonight when you're with him," Jev murmured, the words too quiet for the guards to overhear.

"Why?" A surge of worry flowed into her limbs. "What happened?"

"Nothing... exactly. But I talked with him a few minutes ago and noticed he was sweating. He promised he was just nervous, but I—" His lips flattened together. "That was one of the symptoms. Fever and sweating."

"Did you touch his forehead?"

"He's my liege lord. That seemed presumptuous."

"Do you want me to touch his forehead?"

"Yes."

Zenia snorted. "It's all right for me but not for you?"

"Yes, because he'll be too busy looking at your female bits to notice."

"I feel like it would be appropriate for me to swat you on the chest, zyndar or not."

"Very appropriate." He smiled as they stepped into the ballroom, then nodded toward the only man wearing the royal colors, rich purple and blue with gold trim. "There he is."

Zenia let Jev guide her toward Targyon. "What will you be doing while we ask people questions?"

"Standing by a wall or column and watching to make sure there's no trouble afoot. Much like Drem there." His eyes narrowed as he gazed past knots of well-dressed people toward a portion of the wall where Lunis and another agent watched the proceedings.

Zenia hadn't asked anyone from the office to come. Had Jev? Or Targyon?

They were dressed more like the castle guard than guests, in simple black trousers and jackets. Unlike the guards, they did not carry weapons, at least openly, but they both had the appearance of being on duty.

"Did you assign them this task?" Jev asked.

"No. Did the king?"

"It's possible, but I don't think so. I talked to him recently, and he'd been warned by Lunis to watch for representatives from the criminal guilds."

Zenia wondered if Lunis knew more than she did. She'd read the report Lunis had left on her desk but hadn't found any evidence in there. Simply rumors and gossip shared by various watchmen and spies around the city about the Fifth Dragon's activities and how they might relate to the castle and king. Sometimes, rumors and gossip were enough of a lead, but nothing had plucked at Zenia's intuition.

"I'm going to talk to her," she said.

"I think Targyon is waiting for you." Jev lifted a hand, acknowledging Targyon, who was looking over at them while speaking with a couple wearing the mustard yellows and browns popular among the leaders of the desert tribes to the south. Diplomats?

"Tell him I'll be there in a moment, please."

Jev frowned, and Zenia agreed that it wasn't a good idea to make the king wait, but the instincts that had been silent while reading

Lunis's report started jumping up and down and hollering now. Maybe she should have been reading about Lunis's background rather than focusing on Brokko and Garlok. Zenia didn't want to suspect Lunis of anything—damn it, she wanted Lunis to be her first friend among the Crown Agents—but having her show up here without asking permission made Zenia uneasy.

Was she simply showing initiative? Or was she up to something dodgy?

"Hope not," Zenia muttered, heading across the ballroom as Jev veered over to join Targyon.

She was aware of them talking and pointing after her, but she kept her focus on Lunis. So much so that she almost missed the sea-blue robe stepping out of a gathering of people.

Zenia halted as Archmage Sazshen stopped in her path. *Blocked* her path.

"Archmage." Zenia made herself curtsy, though she had no interest in sharing social niceties and didn't think, from the dyspeptic twist of Sazshen's mouth, that her former boss wanted to engage in them either.

"*Captain*, is it now?"

"Yes, ma'am."

"An odd rank for a woman, considering women can't join the army."

"The watch has ranks similar to those of soldiers, and women can join the watch."

What a ridiculous discussion to be having now. Zenia looked past Sazshen's robed shoulder to where Lunis had been standing, but Lunis wasn't there. The male agent remained by the wall, but where had Lunis gone? There were a couple hundred people in the ballroom, and all the columns, with purple, blue, and gold banners draped around them, offered plenty of obstacles to one's view.

"Fascinating, I'm sure. I won't hold you up for long." Sazshen, noticing Zenia's distracted glances around the ballroom, frowned. "I'm sure you're busy, though doing what, I can't imagine." She pursed her lips and frowned her disapproval at the sausage-casing dress. "I do want to make sure you know that I would be extremely displeased if all of the Water Order's secrets became common knowledge to the king."

"I know precious few secrets, Archmage. If I'd known more, perhaps the search for that artifact wouldn't have turned into a ludicrous man hunt."

"The artifact that is now founders know where." Sazshen shook her head. "Tell me if the king saw it, if he knows what it contained."

"The visions it shares? The elf princess who came to retrieve it said she was going to show him. I don't know if she did."

"I see," Sazshen said coolly. "I see."

"I have other matters to worry about tonight, Archmage." Zenia walked past Sazshen without waiting to be dismissed as she once would have done.

She strode to the wall where the male agent stood. Khomas. She had recently learned he oversaw tax collection from the zyndar and common subjects around the kingdom. She stopped in front of him. "Good evening, Khomas." She forced herself to sound civil and not make accusations. "I didn't realize anyone else from the office would be here tonight."

Unlike Zyndar Garlok, Khomas did not carry a dragon tear. Zenia willed hers to lend her the power to see the truth or lack thereof in his words.

"Hello, ma'am." He smiled, but she sensed that he didn't like having to call someone younger than he and far newer to the job *ma'am*. "Lunis talked me into coming up here instead of going home for the night." True, she sensed. "She's real worried that, uhm. She just thinks maybe people aren't paying enough attention to the threat from the criminals in the city."

Also true, at least insofar as Khomas knew. Zenia could tell that he hadn't wanted to come and that he didn't know if the criminal organizations were truly a threat to the king or would make trouble at this reception. He'd come up as a favor to Lunis and hoped to leave before the event ended.

"Where did she go?" Zenia asked, pleased to have a dragon tear's assistance again.

A little trill of warmth came from the gem, as if it was pleased to assist. Maybe that was her imagination. She still needed to spend a couple of days meditating and opening her mind to the dragon tear's magic.

"Said she wanted to check the food." The agent pointed toward the long buffet table stretched along one wall. Lunis wasn't there. "Not sure where she is now. Maybe she got distracted."

True.

Zenia wished the man knew more, but at least she'd found out quickly that he didn't. "Thank you. Let her know I'm looking for her if you see her, please."

"Yes, ma'am."

Zenia turned to check on Jev and Targyon, but a new sensation emanated from her dragon tear. It drew her awareness away from her body and outward, out of the ballroom, through the hall, and toward the castle courtyard. Suddenly, with certainty, she knew Lunis was out there. She didn't have a dragon tear, so she lacked a magical presence acting as a beacon, but somehow *her* dragon tear knew who she was looking for. And where she was.

Had Lunis run off after a suspect? Had she seen Iridium or a known cohort of hers?

Zenia took a step toward the door, tempted to run out and check, but she spotted Targyon talking to someone new. A tall, lean man in an elegant green robe. Pointed ears poked up through his silver hair. The elven ambassador.

Jev stood slightly behind Targyon. He noticed Zenia looking their way and lifted a hand, gesturing for her to join them. His eyes bespoke urgency.

Finding Lunis would have to wait. Zenia strode over to join the men.

CHAPTER 18

J EV LET OUT A SLOW, relieved breath when Zenia headed
toward them. She had appeared agitated, almost as if she meant
to race out of the ballroom, and he hadn't been certain she would
see him waving. Targyon and the ambassador—Lord Shoyalusa, he'd
introduced himself as—seemed to be nearing the end of their small talk.
Targyon wouldn't want to ask anything potentially incendiary without
Zenia and her dragon tear there.

Unfortunately, as Lornysh had promised, Shoyalusa wore a dragon
tear of his own, the gem displayed prominently on a silver chain around
his neck. A tree was carved into the front of the gem. Jev had no idea what
powers a tree might grant a person, but he had no doubt the ambassador
would be experienced at defending himself from threats.

The elf looked at Zenia when she approached, and his eyes narrowed.
Jev had received a similar look. He had a feeling the ambassador knew
the identities of the people responsible for the incident in his garden the
day before.

"Ah, Captain Cham." Targyon smiled and waved her closer.

Zenia managed to return the smile and frown with concern at the same
time, her gaze flicking toward his forehead. A gleam of sweat lurked there
again, and Jev thought Targyon appeared flushed. Founders, what would
they do if Targyon had been infected with the same magicked bacteria
that had killed his cousins? The idea of losing his young lieutenant—
and his new liege lord—made Jev's heart heavy. Almost as bad was the
knowledge that he would have failed Targyon. He'd been on the case all
week and hadn't found the insider *or* the outsider responsible.

"Captain Cham," Targyon said, "this is Ambassador Shoyalusa. Ambassador, one of the leaders of my security forces."

Security. Not special agents. Understandable to play down what they did, but Jev doubted the ambassador would be fooled.

"And do your forces typically trespass on embassy property and start skirmishes with its guards?" Shoyalusa asked coolly.

Since Jev hadn't explained that incident to Targyon yet, he rushed to answer. "I was merely attempting to knock on the door to see you, Ambassador. It was your guards who started a skirmish."

"Because you, for no reason whatsoever, *chased* after one my guests."

"One of your guests who was skulking away and trying to avoid chatting with us."

"My guests are not required to chat with you. And did you not just say that you came to see *me*? Not anyone else staying at the embassy?"

Targyon lifted a placating hand, his mouth opening, but Zenia spoke first.

"If there are criminals staying at your embassy, Ambassador, it is, of course, within your right to house them, but I posit to you that this isn't a wise course of action. King Targyon is eager for peace, and it's my understanding, having spoken to one of your princesses, that the majority of your people seek that too. For one of your kind to cause trouble now… It could be misconstrued."

Zenia held the ambassador's gaze as she spoke, her green eyes boring into his. Shoyalusa threw back his shoulders and returned her stare, not looking flustered.

"There will be no more trouble if you simply let bees in their hive stay there," he said. "Trust that my people will handle any problems among our own kind, and we have no need of human intervention."

That wasn't the answer Jev had expected. It almost sounded like an admission. Had that furtive elf truly done something criminal? Something the ambassador didn't approve of?

"Normally, we are happy to let your people handle your own kind," Targyon said when Zenia didn't reply right away—she and the ambassador were busy staring at each other, as if they were locked in some magical mental battle. "But you can understand how important it is for me to bring to justice whomever is responsible for the murder of my cousins."

Jev thought the ambassador's nostrils would flare in indignation at the statement, or maybe he would flinch if he knew something about it, but he did neither. He did not even seem to hear the words. His gaze was still locked with Zenia's.

Targyon looked at Jev. As if *he* knew what to do.

A faint blue glow seeped out through the front of Zenia's dress. A green glow emanated from the dragon tear on the elf's chest. The glows mingled in the air between them like mist rolling in from two fog banks.

Jev was not wearing any weapons, but he tensed, ready to spring to protect Zenia if the mental sparring match started to look dangerous.

"Ambassador," Targyon said firmly, attempting to draw the elf's attention, "what do you know about the deaths of my cousins? Was one of your people responsible?"

Zenia staggered back, lifting her hands as if to defend herself. Jev jumped forward, whirling toward the elf as he placed himself between them. But the ambassador also staggered back, raising his hands defensively.

He recovered before Zenia did, snarling and pointing past Jev's shoulder at her as he glared at Targyon.

"That's quite a bauble you gave your *forces*, King Targyon. Do you know the lineage on it? I'll wager I can figure out which of my people it was originally stolen from."

Targyon flinched, no doubt remembering the elf princess and the vision the artifact would have shared with him, but he did not retreat from the ambassador's glare. "Do not change the subject, Shoyalusa. Tell me what you know of the deaths—the *murders*—of the princes."

"I know nothing of their deaths. My kind only monitor the goings on of humans so best to know when you intend to make war on us. We do not interfere with your rule, and we do not *murder* people." The ambassador backed several more steps, glancing at Zenia as he did so.

She had lowered her hands, the pained grimace on her face disappearing. Now she gazed calmly at the elf. Knowingly? Jev hoped so.

"Since this *reception* of yours was a thinly veiled excuse to interrogate me, I will depart now." The ambassador glanced at Zenia—no, at her chest and the faint blue glow still escaping the confines of her dress. "I'll be certain to send you the details of that dragon tear when I learn them, so it can be, if you are an honorable ruler, returned to the family of its rightful owner."

"A dwarf, right?" Jev asked. "According to the vision *I* saw, dwarves mined out all the dragon tears and only gave them to elves for safekeeping."

Targyon cleared his throat. Right, this wasn't what was important tonight. The elf was trying to divert their attention.

"Ambassador," Targyon started, but Shoyalusa thrust up a hand.

"I'm done here. Goodnight." He bowed like he had a board glued to his spine, then stalked out of the ballroom.

"Zenia?" Jev hoped she'd learned what they needed. Had she found a way past the elf's dragon tear for a mental probe?

Targyon coughed, drawing a concerned look from both of them.

"Sire?" Jev rested a hand on his shoulder as four of his bodyguards approached. "Get a doctor," he ordered one of them.

"No, no," Targyon rasped, lifting a hand. "I'm fine."

"Get a doctor," Jev repeated, using his sternest commander's voice.

He braced himself, expecting Targyon to argue further and expecting the bodyguard to be unwilling to disobey him. But one of the men ran off, not waiting for a counter order.

Targyon sighed at Jev, but all he did was wave the other three bodyguards back and focus on Zenia. "Did you learn anything useful, Captain?"

Zenia nodded. "He's not positive, but he believes one of his guests created the modified bacteria that was used against your cousins."

Targyon clenched his jaw and glanced at the exit the ambassador had taken, as if he meant to chase after him. Jev tightened his grip on Targyon's shoulder. He and Zenia would handle the ambassador, if he needed to be handled. It was that wall-climbing cloaked elf that they truly needed to locate.

"I didn't get a chance to ask him if he knew if the guest had delivered the infectious agent or if he had inside help. It's likely he doesn't know. The guest—I'd recognize him if I saw him because his face was clear to me in the ambassador's thoughts, despite his attempt to block me—has spiky brown hair, not typical for an elf. He's a renowned scientist, or was, back in his homeland, but he joined the—I can't pronounce it, but I think it's their word for the young elves who wanted to *do* something about humans."

"*Xilarshyar*," Jev supplied. "They're the ones who, with their anti-human talk, caused King Abdor to preemptively and perhaps prematurely start a war. I don't know if they were ever actually going to be a threat."

This new development made Jev wonder if perhaps Abdor hadn't been premature, after all.

"He's no longer welcome in his homeland because of his association with them. That's all the ambassador knew for certain. This guest—I believe it *is* Yilnesh, the one you saw—didn't confess anything to him. He simply showed up, asking for asylum, and the ambassador granted it without question, as that's their way." Zenia met Jev's eyes. "If we could find this elf, and *I* could question him, perhaps we could get a confession."

"And he could tell us who his inside ally is," Jev said grimly, looking at Targyon, at the sweat gleaming on his forehead. "And if that ally just struck again."

Targyon grimaced, but he didn't deny the possibility. Maybe he knew in his heart that someone had gotten him. Damn it, how? Jev knew he was being careful—he'd seen Targyon carrying around a sealed water bottle that he'd pulled up from a well himself. And Jev hadn't seen him eat anything lately.

Zenia looked toward one of the exits. It was the one the ambassador had gone out. Two guards in the hallway were whispering to two more guards stationed inside the door.

"Trouble outside," she whispered, a distant aspect to her eyes. Her dragon tear glowed softly again.

"Sire?" Jev considered the nearby bodyguards, wanting to know they were capable, determined, and deadly before leaving Targyon. "Will you excuse us?"

Targyon waved them toward the door without hesitation, but he added, "Don't dally for long. I have more people I want Captain Cham to help me drive out of the ballroom."

"She would be happy to do so, Sire."

Zenia gave him a dirty look but strode for the exit without responding.

Jev hurried after her. As soon as they stepped into the hallway and out of sight of the guests, her walk turned into a run.

"I sense—er, my gem does—that there's magic being used in the courtyard."

A distant crack sounded, muffled by intervening walls.

Jev grimaced, running to catch up with her. "I sense that there are *guns* being used in the courtyard."

Castle guards flowed out of side passages ahead of them, the armed men also sprinting toward the courtyard. More shots rang out, louder as Jev and Zenia drew closer. He passed her and raced out on the heels of the guards.

The uniformed men drew pistols and ran straight across the garden-filled courtyard after a cloaked figure sprinting for the front gate. There should have been guards standing at that gate, but Jev only glimpsed one man, and he lay crumpled and unmoving on the ground.

Jev ran after the guards, intending to join them in chasing whoever was fleeing, but a gasp from one of the garden aisles made him pause. A familiar young woman lay on the ground, slumped against the side of a fountain and clutching her abdomen.

"Lunis!" Zenia yelled, racing up behind Jev.

The young woman grimaced and shook her head. By the light of the lanterns burning along the walkways, Jev could see blood on her fingers.

He stepped toward her, but Zenia gripped his shoulder.

"Go after that elf," she ordered. "I'll take care of her."

"You're sure that was him?" Jev flung a hand in the direction the cloaked figure had gone.

"I'm sure."

"Think he'll be heading back to the embassy?"

"Or fleeing the city. But start there. He may have belongings to collect." Zenia ran up the garden aisle to kneel beside Lunis.

Jev raced toward the gate. Just as he was thinking that a horse would make chasing down a criminal easier, two guards rode around the castle from the direction of the stable. They stared intently at the gate even though the elf had disappeared through it already.

Jev lifted his hands and stepped into one man's path. "Hold!" he cried, hoping he wouldn't spook the horse. "I'm Zyndar Dharrow, and I know where that elf is going. I need a mount."

"Elf?" one of the guards blurted. "It was an elf? Did you see—"

Jev ran to the man's side and dragged him off the horse. There was no time for chitchat now.

Fortunately, the guard didn't fight him. His comrade was already riding through the gate. Jev guided his horse to follow him, hoping they could overtake the elf before he made it to the city walls.

But as soon as Jev cleared the castle, he saw the cloaked figure far, far down the road. He was on horseback too.

Jev nudged his mount into a gallop and leaned low over the horse's neck. He doubted he would catch his fleeing foe before he reached the city, so he hoped he knew where the elf was going.

Zenia gathered Lunis in her arms, her gut lurching at the sight of blood—so much blood—smearing the young woman's hands and leaking onto the flagstones.

"What happened?" Zenia knew Lunis would want a hospital, not an interrogation, but she had to find out what was going on, how that damn elf had sneaked into the castle, and if he'd been there long enough to infect Targyon with more of that bacteria.

"I... screwed up." Lunis squinted her eyes shut, and tears leaked from the corners.

"It's not your fault that you didn't get him. He's evaded all of us so far."

Zenia closed her own eyes, listening as the sound of hoofbeats faded, and brought one hand up to her dragon tear. She had absolutely no knowledge of how to use magic to heal wounds, but so far, the gem had shown itself powerful and versatile. Was there any possibility it could heal Lunis?

Unfortunately, she received a sensation of uncertainty, followed by apology.

Not your fault, she told it silently. *Can you sense anyone around with a dragon tear geared toward a healer?* Doubting the gem understood the Kingdom Tongue, she changed the words into thoughts, hoping the dragon tear could work through her to do as she wished.

"It is my fault," Lunis whispered after a long pause. "I knew he'd be here, but I still missed finding him. I should have warned the king. I just couldn't without..."

Zenia shifted her attention to Lunis, to her face, but she hadn't opened her eyes.

"Why didn't you?" Zenia asked quietly.

She wasn't sure how, but she had the sense of another dragon tear in the castle on the move. Coming toward them?

"Ma'am?" a guard asked, one of the men who had come too late to chase after the elf. Other guards were lifting the fallen man at the gate. To take to a healer? Or to bury? "I can carry her inside."

"I don't think it's safe to move her," Zenia said, hoping she understood her dragon tear correctly and that a doctor was coming to them. "If you see any doctors, please send them. Agent Drem took a gut wound. It's bad."

"I see, ma'am. I—all right, stay there. I'll be right back."

"Lunis?" Zenia prompted again as the man jogged away. "Help is coming. Don't go anywhere."

Lunis laughed shortly—it sounded like more of a cough—and blood trickled from the corner of her mouth. "Got what I deserve."

"What? Why? You didn't answer my question about the king."

More tears trickled from Lunis's closed eyes. "Do I need to?" she whispered.

It took Zenia a moment to realize Lunis referred to her profession, her ability to interrogate people and read minds with the help of a dragon tear. Something she now had once again.

Zenia hesitated, reluctant to stress Lunis further by poking into her mind, but she suspected she needed the answers locked away in there. And she also sensed Lunis wouldn't say any more. Why?

Images floated into Zenia's mind, more vividly than she had ever experienced when seeking out truths with her old dragon tear. Instead of simply getting the gist of whether someone was lying or telling the truth, along with a few fleeting thoughts, it was as if she relived Lunis's memories with her. More, she could pull up the memories she wished... Such as one from the month before.

Lunis was at her home in the city, a modest one-room flat that she'd had since she'd first become a detective for the watch. She could afford a larger place now that she received a Crown Agent's salary, but she was comfortable here, and didn't see a need to move. Perhaps one day, when she found an endearing man to share her life with, she would consider a change. Or if her father ever relented and agreed he should stay with someone who could help him. She'd stopped by to visit him on her way home from work, but, oddly, he hadn't been there. With his missing leg, lost in a factory accident, he rarely went anywhere, not wanting to deal with the stump and cane.

A knock sounded at the door, and Lunis rose, wondering who would visit her an hour after dark. A stranger stood in the hallway outside, wearing a hood and a cloak. She glanced toward the chair where her weapons belt hung, the pistol in its holster.

"There is no need for a weapon," the cloaked figure said in a lilting accent. "Not if you cooperate."

Lunis frowned and stepped casually toward the weapons belt, but the figure's hand darted out, capturing her wrist before she realized he'd moved. With his other hand, he pushed his hood back, revealing short brown hair that stuck up in spikes around his head—and around his pointed ears.

She gasped and tried to yank her wrist away. He appeared slender, but a grip like iron held her tight.

"That is not cooperating," he said coolly. "Your father would not approve."

Lunis froze. How could this strange elf know about her crippled father? For that matter, how did he know her? *Why had he come, and what did he want?*

He smiled, a cold smile, and withdrew a vial from a pocket. "I need you to deliver something for me."

She shook her head.

"If you don't, your father will never be returned to you. Nor will he see another sunrise."

Ice ran down her spine. "Where is he?"

"Safe. For now. As long as you do what I say." The elf tilted the vial so she could see murky liquid inside. "You work in the castle and can get close to the princes whenever you wish."

Four founders, what horror had come stalking her?

"Not easily," she whispered. "I work in the basement."

"You are trusted. You've worked there for two years. Your colleagues—and the princes—find you earnest and attractive." He smirked, an unfriendly smirk.

How could he know all this?

The inside of her skull itched, answering the question for her. He was an elf. He had magic. Maybe mind-reading magic.

"I need you to divide this into three doses and slip it into the drinks of the three princes. All on the same day. Tomorrow."

She shook her head again, and his grip tightened painfully on her wrist. She bit her lip to keep from crying out.

"You will do it, or your father will not live."

She blinked, trying to keep tears of pain and horror from forming in her eyes. "I can't betray my oath, my king, or his sons."

"You'll be betraying nothing. All this will do is make them more willing to listen when my ambassador goes to visit them this week, to make another attempt to end this war your people have started and dragged on and on."

"The princes aren't the ones who made that decision. The king—"

"If it works on them, we'll then use it on him. I'm a scientist, you see, and I've made a serum specifically for those of their bloodline."

"A negotiation serum?" she asked skeptically. She had never heard of such a thing.

"It is merely designed to make them more agreeable, more sympathetic to my people."

A thousand objections sprang to her lips, but his grip tightened again, and he leaned forward, holding the vial before her eyes.

"The choice is yours."

He pressed it into her hand, then strode out, disappearing into the hallway.

"Some choice," she whispered, staring down at it.

"It wasn't a serum," Lunis whispered, finally opening her eyes, though they were glazed, and Zenia worried she didn't see her, didn't see anything anymore. "It was a poison."

"Actually, it was a bacterium," Zenia said, aware of someone walking up behind them.

"I'm Dr. Hy," a woman said.

Zenia knelt back from Lunis so the healer could get close.

"The result was the same," Lunis whispered, not acknowledging the doctor even when she knelt on her other side and helped lie her flat on the flagstones.

Zenia sensed Lunis hoped the doctor wouldn't be able to help her.

"Lunis…" Zenia whispered.

"I'm sorry I sent that message," Lunis whispered.

"What message?" Zenia thought of the man who'd come out to the Nhole cottage. "The one threatening Targyon?"

"Just a bluff. I swear. I knew you'd find out eventually that I'd done it if you kept picking at the loose threads. I knew... I love this job, this career. I wanted to be an agent forever. Maybe one day captain of the agents. I worked so hard as a detective and then here. I just wanted to be someone. Can't you understand? My family... We were nothing."

"I can understand." Zenia did her best to keep judgment out of her tone, but it chilled her that Lunis could have sent the threat. She must have known it would be the end of her career, if not her death, if she were caught. But then, what more did she have to lose? Lunis was right. Zenia and Jev would have figured it out eventually.

"It wasn't worth it," Lunis whispered. "My father..."

"The elf killed him?"

"No. Oddly, he kept his word on that, even though he lied about what the liquid would do. He returned my father to me, but Father was irate. He said I'd given in to a coward and an elf. It would have been better if I'd let the elf kill him. It—"

Her voice broke off in a choke or a sob—or both. The doctor frowned at Zenia, as if it was her fault she was upsetting her patient. But Lunis had been upset for weeks. It was amazing she'd held it together in the castle, kept playing the role of the earnest agent, trying to deter Zenia and Jev by putting forth the criminal organizations as the lead suspects.

"He said I'd ruined my life for nothing. We haven't spoken since."

"Were you the one to light the farmhouse I was staying at on fire?" Zenia said.

"No." Lunis bit her lip and turned her head again. "Not on purpose. I hired the Night Travelers to scare you. That was all. Nobody was supposed to be hurt. I just hoped... I hoped you'd be scared enough to go back to the Water Order and give up the case."

As if Zenia could have gone back.

"There was nothing to be gained by solving the mystery," Lunis said. "Why couldn't you all see that? The princes were dead. Targyon should have been happy he inherited power he never could have dreamed of receiving."

Power that he didn't, Zenia was fairly certain, want.

"If you'd known me better, you would have known threats and scare tactics wouldn't make me cast aside an assignment, certainly not one given to me by the king." But might Zenia have cast it aside if her mother had still been alive and someone had kidnapped her and threatened to kill her? She didn't know whether to be relieved or not that her mother hadn't lived long enough to be used as a handle on her by some blackmailing criminal.

"I guess, but I had to try. It was either that or flee the kingdom in ignominy. Exile forever with the fear that the agents would one day catch up with me." Judging by the wistful expression that crossed Lunis's face, she wished she'd made exactly that choice.

"Did you dump a vial into Targyon's drink today?" Zenia asked.

If Lunis had, neither Zenia nor Jev nor anyone they had talked to knew of an antidote. Not to a bacteria protected by some elf's powerful magic. Some elf that seemed to have a vendetta against the entire royal family. *Why?*

"No." Lunis lurched upright, her shoulders lifting from the ground. "I tried to save him. To make up for—" A coughing fit stole the rest of her words.

"Easy, Agent Drem," the doctor said, frowning and pushing her gently back down. "You were stabbed in the gut. Even with a dragon tear, this will not be a simple procedure. Please cooperate."

Lunis, her gaze locked onto Zenia, did not look at the doctor. "Please believe me, Captain Cham. You must, right?" Her gaze dipped toward Zenia's dragon tear. "*Must* see the truth?"

"Tell me, and I'll know if it's the truth." Zenia thought about willing the gem to let her dip into Lunis's memories again, but she feared that had taken several long minutes, and she was worried about Targyon—and also about Jev. He'd ridden off after a murderer, someone who might have an ally in the elven ambassador. "Tell me," she urged, putting some of the dragon tear's power into the command.

"He came to me last night, the elf scientist. I did research on him afterward to learn what he's capable of. I believe he may have been testing his concoction on the princes. With the intention to use it on the king if it worked. He said as much, even if he was lying about what it did. He knew I never would have... Zenia? I never would have done it if I'd known it would kill them. Not even for my father."

"I understand," Zenia said, struggling again for neutrality. It would be up to Targyon to decide what would happen to Lunis after this. Assuming she lived. "Did he come here to infect the king himself?"

"Yes. I told him to stuff his vial up his ass. If I hadn't been such a coward, I would have come to you today, told you everything. I almost did. But I thought I could catch him if he showed up. Maybe if I caught him, and he was interrogated and explained how he'd made me..." Lunis rolled her head to the side. "Maybe the king would understand. I never meant to hurt him."

"Did you see the elf pour a vial into something?" Zenia asked. "The king's bottle of water?"

She'd witnessed Targyon being careful about what he drank, but maybe with magic, this elf could have uncorked Targyon's water bottle and floated his vial over to dump in the contents. Maybe he could have done that without being in the same room.

Lunis didn't answer aloud, but Zenia still had a slight link to her thoughts, and she sensed the answer. No, Lunis hadn't seen the elf get close to Targyon or his water bottle. He'd appeared for the first time, lurking in the hallway outside the ballroom, and she'd taken off after him.

"I think you've asked enough questions for now, Captain," the doctor said, her eyes closed and her hands resting on Lunis's bloody abdomen.

"I need to know why this elf wanted Targyon dead," Zenia said. "I can understand one of their kind targeting Abdor, and if this scientist was truly testing his bacteria before using it on the king, I guess I can understand him targeting the princes, but what would be gained by continuing to attack the royal family? Especially when they have someone reasonable on the throne now, someone who might want peace between our peoples?"

"I don't know," Lunis whispered, her head still turned. She gazed blankly at the side of the fountain gurgling next to them, her blood staining it.

"Captain Cham?" a guard asked from behind them.

Reluctantly, Zenia pushed herself to her feet.

"Does she know..." The guard frowned down at Lunis. "The king has retired to his rooms. He doesn't look well. Another doctor is in with him, but there was a doctor with the princes, too, and they didn't make it."

"I know." Zenia pushed back her hair, wishing she had a clip or tie for it. And wishing she wasn't stuck in the sausage dress now. "The bacteria that infected the princes was magically altered. I'm not sure there's anyone here who can thwart it." She looked at the doctor working on Lunis.

The woman lifted her gaze briefly, but only long enough to shake her head. "It wouldn't be me. If Dr. Bandigor couldn't unravel the mystery, I'm afraid I wouldn't be able to."

"We can't just let him die, ma'am," the guard said. "We'll have failed him, and he's a good boy. King. He will be. I know he's young, but he fought in the war. He deserves to be here, to *live*."

Zenia agreed wholeheartedly. "He will. We'll—"

She halted, the guard's words ringing in her mind. "He did fight in the war, didn't he?"

"Not as long as some, but for two years."

"Long enough to have killed a few elves," Zenia guessed.

It was hard to imagine young Targyon firing into the trees and jumping up and down with bloodlust, but if one was thrust into the middle of a battle, what choice did one have but to defend oneself? And those one cared about.

"I imagine so, ma'am. He's a hero."

Except to those on the other side. Such as this elf scientist? Had he looked into Targyon's past and decided that he didn't want someone ruling over Kor who'd fought against elves? Maybe *killed* elves?

"There has to be a cure," the guard added.

"If there is, there's one person who'll know what it is."

The person who'd tinkered with the bacterium in the first place.

"Will you get me a horse, please? I'm going after Zyndar Dharrow. I've got to find him before he and those guards catch up to that elf and kill him."

If the elf died, the cure would die with him.

CHAPTER 19

J EV ARRIVED AT THE ELVEN embassy with the only castle guard who'd been able to keep up with him, the other man with a horse. As they dismounted in front of the gate, images of the hulking creature springing to mind, Jev worried that it wouldn't be enough. He hoped Lornysh was inside, sipping elven wine and reading the brochure from some museum, and that he would be willing to raise arms against his own people.

Only one side of the double gate was closed. The other banged gently in a salty breeze sweeping up from the docks.

"It's not a haunted tower, is it?" his companion asked.

"Just protected by archers, magic, and a man-eating creature."

"That's a relief."

Jev, eyeing the garden foliage visible from the gate and certain he saw something stirring back there, would have preferred to deal with a haunted tower, especially since he'd never seen a ghost, if such things truly existed, or had one attack him.

"We could use some reinforcements, Corporal," Jev admitted, glancing at the guard's uniform to see the rank on his sleeves.

"Tames, sir. It's an honor to work with you."

"Will it still be an honor if we get eaten by a monster?"

"My boss says the greatest thing we can do is give our lives to save the king. I'm less certain about saving zyndar agents working for the king."

"If we catch up with that elf, we might very well be able to save the king." Jev sure hoped so. The elf had to know how to counteract his own concoction, didn't he?

Jev drew his pistol and was tempted to sprint for the front door, but that approach hadn't worked last time, and he suspected the same guards were on duty. And—yes, damn it—there was a glint of something yellow in the shadows. Two somethings. Eyes.

He thought about sending Tames to run in one direction as a diversion but well remembered how his bullet had done nothing to stop the creature. He might be sending Tames to his death.

Raucous laughter came from the tavern down the street, its door open and tobacco smoke wafting out along with the noise. Jev glared briefly in that direction, annoyed that people were obliviously getting drunk while Targyon was in danger. They ought to—

"I have an idea," he blurted.

Tames looked warily at him. "It doesn't involve me sacrificing myself so you can get in, does it?" The guard must have been having thoughts similar to Jev's. "Because I've noticed how in all the children's stories, the nameless castle guards usually die while the zyndar heroes save the princess."

"Fortunately for you, you've told me your name, and no princesses are in jeopardy tonight. Tames, go meet me around back."

"There's not a gate on the other side. I've been here before."

"I know, but we'll go over the wall. Once I arrange a diversion." Jev slapped Tames on the shoulder and raced to the tavern. He hated wasting time, but if he couldn't get inside the tower, he might never find that elf. Would he stay locked up inside once he believed he was safe, or would he merely grab his belongings and sneak out of the city? As old as that tower was, there might be a secret passage into the tunnels under Korvann.

Jev ran into the noisy taproom and jumped onto a table with two people sitting at it—it was the least empty of the options near the door. They cursed and grabbed their steins to protect them.

"What're you doing, you loon?" one cried.

"Subjects of Kor!" Jev yelled, waving his pistol while wishing he had an old broadsword to wave instead. Giant blades were better at getting attention than little firearms. "The king has been poisoned!"

He worried the boisterous drinkers would ignore him, no matter how loudly he yelled, but steins clunked down to tables, and people turned toward him.

"I am Zyndar Jevlain Dharrow and have been tasked to capture the elf who poisoned him. I have to drag him back to the castle because only he knows the cure."

"An elf! Those dragon-humping bastards!"

Dozens of similar oaths of agreement erupted from the mouths of the patrons.

"I need your help," Jev yelled over them. "He's in the embassy tower, but it's guarded by elves and a huge fanged monster."

Technically, Jev hadn't seen the fangs last time, but he assumed they were there. What kind of guard monster wouldn't have fangs?

A testament to the men's bravery—or drunkenness—they didn't immediately throw up their hands or look away.

"I don't want you to get hurt," Jev said. "Just keep that monster distracted. Throw rocks from outside the gate and taunt it. I'll buy you a round of drinks afterward."

"Death to the elves!" someone cried.

"We'll get rid of those stinking elves."

Men sprang from their chairs and raced for the door. Jev realized he needn't have promised drinks. These men probably glared at that tower every time they came to the pub.

"Just the monster," Jev yelled as men flowed past him. "And you don't need to kill it. Just distract it."

But the shouting men didn't hear him. One broke a chair and turned the legs into four clubs. He kept one for himself and thrust the others at comrades. Other men pulled knives as they raced out the door.

Jev grimaced, afraid of what he'd just launched. He glimpsed the bartender glaring at him with his fists on his hips. Because of the broken chair and the loss of clients? He seemed to have gotten over the attraction he'd admitted to last time.

Jev jumped down from the table and pushed his way into the flow of men. He almost took an excited elbow in the eye.

As soon as he made it outside, he veered away from the river of men rushing toward the front gate. He sprinted around the walled compound, not certain how much time these men would buy him. Would the elves— and creature—inside even be fooled?

Tames waited on the far side of the compound, and Jev pointed toward the top of the vine-covered wall. Tames crouched and cupped his hands. Jev raced up, stepped into his grip, and Tames hefted him into the air.

It wasn't enough of a boost to reach the top, but Jev gripped a couple of the sturdy vines and pulled himself up the last two feet. He flung himself atop the wall and reached a hand down to help Tames as he peered into the interior of the garden.

The trees and brush were thick back here, flowers and foliage blocking much of the view. He could barely see the tower through it, but he glimpsed a path not far from the wall. He also glimpsed someone running along it. One of the guards.

Jev grimaced. Even with the clamor at the front of the compound, he doubted he would be able to walk up to the front door. As Tames reached the top of the wall, Jev looked toward the tower, toward the fourth-floor windows. One of those windows ought to belong to Lornysh. Even if he wasn't home, his room should be safe to invade.

Jev and Tames slithered down the back side of the wall and crept through the trees. A heavy crunch sounded to one side, and Jev froze. The creature? Or *another* creature?

Twigs snapped, branches rattled, and whatever it was charged toward the front of the tower. Jev continued on, angling toward the back of the structure. He darted across the path he'd seen and pushed into the brush on the other side. Thorns and branches clawed at his clothing.

"We're climbing?" Tames asked as they reached the stone wall of the tower.

Jev ran his fingers over the ancient stone and the mortar that had been reapplied in a more recent century. He wouldn't want to scramble down the outside of the tower, as the handholds were scant at best, but he thought they could make it up.

"Only halfway."

"I don't see any doors."

"We're aiming for that window." Jev nodded toward the visible one. "Or maybe the one on the other side of it." That was the one that faced the tavern rooftop, the one Cutter could conceivably hit with pebbles.

"Your certainty is reassuring, sir."

"I'm glad to hear it." Jev found his first handhold and pulled himself up. "You might want to climb off to the side. In case I fall. Then I won't fall on top of you."

Tames grumbled something under his breath. Jev didn't hear the word *reassuring* again. He might have heard the words *zyndar idiot*.

Shouts and bangs echoed from the other side of the garden. Thanks to the curve of the tower and all the foliage, Jev couldn't see his volunteer legions yet. He wasn't sure he wanted to. He hoped they were staying outside the gate and that none of them would be hurt.

He also hoped neither guards nor monsters thought to look up at the side of the tower. Most of the trees in the garden weren't that tall, and they would be visible once they passed the third-floor windows.

Tames cursed several times as he climbed up beside Jev. Jev's fingers already ached, so he couldn't blame the guard. They struggled to find footholds to support their weight so they had to rely on their arm strength.

"Just a little further," Jev whispered, not sure if the words were for Tames or himself.

Jev waited until he reached the fourth floor before angling around the structure toward the front window. A thud sounded almost directly below him, and he froze, terrified Tames had fallen. But Tames was frozen to the side of the tower like a tick. They were above the tower entrance now, and two elves had sprinted out, slamming the door behind them.

For a wild second, Jev envisioned leaping down and running in through the door, but he would feel a fool if they had locked it as they ran out. Besides, if Lornysh was here, he ought to be in his room. An ally would be very helpful right now.

As soon as the two elves ran around a bend in the path, Jev continued over to the window. He gripped the sill and with forearms trembling pulled himself high enough to try to tug one side of the window frame open. It was locked. He growled and let go with one hand, dangling four stories above a thorn bush, and pulled his knife out of its sheath. He slid it into the gap between the frames, hoping for a simple latch inside.

There. It gave way, and one side of the window opened.

Jev sheathed the knife and pulled himself onto the sill, slithering over it like a snake. Or a drunken mongoose. It was a tight fit, and he almost got stuck. Finally, hoping this was the right room, he tumbled inside, bumped against a desk, and landed on a carpet.

The tip of an arrow filled his vision as someone aimed a bow at him.

"Jev?" The arrow shifted away from him.

Jev slumped against the desk in relief. "Hello, Lornysh. Hope you don't mind the intrusion."

Lornysh was barefoot and bare-chested, having apparently turned in early for the night. He glanced through the window, his sensitive ears perhaps picking up the sound of Tames climbing up, or maybe he was listening to the ruckus coming from the gate.

"If I'd known you were with that riffraff…"

"You would have come down to help us?"

"I would have arranged to be out for the evening," Lornysh finished.

"Glad to know you're always eager to help." Jev pushed himself to his feet, making room for Tames.

Lornysh grunted, turned up a lamp, and reached for his shirt and boots. "I'm more eager to help against enemies than my own people."

"I think you would consider this scientist an enemy. He was responsible for the deaths of the princes, and I think he poisoned Targyon with his magical bacteria. Also," Jev added, realizing Lornysh didn't have a reason to care much about the royal family, "I believe you said, he's a member of those rebels."

"The *Xilarshyar*."

"You don't like those elves, right?"

"They're brash, irrational, and xenophobic."

"I'll take that for a yes."

"I would help simply because Targyon is at risk."

A scream echoed from the garden, and Jev jumped.

Tames had made it through the window, but he leaned back out to look. "Looks like your new friends are running around on the paths down there and encountered your monster. Or maybe those are the elves you talked about."

"Damn," Jev said, "I told them to stay outside and just throw rocks." He hadn't believed the creature would leave the elven compound. "I didn't want anyone getting hurt."

"Look at all those torches," Tames said. "Must be a hundred people down there. A group made it to the door, and they're banging at it, demanding the elves send out the king's murderer." Tames frowned at Jev. "Murderer? Is Targyon…?"

"Not yet. It's possible my message got distorted as it was relayed." Relayed to *whom*, Jev didn't know, but he was positive there hadn't been a hundred people in the tavern. "Lornysh, can you tell where this Yilnesh is?"

It occurred to Jev that he didn't *know* the elf was here. Maybe it had been the ambassador who had hurried inside so quickly that he forgot to latch the gate. If the scientist hadn't come back here…

"I sense him upstairs in his room," Lornysh said, his eyes focused on the ceiling. "Seventh floor. I think he's packing."

"Tames?" Jev ran toward the doorway, having no intention of letting that elf leave the tower unless he was in handcuffs.

"The ambassador has also returned," Lornysh said. "He's coming up the stairs to—ah. I believe he's coming to find me. Or you."

"Distract him, will you? He was protecting that lake-water-licking mongoose molester."

As Jev opened the door to peer outside, Tames came up behind him, a short sword and pistol in hand. "Zyndar really know how to curse, don't they?"

"My mother told me not to be obscene in the company of others."

Jev stepped out onto the landing. Only one other room shared it with Lornysh's room, and wooden stairs spiraled up and down toward other levels. Not hesitating, Jev headed upward. Tames followed on his heels.

Jev would have preferred to have Lornysh at his back in a fight, but if he could keep the ambassador from charging up to assist Yilnesh, that would be a tremendous help.

As the stairs curved and Jev had his last glimpse of the landing, he saw Lornysh standing there, fully dressed and facing the downward set of stairs. He hadn't drawn any weapons, but he stood with his arms over his chest, blocking the path.

"Thank you, Lornysh," Jev said quietly, trusting his elven hearing would catch the words. He hoped his friend wouldn't get in too much trouble over this.

Jev charged past closed doors on the fifth and sixth landings without pausing to see what lay behind them. He envisioned springing into Yilnesh's room and taking him by surprise, cracking his pistol against the back of his head, knocking him out, and dragging him back to the castle by his ankles.

A *click* came from the landing above him followed by the shattering of glass.

"What was that?" Tames whispered.

"Nothing good, I'm sure," Jev muttered.

He kept going, but he sniffed the air gingerly, imagining some virus or infection having been unleashed.

A faint greenish smoke drifted down from above as a pungent odor assaulted Jev's nose.

"Cover your mouth," he ordered over his shoulder and yanked his shirt up over his own mouth.

Fearing that wouldn't be enough protection, Jev held his breath as he charged up the last of the stairs. The air grew thicker with green smoke. His skin itched, his eyes burned, and his nose ran.

Jev envisioned the stuff flaying his flesh right off his body, but he refused to turn back. He reached the seventh-floor landing, and his boot crunched on something. The glass of the broken vial. He waved at the smoky air, squinting though his tears to see that one door was closed and the other open. He raced to the open one, leading the way with his pistol.

But the room, a library with laboratory equipment set up on tables, was empty, the window closed and shuttered. Tames reached the other door first but found it locked.

He turned teared, bloodshot eyes toward Jev. "Key?"

Jev, his skin shifting from itching to burning as if he were smothered in acid, shook his head. He had no intention of running back down to ask the ambassador for a key.

"Move," he rasped, waving Tames back.

He channeled his pain and frustration about how the day had gone into a single powerful kick. His heel slammed into the door, and something snapped. With another kick, he knocked it open.

Jev ran inside, pointing his pistol with one hand and keeping his shirt over his mouth and nose with the other hand. For all the good it was doing. His nostrils burned as if a volcano were spewing lava into them.

He looked around, expecting to find his foe crouching behind the bed and ready to shoot at him. But the room was empty of everything except furnishings. Yilnesh was gone.

CHAPTER 20

ZENIA DIDN'T HAVE THE PATIENCE to wait for a guard to bring her a horse. She raced around the castle to the stable in the back. Horse whickers and arguing voices escaped through its open door.

She ran inside, intending to grab the first saddled horse she saw, and she almost crashed into a big man's back. She lurched to a stop, and he turned, frowning at her. Zyndar Garlok.

A stable boy hurried toward him with a horse in tow.

"That's for Captain Cham," the guard she'd sent on this errand said, pointing at the animal.

The stable boy, who couldn't have been more than thirteen, shook his head and led the horse around the guard. "Zyndar get priority over captains and anyone else except the royal family. That's the rules."

Garlok, who was looking at Zenia in narrow-eyed contemplation—or was that simply distaste?—smirked slightly at the boy's words.

"I have to catch up to Jev—Zyndar Dharrow," Zenia said, running toward a second stable boy who was preparing another horse. "He went after the elf that may have infected the king with deadly bacteria. I need to get to him before he's killed. Nobody else will know how to cure the king." She was tempted to grab the horse Garlok had claimed but feared he would make a tug-of-war match out of it, and she didn't have time for that. The second horse was almost ready.

"You know where they went?" Garlok asked.

She hesitated. Of all the people whose help she would have liked, he wasn't anywhere on the list. Worse, she remembered his comment about her and Jev quitting or *disappearing*. She wouldn't trust him behind her in a fight. Or at all.

"Tell me," Garlok growled.

"I am your employer, not the other way around." Zenia accepted the reins for the second horse and hurried for the exit, hoping Garlok wouldn't impede her.

"I am zyndar, and you are a commoner."

"I *am* a commoner, but what you are is an ass." She glared. The bastard was deliberately blocking the exit.

One of the stable boys let out a short laugh before catching himself and clapping a hand over his mouth.

"Get out of my way." Aware that there could be ramifications for insulting a zyndar, Zenia forced herself to add, "Please."

"Where did Dharrow and that elf go? I know you know."

"Then follow me if you want to find out, but don't delay me. The king's life is at stake."

His eyes narrowed further, as if he suspected her of lying. Why, by all four founders, would she lie about *that*?

She was debating kicking him in his big, hairy shin when he stepped to the side.

"I *will* follow you."

"Wonderful." Zenia hiked up the hem of her dress to her waist, not caring that she gave everyone a view of her legs, and swung up on her horse.

"Do you need more men, ma'am?" the guard called, hustling to ready a horse for himself. The second one likely had been for him.

"Grab anyone you can find and meet us at the elven embassy," she called as she rode away.

"You tell him and not me?" Garlok growled, matching her pace.

"I trust *he* wants to help the king." And to help me, she added silently.

"What in the hells does *that* mean? I am loyal to the king, no matter who he is and how young he is. That's the oath I swore long ago." Garlok curled his lip at her, reminding her of how affronted Jev got when his honor was questioned, until he added, "Common filth."

She urged her horse to greater speed, hoping it might outdistance his since she weighed much less than he did. But as she charged through the open gate—new guards were posted there now, and she didn't see Lunis or the doctor in the courtyard—she spotted someone jogging up the road on foot. Zenia glimpsed blue monk's robes as the runner passed under one of the street lamps.

"Rhi?" she wondered, not sure who else from the temple would be running up here on foot.

"Zenia!" Rhi yelled, waving a hand as they drew close enough for communication.

Zenia slowed her mount, though she winced when Garlok took advantage and rode past her without waiting. Now, she wished she hadn't revealed the elf's destination. What if Garlok arrived first and hindered Jev instead of helping him? Did he resent them enough that he would risk the king's life?

"What is it?" Zenia asked.

"Here." Rhi pulled an envelope from inside her gi. "Someone sent you mail at the temple, and Mage Darishia told me to bring it to you. I don't think she knows the archmage forbade me from talking to you."

Zenia, aware of Garlok speeding down the road and into the city, accepted the envelope but merely stuffed it into the top of her boot—the stupid dress didn't have pockets or any extra room to hold anything. There wasn't enough light to read it, nor did she have time.

"Jev needs help." Zenia offered her hand. "Do you want to come?"

"Of course."

Rhi swung up behind her, and Zenia rode after Garlok at top speed. Unfortunately, she no longer could claim less weight for her horse, and they weren't able to gain ground.

"Do we get to heroically save his life?" Rhi yelled to be heard over the thundering hooves.

"Let's hope he's not in that much trouble."

"Too bad. I think the journalists would write me up in the newspaper if I carried him out of a burning building over my shoulder."

"He's a bit heavy for that."

"You don't think I can manage it? I'll bet you twenty krons, I can heft him over my shoulder."

Zenia shook her head, not wanting to banter now. She wanted to catch up with Garlok and get that elf.

They tore through the streets, people scattering as first Garlok and then Zenia raced through. A woman yelled curses at Garlok for almost running her over. He yelled back that he was zyndar, presumably implying it was inappropriate for her to curse him. She waved her fist and called him a donkey's teat.

Being zyndar didn't mean quite what it had in earlier generations.

The smell of smoke reached Zenia's nose before the elven tower came into sight. She told herself it was woodsmoke from people's cookstoves, nothing more, but the memory of the burning farmhouse flashed into her mind.

"Uh oh." Rhi pointed over Zenia's shoulder.

They turned onto a street a couple of blocks down from the tower, but they could already see flickering orange light within the garden walls.

Zenia urged her horse onward, dread filling her gut.

Multiple fires burned in the elven courtyard, flames leaping from the branches of trees and threatening to spread over the walls and into the city.

The bedroom window was open, a faint breeze stirring the hazy green air.

"That fool jump from the seventh floor?" Jev muttered, his throat raw. He ran for the window, wanting fresh air as much as to see where Yilnesh had gone.

He stuck his head out, inhaling deeply and looking down. The smoky air outside wasn't much fresher than the green miasma in the room, and he winced, spotting multiple fires burning in the garden. But he also spotted a spiky-haired elven face peering up at him from the side of the tower below.

Yilnesh was climbing down without a rope, a pack and weapons strapped to his back. Unfortunately, he was efficient at it, and after that quick glance at Jev, he kept descending.

Jev pointed his pistol at the top of the elf's head but growled in frustration. He couldn't shoot to kill, not when Yilnesh was the only one who knew how to cure Targyon. He shifted his aim toward the elf's shoulder, though even then he hesitated, envisioning his foe falling four stories and breaking his neck when he landed.

No, Jev decided. He was an elf. He was agile. He would land on his feet.

As he squeezed the trigger, a wave of power slammed into him, knocking his arm against the window frame and almost hurling him to the floor. The firearm went off, but the bullet flew wild.

"Zyndar?" Tames gripped him, offering support. "What happened?"

"Magic happened." Jev growled and peered out the window again. Yilnesh was gone.

He must have jumped and disappeared into foliage. Damn it.

"From the elf we're chasing?" Tames asked. "Wasn't he hanging on the side of the wall?"

Jev thought of the mental showdown between the ambassador and Zenia in the ballroom, the way the elf's dragon tear had glowed with green energy. "I'm guessing the landlord was responsible. Or another elf in here."

Jev did not want to risk dealing with the ambassador by taking the stairs back down. Besides, even with all the chaos down there, it wouldn't take Yilnesh long to escape. He might even find it *easier* to escape with so much going on in the garden. Jev grimaced, not feeling quite so wise now for orchestrating that.

"We're following him." Jev slung his leg over the window sill.

"Down seven floors? Founders, sir, you'll get yourself killed. I can't allow that."

"You're the king's guard, not mine, but thanks for the sentiment. I— oomph." Jev's hand slipped on an oily sheen covering the sill, and he almost pitched out the window.

Tames lunged forward and caught his arm.

Jev cursed as he also found something slick on the tower wall. He didn't know how far down it extended, but he wagered it was far enough to deter them from following.

"The stairs," he barked at Tames, lunging back inside. "Go."

"What made you change your mind, sir?" Tames asked they he ran for the door.

"I didn't want you to have to explain my death."

They sprinted down three flights of stairs without encountering anyone. Jev prayed to the Air Dragon that Lornysh had somehow pulled the ambassador out of their route. But when they reached the fourth-floor landing, they almost ran into Lornysh's back.

He faced the ambassador, who stood several steps down with two dour-faced elves behind him. The ambassador's dragon tear was out, the tree carving on the front glowing an intense green. Lornysh had no visible gem, but his face was tight with concentration. Working some magic of his own?

Jev thought about slipping past him and attempting the brute force method of bowling into the elves, but he would likely earn a knife between the ribs that way. He was the intruder here, and they would feel justified in attacking him. Unfortunately, he knew he would get in trouble if he attacked *them*.

Hoping he wouldn't kill himself, Jev jumped past Lornysh and onto the railing, then off it, hoping he could land on the spiral stairs *behind* all the trouble. He made it to the railing behind the two assistant elves, but they whirled toward him as he jumped down onto the steps.

He lunged upward, surprising them, and rammed a fist into one's stomach. The elf grunted and doubled over. Jev shoved him toward his comrade.

They might have recovered and put their superior agility to use, but Tames pursued the tactic Jev had rejected. He lunged past Lornysh, almost knocking him over, and flung himself into the ambassador. On the stairs, even the agile elf couldn't evade him. He stumbled back into the other two elves who were trying to capture Jev.

Jev blocked a grasp and landed another punch, silently thanking Tames for jostling them and distracting them. Fortunately, they did not appear to be some of the Taziir's elite fighters, and they must have had orders not to pull bladed weapons on zyndar intruders. Thank the founders for that. Jev held his own with them, even connecting solidly with an uppercut that knocked one to his ass.

Instead of pressing the advantage, he whirled and sprinted down the stairs, his original mission in mind. He feared it was too late, that Yilnesh had been given far more time than he needed to escape the compound. And Jev hadn't the foggiest idea where he would go once he left.

Running so fast he tripped twice, Jev made it to the bottom floor. As he sprinted for the door, the air in front of it flashed with dozens of tiny yellow motes. Jev lunged for it, but he crashed into some invisible barrier.

He cursed and yelled, "Lornysh!"

A cry of pain and rage came from above. The motes disappeared.

Jev yanked the door open and sprang out into air choked with smoke. Flames from a dozen fires lit the night, and wood snapped and crackled, half of the garden on fire. The realization that he would get in trouble for laying waste to the politically designated sanctuary of another race passed through his mind. None of this would be worth it if he couldn't catch the elf and save Targyon.

"I'll get you, you bastard," Jev growled and sprinted down the path.

The open gate came into sight. Had the elf already exited it?

A huge dark figure leaped out of the trees and onto the path ahead of Jev. The creature.

CHAPTER 21

ENIA, RHI, AND GARLOK RODE up to the walled compound, flames visible in the canopies of the trees and shouts echoing through the open gate. Garlok sprang from his horse's back, not pausing to tie the animal anywhere, and ran through the gate. Zenia, not certain if a full-blown battle was underway inside, stopped several yards away and gripped her dragon tear. It was the closest thing to a weapon she had with her, but more than that, she hoped it would tell her if their enemy was inside.

She was aware of Rhi sliding off behind her, bo in hand, and jogging to the gate, but Zenia focused on the gem while picturing the spiky-haired elf in her mind.

"Where is he?" she murmured.

The dragon tear vibrated against her palm and drew her awareness away from the gate and toward a portion of the wall closer to the intersection they had just passed. The fires burning in the garden provided more light than normal, and Zenia gasped when she spotted a hooded figure crouching atop the wall. It—*he* sprang down to the street.

"Stop!" Zenia cried as the elf turned to run up an alley. She drew upon the dragon tear, just as she would have done with her old gem, adding its power to her voice.

The elf halted so abruptly, he almost pitched to the cobblestones.

Zenia wheeled her horse about and raced toward him, afraid the magic would wear off quickly, that his innate elven powers would allow him to overcome it.

The elf recovered and spun to face her. His hood had fallen to his shoulders, revealing his spiky brown hair and pale, icy eyes that bored into her with hatred.

He lifted an arm and threw something at her.

Anticipating some vial of acid, Zenia willed the dragon tear to protect her.

The vial flashed and exploded in the air several yards away, a boom ringing out as smoke flooded the street. Her horse shrieked in alarm and reared onto its hind legs. Zenia pitched backward before she could tighten her grip on the reins.

As she tumbled off the horse, she tried to twist in the air to land on her feet. But the ground came too quickly. She cringed, expecting to strike shoulder-first. Something cushioned her, and her shoulder stopped a foot from the cobblestones. For a second, she hung sideways in the air above the street.

A surge of indignation flared in her chest—no, that came from the dragon tear. The elf was getting away—and the gem didn't like that.

Zenia scrambled to her feet, and they touched down on the cobblestones. But only for an instant. Something propelled her from behind, and she found herself running through the smoke at three times her normal speed.

She came out of the haze in time to see the elf darting into an alley. She raced after him, wildly out of control, fearing she would carom off the whitewashed walls.

"Stop!" she yelled again.

The elf had been about to race out of the alley on the far side, but once again, he lurched, frozen for a second. It was enough for Zenia to catch up to him. And barrel into him. She couldn't stop herself in time, and they crashed to the hard cobblestones together.

Her enhanced speed startled the elf, but he recovered immediately, rising to one knee and twisting toward her. He punched her in the face, and she gasped as pain exploded in her cheek. The dragon tear might have shielded her as she fell from the horse, but she'd let her concentration lapse. She tried to channel it once again, not just to defend herself this time, but to attack. She couldn't let the bastard escape into the city, or Targyon might be lost to them forever.

Zenia tucked her chin to protect her throat as the elf reached for it, and she pummeled him with punches. It had been months since she'd grappled with Rhi on the practice mat, but she tried to pretend she faced no more dangerous a foe than a sparring partner in the temple.

The agile elf should have had the advantage and should have flung her away—or knocked her out with a well-placed blow—but energy from the dragon tear flowed into her limbs. Zenia attacked with punches far faster and more powerful than usual. Soon, the elf jerked his arms up, protecting his head. She rained blows onto his abdomen and sides.

"I surrender!" the elf cried in accented Korvish.

The dragon tear exuded glee as well as energy, some strange satisfaction at pummeling an elf, and Zenia struggled to gain control, struggled to stop hitting her foe. Fear coursed through her as her fists continued to land against her wishes. Her knuckles ached, bruises blossoming, and the elf did his best to curl into a ball and ward her off.

Stop, she silently ordered the gem, throwing all of her will into the command.

She sensed a reluctance from the dragon tear, but her fists slowed, and she regained control of her body. She knelt back from the elf, her breaths ragged. Blood smeared her throbbing knuckles. His or hers? Both?

The elf didn't move. He emitted faint whimpers.

Zenia swallowed and rose to her feet, her legs shaky. The dragon tear had slipped free from her dress, and it glowed blue on her chest.

Prisoner.

Zenia didn't know if the thought was hers or came from the gem, but she nodded and grabbed the elf's arm. "Get up."

She hadn't intended to put magic behind the command this time, but blue light flowed from the gem and wrapped around her prisoner in concentric tendrils. The elf rose to his feet. Under his own power? She didn't think so. His eyes were glazed, and he barely appeared conscious.

Zenia looked down at her chest. "You're a lot more powerful than my old dragon tear," she murmured.

More than that, it seemed capable of far more than she'd ever heard of dragon tears doing. Targyon ought to have claimed it for himself and learned how to use it instead of giving it to her. She wasn't...

No, she decided. She *was* worthy. She would learn to master it, and she would use it well.

A scream came from the direction of the tower. A man's scream? Jev?

"Let's go," she said, trying for a brusque tone and not to let any worry show, not to her prisoner.

Though she wanted to leave him there and sprint for the front gate to check on Jev, Zenia gripped the elf's arm firmly and marched him toward the tower.

The creature reared up on its back legs, raising its hairy arms high, claws gleaming in the light of the fires dancing in the trees. One huge paw swiped toward Jev's head.

He flung himself backward, rolled, and came up on one knee, facing the creature. As it sprang after him, he fired his pistol straight at its black barrel chest.

It did not slow down. Its yellow eyes did not even show pain. They seemed to glow with some unearthly, otherworldly hunger.

Jev scrambled off the path and behind a tree. As it lunged after him, he fired at one of those yellow eyes, hoping they would be a more vulnerable target. But the creature dipped its head as it charged at him, and the bullet struck it in the skull. Again, not hurting it.

The creature slammed into Jev's tree with a massive shoulder. Jev leaped back into thick brush, and leaves and twigs rained down on him.

"There it is!" someone cried.

People with torches and clubs ran into view on the path, some shouting and waving uselessly, a few braver ones jumping in to strike the creature. Their efforts were equally useless.

Jev backed farther into the brush. He held his pistol ready to fire but waited, wanting a clear view of the creature's eyes. It shoved over a sapling, tearing the thing from its roots as it pushed closer to Jev. He darted behind two thick trees, hoping his monstrous foe wouldn't be able to knock them over easily.

Something brushed Jev's shoulder. He gasped and jerked to the side, envisioning some other creature poised to attack him.

But Lornysh stepped up beside him, his bow in hand. "Greetings, Jev."

"Greetings. Did you finish your meeting with the ambassador?"

"We were at an impasse." Lornysh fired an arrow.

It pierced the creature's hairy black throat, and finally, it reared back and yowled in pain.

"Your arrows work better than my bullets?" Jev complained. "How is that possible?"

As the creature landed, its head swung toward them, its eyes blazing with fury. For a split second, its head was still, those eyes a perfect target. Jev fired. This time, his bullet successfully slammed into one of those yellow orbs.

The creature screamed.

Finally.

"No," Lornysh said, "but the throat of the *zarl* has thinner skin than elsewhere on its body."

The creature roared and clawed at its face, ignoring the people jumping in to thump its legs with their makeshift clubs. Founders, that man from the tavern still had a broken piece of chair leg.

The creature must have had enough because it sprang into the brush on the far side of the path. Howling and rattling the trees, it left a trail of broken foliage as it disappeared into the undergrowth.

"Let it go," Jev yelled when a few of his enthusiastic recruits turned to follow it.

"Get off elven land," came a booming cry from the direction of the front door.

"Care to resume your chat with the ambassador?" Jev whispered to Lornysh, then pointed to his right, in the direction of the front gate. He still needed to try and catch the renegade elf. By now, he feared it would be too late.

"Go," Lornysh said. "I'll do my best to distract him again."

Jev pushed through the brush, angling to come out near the gate. But going through the undergrowth was harder than walking along the path, and when he came out of the trees near the gate, he groaned. The ambassador stood in front of him, glowering straight at him. The gate was open, but he blocked it.

Jev glanced over his shoulder. Lornysh stood behind him on the path, the two elven guards to either side of him. One had taken his bow. Or perhaps Lornysh had let them take his bow. Jev knew he didn't want to fight these people.

But Jev had no choice. He bit his lip and considered running straight at the ambassador. He couldn't let the damn assassin elf get away.

"Jev?" came a familiar voice from behind the ambassador.

"Zenia!"

When had she gotten here?

The ambassador turned, looked through the gate for several long seconds, then sighed and stepped to the side. Zenia walked through the gate while gripping the arm of a prisoner, a spiky-haired elven prisoner with split lips and contusions all over his face.

"Damn," Jev said, "did Rhi do that?"

"Not me," Rhi said from the brush. She walked out with her bo, a contusion of her own swelling at her temple. She must have encountered the creature as well. And was that Zyndar Garlok coming out behind her?

"It was... the dragon tear," Zenia said quietly. She looked warily at the ambassador.

Shoyalusa gazed at his fellow elf, but Zenia's new prisoner appeared too dazed to realize he was there.

"The dragon tear beat someone up?" Rhi asked.

"It's a long story," Zenia said.

"It can't be that long. It's only been three minutes since we parted ways."

Zenia managed a faint smile, though she looked a little dazed too. "At least six."

"Is that the rat that poisoned the princes?" Zyndar Garlok thrust a finger at Zenia's prisoner. His other hand curled into a fist.

"Yilnesh," the ambassador said, sighing again. "My understanding is that it wasn't a poison, but you'll have to get the details from him. He's been evasive, even with me."

"Yet you protected him," Jev said, wondering if the ambassador might try exactly that again.

"He is an elf," Shoyalusa said, as if that explained everything.

"A *criminal* elf. Why protect him? Don't your people—the majority of them—want Targyon on the throne? A king that has nothing against your kind and will likely do his best to keep Kor from jumping into any new wars?"

"It is early to judge what he will or will not do," the ambassador said. "As for the rest, I do not turn on my own kind. Any elf who needs my help may find refuge and safety here." He looked at Lornysh, his lips thinning. "That is the way of the embassy, the way of our people."

Jev shook his head but dismissed the ambassador for now. "Zenia, can you question Yilnesh?" He pointed at the dazed elf. "We need a cure for Targyon."

"I know, and I think so. Will you...?" She nudged the elf toward him.

Jev jogged up and grabbed Yilnesh, turning him so he faced Zenia. He didn't think he was overly rough, but the elf gasped in pain, and his knees buckled. Jev had to hold him up to keep him from toppling to the ground. Later, he would ask Zenia if an elephant had fallen on him. He couldn't see how a dragon tear could have pummeled someone.

"What do you intend to do?" the ambassador asked.

Zenia lifted her chin. "Question him."

"You've brought him back onto embassy soil. Where you are trespassing without permission. I forbid you to interrogate an elf here."

Mumbles came from the growing crowd, Jev's club-wielding recruits from the tavern. They eyed the ambassador and also Lornysh and the two elven guards while fingering their makeshift weapons.

Jev strode toward the gate, pushing his prisoner ahead of him. The ambassador's eyes narrowed, but he did not try to stop him. Was he giving up? Or did he have another chip to play?

As soon as Jev passed through the gate, he turned the prisoner to face Zenia again.

"Go ahead," he told her. "I'll make sure you're not interrupted."

Zenia took a deep breath, glanced at the ambassador, but then focused on her prisoner.

"Be quick," he added quietly. "If you can." He thought of the sweat glistening on Targyon's forehead. "We may not have much time."

CHAPTER 22

ZENIA GAZED AT THEIR ELVEN prisoner and brought her fingers to her dragon tear. After the way it had taken over during the skirmish, she was apprehensive about drawing upon its power again, and she wished she had more time to familiarize herself with it in a calm setting. But she didn't.

The elf—Yilnesh, she reminded herself—glowered back at her. He radiated pain and discomfort as he stood, Jev locking his arms behind his back, but he had recovered enough to appear coherent. Zenia feared he would fight her, but she believed she, with the dragon tear's help, was his match. She just hoped the gem didn't try to take over again. Already, she worried about explaining how the elf had come to be so battered. What would Jev think? That Cutter had been right?

"Where did you get the lake water that you used to poison the princes?" Usually, Zenia would have started with more basic information that the prisoner wouldn't object to answering, such as his name and where he'd been born, but Jev's words rang in her mind, the reminder that they might not have much time.

The elf sneered.

"Where?" Zenia demanded, drawing upon the dragon tear's power.

It flowed into her without a hitch, more than she would have called for.

"Lake Eskalade on your southern border," Yilnesh blurted, gripping his chest and almost pitching forward.

The ambassador stirred, frowning darkly at her.

Easy, she silently told the dragon tear. *Easy.*

"A long way from your home up north," Zenia said.

"I have no home anymore. They cast me out because I was sympathetic to the *Xilarshyar*, agreed with their concerns. But I knew my people would thank me when—" The elf choked off his words in mid-sentence.

Zenia frowned, thinking he was fighting her, but then she sensed an outside influence. The ambassador. To anyone else, he would merely appear to be standing there with his hands clasped behind his back, but she sensed him interfering, trying to wall off Yilnesh's mind from her.

"Lornysh," she said without taking her gaze from Yilnesh, afraid she would lose her touch on him if she broke eye contact. "Would you invite the ambassador to go back inside with you, please?"

"Uh, Lornysh is imprisoned, I believe," Jev said.

"I know the elves would prefer to go back inside and let us handle this." Once again, she drew upon the dragon tear to add power to the words, trying to influence the guards and the ambassador all at once. She never could have affected more than one person at a time before, but she thought it might be possible now.

The two elven guards said something in their language, then slowly turned and walked toward the front door. They took Lornysh's bow but did not drag him along with them.

"Ambassador?" Zenia looked at him, knowing she would have to make eye contact. She remembered their battle of wills in the ballroom and knew it had only been the fact that her dragon tear was stronger than his that had allowed her to extract information from his mind. "Go inside. You are defending a criminal. A murderer. Do not sully your reputation this way."

The ambassador's dragon tear glowed on his chest, and Zenia sensed him wrestling, not with her this time, but with himself. Did he continue to defend someone who'd committed a crime he didn't approve of? Simply because he was an elf and they were from the same homeland?

A branch snapped in the garden, reminding her that a creature guarded the compound. Unless her friends had slain it? She looked at Jev, hoping he would say she had nothing to worry about, but he eyed the foliage with concern. Could the ambassador telepathically call the creature forth?

"Do not fight us further, Ambassador," Zenia said.

Rhi fingered her bo and stared into the garden as the leaves rustled. Garlok gripped a pistol.

Yilnesh surprised her by speaking to the ambassador. She couldn't understand any of the words, but they sounded defeated. Or so she hoped. If the elf begged the ambassador for help, would he sic the creature on them?

The ambassador arched his silver eyebrows and asked a question in Elvish. It sounded like, "Are you sure?"

A single-word response.

The two elves locked gazes, and for a moment, the only sounds came from the crackling of the fires in the garden. Finally, the ambassador turned away from them and walked up the path toward the tower. The rustling in the foliage stilled.

Zenia let out a slow breath and focused on her prisoner again. "Continue. Your people would thank you when what?"

"When Abdor was dead." The elf wasn't fighting her anymore. He responded promptly, his shoulders slumped. "Even if it meant being an outcast, I vowed to help my people, to defend them against humanity's tide."

"Abdor. Why did you kill the princes if he was your target?"

"I had to make sure it would work. They shared their father's blood."

"Why infect all three of them?"

The elf's shoulder twitched with indifference. "Had to make sure it worked and didn't want to leave angry kin alive to come after me, wanting to avenge their brother's death." He sneered again. "I didn't think whatever cursed cousin your people picked would care about hunting down the one responsible. He ought to be delighted to have the throne handed to him by an elf."

Zenia shivered, remembering that Lunis had said almost the same thing. Did everyone think being a king was such a wonderful thing? She couldn't imagine wanting the responsibility.

"Why did you come to the castle today?" she asked. "To target Targyon?"

"Yes. He kept meddling. Kept sending *you* to meddle." He glared at her and flicked his fingers toward Jev, as much as he could while he was held captive. "Why couldn't he leave well enough alone and be glad he was king and he was safe?"

"He didn't know he was safe," Jev growled. "How could he?"

"I would have been content to leave him on the throne if he hadn't meddled. It was far more than he deserved, the elf killer. I know he was in Taziira. That he fought with your army. He's not the one I thought your people would choose to lead them, but I shouldn't be surprised. Humans love elf killers, don't they?"

"What's the difference between a human that kills elves and an elf that kills humans?" Zenia asked.

Yilnesh curled his lip and gazed past her shoulder and into the distance. As if to say the interrogation was over.

Not yet it wasn't.

"You poisoned him today," Zenia said. "How do we kill your enhanced bacteria and heal him?"

The elf's brow furrowed as he looked back to her. "What are you talking about?"

"He's sick. We know you poisoned him."

"I did not. Your agent chased me off before I could."

"He's sick," Zenia repeated.

"Not by my hand."

Certain the elf was lying, Zenia channeled the power of the dragon tear into scouring Yilnesh's memories of the day. Of how he'd prepared a new vial in his room. Of how he'd gone over one of the castle walls, slipping through the shadows as guards were distracted by arriving guests. Of how he'd slunk through the halls of the castle, avoiding notice until he tried to slip into the ballroom. Then Lunis had spotted him and given chase, ruining it all.

Zenia frowned, going over his memories twice to be sure he wasn't evading her somehow, keeping her from seeing a moment when he'd slipped the contents of his vial into Targyon's drink. But it wasn't there.

"Zenia?" Jev asked quietly.

"He's telling the truth."

"Then... Did someone else poison Targyon?" Jev shifted his focus to the tower, the fires burnishing its stone walls. Did he think the ambassador might have been responsible?

Zenia shook her head slowly, believing she would have seen that in the ambassador's mind when she had confronted him.

"Could he just be sick?" she wondered. "From a normal virus?"

She looked at Yilnesh, but he only shrugged.

"I guess we can go back to the castle and check him for pustules," Jev said.

"Gross," Rhi said. "I volunteer not to do that."

Garlok frowned at her.

Zenia lowered her hand from her dragon tear. "We can take the prisoner back and question him again if we find out the king's illness isn't natural."

"*I'll* take him," Garlok growled. "He's going in a dungeon for what he's done. And then, once we know the king is well, to an executioner."

Surprisingly, the elf didn't balk when Garlok approached. Zenia didn't know what Targyon would decide about Yilnesh's fate, but she couldn't argue for leniency for someone who had so blithely taken the lives of three men.

"Rhi?" Jev asked after Garlok gripped the elf and marched him away. "Go with the zyndar, will you? In case he needs *help*." Jev narrowed his eyes, giving that word special emphasis.

Zenia figured he didn't trust Garlok either and was loath to let the zyndar take their prisoner off by himself.

"As long as it doesn't involve a pustule check," Rhi said with a shrug and headed after Garlok.

"You there," Jev said to a soot-faced man carrying what looked to be a piece of a chair. He dug into his purse and dumped a few coins into the man's hand. "See to it that everyone who helped gets a drink."

"Yes, Zyndar," the man said brightly. "To the pub, everyone!"

The crowd cheered and quickly funneled out of the compound, leaving Jev, Zenia, and Lornysh alone.

"Thank you for your help, my friend." Jev patted Lornysh on the shoulder. "I know you would have preferred not to fight the ambassador."

Lornysh hitched a shoulder. His face was a mask when he said, "He's not the first of my people I've fought."

"I know that well," Jev said quietly, then lifted his eyebrows, as if inviting his friend to explain further.

"You had better go check on Targyon," was all Lornysh said. "I helped keep him alive in Taziira. It would be irritating if he got himself killed in his own castle."

"Indeed."

Lornysh lifted a hand and walked off, muttering something about finding his bow.

"Shall we?" Jev touched the small of Zenia's back and extended his other hand toward the street and the way back to the castle.

"Definitely." Even though she believed Yilnesh had told the truth, she wouldn't breathe a deep sigh of relief until she saw Targyon healthy and happy. Though he didn't seem to know how to be the latter. Poor kid. "What did he say? Yilnesh. When he sent the ambassador away."

"That it was over and not to make it worse. That there was no place left for him in the world. He apologized for bringing trouble to the ambassador's doorstep."

"Ah." Zenia didn't know what else to say. She couldn't condone anything the elf had done, but she did understand why his people, at least some of them, hated humans right now. A part of her wondered if maybe things would have been better if Targyon hadn't ordered her and Jev to investigate. But no, the elf had committed a crime, and even if his hatred was understandable, his choice to kill—to *murder*—was not. She couldn't regret finding him and bringing him in. She did regret that Lunis would lose her career, if not her life, for the role she had played in all this.

"I'm glad you followed me down," Jev said as they headed off to find their horses. "I'm ashamed to admit that he would have gotten away."

"Did you get stuck fighting that monster?"

"After a detour through the tower, yes."

They passed under the light of a streetlamp, and Jev paused, frowning at her cheek—was it already swelling?—and then down at her side. He grasped her arm lightly and held up her hand. Zenia grimaced as he looked at her bruised knuckles, now visibly swollen and discolored.

"You *did* beat him up," Jev said.

Zenia couldn't tell if he sounded awed or concerned. Maybe both.

"The dragon tear helped. I've boxed and wrestled with the monks in the temple, especially when I was younger, but I wouldn't have bested an elf without magical help." She lowered her voice to add, "More than help."

That was definitely a concerned wrinkle to his brow, but all he said was, "We'll find you a healer."

He let her arm go, and they resumed walking, but he glanced at her chest, and she knew it wasn't to ogle her curves. He was worried about the gem. Maybe she was a little worried about it, too, but for now, she just wanted to check on Targyon and make sure he would be all right.

After being waved in by one of the bodyguards, Jev led the way into Targyon's sitting room and then bedroom. Zenia and Rhi followed, though the guards stopped Zyndar Garlok. Jev didn't know if Targyon had put him on a list of suspicious persons, but the sound of the man's pompous indignation trailed them inside. Rhi shut the bedroom door firmly on it.

Targyon lay in his great canopied bed, a sheet draped across his form, and cups of water and juice on the table beside him. They didn't appear to have been touched. Maybe he feared another dose of some bacteria or poison?

"Drink up, Sire," Jev said, stopping beside the bed and bowing. "You'll need liquids to feel better. And grapefruit. My grandmother swore by juice made from the stuff. And then there's gort. Nothing like a steaming pile of green vegetables to get some nutrients in you."

Targyon, looking particularly wan, turned his head toward Jev, just enough to display the disgusted expression on his face. "I don't think it's within your right as a zyndar to make me throw up."

"What? You don't want steaming piles of green mushy things?"

Targyon's gaze shifted toward Rhi and Zenia. They had both stopped inside the door but curtsied when he looked at them. Rhi's bo clunked on the base of the wall. There was something odd about seeing a monk curtsying, even a female one, and she clearly wasn't practiced at it.

Jev smiled, remembering Rhi's brief conversation with a bodyguard who'd insisted she not take a weapon into the king's presence. She'd demonstrated how she needed it as a walking stick, accidentally dropping the butt on his boot in the process. Jev had waved for it—and Rhi—to be allowed in and had been somewhat surprised when the bodyguards listened.

"Did you find the ambassador?" Targyon asked.

"Yes, but he wasn't the one who tampered with some lake bacteria to deliver those deadly infections to your cousins," Jev said. "It was an elven scientist who was on the outs with his people, the majority of his people, that is. It's possible the *Xilarshyar* approved his tactics."

"Did you *find* him?" An exasperated, or maybe that was impatient, note colored his voice. More softly, he asked, "Did he have a cure?"

"To the common flu? No, I don't think so, Sire." Jev smiled, waiting for Targyon to catch on.

He must have felt a touch addled by the illness because it took a few seconds for Targyon's forehead to unfurl.

"Are you saying…?"

"I questioned him, Sire," Zenia said, speaking for the first time. "With the help of the dragon tear you gave me." She touched her chest where the gem lay. "He *did* intend to slip one of his vials into your drink tonight, using magic to manage the task unnoticed, but one of our agents spotted him before he got close to you." Zenia hesitated. "Lunis Drem. She scared the elf into running, getting stabbed in the process. The rest of us—" Zenia waved to include Rhi and Jev, "—chased him back to the embassy where we finally caught up with him."

Jev waited to see if Zenia would explain what else Lunis had done in recent weeks. On the way back to the castle, she'd explained that Lunis had been the unwilling but effective insider. He hated the idea of her being punished, but he couldn't condone a coverup. Targyon would have to be told the truth. Lunis couldn't be allowed to keep working here. By kingdom law, she ought to be put to death for her role in killing the princes, but Jev couldn't argue for that, not knowing she had been blackmailed.

"Then perhaps I should give her a raise," Targyon murmured. "Or a promotion."

"I don't think so, Sire." Zenia took a deep breath, then told Targyon everything she had told Jev.

Targyon's already pale face grew paler.

"I liked her," he whispered. "I mean, I thought she really enjoyed the job and could be trusted. I… if she'd wanted to come into my office and talk to me, I would have allowed it." He eyed the untouched glasses sitting on his bedside table.

"Fortunately, she refused to be used that way again," Zenia said. "*Tricked* that way."

"When you're feeling better, Sire, you'll have to decide what punishment is fitting," Jev said.

"Founders." Targyon looked bleakly up at the canopy. "I knew the time would come when I would have to make life or death decisions for people. I just thought I'd have more time to get used to all this. I'm not even used to the pajamas yet." He lifted an arm covered in a silken crimson sleeve with a gold hem.

"They look soft and comfortable," Jev offered, even as he imagined his father rolling his eyes at the notion of wearing such garments.

"They're weird. All cool and silky. They feel funny against my—" Targyon glanced at Rhi and Zenia. "Never mind."

Jev smirked. "There are worse materials to have rubbing your balls when you walk."

Targyon groaned and dropped a hand over his face, but not before Jev caught his cheeks growing pink.

"Perhaps," Zenia told Jev, "you would like to inform the king how we *know* he hasn't been infected with any magical lake bacteria."

"I'll let you do that since you and your dragon tear interrogated the elf. My job as zyndar is to make the king uncomfortable in front of women."

"I had no idea the nobility had such expansive duties."

"The job is an honor and a burden."

Targyon lowered the hand covering his face, squinted at Jev, then looked at Zenia with hope in his eyes.

"Sire." Zenia stepped forward. "We captured the elf, and I questioned him. Since Lunis refused to do his bidding again, he was denied the help of an insider, and he wasn't able to get in to see you easily. He never touched any of your beverages. So, unless you believe someone else might have felt the urge to poison you, it's likely you have a simple virus."

"An inconveniently timed one, then." Targyon touched his forehead.

"Might I suggest that the stress and worry you've been feeling the last few days may have weakened your immune system?" Zenia asked.

Targyon grimaced. "If so, it's not heartening to know I have the immune system of a doddering geriatric."

"I won't tell anyone," Zenia murmured.

"I might." Jev winked and thumped Targyon's shoulder. He firmly felt that humor was the way to deal with the night, at least around Targyon. If he had spent the day believing himself poisoned and dying, a laugh was exactly what he needed. Now, if he would simply cooperate and let out a little chuckle...

He looked more like he was once again contemplating vomiting. Maybe they ought to leave him alone until he felt better.

"You should try meditating, Sire," Rhi offered. "To calm and center yourself. I meditate, and I never get sick."

"I've seen you meditate," Zenia murmured. "You sing to yourself and sway while tapping out beats on the tile floor with the butt of your bo."

"So? The Codices of the Monk only say you have to meditate, not that you can't sing while doing so."

"Are you sure there's nothing about silence?" Zenia asked.

"Absolutely."

Targyon was gazing at the canopy again, his eyes sad and distressed. Since humor wasn't working, Jev asked more seriously, "Will you be all right, Sire? If it's the flu—and we've got a doctor coming up to make sure—you should feel better in a couple of days."

"Yes. I was more concerned about... I'll have to consider what to do about Agent Drem. And I guess I'd like Agent Cham to interview the rest of the Crown Agents to make sure they're all loyal and ask them about their backgrounds too. See if anyone has any levers that can be pushed using friends or family. We can't fire people if they do, but it would be good to be aware of it."

"We can do that, Sire," Zenia said gravely.

"We might need to hire some more people too. Trustworthy people. I'll put you two in charge of finding and training new agents."

"Training?" Jev asked. "Shouldn't we be trained ourselves before we train other people? So far, we've been, uh, winging it."

Zenia's mouth twisted in wry agreement.

"You're doing fine." Targyon said. "Both of you. But I did ask Zyndar Garlok to bring up the handbook before he— Well, he talked me into letting him stay, so he's not leaving. Make sure you interview him first, please. He was contentious when we spoke. I wasn't sure if he was truly affronted because I was questioning his honor, or if it was an act, and I have to worry about him."

"I'll be happy to interview him, Sire, and did you say someone knows where the handbook is?" Zenia's eyebrows rose hopefully.

"Zenia has been looking for it since we first arrived," Jev said dryly. "I believe she's hoping for something organized and cohesive with strict rules and guidelines for us to follow."

Zenia nodded. "I like structure."

"I'm not certain the handbook Garlok brought up will provide that," Targyon said, "but you're welcome to update it as needed."

"Thank you, Sire." Zenia peered around the room, even glancing under the bed's canopy, as if Targyon might have put the precious item in a hidden spot up there for safe keeping. "Is it here? Do you have it now?"

"It's on one of the bookcases in my office," Targyon said. "Please grab it on the way out."

"*Thank* you." Zenia turned, as if she would sprint for the office that very second.

Rhi cleared her throat and shifted her bo to block the door. She tilted her head toward Targyon.

Jev watched curiously.

"Oh." Zenia turned back to Targyon. "Sire, you said we might need to hire new people? Would they all need to be previously trained as intelligence gatherers? Or could someone with more of a meditating, martial background be taken on?"

Rhi shot Zenia a suspicious look at the meditation mention, but when Targyon gazed toward her, she stood up straight and brought the bo to stand vertically next to her, like a second lieutenant assigned the duty of displaying the company colors in formation.

"If you find someone you believe you can train to be a good agent, I see no reason to object," Targyon said. "Right now, finding people I can trust means more to me than pedigrees."

Zenia nodded thoughtfully and looked like she was trying to find a way to officially ask if she could hire Rhi.

Since Targyon had dark circles under his eyes, Jev decided to use zyndar bluntness and move things along. "Rhi, you want a new job?"

"Yes."

"Good. You're hired."

"Good." Rhi nodded curtly.

Zenia blinked a few times at this abrupt job interview. Targyon smiled faintly. It wasn't the chuckle Jev had hoped for, but at least he seemed to have relaxed.

A knock sounded at the door. "The doctor's here, Sire," a bodyguard called.

"Send her in," Targyon said.

"We'll leave you to get checked out by the doc," Jev told Targyon. "If there are any problems you need solved while you're recuperating, you know where to find us."

"Are you sure he's not waiting for a solution to the silk pajamas?" Rhi murmured as their little group turned for the door.

"I trust he can figure out that going naked is the only logical solution," Jev said.

"That might alarm the lady doctor," Rhi said.

"Nah, Targyon is a pretty boy. She'll like it." Jev looked back over his shoulder to find Targyon's hand over his face again. "Goodnight, Sire."

"Goodnight, Jev." Sarcasm dripped from Targyon's farewell. "I may fire you in the morning."

"So long as you're alive to do so."

EPILOGUE

ZENIA BREATHED IN AND OUT slowly, trying to calm her mind and seek the steadying peace deep within herself. She hadn't meditated in weeks, and it felt strange doing it here, in front of a single candle and a tiny dragon figurine instead of in the temple with all its candles and the massive statue of the Blue Dragon founder. Still, she found she liked the privacy, liked that she had been given a room in the castle with enough space for a bed, a desk, bookcases, and a small shrine in the corner with a pillow on the floor for her knees.

The comfort of meditating in a private space wasn't enough to keep her thoughts from straying and her nerves from bouncing around in her stomach. Tonight was her first date with Jev.

It had been four days since the elf scientist had been arrested, his fate not yet determined. He was currently residing in a cell in the castle's dungeon. Lunis, though she may have wished otherwise, had survived the gut wound and was recovering under the watchful eye of a healer. Once she was well, she would leave the capital—and the kingdom— forever. Targyon hadn't had the heart to order her execution, but he had exiled her. Zenia thought it was the right decision and hoped Lunis would be able to start over and find a new life in another kingdom.

With these matters settled and the investigation officially closed, Jev had pointed out there was no reason they couldn't go on their date. And Zenia had agreed.

Giving up on meditation and any hope of achieving inner calmness, she rose to her feet. She stepped in front of the mirror to check the makeup she'd used to conceal the faint bruise left from Yilnesh's punch. Her cheek appeared normal. A good sign.

She smoothed her dress, a loose, flowing red and cream garment that didn't suffocate her as she wore it, nor did it push her breasts so far north that they were in danger of falling into the Anchor Sea. She'd recently purchased it, so it was a current fashion, and she liked how it hung on her, though the way it left one of her shoulders bare did seem risqué to her. She hoped Jev would like it.

But maybe it would be better if he didn't like it too much since she had to tell him... Well, she hadn't figured out *what* she would tell him yet. But if she kept kissing him, he would surely expect it to lead to sex. And while the primal part of her, the part of her guided by instincts and a yearning for pleasure, would like to engage in that with him, she couldn't. Not unless he had marriage in mind, and she feared he did not. She was reluctant to bring it up, for she would be disappointed when she found out for certain, but tonight, she would tell him her stance.

"Rotten gort of a topic for a first date, eh?" she muttered to her reflection in the mirror.

But after all they had been through together, this had to be more like their tenth date. Would he expect it to lead to more than kissing? She lifted her chin. If he did, he wouldn't by the time the night was over.

She grabbed her brush off the bureau, glancing again at an unfolded note atop it as she brushed her hair. It was the message Rhi had delivered the night of the reception. Zenia had forgotten about it until she removed her boots late that night and the envelope fell out. The single small piece of paper that had been inside read: *Do not trust Agent Drem.*

That was it. No signature or seal on the envelope, nothing. Days later, Zenia still had no idea who had sent it. Rhi hadn't known how or when it appeared on Zenia's bed in her old room in the temple. It could have been there for days before someone noticed it. What Zenia couldn't understand was how the sender had known about Lunis's betrayal and that Zenia was now an agent interacting with her but hadn't known she no longer lived at the temple. Had it simply been easier to deliver a message there than to the castle? Had the person assumed someone would send it right over to her?

She set down the brush, leaving the mystery for another time.

A rhythmic knock sounded at the door, and she knew it was Jev. The pattern contained his irreverence.

"Come in, Jev," she called, smoothing her dress one last time before turning to face the door as it opened.

Jev smiled at her, a picnic basket in one hand and something flat wrapped in brown paper and ribbon in the other. The ribbon came together in a lopsided bow that hung limply off-center, and she could tell he'd wrapped the gift himself. Zyndar weren't likely schooled on such things as children, having legions of servants who could wrap presents for them.

"You're supposed to be looking at my dashing figure rather than my mangled bow," Jev said, following her gaze.

She grinned at him. He *was* dashing. He wore slacks, a tunic, and jacket in his family colors, a less formal version of the quasi-military outfit he'd worn at the reception. The lines of the garments drew the eye to his broad shoulders, narrow hips, and flat stomach.

She felt a twinge of disappointment that she *wouldn't* be having sex with him tonight. Also a sensation of panic that if she didn't have a relationship with him, the only man who hadn't found her career as an inquisitor daunting, nobody else would ever be interested. Not that she wanted someone else. He was someone she trusted and cared about more than she would have thought possible after such a short time. *Especially* considering he was zyndar.

She tried to refocus her panic by pointing at the gift. "You brought me something?"

"I did, but the fact that you didn't agree to my self-assessment of dashingness makes me have second thoughts about giving it to you."

"Oh? You only give gifts to people who agree with your delusions?"

"They are the *best* kinds of people." Jev walked into the room, holding the gift out to her as he looked her up and down. "You are beautiful. New dress?"

"It is. I got my first pay as a Crown Agent, so I mustered all the feminine blood in my veins to go shopping. Rhi went with me, though not to the hoity toity Silver Ridge district this time." Zenia had been tempted to visit the jewelry store there to show off her new dragon tear, but it was technically the king's dragon tear, and who knew what people would assume if she admitted she was carrying it for him? Probably that she was his mistress rather than his agent. "Weavers' Row had an excellent selection and more reasonable prices."

"It's a lovely dress. Is your pay adequate?"

"The same as yours, I imagine." She had received a slightly higher purse than she'd earned from the temple, and now that she had a room at the castle and was allowed to dine with the staff here, she was coming out ahead.

"I don't get a salary." He smirked. "It's my honor as zyndar to serve."

"Does that mean you have to rely upon your father for an allowance?" She knew his family had land and money aplenty, but she was less certain how much of it Jev had access to until his father passed. She could imagine him resenting a lack of independence in that regard.

"Nah. I own the majority shares of a couple of the family businesses that my grandmother and grandfather on my father's side left to me and my brother." His smirk faded. "They've all fallen to me now with his passing. Not that he ever paid attention to them anyway. Admittedly, I haven't paid attention to anything these last ten years either. I'm lucky my cousins Wyleria and Neama keep an eye on things. They have hefty shares, too, and we split the profits at the end of the year. Whatever doesn't get invested back into the businesses."

"What types of businesses are they?"

"Some are gold and silver mines in the Erlek Mountains. Big, burly, and manly mines."

Zenia arched her eyebrows. "Am I to assume from that addition that you also own businesses that don't fit that description?"

"Possibly. And maybe it's ironic that the mines actually came from my grandmother? Grandpa Jev, the man I was named after, left me an herbal shop known for making blends to help women with, er, female problems. There's also a chandlery, a meadery, and a seamstress shop that specializes in sewing dolls."

"Are the dolls manly and burly?"

"They actually feature monks and mages from the various temples." His smirk returned. "Perhaps I'll request a Water Order inquisitor for next season's offerings."

"I'm not sure many little girls would want to play with an inquisitor."

"The blue robe is kind of pretty."

"I do miss it sometimes." She decided not to mention that it still stung to have gone from being someone in the city famous for her job to someone who probably wasn't supposed to mention that her job existed.

"It couldn't have been nearly as exciting as your new job. We stormed an elven tower together. Next thing you know, we'll be sent into dragons' caves to retrieve the treasures for the king."

Zenia thought of the warning Cutter had given her about her carving and decided she wanted to stay as far away from dragon caves as possible.

"When I was an inquisitor," she said, "I got to run through mangrove swamps with criminals."

"I assume you refer to the Fifth Dragon thugs who were chasing us rather than to me. Since I was *never* a criminal."

"Hm."

He squinted at her, then handed her the gift. "If you don't open this soon, I'm going to assume you don't want it and keep it all to myself."

"Is it something you'd want as much as I would? Such as an inquisitor doll?" She accepted the gift and decided it was a book rather than a doll. A large, heavy book.

"I prefer the real thing to dolls, but if you keep teasing me about it, I'll make sure the shop makes some soon. And then give you a bunch of them. You can line them up on that wardrobe there, and the dolls can ask you deeply personal questions."

Zenia, busy unwrapping the book, did not reply. She soon discovered a brand-new, leather-bound tome with Alderoth Castle embossed on the front.

"Crown Agents Operations Handbook," she read the title, then grinned as it sank in. "Is this—?" She flipped through the pages. "Everything that was in that mess of a handbook in the king's office?"

"It is. Organized, updated, and printed by a scribe with a neater hand than a press. The three agents I put to work on this kept sending me murderous glares until I promised they could take a couple of days off after they finished. That worked on two of them. Zyndar Garlok is still giving me murderous glares."

"You had *him* do it?"

"He's the one who let the old one become a mess. He deserved the job."

"I won't disagree with that, but are you allowed to make zyndar do tedious things like organizing notes?" She paused to lovingly touch a page full of charts, then flipped to the back and found an index that included several appendices of supplementary material. She hummed with approval and pleasure at the organization.

"Certainly. As zyndar, it's our job to serve the king, whether it's tedious or not. In Taziira, I once spent three days stirring a pitch concoction we made to repair our tents after hail the size of dragon heads attacked the camp with greater fervor than the elves ever did. Now, my lady, if you're done caressing my gift, may I escort you to the library where you can caress something else? My salami, perhaps?" He waggled his eyebrows at her, hefted the picnic basket, and tipped his head toward the door.

Zenia almost dropped the book at the blunt innuendo, and her concerns that he would expect to have sex with her tonight rushed back.

"I refer," Jev said, lifting the lid of the basket and delving inside, "of course, to the dinner salami." He waved a large wrapped log of cured meat before returning it to its home. "I also have cheese, grapes, laffa bread, and honeyed pastries. You can caress whatever appeals most to you."

"You're a naughty man, Jevlain Dharrow." Zenia lost that edge of panic that had lurched back into her mind, but she still felt ridiculously nervous over the conversation she needed to have with him.

"I don't have the faintest idea what you mean." He closed the lid of the basket and extended a hand toward the hallway. "Shall we?"

Zenia smiled. Despite her nerves, she looked forward to spending time with him, quiet and relaxing time, with neither an unsolved case nor threats to the king looming over their heads.

She stepped into the hall with him and took the arm he offered. "I'm ready."

After all Jev and Zenia had been through together in the last couple of weeks—by the founders, had it even been two full weeks yet?— he shouldn't have been nervous about spending time alone with her. But as they ambled arm in arm through the castle hallways, the picnic basket bumping against the side of his thigh, he struggled to relax. He groped for things to say, discovered them, but then rejected them before uttering them. They all sounded goofy. Like innuendos about salamis. He wanted to be romantic, not goofy.

He also wanted her to find him entertaining and endearing enough that she would invite him back to her room afterward, but he wasn't sure his charm could finagle that. He sensed that she liked spending time with him, even if he was an odious zyndar, but he also sensed... he wasn't entirely sure. Reserve. It had disappeared the times they had kissed, but it had always come back, leaving him feeling like he had done something wrong.

Even though the library where he had arranged to have a private room to themselves was in the same castle where they both roomed now, it was a long walk through hallways and down stairs.

"I hope the fact that you're bringing that along doesn't mean you anticipate being bored tonight," Jev finally said, worried the silence had grown too long.

Zenia glanced at the handbook resting against her hip and smiled. "Maybe I'm so delighted by my gift that I can't stand the idea of being parted from it. Or maybe I'm worried someone will steal it if I leave it in my room."

"Yes, I hear theft is rampant in the king's castle. Why would burglars want to target the infrequently visited and often vacant townhouses of zyndar families when they could truly test themselves against the legions of guards and bodyguards here?"

"Are you teasing me, Jev?"

"Would I do that?"

"Because if you were," Zenia said, "I believe it would be within my right to beat you over your head with your own salami."

As she finished the sentence, a couple of maids entered the intersection ahead, their route taking them past Jev and Zenia. They arched their eyebrows and looked curiously at them. One glanced in the direction of Jev's salami. Not the one in the basket.

"I admit," he said as they passed, "I would be somewhat alarmed if you beat me with a salami."

"You're not that adventurous?"

"I'm afraid not."

"The bartender in that tavern will be disappointed."

"Uh, I believe my performance there the other night assures he no longer has an interest in me." Unless it was to send an invoice for that broken chair and his lost business.

"Performance? Did you take your shirt off for him?"

"I only do that for pretty women."

They reached the double doors of the library, and Jev opened one side for Zenia.

"Any pretty women?" she asked. "Or do you have to know them first?"

"I'd like to say only women I like, but I was naked—reluctantly naked—for that dreadful Iridium." Jev was glad she hadn't ended up having anything to do with the bacterial poisonings, if only so he hadn't had to deal with her again. Alas, they would probably cross paths in the future. At least his job was to monitor the work of foreign spies rather than worrying about home matters. *Zenia* had that task. She could deal with her.

Jev smiled agreeably at the thought. Zenia might like finding an excuse to arrest Iridium.

"I hope that doesn't become a trend for you," Zenia said. "Getting naked in front of enemies."

"It was difficult staying clothed in the elven tower, but I did manage."

She grimaced. "Do you think we'll get in trouble for all the damage to their compound?"

"I talked to Targyon about that, and the ambassador hasn't brought it up. He may feel that since one of his so-called guests was responsible for the princes' deaths, he can't truly raise a fuss."

"I did sense that he didn't like what Yilnesh had done and even contemplated turning him over to the king at one point. When the ambassador was defending him, and buying time for him to escape, it was more that he felt honor-bound to protect his own kind than that he condoned the crime."

Jev hadn't sensed that. Maybe because he didn't have a dragon tear. Or maybe because the ambassador had kept hurling magic at him.

"Where shall we set up?" Zenia asked.

"In there."

Jev led her toward the room he'd reserved, one of several in the great library that could house meetings or game nights, or simply afforded people a secluded place to lounge on a sofa and read. This one had two sofas, a large table, a hearth with a fire crackling in it, along with two tall doors that one could close for complete privacy.

He smiled as they entered and did just that. He'd only spotted one other person as they walked through the main library, but he didn't want any intruders peering through the doors at them.

"A private room with doors that close and a fireplace," Zenia said. "This is precisely what Rhi recommended." She smiled, but it seemed a little uncertain.

Jev hoped she didn't think he was assuming... things. As much as he would be delighted to do *things* with her, he would understand if she wasn't ready. After so long without intimate female companionship, he would be disappointed, but he would understand. After her earlier hesitancy, he was pleased she had agreed to the date. He'd worried she might decide that intimacy wouldn't be a good idea since they worked together. Or just because his charms weren't as wonderful as he thought they were.

"You told her about our date?" Jev set the basket down on the table.

"I don't remember telling her, but somehow she knew." Zenia looked curiously at him.

"*I* didn't tell her. I'm a private and circumspect man."

"Hm."

"Maybe, now that she's in and out of the agents' office, she caught you gazing longingly at me across your desk, and she just assumed."

"Yes, I'm certain that's it."

"Your voice was depressingly deadpan when you said that." Jev wondered if she'd ever gazed longingly at him, maybe when he hadn't been paying attention.

"Was it? Odd." Zenia touched the basket. "Should we set up on the floor in front of the hearth? It seems strange to eat a picnic at a table. On her days off, my mother used to make stuffed gort leaves and thumbprint swirl cookies, and we would take them to the park on Sunset Street to eat."

"Sounds lovely." Jev did not mention that the only time he had been to that park, it had been full of homeless people. He suspected most parks in the city were like that, and it might be considered snooty and zyndar-ish to point it out.

"We would eat, and then I would ride the dragons." Zenia found a folded blanket on one of the couches and spread it in front of the hearth.

"Not real ones, I assume." Jev left the picnic setup to her and added a few logs from the wood box to the fire.

"The park has a carousel with wooden ones. I believe the real ones are known more for eating people than letting them ride them."

"Yes, except for Vraggorth the Valiant and his scaled mount Myscopia."

"I don't think it counts if you sneak into a dragon's cave, steal an egg from its mother, and raise the dragon yourself. And as I recall, that still didn't turn out well in the end."

"It depends on how partial you were to the monarch of the time period," Jev said. "If the stories are to be believed, there was cheering in the streets when the dragon ate King Draxmoroth. A shame Vraggorth was punished for the deed, but at least his dragon fled into the wilds instead of allowing itself to be shot. Wild creatures are wild, after all."

"Yes." Zenia reached up to her chest and touched the little bump under her dress, then knelt on the blanket and dug into the basket.

"Are you having any trouble with the dragon tear?" Though Jev had only seen it help Zenia so far, he still worried about the tale Cutter had told and the possibility that it somehow had the personality of a *real* dragon.

"No, but it's definitely... different from my last one."

"That sentence would have made me feel more comfortable if the period had come after the no."

"Sorry. You can pretend it did if you wish."

"Too late. You can't just shift punctuation around left and right after the fact."

Zenia patted the blanket and offered him a plate. She'd laid out the salami and cheese on a cutting board and stuck spoons into the bowls of different types of salads. She pulled out a couple of wineglasses, followed by an elven red Jev had pilfered from the family cellar. He'd been pleased to find it, as he'd worried his father might have gone on a rampage and destroyed all the bottles from elven vineyards. Fortunately, the old man didn't drink wine, so he hadn't likely been in the cellar for years.

"Is it difficult to find elven wine these days?" Zenia asked.

"I imagine so," Jev said. "I heard from my business-savvy cousins that exports from Taziira are all but nonexistent right now. Maybe Targyon will lower the tariffs to encourage trade again."

"I'm surprised elves grow grapes and make wine. I wouldn't have guessed their chilly climate and thick forests would provide the natural habitat for them."

"I've seen their vineyards in Taziira. The elves train the grapes to grow in sunny spots in the forest, vining up trellises made from living trees. You can be standing in the middle of a vineyard before realizing what it is. I do think grapes prefer our climate, but I've heard the elves use a little magic to encourage growth."

For a few moments, they were silent as they piled sliced meat and cheese and scoops of vegetables onto their plates and sampled the fare. Zenia settled her back against the sofa, and Jev did the same after opening and pouring the wine. Jev was glad she had pulled out two glasses. He remembered her once saying inquisitors didn't imbibe alcohol, so he hadn't been certain she would share a bottle with him.

"So fancy," Zenia murmured, lifting her glass to consider the wine by the firelight, or maybe the glass itself. The crystal had a pattern of gold flakes around the middle. "I suppose I should enjoy it instead of thinking about how one of these glasses could be sold for enough money to…" She shook her head and trailed off.

Since she'd mentioned her mother earlier, Jev wondered if her thoughts were on the woman tonight, on the death that could have been averted if they'd had enough money to pay for the hospital bill. He still hoped they would be strolling through the city together one day and come across her degenerate zyndar father so Jev would have the chance to punch the man in the nose.

"Maybe in your next report to the king, you can suggest Targyon sell the castle's wineglasses and donate the money to the Orders."

Zenia sighed. "It would be better to stand in the park and hand out coins to those who need them. I know Archmage Sazshen doesn't embezzle from the donation trays, but I've heard that other archmages lead suspiciously opulent lifestyles." Her lips pressed together in disapproval.

She hadn't tasted the wine yet. Maybe Jev should have filled the picnic basket with food purchased from street vendors and wrapped in greasy paper. He hadn't intended to remind her of the differences between them, that he'd grown up unaware of poverty and the value of things around the castle that he took for granted.

There were stories out there and even novels written of common women falling in love with zyndar men, and of the women being captivated by the zyndar lifestyle as if it was as much of a prize as the men that came with it. Or more of a prize. Somehow, Jev didn't think Zenia had read many of those stories.

He searched for another subject to discuss while they ate.

She finally took a sip of the wine, then asked, "Have you ever had a picnic with a common woman before?"

He stifled a grimace. That sounded like more of the same subject, the one he wanted to avoid.

"I've had picnics with scant few women of any class," Jev said truthfully. "A lot of meals shared outdoors with common men. In between elves shooting at us from the trees."

"Sorry." She lowered her glass. "I'm dwelling on unimportant things. I just... I guess I've had something on my mind, and I'm looking for a way to tell you, but all I keep thinking about is all the reasons you—we—can't... can't."

"Can't what? Join together in passionate union? Because I assure you none of those arrows delved into that territory, and I'm fully functional." He smiled to hide the panic her words inspired. They'd sounded far too much like the words of a woman about to suggest they go separate ways. Or at least *unromantic* ways. Since they both lived and worked in the castle now, they couldn't be too separate.

"I'm sure your future wife will be glad to know that." She glanced toward his fully functional parts, then hurried to look away, studying the fire with far more scrutiny than it deserved.

"No chance of *you* being glad to know it?" he asked quietly.

Her gaze dropped to her glass, and his stomach sank before she even spoke. What was it? She liked him but couldn't see loving him? Because he was zyndar? Because they worked together? Because his beard was too short? No, she wasn't a dwarf. That wouldn't be it.

She shifted her gaze to him, and he wrestled a smile into place. By the founders, why did she look like she wanted to be somewhere else? To avoid speaking with him? He'd wanted this evening to be light and fun. They *deserved* light and fun after the last couple of weeks.

"I can't have sex with you, Jev," she finally said, the words falling out in a tumble.

He opened his mouth to respond, but he had no idea what to say. That wasn't even remotely what he'd thought *she* would say.

"I told you about my mother and how I came to be." Her gaze slipped to her glass again.

The determined woman who could face down criminals, zyndar, and elven ambassadors was avoiding his gaze. Why did he once again feel like he'd done something wrong?

"Yes," he said carefully when she paused.

"At the temple, I saw a lot of that. Not necessarily mothers dying of illnesses, but mothers bringing their babies or children in for us to care for because they couldn't figure out a way to keep them fed and clothed by themselves."

He didn't know where this was going and felt confused, but he shifted to face her, resting his elbow on the sofa, so she would know he was paying attention.

"They were all children whose mothers were not married. I'm sure they hadn't all been mistresses, but for whatever reason, the fathers hadn't chosen to care. Or they hadn't even told the fathers because... the relationships they'd had hadn't meant anything, I guess." She rubbed the gold flakes on the side of the wineglass with her thumb. "A long time ago, I vowed that I wouldn't have sex with anyone outside of marriage. I didn't—don't—want to risk having children outside of marriage. I know there are various teas that are supposed to prevent conception, but I also know they don't work all the time. As so many of the mothers leaving their children at the temple pointed out."

She looked at him. To see if he was tracking? By now, he was, and he couldn't help but feel disappointed. It made sense, and he couldn't begrudge her choice, but he couldn't deny that he'd hoped their date would end up with them back in his room, limbs entangled as they explored all the creative things one could do on the small guest bed.

"I can understand not wanting to raise a child by yourself," he made himself say.

The last thing he wanted her to know was that he was disappointed. And now, he felt like an ass for that comment he'd made in the carriage about fantasizing about her. Did this mean she was a virgin? Unless she had past marriages she hadn't spoken of, it had to, didn't it? He rubbed his face, hoping he hadn't scared her with that comment. Damn. He had not envisioned fearless and determined Zenia as someone inexperienced with men. Or with *anything.*

Her kisses hadn't been chaste or uncertain. Of course, just because she hadn't had sex didn't mean she'd never kissed anyone before. She'd dated, surely, and maybe she'd explored the various things a man and woman could do that would be satisfying without any chance of pregnancies coming about. Maybe she would consider exploring such things with him.

No, damn it, he growled to himself. He needed to ratchet down his libido and listen to her. Listen to her concerns and figure out how to say something supportive and un-asshole-y. He could do that. He wasn't an ass. He wasn't that damn Zyndar Morningfar who had treated her mother so poorly. And her.

"For most common women, it's not even possible," Zenia said quietly. "Women aren't paid that well, in general. As an inquisitor, I had a better job and career than most, but my guest room here at the castle is larger than my room in the temple was, if that tells you anything. And there's no way I could have chased criminals all over the city, and sometimes out of it, while still nursing a baby."

"That might slow you down a little," he agreed, offering what he hoped was an understanding smile.

"I know—or I've gotten the notion, now that I've talked to you about it—that you are expected to marry a zyndari woman. And from the haunted look you get in your eyes when this comes up, I don't think you want to marry *anyone* right now."

"It's true that I was hoping to relax and settle into my new life before contemplating marriage and children." He remembered Dr. Nhole's mother, and hoped the zyndari mothers out there didn't start sending propositions to his father, something Jev still needed to discuss with the old man.

Zenia nodded as if she'd already known that. He supposed she had. He almost said that he would consider marrying a common-born woman, if he found the right person—was it possible *she* wanted to become the right person? He'd already hinted of that to her, hadn't he? But he didn't want to promise her something he wasn't ready to promise. Especially since it could mean giving up so much if his father didn't approve. And he had to admit that even if his father could be brought around to the idea of Jev marrying a common woman, the old man loathed Zenia right now. Rhi might have been the one to kick him into the fountain, but he knew Rhi had been working for Zenia.

"I'm sorry this has put a damper on our date," Zenia said, "but I needed to tell you because... I like it too much when you kiss me."

He almost laughed, his ego appreciating the admission, but then he realized what she was doing in telling him everything. He was sworn to obey the Zyndar Code of Honor, and that meant not only defending his own honor from all threats; it meant defending the honor of women too. And if he tried to seduce her, inadvertently or not, it would be an attempt to make her break the promise she'd made to herself.

"Well." He cleared his throat, surprised at the emotion filling it. "At least I know you don't find my kisses loathsome and have been searching for a way to toss me overboard."

"No." She smiled sadly, her gaze settling on his lips. "They're not loathsome. *You're* not loathsome. It would have been easier if you were."

The words stabbed him in the heart, but he managed to stifle his instinct to wince. "I can't claim to be apologetic about not living up to your expectations of zyndar."

Still smiling, she touched his cheek.

"Listen, Zenia." He lifted his hand to hers, holding it there. "It's true that marriage hasn't been on my mind since—well, I told you. I planned on it once before, and it didn't work out. She didn't wait— didn't even wait a full year—before going into the arms of another man, and it crushed me." He swallowed, almost admitting that he'd gone to see Naysha, to *spy* on her, just in case it turned out she needed saving from a dreadful husband and a dreadful life, but he didn't want to make that admission. It might hurt Zenia. As strange as that seemed since she was in the middle of rejecting him. "I just hadn't planned to get that involved again so soon. To put my heart out there and risk getting it trampled." That was more honesty than he'd meant to share. "But can't we still *date*? Have picnics in the library? Spend time together? And see if... I don't know. It seems a shame to say no forever before we've even had our first glasses of wine, doesn't it?"

"Do you truly want to have wine with someone who won't sleep with you?"

"Just because you don't want to risk getting pregnant doesn't mean there aren't intimate things we could do together. Sleeping, for example, rarely gets *anyone* pregnant. I could wear some of those royal pajamas that caress a man's balls to make sure everything stays properly restrained."

That surprised a laugh out of her. He grinned, delighted to hear it. She'd been so incredibly serious since they started talking about this. It was a serious topic, of course, but he worried that her grave attitude meant she'd already given up on him. On them.

After she laughed, she tilted her head thoughtfully. Was that intrigue in her eyes? Maybe she wanted to see what intimacies he had in mind that wouldn't result in surprise children.

He took his hand from hers and touched her cheek. Her cheek was far more appealing than his.

When she didn't draw back, he leaned forward slowly, watching her eyes for signs that he should stop. For a moment, she seemed hesitant, but she parted her lips when his came close. He closed his eyes and kissed her. And his wounded heart took solace in the fact that she kissed him back. When her arms came around his shoulders, he believed maybe this could work, maybe they could still spend time together. Get to know each other more intimately. And he could find out if she was the one to replace the one who hadn't waited for him. Maybe even to become more than the one had ever been. Because if he found the new one, it would be worth doing anything, and giving up anything, to be with her, wouldn't it?

Especially when her kiss was so appealing. As was the way her hand drifted to the back of his head, and her fingers pushed through his hair. Appealing and... arousing. Founders' fiery breath, it would be hard not to let kisses turn into more than she wanted, and he was already questioning his words about sleeping together without having sex. Memories of her naked sprang to mind and how much he would like to hold her naked body in his arms, to let his hands explore every part of her, to have her explore him back, to—

Zenia squeezed his shoulders and pulled away. He almost moaned his objection.

She stared at him, her moist lips parted, her breaths quick. He realized his were quick, too, and that his hand had found its way to her waist, scooting her closer to him, almost pulling her into his lap.

"I can't, Jev," she whispered, pushing him farther away. "It would be too hard not to... just not to."

"Zenia..." He wished he could muster more of a protest, a logical argument, but he feared she was right.

She scrambled to her feet, almost knocking over the wineglass she'd set aside. "Thank you for dinner. I have to go."

"Zenia..." he groaned again.

But she rushed around the sofa, bumping the end with her hip, and kept going without looking back. The door creaked faintly as it opened, and then she was gone.

Jev slumped back against the sofa, utterly defeated.

For several long moments, he sat there, the fire crackling cheerfully to mock him.

A throat cleared in the doorway. For an ecstatic second, he thought it was Zenia, that she'd come back to tell him she'd changed her mind, but he knew before he looked that it wasn't she.

A young woman wearing a page's uniform peered hesitantly in at him and lifted an envelope that she carried on a silver tray. "My pardon, Zyndar Dharrow. I heard you didn't want to be disturbed, but, uh..."

The page looked in the direction Zenia had gone. Great. She'd probably seen Zenia fleeing from the room they'd shared and wondered what monstrous thing he'd done to her.

"Go ahead." Jev waved to the envelope.

"This was delivered for you, Zyndar." The page strode in and presented the tray.

He thought about asking her for more details but doubted she had any. As soon as he accepted the envelope, she hastened away, almost jogging.

What a touch he had tonight. All women were fleeing from him.

Sighing, he looked at the front of the envelope. All it contained was his name, but he recognized the flowing script. Lornysh.

Jev needed to talk with Targyon to see if there was a way to get Lornysh and Cutter access to the castle. Especially tonight, he wouldn't have minded some company, someone to listen to him explain his woes while they imbibed the nearly untouched bottle of wine.

Targyon ought to be able to make sure an elf could come and go without guards perforating him with arrows. Maybe Jev could even suggest him as one of the Crown Agents, should Lornysh want to stay in the city for longer than a few weeks.

He wasn't sure what he expected from the message inside, but it wasn't what he got.

Cutter is missing. So is Master Grindmor.

Jev slumped back against the sofa again. He promptly felt like an ass because he hadn't seen Cutter in a couple of days and hadn't thought anything of it. He'd been too busy wrapping things up with his case and planning his *date*.

How long had he been gone? Was it related to the master cutter's missing tools? It had to be if she was missing too.

Reluctantly, Jev rose to his feet and abandoned the picnic.

"No rest for the king's agents," he murmured and headed for the door.

THE END